By David Sherman and Dan Cragg

*Starfist*
FIRST TO FIGHT
SCHOOL OF FIRE
STEEL GAUNTLET
BLOOD CONTACT
TECHNOKILL
HANGFIRE
KINGDOM'S SWORD
KINGDOM'S FURY
LAZARUS RISING

By David Sherman

*The Night Fighters*
KNIVES IN THE NIGHT
MAIN FORCE ASSAULT
OUT OF THE FIRE
A ROCK AND A HARD PLACE
A NGHU NIGHT FALLS
CHARLIE DON'T LIVE HERE ANYMORE
THERE I WAS: THE WAR OF CORPORAL HENRY J. MORRIS, USMC
THE SQUAD

*Demontech*
ONSLAUGHT
RALLY POINT

By Dan Cragg

Fiction
THE SOLDIER'S PRIZE

Nonfiction
A DICTIONARY OF SOLDIER TALK
GENERALS IN MUDDY BOOTS
INSIDE THE VC AND THE NVA (with Michael Lee Lanning)
TOP SERGEANT (with William G. Bainbridge)

# STARFIST

## Book IX

# LAZARUS RISING

## DAVID SHERMAN AND DAN CRAGG

BALLANTINE BOOKS • NEW YORK

A Del Rey® Book
Published by The Random House Publishing Group

www.delreybooks.com

ISBN 0-345-44373-X

Manufactured in the United States of America

First Edition: December 2003
First Mass Market Edition: December 2004

OPM 9 8 7 6 5 4 3 2 1

Dedicated to:
Lieutenant Commander John G. Hemry, USN (ret)
An officer who knew what was real
And what wasn't—
And made his beliefs known.

# PROLOGUE

Arrogant unbeliever! Lesser Imam Shammar thought as he shivered under dripping fronds, watching Gunnery Sergeant Bass place sensors in the soggy ground. The Marine had ordered Shammar to place his five soldiers as security so he could fiddle with the sensors, but the lesser imam had simply dismissed the soldiers farther into the undergrowth then used the cover provided by the vegetation to spy on the two Marines. The lesser imam was tired of taking orders from an off-world "gunnery sergeant." What's more, the man was not a proper sword. The off-worlders didn't even have proper titles of rank; in the lesser imam's world, a "sergeant" was somebody who groveled before a judge in the courts. Shammar cast a longing glance at the armored personnel carrier. He wanted to return to it; inside, it would be warm and dry.

There was a brilliant flash, then a wave of searing heat.

"Gunny," Dupont said, "the UPUD's picking up motion deeper in the trees."

"It's probably the soldiers; they don't have good field discipline."

"I don't think so, Gunny; what I'm picking up is farther into the trees."

Bass grimaced. "I don't trust that damn thing." He was reaching into a cargo pocket for his personal motion detector when it felt like his entire arm was being torn off. Simultaneously, something ripped off his helmet and threw him to the ground. As he lay, dazed, just meters away, he saw two

1

shreds of gore, one lying on the ground, the other hovering above it. They struck him as very curious, in a distracting kind of way. When he managed to focus on them, he saw two ankles sticking out of a pair of chameleon boots. Idly, he wondered if Dupont had blisters on his feet and had taken his boots off to ease the pain. But if Dupont had taken his boots off, why had he left his feet inside them?

A sudden, horrible wave of pain washed over Bass, and then he lost consciousness.

# CHAPTER
# ONE

The navigator on the Amphibious Landing Ship, Force, CNSS *Grandar Bay*, was very good at his job—he jumped the starship out of Beamspace barely more than two days' travel from the world called the Kingdom of Yahweh and His Saints and Their Apostles.

Those Marines who knew anything about the mechanics of the jump reasoned that the closer they were to Kingdom when they came out of Beamspace, the sooner they'd get to somewhere they'd rather be. And after the campaign the Marines of the 34th Fleet Initial Strike Team had just fought against the Skinks, the Marines were anxious to get back to Camp Ellis, their homeport on Thorsfinni's World—despite the fact that the Marine Corps rated Thorsfinni's World a hardship post.

The stop at Kingdom was too brief for Marines or ship's crew to be granted shore liberty. Brigadier Sturgeon, commander of 34th FIST, and a few members of his staff made planetfall to report to Confederation Ambassador Jayben Spears and the leadership of Kingdom's ruling Ecumenical Council. Before lifting off again, Sturgeon took the time to share a glass of wine and a cigar with Spears.

"One more thing before I leave, Jay," Brigadier Sturgeon said when the wine and cigars were almost gone.

"Anything in my power, Ted."

"I need to send a backchannel. Can you handle it for me?"

"Of course."

"Thank you, Jay. I haven't the words to tell you how important this message is to 34th FIST." He handed over a crystal. "It's for Andy again. He'll get my official report, of course; that was dispatched via Navy drone from the *Grandar Bay* as soon as we reentered Space-3." He tapped the crystal. "Go ahead and read it."

Spears rose, went to his desk, and popped the crystal into his reader. He raised his eyebrows when he began reading. The headers on the message weren't in normal military format, but that of a personal letter.

Spears looked up at the Marine commander. "I hadn't realized how close you are to the assistant commandant."

"On my leave to Earth we became friends." Sturgeon nodded for Spears to continue reading.

The ambassador read:

Andy,

First off, let me thank you for sending 26th FIST so quickly. Jack Sparen and his Marines really saved the day; we couldn't have done the job by ourselves.

That's an understatement. If you hadn't expedited reinforcements, there's an excellent chance the Skinks would have wiped us out. By now I imagine you've seen my draft report on the Kingdom Campaign. Take my word for it, as hairy as that report reads, the reality was worse. This one was more of a meat grinder than the Diamunde Campaign, if you can imagine that.

I lost a godawful lot of men. You've seen the details in my report. Andy, I've never had such losses on one campaign, and I doubt that you have either. Now, I know that as soon as my report filters through to Personnel they'll start sending replacements to 34th FIST. But that'll take a lot of time since 34th FIST has been removed from normal personnel rotation. That's time that my Marines will be spending in Barracks with a lot of empty racks.

I need bodies in those racks to distract my Marines from their losses. Andy, if it's at all possible, please goose Personnel and get me Marines to put in those racks. My Marines aren't the only ones who need them. I'm going to really hate it when we hold our first FIST formation back at Camp Ellis and see how much smaller we are now than we were at the last.

With many thanks in advance,

Ted

Spears looked up when he finished reading. "I'll get this out today." He popped the crystal and put it with the materials he was readying to send by diplomatic pouch. "Do you think they're going to lift the quarantine on you now?"

The very existence of the Skinks Sturgeon's Marines had just fought on two worlds was a tightly guarded secret. The only earlier contact with them had been made by the third platoon of Company L of 34th FIST's infantry battalion. Fear of widespread panic caused the government to tightly seal everything having to do with that contact—including canceling all transfers and retirements out of 34th FIST and slapping an involuntary extension of service "for the duration" on all members of the FIST. Thorsfinni's World itself barely escaped the strictures.

Sturgeon shrugged. "Who knows what politicians will do? They should lift the quarantine since they won't be able to keep the secret now."

"If they quarantine 26th FIST, the *Grandar Bay,* and Kingdom, they can keep it secret for a while longer. They'll think of that, you know."

A hard smile creased Sturgeon's face. "The more people they quarantine, the sooner someone will notice. And what will they do to *you*?"

It was Spears's turn to shrug. "They want to put me out to pasture anyway. They might see Darkside as a good grazing ground for me."

The *Grandar Bay* left Kingdom's space after less than twenty-four hours in orbit.

The Marines of 34th FIST were somber on the return voyage to Thorsfinni's World; the Kingdom Campaign had been costly. The first phase was especially brutal. They'd been surprised to find themselves fighting Skinks instead of the peasant revolt they'd expected. They wouldn't have suffered so severely had they just gone up against the Skinks the same way Company L's third platoon had fought them on Waygone, the exploratory planet Society 437. Horrible as they were, the Skinks' acid guns were short-range weapons. Under those conditions, if the Marines found the Skinks at a great enough range, they could destroy them before the aliens got close enough to use their weapons. But on Kingdom the Skinks also had rail guns. The Marines' body armor was ample protection against normal projectile weapons, but it was worthless against the rail guns, which had killed and wounded a lot of them before anyone found a way of putting the guns out of action.

More than two hundred Marines had been killed or too badly wounded to return to active duty, mostly from the infantry battalion. Mike Company had suffered the most—more than an entire platoon had been wiped out when the Skinks sprang their first ambush in the Swamp of Perdition.

That didn't mean other units hadn't suffered severely. Company L's third platoon had lost PFCs Hayes and Gimble; Lance Corporals Dupont, Van Impe, Rodamour, and Watson; Corporal Stevenson; and Gunnery Sergeant Bass.

Gunny Bass. Damn.

Corporal Goudanis and Sergeant Bladon were wounded badly enough that they'd been evacuated off-planet. They had survived their wounds, but would they ever return to third platoon, or even to active duty? Nobody knew.

Gunny Bass. There was hardly a man in the entire company who wouldn't have been happy to be in his platoon. And now he was gone.

PFCs Longfellow and Godenov, Lance Corporal Schultz, Corporals Linsman and Kerr were wounded during the first phase of the campaign but returned to duty, and Linsman and Godenov were promoted to sergeant and lance corporal respectively.

Eight Marines killed and two wounded so badly they were totally gone. Ten men out of a thirty-man platoon. Third platoon hadn't lost that many men even in the fierce antiarmor fighting in the war on Diamunde. The loss that hurt the most, though, was Gunny Bass.

Thirty-fourth FIST was reinforced by 26th FIST for the second phase of the Kingdom Campaign, and the tide of battle turned, resulting in victory for the Marines. In some ways, even more welcome than the addition of another FIST, was the new weapon they brought with them to combat the Skinks. It wasn't an offensive weapon, it was defensive: chameleon uniforms that were impervious to the acid from the Skink short-range weapons.

Thanks to the new chameleons, and newly discovered means of defeating the rail guns, casualties dropped dramatically in the second phase.

PFCs Gray, Shoup, and Little, all replacements who came in with 26th FIST, were wounded. So were Lance Corporals MacIlargie and Kindrachuck, and Corporals Pasquin and Doyle. Sergeant Linsman must have thought the Skinks had it in for him personally when he was wounded a second time. But thanks to the impregnated uniforms, no one in third platoon was killed in the campaign's second phase.

And at least they couldn't lose Gunny Bass again.

Brigadier Sturgeon knew full well how his Marines felt. He knew because he felt much the same way. Never in his four decades in the Confederation Marine Corps had he commanded or been a member of a unit that had sustained such heavy casualties. He'd seen in the past how the survivors of a brutal campaign could suffer in the aftermath if they were allowed to be alone with their thoughts, how unit cohesiveness and discipline could be damaged, even destroyed.

On the second day out from Kingdom, before the *Grandar Bay* made the jump into Beam Space for transit to Thorsfinni's World, he went to see Commodore Borland.

They met in the captain's dining salon. Sturgeon gave the genuine mahogany wainscoting on the bulkheads an appraising look when he entered. He speculatively eyed the painted portraits of ships and navy officers that hung on its walls, took in the polished hardwood sideboard and chairs, and almost smiled at the sterling silver flatware on a dining table that was covered by a white linen cloth with a damasked pattern.

"Welcome, Brigadier," Borland said as he strode the few steps from the sideboard opposite the hatch to greet the Marine commander with outstretched hand. He noticed the way Sturgeon looked the room over. Since he'd been there before, the appointments of the captain's dining salon shouldn't have been a surprise to him.

"Thank you for agreeing to see me on such short notice, Commodore," Sturgeon said as he gripped the proffered hand.

After shaking, Borland looked at the table, then at the steward who stood at attention after pouring coffee into fine china cups and placing slices of deep-dish apple pie on plates at the table settings.

"Will there be anything else, sir?" the steward asked.

"That will be all, thank you. You may return to your station. I'll signal if I need you for anything else."

"Aye aye, sir." The steward marched from the salon and quietly closed the hatch behind him.

Now that they were alone, Borland dropped all formality. "Have a seat, Ted. That's real coffee, you know; don't let it get cold on you." He went to the sideboard and opened it while Sturgeon took a seat and a first sip of the coffee.

"What do you think?" he asked as he bent over to fish something out of the sideboard.

"The best I've had since the last cup I had with you." Sturgeon took another sip and sighed contentedly.

Borland straightened up and displayed a clear glass bottle filled with a dark amber liquid. "Would you like to give it a bit of a sweetener?" he asked.

Sturgeon raised an eyebrow at the bottle. "Is that . . . ?"

"Real Earth cognac from the region called France."

The tip of Sturgeon's tongue involuntarily moistened his lips. He looked from the bottle to his cup and back. "I don't know, Ralph. When you mix two good things together, sometimes you detract from both."

Borland grinned. "Easily enough resolved." He reached back into the sideboard, withdrew two crystal snifters, closed the sideboard doors with a knee, and carried the bottle and snifters to the table. Borland broke the bottle's seal and opened it with a theatrical flare, then poured an ounce of cognac into the snifters with all the dexterity of a career steward. He remained standing as he handed one to Sturgeon, who took it and rose to his feet.

"A toast," Borland said, lifting his snifter.

Sturgeon held his own up and out.

"To fallen comrades."

"To fallen comrades," Sturgeon echoed solemnly.

They touched their snifters together, then inhaled the aroma and sipped.

"Please, Ted." Borland waved a hand, and the two sat—his voice was suddenly thicker than it had been. The Marines weren't alone in suffering severe losses in the Kingdom Campaign. The Fast Frigate *Admiral J. P. Jones,* the *Grandar Bay*'s sole escort, had been destroyed by the Skinks during their fighting evacuation of Kingdom—all but seventeen of her two hundred officers and crew were killed when the ship exploded.

The two commanders sat for a long moment, each reflecting on the lives of their people who had died in the fighting. Almost as though on a secret signal, they shook themselves out of it and each reached for his coffee—lost lives were a part of combat that Marines and sailors had to accept, or else get out of uniform altogether; dwelling on losses could lead to insanity.

"That's the problem with fine china," Borland said after he took a drink. "It doesn't keep coffee hot."

Sturgeon chuckled. "After some of the kaff substitutes I've drunk in the field, real coffee is delicious even cold."

Borland had an idea why the Marine had wanted to see him. "You've had to drink kaff substitutes in the field, and we were silent for a while there, thinking things no man should have to think," he said. "I think if I put those two things together, they'll bring us to the reason for your visit."

Sturgeon nodded. "My Marines just went through some of the fiercest, most costly fighting I've ever seen in my career. Honestly, Ralph, I've never been on an operation that caused such heavy casualties. It's been playing on my mind, and I know it's bothering my people even more."

Borland nodded. Sailors didn't lose men the same way the Marines did—except for an occasional individual, mostly medical corpsmen, who served with Marines on combat missions. Most navy deaths and injuries were caused by shipyard or shipboard accidents. On the rare occasions when a ship was killed, there were few if any survivors left to suffer the loss of their shipmates. But he was the commander, and he deeply felt the loss of lives when the *Admiral J. P. Jones* was killed. He had personal knowledge of what Sturgeon meant.

"I've got one officer and sixteen sailors off the *Jones* who're undergoing intense therapy to help them through the death of their ship and shipmates. So how do you think I can help you with your Marines? My medical staff is stretched to its limits tending my people."

"On my way here," Sturgeon said, "I saw members of your crew cleaning the passageways and doing a lot of polishing."

"Keeping the *Grandar Bay* shipshape is a never-ending chore. There's always work for the crew to do."

"I dare say it takes a goodly number of man-hours to keep this compartment sparkling." Sturgeon waved a hand, indicating the highly polished wood and other appointments.

Borland bit back a smile but couldn't keep a twinkle out of his eyes. "And what might this have to do with your Marines?"

"The *Grandar Bay* took significant battle damage, didn't she?"

Borland simply nodded.

"Far be it for this old Marine to butt into the business of running a starship"—Sturgeon held back his own smile—"but it seems to me that the *Grandar Bay* would be better served if her crew devoted more of its time and effort to repairing and policing battle damage and less to spit and polish." Now a smile did crack his face, and he held up his hand to forestall Borland's next comment. "Commodore, we Marines spend too much time on deployment these days to apply ourselves as much to 'spit and polish' as earlier generations of Marines did, but from the earliest days of the Royal Marines, Marines have been noted for 'spit and polish.' I'd like your permission for my Marines to take that chore off your sailors' hands."

Borland beamed at him. "Ted, you just proposed a time-honored method for curing what ails battle-weary troops. I agree, my sailors could be put to much better use working on repairs to our battle damage."

He reached across the table, and the two commanders shook hands.

# CHAPTER
# TWO

First Acolyte Ben Loman stood in the observation cupola of his command car and scanned the foothills before him. He had halted his reconnaissance platoon just behind a low ridge and positioned his lead vehicle so he could see over the military crest. An unmanned reconnaissance aircraft had spotted something out there, and he had been sent to investigate. His heart thumped heavily inside his chest out of fear and excitement: fear that they had at last found some surviving demons, and excitement that this time they would have the killing edge. The demon host had been defeated, and First Acolyte Ben Loman's platoon, one of many recon units searching for demon survivors, might today be the first element of the Army of the Lord to make contact with the vile creatures.

Ben Loman was no fool. He knew that the demons at the height of their power were more than a match for anything the Kingdomite army could throw at them. But the off-world Marines had broken the siege of Haven and crushed the demons, who had fled with the Marines in hot pursuit. If any demons were still on Kingdom, they would be demoralized and underequipped for battle. Ben Loman was hot for revenge and eager to prove himself in battle as an officer of the Army of the Lord.

His headset crackled. "Sir, we await your orders," Senior Sword Raipur announced.

Ben Loman winced at the insistent tone in the senior sword's voice, as if the enlisted man were *reminding* him to get on with his mission. Raipur was a capable but overcautious noncom, always reminding his platoon commander that his mission was to find the enemy, not engage him. Senior Sword Raipur seemed actually *afraid* they might make contact with the demons.

They'd been on patrol for three weeks and were some 1,200 kilometers from the capital city of Haven. The main body of the Burning Bush Regiment was positioned sixty kilometers to their rear, eyes, ears, and weapons at the ready. Everyone's nerves were on edge, expecting any moment to run into the enemy. But so far, maybe until this moment, none had appeared. Other regiments in other sectors were also coming up negative, although they were finding isolated groups of refugees everywhere, people who'd fled into the wilderness when their settlements had been destroyed by the demons. Many had been killed by troops with itchy trigger fingers, shooting first and checking later. Those unfortunate incidents were proof, if any were needed, that the soldiers of the Army of the Lord were still scared witless by the thought of the demons, the alien creatures the off-world Marines called Skinks.

And the men were nearly exhausted.

"Hold your position. I'm coming back there." Ben Loman threw off his headset with a loud bang that made his driver and gunner look up suddenly. "Take over the surveillance," he curtly told the driver. He grabbed his map unit and climbed out of the cupola. "If you see anything, get on the horn. I'll be back with the senior sword." He stepped lightly out of the vehicle and walked quickly back to Senior Sword Raipur's position. The senior sword saw him coming and dismounted.

"Have you seen them, sir?"

"Come over here and I'll show you." Ben Loman guided the noncom into the scrub about twenty-five meters from the vehicles. They crouched in the shade of a small tree and Loman activated his terrain unit. "It's just like the colonel deacon told us back at the CP." A three-dimensional overlay of the foothills three kilometers to their front appeared on the screen. "The bird spotted infrared signatures in this box canyon here." He zoomed in on the suspected area. The canyon walls were steep and massive, the passage through it narrow and littered with rockfalls.

"Yessir. The only way in there is on foot," Senior Sword Raipur said. His voice betrayed his anxiety at the thought of so small a force negotiating that narrow space between the canyon walls.

"Well, swordie, we're going to have to go in there; that's what we're here for," Ben Loman responded. He looked into his senior sword's eyes, and after a moment the noncom dropped his gaze to the display on the terrain unit. He's afraid, Ben Loman thought.

"Why don't we just call in air or artillery?"

"We are here and we're going in there."

The senior sword had a worried expression on his face. "Sir, I recommend we call for reinforcements from regiment," he said at last, forcing the words out. That was standing operational procedure for a reconnaissance unit—find the enemy and call in the heavy stuff, not engage if a fight could be avoided.

"We will, when I give the word. But I'm not causing the entire regiment to deploy until I know for sure what's up there. If they are demons, they'll be demoralized, and if we have to fight them, we can." Ben Loman glanced at the sun, hanging just above the horizon. "It'll be dark in another hour. We'll go in under the cover of darkness."

Senior Sword Raipur said nothing. They had excellent night optics, thanks to the Marines, but still . . .

"Look, it's probably nothing, probably wild animals nested up there. Or refugees. But if it is the demons, we're alert, heavily armed, and ready for combat. Go back to your vehicle, get some rest, and when it's full dark we'll go in." Ben Loman spoke gently. He could not afford to have his senior enlisted man get cold feet now. "We're just going to go up there, see what's at the end of that canyon, and get out. Okay?"

"Yessir." Raipur did not trust his commander; the young officer was too eager for a fight. And he did not like night operations.

Back in the command vehicle, Ben Loman continued scanning the foothills, plotting an access route into the canyon. They could drive about halfway up before they'd have to dismount. He would take half his men with him and leave the rest behind as a reserve. Senior Sword Raipur would go with him; Sword Abshire would remain behind with the vehicles. Abshire was a steady, unimaginative noncom who'd follow orders and remain steady under fire, if it came to a fight. Ben Loman made a mental note to ask the colonel deacon to transfer Raipur once they got back to the regimental base camp. Even though Abshire belonged to the Disciples of Hogarth, an offshoot of the Protestant Baptist denomination, he would make a good senior sword.

The shadows were lengthening quickly by then. Ben Loman thumbed his throat mike. "Listen up! Saddle up! Drivers, put your engines on silent running. Follow me and keep your intervals." First Acolyte Ben Loman bowed his head in the proper nondenominational prayer. "Heavenly Presence, watch over us tonight." He paused. "*Please* let there be demons!" His heart raced. "Great One, Holy One, *give us victory!*"

Great Shaman Hadu, the last shaman, as far as he knew, of the Pilipili Magna, raised his arms above his head. "Great Lord, Kuma Mayo, you have blessed your people beyond measure!" he intoned. The few dozen wretches squatting about the fire, all that remained of the Pilipili Magna, listened intently, their wet eyes reflecting the bright firelight. An infant wailed and its mother put her nipple to its mouth. The Great Shaman smiled. Life was going on. The people lived!

The Great Shaman looked upon his people. They were emaciated, their starvation barely covered by rags that had once been festive garments. But they had survived! The great evil that had descended upon their fields and villages from the sky had passed over these fortunate few. The canyon where they'd found refuge had fresh water, caves for shelter, and a few hectares of arable soil where crops were already beginning to grow. By next harvest they could emerge from hiding and reclaim their fields.

*"Kuma mayo embovu!"* the Great Shaman intoned, raising his face to heaven. In his solemn rituals, the Great Shaman reverted to the ancient language of his East African ancestors. Few of the people spoke the old tongue anymore, but they all knew the ritual language by heart.

*"Tini maji!"* the people shouted in response.

*"Juu povu!"* the Great Shaman shouted. Behind him the flickering firelight cast his shadow hugely upon the canyon wall. Far above, the stars glittered in astonishing profusion. The warmth from the fire embraced the people. Sparks from the burning wood rose into the air in a festive display.

*"Illi yokuzaa, emziavoo!"* the people shouted with joy, in the comforting age-old ceremony of obeisance to their God.

The people lived!

The farther they climbed up into the canyon, the more difficult it became, as the reconnaissance element negotiated the detritus that littered the floor. Along the north wall a mountain stream gurgled and splashed its way to the valley below, helping somewhat to cover the inevitable noise of their ascent.

"Easy does it!" Ben Loman whispered into his command net as one of his men slipped on some loose shale and his equipment clattered. "Halt!" he said. "I told you all to fasten down your gear before we started the climb. The next man who makes a noise is going up on a charge!"

"Acolyte!" the point man just around a bend in the canyon wall whispered into Ben Loman's headset. "I see them! I see them!"

"Senior Sword, take charge, I'm going on point," Ben Loman said.

The point man crouched amid a jumble of boulders that had fallen into the canyon ages ago. A hundred yards in front of where the point waited, Ben Loman saw a bright fire flickering in the blackness. "God save us!" he whispered. A figure, its grotesque shadow cast menacingly upon the rock wall behind it, stood before the fire, gesturing wildly. *"It's them!"* Ben Loman breathed. The hand he placed on the point man's shoulder shook slightly. "Raipur!" he almost shouted, momentarily forgetting proper radio procedure, "bring the men up here. Abshire, contact the regimental CP. Tell them we have the demons in our sights and must, repeat, *must* engage!" His voice shook as he spoke into his mouthpiece.

"Sir!" It was Senior Sword Raipur. He crouched beside Ben Loman and whispered in his ear so his voice would not be picked up by the men who were quietly taking up positions to either side of them along the rockfall. "We don't know how many of them there are down there," he hissed.

Ben Loman switched off his throat mike and turned to his noncom sharply. "Count them!" he snapped, gesturing toward the fire with his head.

Raipur's night optics clearly revealed several dozen, possibly as many as sixty figures squatting about the fire. "They outnumber us, sir."

"We have the element of surprise," Ben Loman insisted, his voice edged with the exasperation he felt at his senior sword's despicable display of overcaution.

"First Acolyte, I have seen the demons close up and those don't look at all like them. Besides, Acolyte, *it is not our job to engage the enemy!* We should hold this position and wait for reinforcements!" Raipur was breathing heavily. Ben Loman just stared at the noncom wordlessly. Raipur felt compelled to go on: "I'd say they're refugees from somewhere. They may have intelligence we can use. If memory serves, this region was inhabited by several animist tribes, people too few in number and too insignificant for anyone to bother about. Let me go forward and make contact with them."

Ben Loman's mouth dropped open in surprise. He was speechless for a moment. "Go forward? We lose the element of surprise and you get yourself killed?" He shook his head violently. Then chanting came to them on the quiet mountain air. The sound of the voices caused a chill to run down Ben Loman's spine. The others heard it too. "Is that the voice of mortal man, Senior Sword?" Ben Loman asked triumphantly. He switched his mike on. "On my command, at a hundred meters, fire when ready!" He turned to the noncom. "Demons? Pagans? I don't care who they are, let God sort them out!"

Great Shaman Hadu's body seemed to fly apart as several fléchette weapons hit him at the same instant. The Pilipili Magna froze in unbelieving horror for an instant, and then as the soldiers' weapons zeroed in on the figures crouching about the fire, they realized what was happening and scrambled in panic for cover, some toward caves in the rock wall, others into the high grass on the edge of the spring that was their water source.

"On your feet! *Forward!*" Ben Loman screamed. The soldiers descended on the camp in a ragged line, firing as they advanced. Suddenly, in that first volley, the weeks of hardship and danger drained away and they felt like giants squashing hideous insects before them. They shouted and laughed and screamed, firing with abandon into the fleeing mob of Pilipili Magna, harmless farmers frightened half out of their wits, not a single firearm among them. But to Ben Loman's men, the figures flopping and twisting in their optics were demons, ugly snouts, beady eyes, rending teeth and all. No mistake. Revenge was theirs at last!

First Acolyte Ben Loman's eyes blazed with fury, and spittle flecked his lips as he fired and fired and fired. What exhilaration! Demons scattered and fell before his onslaught. Before he knew it he was standing at the campfire. Twisted bodies lay all about. An elderly man—for now he could clearly see that his targets had been human beings, not demons—was moaning nearby, his legs neatly sliced off just above the knees. Without thinking, Ben Loman killed him with one shot to the head. Whooping and shouting, his men pursued the remaining Pilipili Magna into the dead end of the canyon, shooting them down without mercy. Gradually the screams and moans of the victims ceased.

Senior Sword Raipur was horrified at what he was seeing. He knew these men, had lived with them for months. They'd been disciplined soldiers, but now they'd turned into animals. He shouted for them to stop and regroup, but nobody was listening. Men were throwing the bodies into the fire! He rushed in and dragged a woman out, screaming for the soldiers to stop. No use, she was already dead. He whirled on the acolyte. "Tell them to stop!" he shouted. "What are you doing? Stop them, stop them!" The noncom was almost in tears as he screamed at his commander.

"On me! Everyone on me!" Ben Loman shouted into the command net at last, his breath coming in heavy gasps. Despite the cool mountain night air, he was perspiring freely. His legs felt rubbery. He steadied himself. He looked down at the old man as if seeing him for the first time. Damn! They weren't demons after all.

Gradually his men came into the firelight. "Senior Sword, are the men all accounted for?" he asked Raipur.

Raipur glared ominously at his platoon leader. He had not fired his weapon, and what he saw in the diminishing firelight sickened him to the depths of his soul. "They were *not* demons," he answered, his voice hard and flat with anger.

"So what? They are infidels, pagans, life that is not even worthy of life! *Are all the men accounted for, Senior Sword?*" Raipur was silent, continuing to glare at his commander. "I asked you a question, Senior Sword," Ben Loman said in his normal voice.

Raipur glanced about him quickly at the troopers gathered around the fire. "Yeah. Sir."

Ben Loman removed his helmet and wiped the perspiration off his forehead. "All right, men. Spread out, look for survivors. Use your infras. We have to finish the job. You." He turned to Senior Sword Raipur. "You take two men and search up there." He gestured toward the canyon wall. "A bunch of them ran that way, probably into caves. Find them. You know what to do."

"Acolyte, if any of the survivors are armed, we could be ambushed. Let me take—"

"No! You take two men, swordie, *you* go up there, *you*

flush them out, understand?" the acolyte sneered. "It'll give you a chance to fire your weapon."

Reluctantly, Raipur selected two men—he'd seen them tossing bodies into the fire—and started out toward the canyon wall. Along the way they discovered several refugees who'd only been slightly wounded. His men killed them without hesitation. No longer worried about being fired on themselves, the soldiers used their powerful handheld torches to light the way. The brilliant beams illuminated two dark openings in the rock face. "You two take the one on the left, I'll take the one on the right." The two soldiers looked at Raipur questioningly. "Go on! You know what to do. I'll be all right."

A few meters into the cave mouth Raipur turned off his light and switched on his infras. Nothing, thank God. He switched the light back on and proceeded farther back into the cave. Everywhere there was evidence that people had been living there—discarded clothing and personal items, fire pits, sleeping places. Raipur shook his head sadly. He switched off the light and stood there in total darkness, listening intently. From somewhere far ahead came the steady, hollow sound of dripping water. Then he heard rocks falling as if someone was scrabbling for cover, and his heart skipped a beat. He took the safety off his rifle. Innocent refugees or not, he was not about to take any chances. He switched his light back on. The scrabbling grew louder and then stopped entirely. He switched on his infras. There it was! Fifteen meters off to his left, a faint glow behind a small boulder.

Raipur grinned. He fired several bursts back into the cave but away from the faint glow that represented someone hiding behind the boulder. The fléchettes shattered against the cave wall in a brilliant pyrotechnic display, suffusing the cave with their pale light. His headset crackled suddenly but nothing came through. Evidently, the rock blocked the radio transmission. He grinned again.

Behind the boulder, cowering in a small ball, lay a young woman, a tiny bundle clutched tightly to her breast. In the brilliant light of Raipur's torch she squeezed her eyes closed and turned her back to him, putting her body between the soldier and her baby, anticipating the shot she assumed was coming and offering the infant the only protection she could give it.

The woman shivered in her rags; not from cold, but from fear. She moaned quietly, anticipating the shot that would end the life of her and her child. Raipur slung his rifle and unfastened a sundry pack from his equipment harness.

"Can you understand me?" he asked. The woman continued to moan and shiver. He nudged her with his foot. "Can you understand what I'm saying?" he asked again. "Answer me!" he commanded. The woman nodded. "Take this. Food in here. Understand? Something to make fire and keep you and your baby warm. Stay here until we're gone, understand? Don't move, don't make a sound." He pulled a ground sheet out of the pack and covered the pair with it. If Ben Loman sent someone else into the cave to double-check, the sheet would prevent their being picked up on his infras.

"Remember: no noise, no move, you understand? Be quiet, like death, or you *will* die." He stood there, looking down on the pitiful pair. "Lady, I'm finished, you hear? I'm putting in for a transfer before that *asshole* can fire me." He paused. Evidently she didn't care about his personal problems. "Woman, put your trust in God, the protector of orphans and widows."

Outside, the other two soldiers were waiting. "We got some!" one gushed. "They were hiding back in there! We cut them up like sausages!" He began to laugh in a high-pitched cackle.

"We lit them up," the other added. "Swordie, we saw flashes from your cave and tried to get you on the horn. You must've got some too, huh?"

"You bet," Raipur answered. "Let's go back and tell the acolyte. We're all done up here."

Hours later the woman removed the ground sheet the soldier had given her. Dimly, the light of day illuminated the cave entrance far from where she lay hidden. There was no sound save the steady dripping of water. Were the killers gone? Wrapping the ground sheet about her like a cloak, she gathered up her child and the sundry pack and stumbled toward the light. Her name was Emwana Haramu, and her child, a boy, was named Chisi.

# CHAPTER
# THREE

Interstellar communications were slow. Messages couldn't travel any faster than a starship or drone traveled through Beamspace—some six and a fraction light-years per day. When a message sent via starship went from the point of origin of a message to the message's destination, it didn't necessarily travel in a straight line. The message might travel on several ships before it got where it was going, and could take a year or more to get there. If no starship routing was available in reasonable time, or the message was time sensitive, it was sent by drone—if a drone was available and the cost justifiable. The Confederation Diplomatic Service, the military, and the Bureau of Human Habitability Exploration and Investigation, and planetary governments, along with the larger interstellar corporations, were generally the only entities that used drones for interstellar communication.

Second Associate Deputy Director for State Affairs Lumrhanda Ronstedt knew this when he overstepped his authority a skosh by stamping a request for Marines from the Confederation Ambassador to the Kingdom of Yahweh and His Saints and Their Apostles "Approved, Office of the President." After queuing it via fast channel for the offices of the Combined Chiefs of Staff—he hadn't been prepared to exceed his authority far enough to queue it "urgent"—he made an entry in his tickler and forgot about the matter.

Ronstedt did such a good job of forgetting that he had no idea why his tickler saw fit to remind him of it nearly a year later, when the first report came in from the Marines dispatched to Kingdom. He looked at the header, saw that the message was from the Commander, 34th FIST deployed to the Kingdom of Yahweh and His Saints and Their Apostles. He recognized the name of the planet, of course—the history of the lesser human worlds was a hobby of his—but had no idea what a Marine FIST was doing there. Being a methodical person who disliked going into anything without as much background information as possible—except when it suited his fancy to see what foolishness humanity was up to next— he went back to his tickler to see if he'd put any notes in it to clue him as to what this was about.

There *were* notes, and *bing!* he remembered. An "urgent" dispatch had come from Friendly Credence, a dead-end diplomat with no experience beyond diplomatic circles, who was Confederation ambassador to Kingdom. Credence had put in a request for Marines to put down a peasant revolt. Absurdly enough, the ambassador had claimed the peasants were armed with weapons more powerful than anything in the arsenal of the Kingdom army. Even more absurdly, he claimed—well, "hinted" might be the better word—that the revolting peasants were actually an alien invasion! Nonsense! *Everybody* knew *H. sapiens* was the only sentience in the known universe. Ronstedt made a quick check in *The Atlas of the Populated and Explored Planets of Human Space, Nineteenth Edition,* and saw that Credence had been replaced by Jayben Spears. He looked up Spears in the *Blue Line of Ambassadors, Ministers, and Consuls,* puzzled for a few moments over Spears's checkered career, and concluded he was either an incompetent or a troublemaker who'd been shunted aside to a nowhere backwater to get him out of the hair of his betters.

This should be interesting, he thought. He smiled and settled back to read the dispatch, despite the fact that it was classified "Ultra Secret, Need to Know" and he wasn't cleared to have the need. He was confident he would get a few chuckles out of the human follies he would read about in the dispatch.

A paragraph into it, his smile was gone. He began swallowing and massaging his suddenly constricted throat. Two paragraphs in, he used a tissue to pat his suddenly damp forehead. A paragraph later a bead of perspiration actually did pop out on his forehead. By the time he finished reading the three pages, sweat was dripping from his brow and flowing from his armpits, his eyes were wide and his pupils dilated, he was mildly hyperventilating, and his heart rate was elevated.

There was nothing remotely amusing in the dispatch. There *was* an alien invasion on Kingdom, and the Marines had suffered heavy casualties and were hard pressed to hold.

Ronstedt was afraid. Had he routed Ambassador Credence's original request for Marines to the analysts in the Office of Senior Military Advisers to the President, as he properly should have, they would have sent an investigation team to Kingdom to determine the degree of need. Given an actual alien invasion, the Confederation would have assembled a major force to deal with it—after sending a diplomatic team to attempt to open communications and bring about a cessation of hostilities in an attempt to avoid military intervention. Instead, an entire Marine FIST was in danger of being wiped out and a human planet completely taken over by a previously unknown alien sentience.

Because of him.

The unpreparedness on the part of the Marines was completely his fault. Because he wanted to privately enjoy a minor amusement. It wouldn't take much investigation to track the routing of the presidential authorization to dispatch Marines back to him. Then where would Second Associate Deputy Director for State Affairs Lumrhanda Ronstedt be? At the very least, a letter of reprimand would be put in his file and he might never be promoted to First Associate Deputy Director for State Affairs. He could even be demoted! Why, he could be dismissed! If someone high enough decided a scapegoat was needed, civil—or even *criminal*—charges could be brought against him!

Lumrhanda Ronstedt was afraid, he was *very* afraid.

He would have prayed that nobody ever undertook an investigation of the routing of the message that sent 34th FIST to Kingdom, that nobody ever discovered that he'd exceeded his authority in the initial authorization to deploy Marines without more information than was contained in the initial ambassadorial request. But though human communities on far-flung worlds worshiped a variety of gods, he didn't believe in any of them. And since he didn't believe in any of those gods, he suspected none of them—if any of them did indeed exist—believed in *him* either, so praying was out of the question. Instead, he merely hoped nobody would look and find him.

The Marines of 34th and 26th FISTs were unhappy—in their spare moments when they weren't outright angry. They were *Marines,* for Cthulusake, not squids! When they were traveling back to home base after a deployment, especially a major campaign like the one they'd just been on, they were supposed to spend their time cleaning and maintaining their uniforms and gear, and filling out "Replacement of Uniform and Gear" chits. Mostly, though, they were supposed to be healing their wounds, resting, eating, and exercising to regain their strength. There was supposed to be a lot of slack on the voyage back after a deployment.

So why were they spending most of their time polishing brightwork, waxing wood, and scraping away imaginary crud and corruption from the decks of passageways and troop compartments? Why were they painting bulkheads and overheads that didn't need painting? Why were they working under bosuns mates, stripping down and reassembling everything in the troop compartments? Why were they doing all that and everything else that was properly squid work?

*Oh, the shame of it! Marines working under the supervision of squids!*

And here they'd all thought Brigadier Sturgeon was such a good commander. If he was as good as they'd thought, he'd go straight to that squid commodore, tell him Marines weren't a ship's maintenance crew, and make him stop misusing Marines!

Corporal Claypoole put down the stripper he'd been using

to clean away the thin layer of floor wax that had accumulated where the deck and bulkhead of a passageway joined—he'd just reached the airtight hatch that marked the end of the area assigned to him. Pushing himself up from all fours to sit back on his ankles, he clamped his hands over his kidneys and groaned as he twisted the kinks out of his spine. Then he leaned forward onto his hands again and levered himself up to shake the kinks out of his hips and legs. It took some effort, but he managed to ignore the quietly snickering squids who briskly walked past as he looked back at the twenty meter stretch of passageway he'd just scraped, both sides, and decided it was good enough—as if it wasn't good enough before he started. If he didn't ignore the snickering squids, he'd be obligated to *do* something about their snickering. He was a *corporal,* he wasn't supposed to *do* scutwork, he was supposed to *supervise* scutwork. And all those snickering squids were prime candidates for *doing* scutwork. Which would just get him in trouble with the ship's command—Sergeant Linsman had made that perfectly clear.

So instead of putting the snickering squids to work doing what was properly their work anyway, he ignored them and quickly used the suction hose to clean up the . . . the . . . Well, there *might* be something on the deck after all the stripping he'd just done. That finished, he started to bend over to pick up the scraper, thought better of further tormenting his back, and squatted to pick it up. Standing again, he began to step through the hatch to make his way to Company L's mess for a drink and some rest. Hey, the squid who put him to work told him when he got the job done he was free.

"You missed a spot, Marine."

The words brought him up, rigid. He knew that voice and hated it. Slowly, he turned around and glared at Bosun's Mate First Giltherr. Giltherr looked back with an evil smirk.

"What did I miss?" Claypoole snarled.

"Right there." Giltherr pointed.

Claypoole clomped stiff-legged to him and looked. "I didn't miss anything. There's nothing there to strip."

Giltherr shook his head. "It's a good thing they give you

jarheads blasters instead of masers," he said. "You can't see well enough to hit a man at fifty meters with a maser. Now do it again. This whole section of passageway. If you missed that spot, I'm sure you missed more."

Claypoole glared at Giltherr again. He wanted to tell the squid to shove it, there wasn't anything to strip, and then *help* him shove it because the squid was probably too damn dumb to be able to find his own ass with both hands. But the squid was a first class, the navy equivalent of a staff sergeant, and technically outranked a corporal. As if *any* squid could out-rank a Marine!

Snarling, he twisted past Giltherr to the far end of the passageway and dropped back to all fours to strip away once more at something that didn't need any stripping.

Staff Sergeant Hyakowa's going to hear about this, he promised himself. I'm going to take this all the way to the brigadier if I have to! It's time somebody told him what's happening. But he stripped the entire section of passageway, all twenty meters on both sides, and the ends. Again.

Brigadier Sturgeon, of course, didn't need to be told what was happening—after all, the "squid work" the Marines were doing had been his idea. He not only knew what his Marines were doing, he knew what they thought about it— the same thing he'd thought about it a long time ago when he was a junior enlisted man and *his* FIST commander made a similar arrangement with the captain of the ship on which they were returning to Camp Smutter on the curiously named *Falala* at the end of a particularly brutal campaign. Thirteenth FIST had lost a lot of Marines—he'd lost a couple of friends himself—and the Marines were dwelling on it. Morale was sinking fast and there was serious risk that 13th FIST would wind up irreparably combat-ineffective. Almost as soon as they were assigned to the heavy duty make-work on the ship the dwelling on injury and loss was turned into anger over what they perceived—rightly, he had to admit— as a misuse of Marines. It was hard, physically and mentally, to do that work. But it accomplished what it was meant to—

it gave their bruised and bloodied psyches relief, let them put some distance between their injuries and losses, and allowed their psyches to begin to scab over.

He could see the same thing happening in *his* Marines. When he went through the troop areas, as he did at least twice a day, everything was more shipshape than it had been following liftoff from Society 362 and until the make-work began. The Marines were standing more erect, they looked more determined, and hardly any of them appeared depressed. Angry, most certainly, but not depressed. That was all he asked for. A rueful smile flickered across his face and he wondered how long it would take for his Marines to figure out he was behind the "squid work" they were doing and transfer their anger to him.

Well, nobody ever said a commander had to be loved by his troops.

Corporal Claypoole wasn't the only Marine in third platoon's second squad who promised himself he was going to take the matter up with Staff Sergeant Hyakowa. He was the second-to-last man to make it back to the squad's compartment, and had to get in line behind Corporals Kerr and Chan and then elbow Lance Corporal MacIlargie out of his way— they were already chewing on Sergeant Linsman, the squad leader, about the squid work they were doing and demanding to see the platoon sergeant.

Claypoole warily looked at Lance Corporal Schultz. Surely Schultz would have blood in his eyes about what they were doing. But no, Schultz was calmly lying back on his rack, plugged into the ship's library, reading who knew what, seemingly oblivious to the indignity of the squid work he'd spent his day at. The tip of Claypoole's tongue peeked from between his lips as he considered Schultz's uncharacteristically mild behavior. It worried him. He sidled a half step away from Schultz, a half step being as far as he could go in the cramped confines of the squad compartment, and turned his attention to the squad leader and the two fire team leaders already chewing on him.

"I'm not putting up with any more of this shit!" a loud voice declaimed from the entrance to the compartment. Everybody—except Schultz—looked at the voice in surprise. Not in surprise at the words, surprise at the speaker. It was Corporal Doyle. Corporal Doyle hadn't been heard to raise his voice since he'd come back from his premature transfer out of 34th FIST when Company L's first sergeant, Top Myer, wanted to court-martial him for insubordination following the Avionia deployment. Before the premature transfer, he'd been the company's chief clerk; after it, he filled a PFC slot in third platoon. And he'd *never* been known to raise his voice in the face of a blaster squad.

"What's *your* problem, Doyle?" Linsman snapped.

"I just spent the day cleaning heads for the damn squids, that's what!" Doyle snapped back. "I left those heads clean enough to eat off. They're probably cleaner than the squids' galleys!"

"I doubt it," Kerr grumbled. "Chan and I spent the day cleaning their galleys."

"See! They're treating us like galley slaves," Doyle declared, unaware of the pun. "I'm surprised they don't have us painting this scow!"

Wordlessly, Linsman pushed back a sleeve and held up his arm to show Doyle the drops of paint spattered on the back of his hand and wrist.

Doyle's eyes popped wide. "You too?" he squeaked. "They've got a *squad leader* doing squid work?"

Linsman nodded. "Rabbit and Hound too," he said, naming the first- and gun-squad leaders. "I'm not sure, but I think the platoon sergeants were doing squid work in the chiefs' quarters and officer country."

There were gasps, and everybody—except Schultz—looked at their squad leader, horrified at the very thought of platoon sergeants doing menial labor.

There was a sudden, albeit restricted, surge of movement away from Schultz when everyone simultaneously realized he hadn't reacted. Surely, Schultz was about to go on a rampage, and nobody wanted to be standing in his path when he launched himself. But, no. Schultz was totally immersed in his reading.

"Then it won't do us much good to go to Staff Sergeant Hyakowa, will it?" Chan asked.

Linsman shook his head. "I don't believe so, no."

"We have to request mast straight to the brigadier," Claypoole said. Every Marine, regardless of rank, had the right to "request mast"—speak to the commander at whatever level, all the way up to the commandant. He had to go through the chain of command to do it, and every level of command along the way would try to resolve the problem and talk him out of going higher—but he had the right, and didn't have to discuss his problem with any lower level on the chain of command.

Linsman looked at him coldly. "Do you really think the brigadier doesn't know what's going on with his FIST?"

Claypoole wasn't going to give up that easily. "Then we request mast to the next higher command."

"That's Fifth Marine Expeditionary Force," Linsman said calmly. "By the time any of us can get to Fifth MEF headquarters, the FIST will have been back at Camp Ellis for weeks, maybe months, and the problem will be over. Do you think Fifth MEF will bother to make the navy issue an apology and promise not to do it again? Would you believe the navy if they did promise?"

"Promise not to do it again until the next time," Kerr added, which elicited some weak laughter.

"But we've got to do something," Claypoole insisted. "I mean we can't just lay back and—"

"Found it," Schultz interrupted. Everyone shut up and looked at him as he rolled to a sitting position. He looked around, holding his reader where he could easily refer to it as he spoke to his squad mates. Satisfied that he had everyone's attention, he said:

"Third Silvasian War?" The question, sparsely worded in Schultz's normal conversational manner, was mostly rhetorical. Not a lot of Marines had fought in the Silvasian wars, but some of them were still around, and their exploits were legendary in the Corps.

Some of the Marines exchanged nervous glances. There were unconfirmed rumors that an army division had mutinied aboard ship on the way back to their base at the end of the Third Silvasian War. Was Schultz about to propose that they mutiny?

"Sturgeon was a lance corporal, 13th FIST."

"Yes?" Linsman drew the word out.

"Heavy casualties." Schultz looked each man in the eye. "Like us."

The sound of their breathing was the only noise in the compartment other than the soft susurration of circulating air. They were becoming more convinced Schultz was about to start a mutiny.

"Brigadier Wainwright was commander. Gave his Marines squid work, got their minds off the war."

"What? Let me see that." Sergeant Linsman stepped forward and almost snatched the reader out of Schultz's hands, barely catching himself in time for Schultz to hand it to him. He scanned the document on the screen, then flipped back through others that Schultz had marked. He read them again more slowly.

"This is 13th FIST's Unit Diary on the return voyage following the Third Silvasian War," he told his men. "Like Hammer said, Brigadier Sturgeon was a lance corporal with India Company. Thirteenth FIST suffered heavy casualties, nearly as heavy as we did on Kingdom. The Marines were brooding over their losses." He raised his eyes to look at his men and said, "Just like we were yesterday." His men looked at the overhead, the deck, bare patches of bulkhead, anywhere but at him or at each other. "Their morale was suffering and Brigadier Wainwright was afraid the FIST was going to collapse from it. So he made arrangements with the ship's commander to put his Marines to work, squid-type makework, to get their minds off it.

"It worked." Linsman handed the reader back to Schultz. "Tomorrow we're going to do more squid work. We can be pissed off at the squids, we can be pissed off at the brigadier, we can bitch about it as much as we want. But we won't request mast. Is that understood?"

The Marines made faces and muttered unkind things about squids and their commanders, even about Marine squad leaders, but they agreed.

"I know some squids better stop snickering at me or they're going to be eating through straws," Claypoole grumbled.

"Belay that, Rock," Linsman said sharply, but not too sharply.

Claypoole grimaced, but nodded acquiescence.

Word got around to the rest of the Marines about what happened to 13th FIST at the end of the Third Silvasian War. They continued with their squid work for the rest of the voyage. They were pissed off at the squids and at Brigadier Sturgeon, but they stopped brooding and nobody requested mast. A couple of sailors who snickered too openly did wind up eating through straws, though. The Marines' psyches were well on their way to being healed by the time the *Grandar Bay* reached Thorsfinni's World.

# CHAPTER
# FOUR

He could feel the cold hardness of a floor beneath where he lay. His ears were ringing and there was a gray haze in front of his eyes, but he knew he must be lying on the ground—and he was naked. But his head was clear of the insistent probing that had filled it since . . . when? He could not remember! He groaned. *He could hear himself groaning!*

He let the air out of his lungs and took a deep breath. The air was dank and smelled of excrement. Wonderful! Feeling began to come back into his limbs, first his fingers and toes, then his legs and arms—oh, God! His body hurt, it burned and throbbed all over! He groaned again. "Oh, shit," someone croaked. The voice seemed to come from light-years away but it echoed inside his head. He could feel his tongue now. It seemed the consistency of tar paper and filled his mouth. He swallowed and it hurt his throat. "Oh, shit," he groaned.

Someone touched him. "Unnnh," he said.

"Are you alive?" Someone touched him again.

He turned his head painfully in the direction of the voice and saw a woman, or something he knew must have been a woman, but this creature with its hair in filthy strings dangling about its haggard, pale face resembled a . . . a . . . He struggled for a word, and the name of a monster sprung into his mind: Medusa. He started in terror at the image.

"You don't look so good yourself," Medusa said. "What's your name?"

"Oh, balls," he groaned.

"Hello to you too, Mr. Balls," Medusa replied.

There were six of them, four men and two women, crammed into an iron cage too small for their number. They lay virtually on top of one another, as if they'd been tossed roughly in there to rot. He scooted into a corner and pulled his legs up under his chin. There were scratches and gashes all over his body, some of them very painful, but the others in the cage with him apparently had fared no better at the hands of their captors. In the crook of each person's arm was a huge black and blue welt where a tube or a syringe had been shoved into the vein.

The cage was placed a few meters inside the entrance to a cave. It was empty and light came in from outside.

"My feet!" one of the men screamed. Balls and Medusa—the other three were still only semiconscious—looked at the man's feet. They were bruised and blistered; shreds of flesh hung off them. "Look at *your* feet!" he exclaimed in horror. Medusa gasped and reached a comforting hand toward her own bleeding feet.

"Jesus Christ!" Balls exclaimed, examining the damage done to his own feet.

"You shouldn't talk that way," the other man said.

"Why not?" Balls asked, unaware he'd said anything.

"Because—Because—you shouldn't. I don't know." The man shrugged. "You just shouldn't." He looked quizzically at Balls, as if *Balls* should tell him why his own language was unacceptable.

"I remember—I remember," Medusa began, scrunching up her eyes as she tried to remember something important. She shook her head in frustration. Her filthy locks swayed obscenely with the motion of her head. Balls could see that once they had been *red. Red hair;* now who did he know who had red hair?

"I can't remember!" Balls said, and smacked a palm into his forehead.

"I remember!" Medusa said suddenly, brightly. "I remember carrying things! Monsters made us carry things! Yes! That's how I hurt my feet!" Her teeth were even and white, except where some had been broken off.

The two men looked at one another. Neither could remember that. "I'll take your word for it," the man she called Balls said at last. He tried, shifting in the narrow confines of the cage, to ease the pain in his feet and thighs, but it was no use, so he flopped back down on his rear with a sigh.

Medusa held out her hand. "My name is—is—" She shook her head again. "My name is—Colleen." She spit the name out hesitantly. "Colleen?" she repeated, as if trying out her name. "My name is Colleen," she said more freely. "I—I don't remember the rest of my name," she added weakly.

"I don't remember my name either," Balls admitted, panic rising inside him, but he took her hand and squeezed it anyway. The other man just shook his head and clasped his arms more tightly about his legs.

"They did something to us, to make us forget," Colleen said.

"I think it's only temporary," Balls said hopefully. He looked at—Colleen—closely. She sat with her legs drawn tightly up to her chin, but he could see the reddish-brown hair down below and something stirred inside him. Well, I haven't forgotten *that,* he smiled to himself. All beat up and her hair in a mess, Colleen, lately Medusa, wasn't all that bad-looking. He thought: I can count on her. He looked at the other man, about forty or so, pale, shivering, eyes closed, lips pressed tightly together. Don't know about that boy, he thought. He decided to call him "Shaky."

Gradually the other three came around. They sat, comparing what memories of their ordeal they could muster among them. The consensus was that they had been taken from somewhere—their former lives—and held prisoner by monsters of some sort, creatures that were able to get inside their minds and probe their thoughts. But none of them had any idea what the monsters wanted or why they did not appear to be around anymore, and if they were gone, whether they would come back again. None could remember anything of his or her former life, and only one of the other three could remember his name, and only his given name—Chet. Somehow, that made the rest of them feel better.

A cold breeze came in through the cave entrance. "The light's going!" the other woman remarked.

"Has anyone tried to see if we can get out of this goddamned thing?" Balls asked. Shaky, the one who had objected to his use of words earlier but had remained silent during the discussions, looked sharply at him again. Balls got painfully to his knees and pushed against the bars. A gate swung open suddenly and he pitched out onto the floor with a surprised, "Ooof!" He lay there for a moment, half stunned, then laughed. "Typical military operation!" he said, half to himself, and wondered, Where did that expression come from? Had he been a soldier once?

One of the other men lunged for the cave entrance.

"Hold it!" Balls said from where he lay. "Night's coming on, we don't know where we are, and we won't be able to find out much in the dark."

"But what if the monsters come back?" the other woman asked.

"I don't think they are coming back," Colleen answered, "or they wouldn't have left that gate unlocked, so let's do as he says and stay put until morning. And has anyone noticed, we're naked? And it's getting cold," she added.

"He's right," the man who called himself Chet agreed. "We'll be warm enough if we stay close together. But whatever you do, *don't shut that gate.*"

"Mr. 'Military Operation,'" Colleen said, extending her hand to help him back inside the cage. "Sounds more like you than 'Mr. Balls.' I'll snuggle up with you tonight." And she did.

The morning dawned bright and warm. The six prisoners hobbled painfully into the open, the stronger ones helping the weaker. They stood blinking in the morning light. They were inside a small compound that consisted of several temporary huts built of metal. Scattered everywhere was the detritus of a hastily abandoned camp. Some of the items lying about were obviously pieces of furniture, but most of the stuff had uses none of them could understand. Whatever they were, the previous users did not seem to need them anymore.

The man they were now calling Military Operation looked up at webbing that was strung from tree to tree. "That looks like it can break up infra signatures," he muttered, and wondered why he thought that and how he knew such a thing.

Not far from where they stood was a high, grass-covered ridge. Behind them, a high cliff formed one wall of a small valley.

"I would like to find something to wear," Colleen said to no one in particular. She headed off toward the largest of the huts. Military Operation hobbled off behind her. The others stood about for a moment before heading for the other buildings, to see what they could find.

"Look here!" the man named Chet called from one of the huts. He was holding up several strips of light metallic material. They had the malleability of tinfoil, but no matter how hard they tried, the strips could not be severed. "This stuff is indestructible," Chet commented. "We can use it to make shoe packs for our feet! And wrap strips around us for clothes!"

For twenty minutes or more the six busied themselves fashioning shoes and garments of sorts from the strange material. Colleen wrapped a long strip of it around herself like an evening gown. The sunlight reflected brilliantly off her "dress."

Military Operation chuckled. "Look at your feet," he said. The packs she had crafted out of the material made her feet look six times their normal size.

Colleen looked down at her feet and laughed too, then hopped from one foot to the other. "But I can walk in them!"

"Where there's life, there's a chuckle," Chet said, coming up to the pair.

"And now," Military Operation said, "let's walk up to that ridge line and see what we can see."

At first it was difficult walking in the packs, but after a hundred yards the material began to mold itself to them, and those who had wrapped it thickly enough about the bottoms of their feet found walking much easier, although they had to go slowly because the injuries to their feet were still painful.

They slogged through deep, early morning, dew-laden, grasslike ground cover, leaving long trails behind them as they moved up the slope. By the time they reached the top, the lower half of their bodies was soaking wet from the moisture. They stood on the ridge at last, breathing heavily from exhaustion and lack of exercise, and surveyed the lay of the land. Off in the near distance they could clearly make out running water flashing in the sunlight.

"A river!" one of the men exclaimed.

"If we follow the river," Chet said, "it'll lead us to the sea, and where the coast is, there're bound to be settlements of some sort."

Military Operation waded a bit farther into the grass and stopped. "Look here," he called to the others. They came and stood beside him. The grass had been flattened where he was standing, as if someone had lain down in it long enough to crush it flat so it wouldn't spring back up. "Someone was here," he said. He followed a narrow path through the grass. "Here! A trail!" he called back to his companions. It was a meter wide and easy to follow, as if a number of people had passed that way recently. And it led in the opposite direction from the river.

"I'd say we should follow this trail," Military Operation said.

"I say we follow the river," one of the other men replied. "We don't know who made this. It could've been the—the—*things* that held us prisoner. We could just be walking right back into their arms."

"He's right," the other woman said. "At least the river goes somewhere."

Colleen, who had walked down the trail a ways called back to them, "Look here!" She pointed to a footprint in the fresh earth. "A human footprint. He was wearing shoes!"

"Did anybody notice, we didn't see a path leading up here

from the compound," Chet volunteered. "So I don't think this path was made by the monsters. And whoever made it came from a different direction than the compound. I think Military Operation is right. Whoever made this trail knew where they were going, and if we find them, we'll be among our own kind at least."

"And that crushed-flat place, maybe that was where they lay in hiding, watching the monsters before they moved on!" Colleen said.

"We need food," the other woman said.

"We can find food in the river! Fish, clams, whatever," one of the other men said.

"Look, this trail is relatively fresh, made within the last day or two at the most," Military Operation said. "If we hurry, we can catch up with them. Goddamnit, we're starving, can't you feel it? We can't find enough food in the river to restore our strength. Besides, if there is a town or a city somewhere along that river, for all we know it could be five hundred kilometers from here—or the damned thing could just empty into the sea without ever passing anywhere near civilization."

"Yes," one of the men said, "but there could be a town only *five* kilometers from here, and I still maintain we'll find more food along the river than along that trail of yours."

"He's right!" Shaky shouted. It was the first words he'd spoken since the day before. "And who put you in charge?" he shouted at Military Operation.

"Well, I'm following this goddamned trail," Military Operation said. Nobody bothered to correct him on his language this time.

"All right. Who's for the river and who's for the trail?" Chet asked. He and Colleen voted for the trail.

The six of them stood silently in the tall grass. "Well, if we find civilization, we'll come back for you," one of the men for the river said.

"Same for us," Colleen answered. They shook hands all around. The three started off for the river, and the three who were taking the path watched them until their figures dwindled in the distance. A last wave and they started out on their own way.

They followed the trail all that day. It was easy to follow. Evidently, the people who had made it did know where they were headed and were anxious to get there. All day long Military Operation constantly scanned the skyline and the surrounding geography, looking for the other people but also just checking. Several times he called for a halt as he went forward to a hillock or a ridge to survey the area before them, acting almost instinctively to avoid being seen until he was sure what lay ahead. He scanned the sky continuously and once shouted for them to fall to the ground. He'd spotted a high flier that turned out to be only a winged creature of some sort, soaring on the thermals, searching for much smaller prey.

"I thought it could be the monsters, or something," he apologized sheepishly.

Toward evening the trail skirted a small pond. The three did not hesitate to drink from it, although it was covered with a green scum, which they brushed aside with their hands to get at the cool water underneath.

They rested on the bank. "At least we won't die of thirst," Colleen said. Military Operation smiled at her and thought, She's a good soldier. The man called Chet was too, he realized. "I'm glad you two came with me," he said. He found himself wondering, for what reason he could not say, if they could handle weapons in a fight. He shrugged. Wherever that thought came from, they had no weapons.

"It'll be dark soon. What do you say we spend the night right here?" Chet suggested.

They pulled up some bushes, gathered leafy foliage, and made themselves a small bower beside the pond, then settled down into it for the night.

The second day dawned overcast and considerably cooler. Two hours into the journey, huge thunderheads rolled up from behind them and the wind picked up. The temperature dropped quickly. All the rest of that day it stormed. The three pressed on. At times they had to hold onto each other to keep from being knocked down by the gusts and the wall of cold rain that lashed at them. They grew faint from hunger and the loss of body heat in the cold.

"I can't go on," Colleen shouted at last, her voice barely audible above the roar of the storm.

"We can't stop," Military Operation yelled back, his words picked up and whirled away in the wind. "If we stop, we'll die from exposure." He and Chet each took one of Colleen's arms and helped her along, but the two men were suffering from hunger and exposure too. Worse, the trail had disappeared in the storm. They lost track of time and direction, concentrating only on putting one foot in front of the other and keeping Colleen upright between them, but soon they couldn't do that anymore either and they all collapsed into the mud in a heap.

"We have to get up. We have to go on," Military Operation gasped, but he made no move to get up or go on, just lay there and let the cold rain wash over him. It had grown very dark, but he wasn't sure if that was due to the lateness of the day or the heavy storm raging all around them. In the dim storm light he could see that Colleen's lips were turning blue and her eyes were closed. He rubbed her cheeks vigorously.

"Chet, help me!" The two men managed to revive Colleen enough so that she groaned.

Military Operation lay back in the mud and cursed. He wondered about the three who'd gone downriver. If they went along the river bottom, they'd have been swept away in the surge. But they would die here too, and once dead, be just as dead as if they'd drowned in the river. The shame of it was, he still had no idea how he'd gotten here or who he was before he was taken prisoner. Maybe we're all criminals, he thought. We'd been in a jail, and belonged there. That made him laugh just as there came a momentary lull in the storm.

Chet looked up from where he lay. "What's so funny?" he

asked weakly, and then began to laugh himself. Both men laughed uncontrollably.

Military Operation laughed so hard he began to cough. He fought to recover himself. "Okay," he gasped at last. "Okay, enough of this! I've never been one to miss cadence on the grinder. Full field inspection in fifteen minutes, goddamnit! I'm getting up and I'm going on." Painfully, he rose to his knees, but could not get back on his feet. The storm returned then in full force and buffeted him onto his elbows. He began to crawl, shouting curses into the wind. In seconds he no longer knew where he was or where the others were. He crawled in a circle.

He paused to get his breath. Someone was shouting. At him? The wind screamed around him and he thought it carried a voice calling "Charlieeeeeee! Charlieeeee!" That name sounded so familiar. He looked into the wind-driven rain lashing his face, stinging like hail and blurring his vision. Wait! Was that someone's *face* out there in the rain? Yes, clearly! It was a young face, a man with red hair, he could see the apparition distinctly! He looked familiar. In reaching out toward the man, he became unbalanced and pitched forward into the mud. He shook his head to clear his vision, and when he looked back into the storm, the face was gone. He felt great disappointment. He knew that face. But who was it? Where had it gone?

"Charlieeeee!" the wind screamed. He realized then that it was the Angel of Death and she was calling to him. He smiled. Well, he'd done his best and now it was time to go. High time. He couldn't feel the cold anymore. He was so tired. He just wanted to rest—forever. The angel came for him and lifted him up and stood him on his feet. *Aw, Jesus, she was beautiful!* He had never seen such radiant beauty. She smiled at him, and the warmth of her love washed over him. I'm going home, but I'm going out like a man, he thought, and he felt very good about that. They would have soup and sandwiches and beer in heaven. The thin metallic sheet he'd wound about himself had come off long ago, and his packs were somewhere behind him, lost in the mud too, but even if he'd known he was stark naked, he wouldn't have given a damn.

At that moment the wind died away and the rain slackened. He turned and looked around.

Before him, a gentle slope rolled away. At the bottom glowed lights in the windows of houses.

# CHAPTER
## FIVE

The four students, naked, arms bound tightly behind their backs, knelt shivering on the cold concrete floor in one of Wayvelsberg Castle's innermost interrogation rooms. Behind each stood a black-uniformed shooter at rigid attention, a heavy, black truncheon at the ready. The boy and his three female companions appeared much the worse for the interrogations they'd just undergone.

"How old are you?" Senior Stormleader Herten Gorman asked the boy. As a senior stormleader, a grade in the Special Group equivalent to that of full colonel in the Confederation Armed Forces, Gorman was the ranking officer in the SG.

"The spirit lives," the young man muttered. "Down with the usurper!" His defiance, although genuine, was somewhat marred by the tears and snot all over his face.

Gorman nodded to the shooter, a rank equivalent to that of private in the army, standing behind the boy, and he jammed his truncheon into the young man's kidneys. The three girls howled in terror. After the boy stopped retching and got his breath back, Gorman said, "I ask you again, how old are you?"

"S-Seven-teen," the young man gasped.

"Good. And what is your name?"

"Down—Down with the usurper," the young man croaked.

Gorman nodded at the shooter, who raised his truncheon again, but Dominic de Tomas, who'd been standing by silently, stepped forward and held up a hand. "That will be enough," he said, and the man returned to the position of attention. Gorman looked questioningly at his leader. De

Tomas nodded. "That will be enough," he repeated. "Tell me your name," he demanded of the young man.

"Chris—Christopher Graf," the boy mumbled.

"They call themselves the Order of the Yellow Rose, my leader," Gorman offered. "They are all second-year students at the College of the Immaculate Conception, a liberal arts school founded by the Fathers of Padua, Cardinal O'Lanners's religious order."

"O'Lanners," de Tomas repeated, and nodded.

"You murdered him!" one of the girls screamed, staring up defiantly at the two. Gorman glanced at de Tomas, who shook his head no; the stormer behind the girl made no move to punish her for the outburst.

Gorman regarded the girl and was struck by the bright blue of her eyes. Her body, despite the recent beatings she'd received, was still in the full bloom of youth. He wondered briefly if she might be the type de Tomas had asked him to find to be his consort, but he rejected that thought immediately. She was less than half his leader's age. They had nothing in common. After sex, what would they talk about? Burning heretics? He almost laughed aloud at the thought. But she'd still be a virgin, unless that boy had already deflowered her, the lucky little swine. The men of the Special Group had strict standing orders never to take sexual advantage of their prisoners.

"Ah, yes, my dear, we executed the dear old cardinal," de Tomas said. "He was just too goddamned stupid to be allowed to live any longer. You are 'students,' then, at this 'College of the Inaccurate Reception'?" A storm man, a sergeant, standing behind one of the girls burst out in laughter at the pun. "Get that man's name, Gorman!" de Tomas shouted, pointing at the storm man, who stopped laughing immediately.

"He is a good soldier, my leader!" Gorman protested.

"I don't know about that, my dear Gorman," de Tomas replied, "but he laughs at my jokes, and I want to keep him close by after this. Very well, then what have these little bastards been up to?"

*"This!"* Gorman held out a crumpled leaflet. "They were caught distributing hundreds of these seditious lies!"

The leaflet read:

THE DAY OF REKONING HAS COME! THE
REKONING OF KINGDOM'S YOUTH WITH THE
MOST ABOMINABLE TYRANNY THAT OUR
PEOPLE HADS EVER SUFFERED! BRING DOWN
DOMINIC DE TOMAS AND HIS MINIONS!
FORWARD IN THE FIGHT FOR OUR FREE
SLEF-DETERMINATION, WITHOUT WHITCH
SPIRITUAL VALUES CANNOT BE CREATED
AND DESTORY THE TERROR OF THE SPECIAL
GROUP BY THE POWER OF THE SPIRIT! DOWN
WITH DOMINIC DE TOMAS.

"They didn't waste any time getting started," de Tomas mused. "Vocabulary, purple. Punctuation unsure. Double-check your spelling," he advised the young man. "You misspelled a word in the final sentence." He crumpled the leaflet and dropped it to the floor. He turned to an overstormer, a rank equivalent to captain in the Marines, who'd been standing by the door. "Clean them up. Take them home. I want you to personally escort each to his home. Leave them in the custody of their parents with a warning—and my best wishes. Accentuate my best wishes to their parents. I am giving them back the lives of their children. Then I want you to take a platoon to the college campus. Hang the dean in the quad. Post a detail to make sure the corpse hangs there until it rots. Let the faculty know, any more of this nonsense and we close down the college." He whirled and headed for the door, Gorman close behind.

"My leader! Those young puppies are traitors! Are you just going to let them go, to continue spreading their treason?"

"They deserve to be hung for their poor prose." De Tomas laughed. "What's education coming to on Kingdom, eh, Gorman?" He paused in the hallway outside and put a hand on Gorman's shoulder. "Look, my dear Herten, we have to have

the goodwill of the people with us to succeed from now on.
We can't get that by killing their children. Those kids, back
there? No, Herten, I think their days of treason are well over
after what your shooters did to them."

Gorman reflected that not so long ago de Tomas would
have fed the students into the furnace and not thought twice
about it.

"I know what you're thinking, Herten." De Tomas wagged
a finger at Gorman. "But we are no longer the Collegium,
with a license to kill whomever we want. That worked fine—
was actually fun, wasn't it?—when there was nobody really
in charge on Kingdom. But all that's changed now." He
paused. "And remember this: every man has his price. You
find out what that is, and he's yours to control. For some it's
money, for others, power, and so on. But the 'price' of all
parents is the lives of their children. Save their children for
them and they'll do anything you want. The word will get
around about this morning's little incident, Herten, and the
parents of those kids will think I'm a saint. One of our major
propaganda themes from now on is that we do what we do
for the 'good of the children.' "

"Well, with all due respect, my leader," Gorman said,
adroitly shifting his argument in keeping with what de
Tomas had just announced, "then executing the dean of the
college might not be such a wise move—in keeping with
your new policy, that is. He is well-respected in the community, and such an action might alienate some of the most
prominent people, people whose cooperation we will need."

"What we need, my dear Herten, is the respect and cooperation of the *ordinary* people. Get that and the upper classes
will follow, and if they don't, it won't matter. Governments
are built on the back of the ordinary people. The average
man does not give a damn about so-called 'higher' education. All he cares about is his family and his livelihood. Our
society operates on the labor of the common man. Oh, he
knows engineers, scientists, and the lot require college edu-
cations, but who does he go to when he needs his plumbing
fixed, his landcar repaired, his garbage collected? He re-

spects practical technology and will master as much of it as he needs to live comfortably. But philosophers? Historians? Political scientists and the like? They could all disappear tomorrow and he'd never miss them. Come on." He started off toward the elevators. "Back to the office! We've got to get organized."

De Tomas continued his monologue in the elevator. The elevators at Wayvelsberg Castle were set to descend slowly but rise quickly. This was done in order to give victims extra time to contemplate their fate as they slowly descended to the interrogation rooms in the bowels of the complex; but staff, returning to the upper levels of the fortress, were expected to be back at work promptly.

"It's the same with religion, Herten," de Tomas said as they stepped out of the elevator. "The average person does not care one atom for theology. He attends his church or temple or mosque or whatever to be reassured that his gods are looking out for him, and to associate with other members of his sect in the rites of their religion—the more spectacular the rites, the better, because most people are captivated by solemn ceremony. Oh, to be sure," he went on as they entered his private office, "some of the sects might have departed slightly from this norm. The Neo-Puritans, for example, who derived their strength as a sect from the fact that they all involved themselves in their theology through very simple ceremony—'meetings,' they called them—and the constant study of their holy book—by *everyone,* since they had no priesthood, can you imagine that? Anybody in the congregation could stand up and 'testify,' as they called it."

"Yes," Herten agreed. "We were never able to penetrate that sect, to weed out the leaders. The animist sects either, but they are all primitive people who live in the hinterlands and never were of much concern to anyone except a few illegal missionary groups. Last I heard, the animists were eating them." They both laughed heartily.

"Well, fortunately for our future," de Tomas said, "the aliens rid us of many of those Bible-thumpers, the Neo-Puritans in particular." He rang for a servant, a uniformed member of the Special Group, who came in bearing a tray of coffee and small cakes. They helped themselves after the man had departed. "Now," de Tomas continued, speaking around a mouthful, "we are in a unique position, Herten. We've cut down the highest leaders of the sects. *We are in a position to end state-supported religion* in this world, and that's just what I am going to do."

Herten paused his coffee cup halfway to his lips. "We are going to create a *secular* government?"

De Tomas nodded and swallowed. "Precisely! Henceforth the sects will be confined strictly to their own internal religious matters, and they will be taxed and regulated by civil authority, just like any other institution. I will establish an entire ministry just for the regulation of the religious orders. We will begin slowly, forcing tiny but acceptable compromises under the guise of good government, until we've enmeshed them totally in a web of regulation. Failure to comply will result in confiscation of lands and properties and, in the case of those brave enough to stand up against us, arrest on charges of malfeasance—or treason. At the same time, we will weaken their authority among the people. I'll do that through regulation but also through a complex of social programs designed to propagandize the population. The Young Folk, our youth organization, will be a key tool in this process. My goal, Herten, is to wipe out the sects."

Gorman shifted uneasily in his seat. "That will be *most* difficult, my leader," he said at last. "The sense of religion is so deeply ingrained in the people, that I fear we cannot be successful."

De Tomas nodded. "It will be difficult and it will take time. It will be a struggle, a 'church struggle,' if you will. But we will move slowly and intelligently, Herten, and we will be relentless."

"But, my leader, what will you replace their faith with? The people must have something to believe in."

De Tomas laughed. "I can't eliminate God, but I will remove Him, It, Her, Whatever, to the sidelines, where God has been all along anyway. I will tone God down in the mind of the average man of this world; I will replace God with a 'clockwork' universe, Herten. Our government will give them bread and work, let them believe what they wish about divinity, but I will brook no interference by the sects in the workings of my world. Now, I wish you to see how I've decided to organize my government." He punched a button on a console, and a huge organizational chart appeared covering one wall of the room.

"At the top is the Leader, Herten. That is, me. Next down is the Deputy Leader. That's you. You are become my alter ego, Herten. You will represent me everywhere you go. You are my heir apparent."

Gorman's heart raced and he leaned forward in his seat, his attention now fully concentrated on the chart on the wall. "I—I have *never* been so honored, my leader!" he gasped.

"Under us will be a series of deputies or ministers such as Propaganda and Culture, Religion, Treasury, Interstellar Affairs, Defense, Justice, and so on. I have already picked the men I wish to hold these positions and I will give you their names shortly, and then we will call them all to Wayvelsberg to inaugurate their offices. You will notice next under these ministers are more levels of organization, particularly the paramilitary and professional groups such as the Special Group, the Young Folk, and organizations for doctors, lawyers, teachers, and so on. The leaders of these groups will all report directly to you as Deputy Leader. You'll see I have organized down to the lowest level, from district leaders to local leaders to block leaders. Hardly any of those positions have been filled yet. I expect you to pick the men and women for those positions, using the various ministers to ensure we get the most highly qualified and devoted individuals."

Gorman caught his breath. De Tomas was way ahead of him. "What form will our new government take?" he asked.

"Socialist," de Tomas replied instantly. "Ours is the Socialist Party of Kingdom, the SPK, if you will, but with one very notable exception: we shall not expropriate private industry. We shall use private industry to finance and support our regime, but we shall essentially leave the industrialists alone to profit from their business schemes. That way we shall win their total confidence. Ah," he raised a finger, "but in social programs, we will be completely organized to penetrate even into the family unit. We shall organize and mobilize the people. In time we will transfer their loyalty from their sects to our party. We will promote the concept that we on Kingdom are all one people, one *folk,* if you will, one Leader, one people, one government, Herten! Henceforth that will be our sacred motto!" He paused and took another cake. "And on our coinage we shall emboss the following slogan: 'The Common Good Goes Before the Individual Good.' That is going to be the watchword of our movement.

"We will organize mass rallies, marches, parades! We will involve everyone in campaigns to help the poor and sick. We'll put Young Folk on every street corner during the winter to collect for the indigent. We'll involve every family on Kingdom, one way or another. We'll imbue the populace with a sense of belonging and patriotism they have never known before! We will have veterans' organizations to honor the sacrifices of those who have served in the armed forces. We will exalt the military virtues over all others, and honor as heroes of the people every man who has served—and in particular those who have died in the military service, whether the stupid sectarian wars that have plagued this world from the first or the recent debacle of the alien invasion. I don't care if a man was shot in the ass while retreating, Herten, he goes into the pantheon of military heroes.

"Oh, yes, something else, Herten." De Tomas handed Gorman a large sheet of parchment. "Read it," he demanded.

Gorman read, and as he did his eyes grew wide. "You can't be serious, my leader!" he almost shouted.

"I am, Herten. That proclamation will be published at noon today." He glanced at his watch. "In fifteen minutes." He chuckled.

The proclamation changed the name of their world from Kingdom of Yahweh and His Saints and Their Apostles to "New Kingdom."

"It is simple and direct and it is not theocratic, Herten. 'Kingdom of Yahweh and His Saints and Their Apostles' indeed." De Tomas snorted. "What idiot thought that up? I've never heard such a mouthful of nonsense, and we are not going to call ourselves by that ridiculous name anymore!"

"This change will require many adjustments," Gorman offered tentatively.

"Let them be made, Herten. People will not only get used to the new name, but in time they'll come to like it, I assure you. Now," he activated his intercom, "send in Archbishop General Lambsblood." He turned to Herten. "We are going to discuss army reorganization."

"I did not call you here to ask for your opinion, General," de Tomas started out as soon as Lambsblood was seated. "We are going to effect some army reforms immediately, and you will carry them out to the letter. I want that understood at the outset."

"Very well, my leader," Lambsblood replied.

"First you will reorganize the rank structure in your army, General. We are no longer a theocracy. I have long admired the Confederation Armed Forces. You will now rename the ranks in your army after theirs." Another chart appeared on the wall showing the conversion. "You are now just a general, 'Colonel Deacon' is now simply 'Colonel,' right down to the enlisted ranks: 'Swords' are 'Sergeants,' and so on down to the lowest enlisted level, which will now be simply 'Private.' All these religious titles will be eliminated. You will also adopt the same badges of rank the Confederation Army uses. Next time we meet, you will wear the four silver stars of a full general. Is all that clear?"

"Yes, my leader. But I must point out that all this will take some getting used to, and there will be grumbling in the ranks."

"Then get used to it, General. And let the ranks grumble. Soldiers aren't happy if they don't have something to grumble about. The conversion will begin immediately. It will take time. You must have the new badges of rank made up in sufficient quantity. Issue them when they are ready, but pursue this as your number one mission. I am going to remove *every* vestige of religiosity from your army. An army must be a secular institution, General. And in that regard, sir, I have eliminated the role of 'religious officer.' " Lambsblood opened his mouth to protest. "*No,* General. No religious meddlers spying on our soldiers from now on. That was another reason your army was so inefficient—you had these fanatics peering over everyone's shoulder all the time." De Tomas smiled benignly. What he didn't tell the general was that he'd have his own spies among his troops.

Lambsblood gestured helplessly. "But my leader, all these reforms so quickly! The entire resources of my army are devoted to searching for any demons left behind—"

" 'Demons'? 'Demons'? *Stop it,* General Lambsblood! There are not now nor have there ever been *demons* on Kingdom! We were invaded by alien sentiences, General. The Confederation Marines came to our aid and chased them off, back to wherever they came from! They are alien creatures, flesh and blood, mortal, just like us. I want no more of this superstitious babble about 'demons,' is that clear, General?"

"Yes, my leader," Lambsblood agreed quickly, and shifted nervously in his seat. "But I must repeat, all my resources are devoted now to searching for any remnants of this, uh, *alien* force."

"Good. But you can do more than one thing at once, General," de Tomas continued. "Next: How are you coming on getting your men to take the new loyalty oath?" The oath replaced the grade reorganization chart. It read:

I swear to you, Dominic de Tomas, as leader of my government and my people, loyalty and bravery. I vow to you and to the authorities appointed by you obedience unto death, so help me God.

Lambsblood shifted uneasily in his chair. "Well, my leader—"

"How many men have sworn the oath, General?" de Tomas asked, his voice deceptively calm.

"Well, my leader, as I pointed out, uh, we have given top priority to searching for any of the de—ah, *aliens* that might have been left behind."

"How many of your troops have sworn the oath, General?" de Tomas asked again.

"I have, my leader!" Lambsblood said proudly.

"Every rank will swear that oath, General. It will be duly witnessed and a statement will be placed in every man's file that he has taken it. All new recruits will swear that oath. Is that clear?"

Lambsblood sputtered, "Clear, my leader, but—but—"

"No buts," de Tomas interjected harshly. "See that it is done at once. Dispatch your staff judge advocates to the units in the field *today* and have them execute the oaths. Your field commanders can cease operations for the few minutes it'll take to get the men to take the oath. Emphasize to them, General, that, once duly sworn, any disobedience will be viewed as *treason,* and treason is punishable by death. If there is any hesitation, any resistance, General, those men will be arrested and turned over immediately to the Special Group. Units of the SG will accompany your SJA for that purpose. If it's any consolation, General, every member of my other government departments has sworn the same oath. There has been some reluctance. Those people were 'transferred' immediately—*downstairs.* Do you understand?"

"My leader," Lambsblood croaked, "the men are very religious. Always before, my leader," he whispered, "the men swore their oath to God."

De Tomas nodded. "Are you *questioning* me, General?" Lambsblood hastened to say again that he had taken the loyalty oath—seriously. "So now they swear to me before God. As the leader of this new government on Kingdom, I am fulfilling God's will, General."

Lambsblood, his face pale, nodded his assent.

"Finally, how many men do you currently have under arms, General?"

Lambsblood hesitated a moment. "As of this morning I believe something just in excess of ninety thousand, my leader."

"Look at this next chart. You will reorganize your army into two groups, A and B, each consisting of 45,000 men and commanded by lieutenant generals. Each army group will be composed of three divisions of approximately fifteen thousand men, each commanded by a major general. Each division will have three brigades of approximately five thousand men commanded by a brigadier general or a full colonel; three regiments to each brigade commanded by either a full colonel or lieutenant colonel. As you can see, the regiments are broken down into companies consisting of platoons and squads. Your individual units will be numbered; no more religious names such as 'Burning Bush Regiment' and so on. Army Group A will have three divisions, One, Two, Three; Army Group B will have three divisions, Four, Five, and Six; and so on right down to platoon level. It's all there in the charts, study them.

"You will implement these reforms immediately, General Lambsblood. You will report weekly on your progress either to me personally, if I am available, or to Deputy Leader Gorman." He nodded at Gorman, who grinned wolfishly at Lambsblood. Lambsblood stared back, astonished. Then he nodded his understanding and compliance.

"As I pointed out earlier, no reason to interrupt your ongoing military operations, General," de Tomas continued. "You can work the reforms simultaneously. Convert the units in the field last. Start at the top, with yourself, and work your way down to the maneuver elements. You can call selected units out of the field for reorganization. That way you can keep a force constantly operating until your searches are complete. I—We—have complete confidence in you, General. But I must emphasize, General, *swearing the oath comes first.* Start that process today, after you return to your headquarters.

"Well," de Tomas sighed, "that's it. Would you join us for lunch, General?"

Lambsblood shifted again in his chair. "No, my leader, but thank you anyway. I should be getting back to my headquarters, to get my staff working on these reforms. Thank you for putting your confidence in me, my leader." He stood, saluted smartly, and walked swiftly out of the room. Inwardly he seethed. He had cast his lot with de Tomas thinking he'd be allowed to remain independent or coequal, but now he saw his role as that of a mere order-taking functionary.

"He's going to have to go," de Tomas said after Lambsblood had left them.

"Give me the word," Gorman said.

"Not yet, Herten, not quite yet. Next a spot of lunch, and then we meet with our newly sworn Minister of Propaganda and Culture, the esteemed but practically minded Reverend Dr. Joseph Oldhouse."

# CHAPTER
## SIX

"Is this the residence of Miss—" the Stormleader, the equivalent of a lieutenant in the army, consulted a slip of paper in his hand, "Miss Uma Devi, ma'am?" Behind him in the gathering darkness loomed the figures of two shooters, armed and in full uniform of the Special Group. In the dimly lighted street the wizened old woman who'd opened the door saw a landcar with at least one other man in it. Her mouth went dry as her heart pounded and her lower lip quivered with fear. She struggled to speak. A visit by men of the Special Group meant only one thing for her granddaughter—death.

The Stormleader bowed politely from the waist. "Ma'am, Miss Devi's presence has been requested at Wayvelsberg Castle. We shall escort Miss Devi there and return her safely to you when the interview is done."

"Who is it, Grandmother?" a female voice said from inside the house. The old woman attempted to block the door by shifting her body in front of the very pretty young woman who had appeared behind her shoulder.

"Miss Devi?" the Stormleader asked. "I am honored to inform you that your presence at Wayvelsberg Castle has been requested. My men and I will escort you there and back again." He bowed politely and gestured with one arm that she should step outside and join him.

The old woman shook her head and moaned softly. The town was abuzz with the news that only that morning the Special Group had hung the dean of the College of the Immaculate Conception and left his body swinging out on the quad. But the young woman looked back at the Stormleader with interest plainly written in her large black eyes.

"Grandmother, the Collegium has been abolished, haven't you heard?" she consoled the old woman. "How long will we be?" she asked the Stormleader.

"I really couldn't say, miss."

"Why am I being summoned?"

"All I know, miss, is that our leader has requested you for an interview. It is a very great honor, miss."

She looked at the Stormleader speculatively, not contemplating flight, but thinking of advantage. Then she nodded. "May I change into something more formal?"

The Stormleader nodded and stepped back from the door, which the old woman closed with a bang. One of his men stepped forward, but he restrained him with a hand. "Go around back, Moses. Just a precaution. She won't run, I'm sure of it. I'll stay here with Hung. No matter what happens, *no force,* do you understand?" The shooter named Moses nodded and walked swiftly around the house into the garden.

Shortly, the door opened and Miss Uma Devi stepped out. She was dressed in a green silk sari that emphasized her full breasts and narrow waist. A green silk shawl completed the ensemble.

The Stormleader smiled and offered her his arm, which she took gracefully. "Moses, join us at the car," he muttered into his throat mike.

"That was hardly necessary." Miss Devi smiled when she realized the Stormleader had posted the second man out back.

"My apologies, miss, but a lady as—as beautiful as you, we were afraid somebody might, ah, try to kidnap you?" The Stormleader laughed. "If we failed to bring you to our leader as ordered, we'd all be executed."

"I wouldn't want that to happen," she said dryly, but she smiled at the officer's attempted gallantry.

The drive to Wayvelsberg Castle took about twenty minutes. It was full dark by the time the vehicle turned off the main road and down a gravel driveway into a ravine behind the fortress. Trees and shrubs grew thickly on both sides of the road. For the first time Uma had doubts about why she was being summoned and what would happen to her. "Wh-Why are we going in this way?" she asked nervously.

"Do not be afraid, Miss Devi. Please. This visit is to be accomplished discreetly, to avoid any possible embarrassment to yourself or our leader." The car pulled up to an unloading dock and they got out. "Wait for us at the motor pool," the Stormleader ordered the driver. Sensors had activated bright lights upon their arrival. The driver turned the car around and drove back up the gravel road, a thin cloud of dust hanging suspended in the air behind it. Uma felt a sinking sensation in the pit of her stomach as the car disappeared down the tree-lined driveway.

"Please, Miss Devi, relax," the Stormleader pleaded as he guided her up a flight of concrete steps to a massive iron door. He punched a code into a keyboard, and a small portal opened at the level of his chest. A bright light scanned his face as he inserted his hand, palm downward into the portal.

"Scans complete, Stormleader Mugabe," a computer-generated voice announced, and the door swung open on its massive hydraulics. It closed solidly behind them. Inside, they stood in a tiny vestibule leading to a narrow flight of stairs that disappeared into the darkness above them. "We are coming up," Mugabe whispered into his throat mike.

"This flight of stairs communicates directly to our leader's private study, Miss Devi. It's precisely 214 steps to the top. I am sorry, we cannot use the elevators, but this entrance is absolutely private and reserved for the exclusive use of our leader. We can pause frequently to let you catch your breath. Believe me, miss, you will find the climb was well worth the effort once you've met the leader."

They started up the stairway.

"You are looking more handsome and younger every time I see you, my leader," Miss Gelli Alois said unctuously as she busied herself brushing Dominic de Tomas's face with makeup powder. De Tomas sat in a barber's chair in the Wayvelsberg studio Gorman had arranged for Miss Alois and her assistants, so they could be ready at a moment's notice to prepare de Tomas for his public appearances. He would soon appear before the media to announce his cabinet and explain the decrees he'd recently issued.

De Tomas glanced at Herten Gorman. He was fully aware of the torrid relationship that had developed between his Deputy Leader and Gelli Alois. He also sensed that Gorman was worried he might decide to appropriate Alois's considerable charms exclusively for himself. He found that amusing. He turned to Miss Rauber, Gelli's assistant, who stood behind him holding a cosmetics tray. "Have you a boyfriend, Miss Rauber?" he asked, winking at Gorman.

"Yes, my leader!" the young woman replied with a curtsy.

"Well, tell us: Is he as handsome as Herten over there?"

"Oh, no, my leader!"

"I am sorry for you, Miss Rauber." De Tomas glanced up at Gelli, and was amused to see her face color slightly with embarrassment. "If that man of yours ever abandons you, Miss Rauber, you come and see me. I'm old and ugly and not half as handsome as Herten, but I feed my women well." He laughed. Miss Rauber, although a very pretty young woman, was a bit on the slim side. Her face turned a deep red, and that caused de Tomas to laugh outright. In fact, the young woman enjoyed de Tomas's banter and looked forward to the makeup sessions. And if he ever asked her into his bedroom— but, alas, he never had.

Gelli, finished, held out a mirror to de Tomas. "Hmm," de Tomas said. "Gelli, you could make a dead man look alive again! I bet when the media see me in a few minutes they'll say, 'You're looking wonderful, our leader! Who's your undertaker?' " Laughing, he threw off the smock, stood up and straightened his uniform. Miss Rauber stepped up and brushed him off. "Away, Herten, away! The people await us in the Great Hall! Ladies." He turned to Gelli and Rauber and bowed deeply. "Thank you once again for resurrecting me!"

Ambassador Jayben Spears and Prentiss Carlisle, his chief of station, sat in the ambassador's suite in Interstellar City and watched Dominic de Tomas's performance on the trid. "Some of this stuff actually makes sense," Prentiss said, his voice touched with awe. "Maybe that army reorganization will make them into real soldiers."

"Don't bet on it, Prentiss. The real military power in this place is the Special Group."

"I can actually follow their rank structure, now that he's converted to the Confederation's system. Acolytes, swords, imams . . . their grade structure was so damned *ecumenical* I could never make any sense out of it, much less remember which was a colonel and which a private."

Spears snorted. "Yes, some of his reforms are long overdue, such as organizing the army under the general staff concept, a system every military has adopted, because it works so damned well, since the Germans invented it back during the nineteenth century." Spears shook his head. "And as an old soldier myself, I appreciate the awards and decorations program he's established, medals for both heroism and meritorious service, and enlisted people can earn them too, not just officers. And I have to admit, Prentiss, were I a Muslim in the Army of God, I don't think being called an acolyte would sit very well with me." He snorted again. Then almost to himself, "In their insane effort to be ecumenical, the previous regime only pissed everyone off; morale in the old army was at a terrible low.

"Prentiss, if only these reforms had been initiated by somebody else. De Tomas is a ruthless murderer, we all know that." He paused. "But nobody ever said he's stupid." Spears had been told of the reforms by his various contacts well in advance of that evening's announcement. What interested him was the men de Tomas had picked for his cabinet posts, whom he'd just introduced, and the justification for the reforms, which he was now putting forth very eloquently and, Spears had to admit, persuasively.

"I'll bet that little bastard there wrote the script for this," Spears muttered, pointing to the screen, "the stocky red-haired guy sitting just beside Gorman." He was referring to the Reverend Dr. Joseph Oldhouse, newly appointed Minister of Public Enlightenment and Culture. Spears snorted. " 'Public Enlightenment and Culture' my ass! The devious little swine is nothing more than a rotten propagandist, opportunistic little . . ." He let the sentence trail off.

Prentiss glanced down at the brief bio sheet the staff had prepared on Oldhouse. "He's known as a prominent theologian," Prentiss offered. "He's published widely."

"Yeah, I read his crap in the papers this morning, *The Theology of Order,* one of the most dishonest justifications for dictatorship I've ever read." But Spears also recognized the article as a very intelligent and convincing argument for the faithful to render obedience to the secular state. The piece started out with a survey of all the major religions on the matter, concluding that each recognized the necessity for secular government, under God, and admitted each person's responsibility to obey the laws of their secular leaders.

"The law of God," Oldhouse had written in his closing paragraph, "binds each of us in the position to which we have been called by God, and commits us to the natural orders under which we are subjugated, such as government, family, people, race . . . It also binds us to a specific historical moment, to a specific moment of our history. This natural order is decreed by God to serve his purpose of binding society together and creating stability. It must be accepted as a human representation of God's will in an imperfect world. For us on Kingdom, that moment is arrived. That moment in history is now, and the representative of God's will is our noble leader."

"Dear God," Spears whispered, "I wish old Ted Sturgeon and his boys were back with us now." The Confederation consulate on Kingdom was too small to qualify for a complement of Marine security personnel. "Prentiss, what I wouldn't give this moment for a few of those good men."

Mugabe called for a halt about halfway up the stairs. "Excuse me, I have to catch my breath," he said with a weak smile. "Miss Devi," he observed, "you don't seem at all winded."

"I am a professional dancer, Stormleader," she replied with a coquettish smile. "Besides, I'm a few years younger and several kilos lighter than you are." In a society that frowned on dancing for pleasure, Uma had made a career as a ritual dancer among the sects, some of which permitted ballet-type performances as part of their seasonal religious observances. Uma was well-known for her practice of that art, and well-paid for it. The dancing she performed during the Tantric rituals, lascivious as it may have been, was still an important aspect of a genuine religious rite, and done only in secret before the sect's devotees.

Mugabe smiled back. This woman knew how to flatter a man. He wondered how successful she'd be using that with de Tomas. Well, Mugabe liked her style. He laid a friendly hand on the woman's shoulder. "Miss, when you see our leader, be honest and straightforward with him," he said. She regarded the officer frankly, then nodded. They continued up the stairway. By the time they reached the top, both were breathing heavily.

"I will wait here, Miss Devi. When you are finished, I'll escort you home." He announced himself through an intercom, and the door to the private study hissed open.

Miss Uma Devi walked in, and the door closed silently behind her. Mugabe sighed and sat on the top step. He wiped the perspiration from his forehead. He could still smell the girl's perfume, something that reminded him of fresh flowers. I need to work out more, he thought, still breathing heavily from the climb. Then: I sure hope this damned meeting doesn't take all night.

There was no one in the study. Uma stood there uncertainly. The room was well-lighted and comfortable; the walls lined with books, the furniture, solid, dressed in leather, masculine but inviting. She wondered if she should call out her presence or sit in one of the armchairs. She decided to remain standing. A full minute went by and still no one came in. She moved to the bookcases on one wall and surveyed the titles on the spines. She pulled one out, *Satan, the Early Christian Tradition*. The cover depicted a horrible horned beast with wide, staring eyes. Quickly she put it back.

"Are you interested in such things?"

She whirled about, and there was the Leader, dressed in a loose-fitting black gown decorated with bright silver goshawks. At first, standing so close to the great man, Uma did not know what to do except stare at him. He smiled at her, and recovering her wits, Uma folded her hands in obeisance and bowed her head respectfully.

De Tomas covered the short space between them in two strides and held out a hand. "Welcome, Miss Devi. It was very good of you to come at such short notice. And I do apologize for the abruptness. I also apologize for keeping you waiting like this. I have just come up from a press conference in the Great Hall. Would you care to take a chair over here and talk with me for a few moments?" Holding her hand gently, de Tomas guided her into one of the chairs. Uma felt a thrill when his hand touched hers. It was warm and strong and transmitted the energy of a forceful personality.

De Tomas sat opposite Uma and gracefully folded his legs. Uma brushed as surreptitiously as she could at a rivulet of perspiration creeping down the side of her face. "It's a long climb up those stairs, isn't it?" de Tomas said. "I apologize for that as well. I find that secret staircase useful for very private meetings. I assure you, Miss Devi, if you ever come back to Wayvelsberg Castle, you will use your own pass to get in through the main entrance and take the elevators," de Tomas said with a laugh. "I am looking for a private secretary, Miss Devi. Would you be interested?"

The question surprised her. "I—I have no experience, my leader," she stammered.

"Yes, yes," de Tomas nodded, "I know. You are a professional dancer and a devotee of Shaktism. When I was Dean of the Collegium, one of the Brahmans on my staff showed me a trid of you participating in the so-called 'left-handed' Tantric ritual. I was impressed."

Uma smiled and relaxed. So that was it! The left-handed Tantric rituals, as opposed to the right-handed, involved erotic and magical practices. The great Leader of Kingdom, lately the Dean of the Collegium and a figure both feared and respected, but mostly feared, wanted a *woman*. Uma ran a pink tongue over her lips and laughed outright. She could handle *that*!

De Tomas's face went hard. Did this woman think all he wanted from her was sex? Did she find that amusing, as if the Great Leader were no more than an ordinary man after all? "Do not get the wrong impression, miss," he said. "You are a beautiful young woman, but there are many beautiful women in this world, and if sex were all I wanted of a woman, I could get it just by snapping my fingers." Then he continued in a softer tone, "If you come to live with me—and you'd live here, nowhere else—you would be my consort, much, much more than a mere bed partner. Do you realize what I am offering you?"

Uma froze. De Tomas was no ordinary cocksman. Mentally she kicked herself for having been caught. In the pit of her stomach she could feel the beginning of a gnawing uncertainty, a growing tendril of fear. This was a man known for sending countless people to their deaths for apostasy. His power now was unlimited, and despite the public image de Tomas had put on recently, she had no desire to displease him.

"I thought I saw something in you, Miss Devi, something that I admired. Oh, your physical beauty, your athletic body, any man would admire that. But I made inquiries. You have a master of arts in philosophy. You are used to making public appearances. You enjoy sex but you have remained single and you live alone, with your grandmother. That indicates to me that you're a woman who values her privacy and who knows what she wants."

De Tomas stood up and extended his hand. "I will have you escorted home. Again, thank you very much for coming here tonight. If you should require anything, anything at all, please contact Stormleader Mugabe and he will arrange it. Good evening, Miss Devi."

The secret door swung open and Stormleader Mugabe stood there. Uma, confused and disappointed, bowed and left the room.

De Tomas swore. Herten Gorman came in. "She was not satisfactory, my leader?" he asked, an anxious expression on his face.

"It was the laugh, Herten, the laugh! I will have *no one* in my presence who dares to *laugh* at me! Laugh *with* me, that's different. But laugh *at* me? She's lucky I didn't have her sent downstairs."

"I am surprised, my leader, that you did not do just that." Privately, Gorman was wondering what had come over de Tomas recently. He was beginning to have the faintest inkling of suspicion that his leader might be losing his edge.

"Well," de Tomas rubbed his hands together, "back to the drawing board, eh? Keep looking Herten, keep looking. Have that cosmetician,"—Gorman's heart skipped a beat thinking he meant Gelli Alois—"what's her name? Rauber! Have her sent up, will you? It's a little chilly in here tonight." He slapped Gorman heartily on the back. "Herten, you are my deputy leader. Do you think I'd use my position to steal your woman? Tsk tsk, I'm getting a bad reputation around here. Guess I'll have to go back to just killing people." He laughed and walked out of the study.

Uma Devi stripped and lay naked on her bed. She knew the Leader had rejected her as a possible companion, but she was still flattered he'd even considered giving her that interview. She had seen and learned some very interesting things. Private entrances, secret stairways—214 steps, wasn't it?— to the Leader's private office. She bet not many people knew about such things, much less had seen them with their own eyes. That information could be very useful sometime. Potentially very useful.

Uma rolled over and spoke into her personal comm. A sleepy male voice answered. "Krishna!" she shouted. "It's Uma! I have some really important news for you!"

"Uma, do you realize what *time* it is? I have a very important meeting with the general early tomorrow morning and—" Uma's brother, Krishna, was a "major" under the new system in the Army of God, or whatever they were calling it these days, an aide to an important general officer. Krishna was considerably older than Uma, married with children. His job as the general's aide had kept him out of the horrendous fighting recently, very disappointing to him, but considered evidence of divine intervention by Uma.

Uma breathlessly told her brother about the visit to Wayvelsberg Castle. A few sentences into the story and he was wide-awake. This was riveting! A private interview with the Leader himself, hidden doorways and a secret stairway! "I'm afraid I upset him," Uma concluded mournfully. "I laughed at him, Krishna, a very bad mistake. So," she brightened, "I guess I won't be going to Wayvelsberg Castle again anytime soon."

"A good thing, Uma. Keep this to yourself, would you? This information could be, ah, well, not good for you, understand? Now look, I've got to get some sleep. You take care, little sister."

"One final thing, brother," Uma said, the tone of her voice serious and confidential. "He was nothing like I imagined him to be, Krishna. He was polite to me, kind to me. And I will confess it to you, if he'd picked me for the job, I'd have taken it without hesitation."

After the call, Major Krishna Devi lay back in his bed and put his arms behind his head. He smiled. That damned sister of his! But that information . . . What did she say, 214 steps to the Leader's private office? He filed that fact away for future reference.

Uma lay back on her bed and regarded the ceiling for a moment, then produced her personal comm and asked to be connected to the number Stormleader Mugabe had given her. He answered immediately. His deep baritone voice sent a shiver through the young woman. "Uma Devi, Stormleader. I'm thirsty."

There was the very briefest silence on the other end, and then, "I get off duty in one hour, Uma. I'll pick you up at your place then."

Brigadier General Ricardo Banks, Confederation Army, regarded General Lambsblood carefully over his coffee cup. General Banks had only recently been assigned to Ambassador Spears as his military attaché, but he had been thoroughly briefed on the New Kingdom reorganization plans. The Combined Chiefs had decided that once the Skinks had been chased off Kingdom, the time was ripe to assign a senior military officer there to "assist" in the mopping-up operations—and to keep a close eye on what was happening in the army under the new regime.

"So none of us is happy with these innovations, General Banks," Lambsblood concluded, "but orders are orders."

"I understand, sir. The changes in your organization and grade structure are certainly far-reaching. I have to confess, though," he chuckled, "that for some reason, I find the new rank system pretty easy to understand."

Lambsblood joined good-naturedly in the laugh. "I guess we'll get used to it. Say, I'm going to visit my units in the field sometime during the upcoming week, General Banks. That loyalty oath business, you know? Would you like to accompany me?"

"Very much so." Banks smiled. "I am here at your disposal, General. I'd also like to visit your training facilities and ordnance depots and such. I might find some interesting ways the Confederation can be of use to you. Once this, uh, new man gets your economy back on its feet, I think some upgrades to your weapons systems might be feasible."

Lambsblood nodded approvingly. "The war with the aliens ruined us. I certainly hope our leader can restore stability and prosperity. Well, I'll have my aide-de-camp set it up, then. Are you returning to Interstellar City now?"

"Yessir. I'm having lunch with Ambassador Spears."

A smartly dressed major wearing the newly approved General staff badge came into the room at General Lambsblood's summons. "Have you met Major Devi?" Lambsblood asked.

"Not formally." General Banks stood up and offered the major his hand. They shook vigorously. Major Devi was a short, well-built man with a very dark complexion and a very black mustache, neatly trimmed, on his upper lip.

"Ima—I mean *Major,* General Banks will need assistance developing an itinerary, first to accompany me next week and then to visit some other places. You are to give him carte blanche and your full cooperation in everything. General, the major is an excellent administrator and you will find his services invaluable." He stood up and offered Banks his hand. "I look forward to traveling with you next week, General."

Lambsblood really did look forward to an association with Banks. He had deeply resented the subordinate role to which he'd been relegated during the war with the aliens, forced to take orders from Brigadier Sturgeon, his army virtually commanded by Confederation Marines. But now that the emergency was over, and especially now that Dominic de Tomas was giving the orders, Lambsblood had reconsidered. Without the Marines, he had to admit, all would have been lost. He was uncertain, too, of his future with de Tomas. He had the uncomfortable feeling the Leader and his deputy were only using him, and that once his usefulness was over . . . This Brigadier General Banks and Ambassador Spears might turn out to be the most valuable allies he'd ever had. It was known that people had been granted asylum in diplomatic enclaves.

On the way to his car Banks chatted amiably with Major Devi. "How do you like the reorganization of your army, Major?"

Devi shrugged. "Well, I never really liked being called an 'imam.' I'm a Hindu, you know?"

"Well, I for one am glad de Tomas made the changes, Major. At least I know who I'm dealing with now." They had arrived at his car. Banks held out his hand. "Major, I really am here to be of assistance." They shook again. "I think I'll like working with you, but please remember, our association is a two-way street." He pointed his forefinger at Devi's chest. "Major, you let me know if I can help you in any way. *Any* way."

All military attachés were spies; Devi knew that. Was Banks offering his help for inside information? If he were to give it, would that constitute treason? Dominic de Tomas, no matter what his image was supposed to be these days, had killed a lot of innocent people in his time. He had seized the government of Kingdom in a coup using the Special Group, as ugly a menagerie of professional killers as anyone could imagine. Life was in no way safe yet on the world called Kingdom.

Major Krishna Devi watched Brigadier General Banks's car disappear down the road. Yes, he thought, yes, I am definitely going to like working with this man.

# CHAPTER
# SEVEN

Emwanna Haramu knew how to survive in the wilderness. The food the soldier had given her helped, but what saved her and Chisi, her baby boy, was her knowledge of her environment, which plants were edible, which had stores of carbohydrates and water a person could survive on without cooking them; she also knew how to construct snares and traps to catch the tiny meat-bearing creatures native to Kingdom that were good to eat. Perhaps most important, she knew how to navigate by the stars and she understood that if she traveled long enough in a certain direction, she would come to a settlement of the Powerful Ones, as her people called the other humans in the world. And of course she knew the proper rites to propitiate the spirits that dwelt in all natural objects.

Emwanna did not thrive on her desert diet, but she survived, as her people had survived for countless generations in the deserts and wild places on Old Earth.

The Pilipili Magna, Emwanna's tribe, had come to Kingdom years before as "domestic" servants indentured to members of the Malakals, a warlike Muslim sect native to the Sudan back on Old Earth. Historically, the Malakals were slavers, although over the centuries, changing times and stricter enforcement of laws had weaned them from that occupation. But on Kingdom the Pilipili Magna had existed in virtual bondage to the Malakals until the Malakals were finally crushed in one of Kingdom's many sectarian wars by a coalition of mainstream—by Kingdom's standards—groups. Afterward the Pilipili Magna, freed from their bondage, fled to the wild and remote regions of Kingdom and resumed the primitive, nomadic lifestyle of their ancestors. Since they were a very small group and dwelled only in the most inaccessible places, nobody had troubled them—until now.

After many days in the wilderness, Emwanna and Chisi found their way to New Salem.

The first few days "Military Operation" was with the Brattles, he ran a high fever and was delirious much of the time. His two companions, who'd been taken into different households to recuperate, were not much better off. Aside from some brief moments of coherence, he muttered and screamed unfamiliar words and phrases sounding like commands and warnings, but nobody could understand them. Gradually, however, the fever subsided and his mind cleared.

"There was a name you spoke while you were delirious," Zechariah Brattle said when Military Operation's fever broke. They were sitting at the table, where Military Operation was drinking broth and eating chunks of black bread. "You said, 'Charlie. Call me Charlie.' Is that your name? Charles?"

Military Operation looked puzzled as he mulled over the question. He became frustrated when he couldn't remember and pounded his fist hard enough on the table to slosh broth from the bowl. He shook his hand and swore at the bruising pain.

"Charles, don't take the Lord's name in vain."

"I don't know," Military Operation moaned, not hearing Brattle's admonition. "I'm Charlie ... Charlie ... God-damnit, I can't remember!"

"Charles, we are a God-fearing people. Please, your language."

"My language?" Charles mumbled, sucking on the edge of his injured hand.

"The Lord's name."

"Oh." He blushed with embarrassment. "I'm sorry, I'll try to watch that."

"Thank you, Charles." So even though he couldn't remember his full name, from then on he was Charles. Watching his language was something else he couldn't remember.

"Goddamn, Comfort, you sure know how to construct a stew," Charles said as he finished the bowl Comfort Brattle had brought to him.

"It's the best I could do under the circumstances, Charles," Comfort said. "Until Father slaughters another cow, we'll have to live on vegetables." She paused. "Charles, I really wish you wouldn't take the Lord's name in vain." Comfort's face reddened and she was forced to look down at the floor in her embarrassment.

"Oh. Sorry," Charles replied. During the time he'd been in the Brattles' care, Zechariah, his wife Consort, and their daughter Comfort had steadfastly refused to call Charles "Charlie," thinking that too familiar a form of address for a person they did not even know. And they had all complained to him about his language. "Well," Charles continued, spooning up the last fragment of potato in thick beef stock, "if it hadn't been for you Brattles, I guess I'd have been standing before Saint Peter a long time ago, explaining myself rapid-fire to get all those black marks against my name erased from his Big Book."

Comfort couldn't help herself and laughed at the idea of the man standing before Saint Peter. Comfort's laugh always made Charles feel better. He'd needed a lot of that laughter—and that stew!—over the weeks he'd been in the Brattles' care. "See, Comfy, we talk like men who live on the edge because . . ." A strange expression came over Charles's face. Carefully, he set the empty bowl down and smacked a palm into his forehead several times.

"Have you remembered some more, Charles?"

Charles shook his head, "I *don't know*, Comfort, I just don't know. That—what I just said? It—It just came to me." He looked up at her imploringly. There was moisture in his eyes. "Sometimes things come back to me, just images I can't identify? I think I was a soldier once, or maybe a policeman, but . . ." He shrugged helplessly. *"I just don't know."*

"Well, whatever you were, Charles," Comfort said firmly, "you have a good head on your shoulders and a good heart. The things you have advised Father to do about our security here have made sense to everyone and we're glad you're here. The Lord looks after His people, Charles, and it was He who brought you here."

He recovered enough to get up and move about, and when he wasn't feeling too tired, he had long talks with Zechariah Brattle. Zechariah had told him about their trek from the Sea of Gerizim and how they'd snuck by the devils'—as he called them—camp, where evidently Charles and his two companions had been held prisoner in the cave. Zechariah told him how they feared a return of the devils, and it was then Charles began to put his mind to the problem of security.

"I think you need watches mounted around the clock, Zechariah. Everyone twelve and up should participate. That way you can divide up the duty. How many people would that be?"

Zechariah counted mentally. "Thirty-five people, not including you and your two companions. Hmm. Well, some of our folks are rather on in years, Samuel and Esther Sewall, for instance, are nearly a century old, but they're spry and they'd hate to be left out."

Charles thought for a moment. "How about two twelve-hour shifts each day, dawn to dusk, five people to a shift? One would be the sergeant of the guard, and four watchers, one for each quadrant. It'll be real hard on the older people, and the younger watchers will have to be supervised closely because they'll have a tendency to get bored, but there's no other way you can organize a watch—your numbers are so small and you have your own work to do during the daylight hours. The sergeant of the guard would continually make the rounds, checking on each watcher and helping observe. Pick your sergeants from the more elderly people in your group.

With thirty-five people, you would have seven shifts, so the duty would come around about once every four days. When Colleen, Chet, and I are up to it, we'll be able to fill in. Who knows, maybe you'll even pick up some more people as time goes by."

Charles was deep in thought for a moment. "We also need some kind of warning system, to alert us if anyone approaches. You don't have any kind of radio communication, do you?"

"No, Charles. But we have plenty of scrap metal lying about. Why not rig up something for the watchers to bang on, something that we can hear even out in the fields?"

"Excellent idea. But remember, if you can hear the alarm in the fields, so will any approaching enemy. We need to train everyone that as soon as the alarm for a ground approach is sounded, to drop what they're doing and take their positions or run to the rally point. And when you place the watchers, we've got to position them from the best places, to get good observation, but we've got to be sure they can't be seen themselves. We should build some kind of shelter for them, to hide them and also to protect them from the weather."

"Yes, something like hunters use."

"Exactly, Zechariah." Charles thought for a moment again. "What's your weapons status?"

Zechariah shrugged. "Two shot rifles, my pistol, and two acid-throwing devices we captured from the devils. None of these weapons have much range, Charles; they're for close-in fighting. Comfort and another man have the rifles. They've actually used them to kill. I want them to keep the weapons at all times."

"Okay. It won't be the job of the watchers to engage the enemy anyway, but to warn us of their approach. Tell me about these 'acid-throwers,' did you call them?" Zechariah filled him in on the captured devices. "I don't think the watchers should take them out there either. Let's hold them in reserve. You don't want to stand on guard for twelve hours with one of those things strapped on your back all the time you're out there. But we've got to be sure *everyone* knows how to use all these weapons. If we ever get into a fight, there will be casualties, and everyone's got to know how to pick up a discarded weapon and use it. We need a fortress or a rally point, a place where we can escape to so we can hide or defend ourselves. We can't do much to defend this village. We don't have communications, too little manpower, and limited ammo, I suspect, for the weapons we do have. Right? We don't have any ammunition for training purposes but we can teach everyone how to dry-fire the weapons. If we fight, we've got to consolidate our forces to multiply and concentrate our firepower and coordinate our defenses. If we flee, we've got to have escape routes and more distant rallying points."

Zechariah smiled.

"What's so funny?" Charles asked.

"You, Charles." Zechariah chuckled. "Where did you come up with all these ideas so *suddenly*? They make good sense to me."

Charles shrugged. "I honestly don't know, Zechariah. Just seems common sense to organize that way, don't you think so?"

"The Lord God sent you to us, Charles, and at the next meeting we are going to thank Him for it."

Comfort stood and took up the empty bowl. "I'll take this to the kitchen."

"No! No, Comfy." Charles took her hand. "Sit here a spell? I—I seem to remember things best when my mind is on something else and, well"—he smiled wryly—"you sure are 'something else,' Comfy." Though the Brattles refused to call Charles by the diminutive of his name, he had no such problem; from the first he had called everyone by the familiar version of their given names. When he'd greeted the widow Flood as "Hannie" at their first meeting, for instance, she'd laughed so hard tears had come to her eyes. Hannah Flood had been a frequent visitor to Charles's sickroom since then, and while Comfort sincerely loved the sturdy old widow, secretly she was a bit jealous of her.

Comfort sat back down. "Well, we have found a lot of potatoes in the fields and the men have managed to get some of the cows back into the pastures. And Father has organized a watch, just as you said we should, and we have people on guard around the clock and he's worked out a roster, to make it fair to everyone, and at night we don't let any lights show, and I'm on the watch too, and I am one of the two gunners we have at New Salem and—"

"Hold it, hold on," Charles said, laughing. "Your tongue will get all twisted up! Tell me about your gun." He put his feet back up on the bed and lay back on the pillows. Comfort told him about the shot rifle and how she'd used it during the engagement with the Skinks—although she called them "devils"—and how her brother had been killed. Where had that word, "Skinks," come from? he wondered, but he didn't pursue the thought.

"Aw, Comfy, I'm really sorry to hear about Samuel," he said, and sat up, taking Comfort's hand in his again. "Comfy, sometimes in combat people, your loved ones get killed and—" He smiled broadly. "Now where the hell did *that* come from? See? See? I remembered something there! I've been in a war! I know it! Holding hands with you is good therapy for me."


"Comfort! Come outside at once!" Zechariah Brattle paused at the door to Charles's room when he saw the two holding hands. The growing intimacy between his daughter and their guest had not gone unnoticed by the patriarch, but he'd kept his peace about it. "Come outside. A stranger has arrived! Charles, come too, if you will."

The small brown woman dressed in rags and carrying a tiny bundle slung on her back stood in the middle of a small crowd, obviously embarrassed at being the center of attention. She was also very relieved to be there, as clearly evidenced by the big smile on her face.

"She doesn't seem to speak English," someone volunteered as Zechariah, followed closely by Comfort and Charles, came through the crowd.

"Zechariah," he said slowly to the woman, tapping his chest. "What is your name?" He pointed at her.

She knew what that meant. "Emwanna," the woman answered. She unslung the bundle from her back and held back the rag that had been covering her child's head from the sun. "Chisi," she said proudly, holding the baby out toward Zechariah. The baby's head was very big and its brown eyes enormous. It blinked at Zechariah.

"The poor thing is starving," Hannah Flood said softly.

"Do you speak English?" Zechariah asked slowly. English was the lingua franca on Kingdom, as it was throughout the Confederation of Human Worlds. All the peoples who'd emigrated there brought with them the languages of their forefathers but everyone used English, if not in their daily lives, then in their relationships with other groups.

"Yes." The woman nodded. "Little." Her voice sounded like the rustling of old parchment. "Water?" she asked. Several of the onlookers rushed off to get the woman water. Someone produced a cup of milk for the child.

"Where do you come from, child?" Zechariah asked.

"Long way. From my people," she rasped, and pointed over her shoulder in the direction from which she had just come. She took the glass of water someone had given her and drank eagerly while one of the women gently removed the child from her arms and fed it milk. She drained the cup and bowed in thanks toward Zechariah.

"Who are your people?"

"Pilipili Magna. But all dead, all dead," Emwanna said tonelessly, and she drank deeply from her refilled cup.

When Charles followed the Brattles out into the street, the first person he recognized was the red-haired woman who'd escaped from the caves with him, Colleen. The Sewalls had taken her in. Charles walked up to her, leaving Comfort with her father. "Long time no see," he said, putting his arm around her.

"Charles, you saw me only this morning!" Colleen laughed and kissed him lightly on his cheek. Comfort noticed the intimacy and chided herself at the feeling of jealousy that surged up within her.

Zechariah stood next to Emwanna and put his arm around her. "Friends, the Lord has seen to deliver this poor soul to us from the wilderness. It is our Christian duty to take her in, as we have Charles and Colleen and Chet. Who among us will care for this woman and her child?"

"I will, Zechariah!" Hannah Flood bustled forward and took Emwanna under her wing. "I'll take that one too." She chuckled, pointing at Charles.

"God bless you, Hannah. I believe—" He paused, looking for the right word, the ghost of a smile on his face. "—that Mrs. Brattle and I have grown very fond of Charles. Even if he does swear like a trooper," he muttered under his breath. "Friends," Zechariah addressed the rest of the crowd, "it's not wise to bunch up like this. Let us disperse to our homes and duties. Hannah will restore the woman and child and then we'll let her speak about her ordeal. Don't forget, guard mount changes in one hour." He beckoned to Charles, who joined him. "Charles, what do you think?"

"I think she is only the first of many who will find their way to us, Zechariah. I think those things that killed your friends and held us in cages have devastated our world and they *will* be back for us." Although Charles could not remember what he had done in his former life, he was sure he was also a native of this world, like everyone else around him.

Zechariah nodded. "The security measures you recommend, Charles, are very wise. You have had experience in these matters at some time in your life, that's obvious to everyone. I pray each night the Lord will restore your memory perfectly. I have a feeling we'll need all the advice we can get in the near future. When will you feel up to taking over the training of our able-bodied people to form some kind of defensive force?"

"Tomorrow, Zechariah."

"Good." He turned to Comfort. "Daughter, you go on watch in one hour."

"Yes, Father." As she walked back into the house she frowned back at Charles.

At first Charles was surprised at the look she gave him, and then his face reddened. Damn, he thought, she saw me kiss Colleen. The girl has a crush on me! He was both amused and alarmed. "Comfort," he called out, "wait up!" and followed her into the house.

Spencer Maynard placed a hand on Reuben Stoughton's arm as they walked down the street. "See that?" He nodded at Charles and Comfort. "She's pretty sweet on that stranger." Spencer was twenty-five years old, and he'd been thinking of courting Comfort long before the community had moved to the Sea of Gerizim.

"You are looking daggers at the man's back, Spencer," the older man observed wryly.

"Lord forgive me for that," Maynard answered. They continued walking down the street. "But Reuben, is there something, you know, *suspicious* about the strangers? I mean, they come to us out of the night claiming they don't remember who they are, and we take them in. We really don't know who they are, do we? I do not trust them. In fact, Reuben," he leaned close and whispered into Reuben's ear, "I think they're *spies*." He nodded firmly.

"Hmm, I'm not so sure," Reuben replied. "They came with no clothes and nearly dead—the other man and the woman would have died if we hadn't found them in the morning—"

"Ah! You need only one man to do the job, but you send three? And what do we know about this 'amnesia,' eh? I looked it up, Reuben. They weren't hit on the head. We've all talked to them and they don't seem to be trying to forget something awful in their personal lives. They don't seem to be suffering from any diseases that would cause loss of memory, and if they were exposed to toxic substances, wouldn't that show up in some way? Oh, they talk about being tortured, but they *remember* that experience, they're not trying to forget it! They want us to believe the devils did it to them, but Reuben, the devils kill human beings, like they did all our friends, they don't just let them go! No, no, there's something about these three that just doesn't add up, Reuben."

"Hmm. Yes, maybe?" Reuben said doubtfully. He looked hard at his companion. He was fully aware that Spencer was jealous of Charles's relationship with Comfort, and he did not discount that as his motive for making such a slander. Still . . . He clapped Spencer on the shoulder. "Let us keep a close watch on the three of them, and if your suspicions grow into facts, we'll talk to Zechariah. Meanwhile, I've got the watch tonight."

Spencer Maynard nodded and smiled. He'd get the facts, all right.

# CHAPTER
## EIGHT

Charles followed Comfort back into the house. She was slinging her shot rifle and picking up her coat when he caught up with her. Outside someone was giving the signal for the relief watch to muster at the meetinghouse—*Bong!*— one, two—*Bong!*—one, two—*Bong!*—one of the several warning signals Charles and Zechariah had worked out before instituting the watch system.

"Comfort . . ." Charles paused, catching his breath. His long convalescence had weakened him. Comfort glared back at him. "Um, is that rifle loaded?" he asked.

Comfort's expression changed to one of bewilderment. The Remchester 870 Police Model shot rifle was based on the simple design of the old-fashioned pump shotgun, with a tubular magazine mounted beneath the barrel; rounds were transferred from the spring-loaded magazine into the breech by working the slide to the rear and then ramming it forward to load the rounds. The Remchester was designed to fire a wide variety of ammunition, from ordinary buckshot to powerful explosive and armor-piercing projectiles. It came in a semiautomatic gas-operated version, but evidently the previous owner of this weapon preferred a pump action, because it was thought to be more reliable, if a bit slower to put into battery.

"Never go on guard mount with a loaded weapon. The sergeant of the guard will inspect—" Charles smiled and held out his hand for the rifle, which Comfort passed over without comment. Then she smiled. He had remembered some more! Charles opened the breech and a live round popped out. "See?" he said, stooping and picking it up. He shoved it into the weapon's magazine. "Leave the action open, so you can look inside and see the round in the magazine and that the breech is clear. Put your finger into the breech to double-check that there's nothing in there. That way there's no chance of discharging your piece by mistake. You'd have gotten a gig for going on guard with a charged weapon."

"What's a 'gig,' Charles?"

"Huh?" Charles screwed up his face. "Oh, well, a 'gig' is—it's, you know, like a mistake? Hell's bells, Comfy, I don't know! It just came to me." He examined a button on the left side of the rifle. It was sticking out. A green strip indicated it was on safe. "How many rounds does this thing hold?"

"Four, Charles."

Charles nodded. "Are these rounds solid shot or pellets?"

"I don't know. I reloaded after the fight with the devils and didn't bother to look. When I used it that day, I just pointed, fired, and worked the action. Afterward I noticed black and blue marks on my shoulder, and Father said it was because I didn't hold the butt end properly. But I killed them, Charles, I killed them."

Charles smiled. She didn't look like she could kill anything, but he'd heard that story many times, and he knew Comfort would never hesitate again in combat. "It needs cleaning, Comfort," he observed sourly. "When you come off duty tonight we'll sit down and run some oily rags through the tube, get the dust and grit out of the action." He pointed the rifle in a safe direction, hefted it and sighted along the barrel. "How do you get a proper sight picture with this thing?"

"You fire when the outline of the stock, or the whatcha-macallit, lines up with the bead on the front of the barrel. Father taught us that, but in the fight, I just pointed and squeezed the trigger and worked the pump back and forth."

Charles handed the rifle back to her. "Well, your father wants me to start organizing and drilling a defense force starting tomorrow. But I'm going to start tonight. I'm going with you. Who's watch master tonight?"

"Reuben Stoughton."

"Let's go."

"Charles," Reuben Stoughton exclaimed in surprise as Charles and Comfort walked into the meeting hall. "What are you doing here?"

"I'm Zechariah's 'military' adviser, Reuben, and tonight I'm starting off my new duty by observing your guard mount."

"Well, we don't need any advice, Charles, we've all done this before." He glanced suspiciously at Comfort, remembering the innuendos Spencer Maynard had made against Charles and Comfort earlier in the evening. Charles noted the look but said nothing.

"That's fine, Reuben. I'm sure you're an excellent watch master. But when the rest of your people arrive, I want to talk to them."

Soon the others—Joab Flood, twelve; Lela Stoughton, seventeen; and Kezia Sewell, twenty—arrived. They were also surprised to find Charles there. He explained his presence in a few terse sentences.

"Effective tonight, we're putting all of our defensive measures on an organized, military footing," Charles told them. "Tomorrow we're having a meeting of everyone in New Salem and we'll go over the details. But tonight I'm going to show you how to mount a proper guard detail—not that Reuben hasn't been doing it right, but I have a better way, and you'll learn it."

Reuben frowned but said nothing; the others looked expectantly back at Charles.

"First, the watch master will inspect your weapons. I know most of you are 'armed' with cudgels, but he'll make sure you have them and that they're serviceable. Comfort has a shot rifle." He took it from her and held it up for all of them to see. "You will all be trained on how to operate this weapon— you may have to in an emergency. But observe how it is now, action open, breech empty. Reuben will make sure, every night, that when Comfort brings this with her, it is in the same condition as it is now—rounds in the magazine but breech empty. She will load it at her post and make sure it's safe. When she goes off duty in the morning, Reuben will ensure that the weapon is made safe before she is relieved."

Joab Flood grinned and looked hungrily at the weapon. He'll make a good gunner, Charles thought. "The watch master each night will make sure you remember which signals you are to give in case of alarm. I know, they're very simple, but in an emergency anyone can forget and give the wrong one. But you won't do that because we're going to drill over and over again. Your first order on watch is to take charge of your post. The second is to remain alert, and so on, and each time you go on duty you will be reminded of these things." He pointed at Lela Stoughton. "Miss, what do you do if you see something coming on the air?"

"You hit the gong, bong—pause—bong—pause—bong," she answered immediately.

*"No!"* Charles snapped, and immediately felt sorry for it when he saw how embarrassed the young woman was. "The signal for an air attack is a quick and vigorous *'Bong, bong, bong!'* over and over again!" he said gently, and laughed. "See what I mean?" He patted the young woman on the shoulder to reassure her that he wasn't angry with her. "I know you won't forget that again, Miss, er . . . ?"

"Stoughton," Reuben said.

"Stoughton. But you see what I mean? We go over and over even the simplest things so that when you are scared to death and every fiber in your body screams that you should *run* to safety, you'll do your duty. You watchers have the safety of this whole village on your shoulders and we're all depending on you to keep alert out there." He turned to Reuben. "How do you post your people to their watch stations?"

Reuben shrugged. "When I see they're all here, I just let them go. They all know where the posts are."

"Tonight we go in a group, watch master. We'll drop them off one by one, and in the morning your replacement will relieve your men in the same way. No more wandering around by yourself out there, especially after dark. I'll stay with you for part of the night. You will check each post every hour. How would you do that?"

"I've been starting with post number one and walking around the perimeter to number four."

"Don't do that. All of you listen to me. Any of you could be a watch master. Never establish a pattern. Vary your route to and from the posts. The watch master is the backup to our system, and he may be the one to discover an infiltrator before anyone else is aware of him." Charles heaved a sigh. "Okay? Now, what are the passwords for tonight?"

"They are 'Night' and 'Day.' When someone unidentified approaches a post, the watcher challenges with 'Night' and the other person answers with "Day.' "

Charles suppressed a sigh. He had discussed the need for signs and countersigns at night with Zechariah but apparently he hadn't been very clear. "When you approach a post in the dark, especially when the watcher is armed with a rifle, you need some way to let him know you're not the enemy, and for sure you don't want the enemy to learn what your passwords are. So you don't want to pick a sign and countersign that're easy for anybody to figure out, like 'Night' and 'Day.' It's logical one follows the other. All right, I know we're just getting started. We'll work all this out in the coming days. For tonight, can you think of passwords that nobody else can figure out?"

"How 'bout 'Genesis' and 'Revelations'?" Joab Flood volunteered. "The first and last books in the Bible. We're all big on Bible readings, we know all the books by heart, but I doubt the devils do."

"Good man!" Charles enthused. He turned to Reuben. "There's officer material in that lad, Mr. Stoughton. Okay, if the person doesn't answer immediately with the countersign, 'Revelations,' you give the emergency signal . . ." He looked again at Lela.

"Two quick bangs, as distinguished from aerial, ground, and muster signals," she answered immediately.

"And run like hell," he added, and Lela grinned triumphantly. "If the weather is bad and the sound won't carry, you run straight for the village to warn the rest of us. And be ready to defend yourself with those sticks. Make as much noise as you can." Charles sighed. "In the future these signs and countersigns will be given to you at the beginning of each watch. Now, one final thing: Why have we laid lines along the ground connecting all the posts?"

"To detect infiltrators and to warn the other posts if we spot anything," Kezia Sewell answered.

"Right. A lone infiltrator may not trip the lines. They'll be just above the ground, and if an infiltrator knows what he's doing, he'll be very careful. Let's face it, if we're being watched, they'll know where the posts are and they may also know we've laid the wire. I doubt it, but it's possible. But you do the best you can in these circumstances. But any sizable force, one big enough to give us trouble, will hopefully stumble over them. And that's another reason the watch master keeps moving between posts all night long." They had carefully strung thin wire cable at about mid-calf to an average man's leg above the ground between all the posts. At close intervals they had hung tin cans containing one or two stones so that when tripped they'd cause a rattling noise at the nearest watch station.

"Hey, it could be a stray cow," Charles continued, "but you react as if it's a whole herd of devils, right?" The watchers all nodded enthusiastically. Charles had their attention and their confidence. "Reuben? You ready? Let's go."

Reuben posted the watchers well, and Charles congratulated him. "You go to your post in the meetinghouse," Charles told him, "and rest for an hour. I'm going to stay out here and check on things. Then the rest of the night is yours. Reuben, I'm not trying to embarrass you or make you feel small. I'm taking my new responsibility seriously and I'm only doing what I think is best for the safety of everyone in New Salem. You do understand that, don't you?"

Reuben Stoughton looked at Charles in the darkness. If this man is a spy, he thought, he sure doesn't act like it. "Yes,

Charles, I do, and I appreciate what you're doing for us."
They shook hands and Reuben walked back to the village.

"Genesis!" Comfort Brattle challenged when she heard someone approaching.

"Revelations," someone answered in a very soft voice.

"Charles! I knew it was you by the sound of your voice!"

Charles came up to her. He could just barely see the outline of her face in the darkness. "Suppose I was a ventriloquist hiding out there in the dark, listening to the challenges?"

"Oh, Charles! Aren't you taking all this too seriously?" Comfort did not expect to be examined that way, and despite the fact that she was ashamed of herself for it, she still burned with jealousy over his close relationship with Colleen. Comfort Brattle considered Charles *her* man. She'd nursed him back to health and he belonged to *her*!

"Maybe, but we're in a serious position, Comfy. We can't—where's your rifle?"

"Leaning up against the wall. It got too heavy to carry."

"Comfort, never, but *never* get away from your weapon when you're on guard duty." Charles could tell from Comfort's voice she was near tears with frustration. He had been carrying on his side of the conversation in a whisper, which Comfort automatically imitated. He leaned forward and put his lips close to her ear. "You have a big responsibility, and I know you're up to it. Just keep your mind on—" She turned her head and kissed him full on the mouth.

Charles stepped back immediately. "Now listen to me, Comfort. You *ever* do anything like that again on duty and you're off the watch, you'll turn in your weapon, and your little ass'll be in the kitchen with Mama." He placed both hands on her shoulders and shook her none too gently.

What is going on? Comfort asked herself. He'd kissed that Colleen woman, she'd seen it! And now he objects to me kissing him? Conflicting emotions of rejection and jealousy welled up within her. She began to cry. "Nobody's ever talked to me like that before and—and—Charles, I—I—*love* you!"

"Now listen to me again: when you're on watch you *watch,* you got that? You don't sit up here and moon about

your lover or your dead brother or your goddamned period!"
Charles paused to catch his breath. The kiss, he admitted,
had been wonderful. He continued in a calmer tone of voice.
"Comfort, you have to be able to separate your duty from
your personal concerns. Now look, everybody in the village
thinks we're soft on one another. I know they're talking about
us. I'm twice your age, Comfort! What do you think people
are saying about us? And we can't have that anymore, now
that I'm responsible for the defense of New Salem and have
to make up duty rosters and order people around. Nothing I
can do will ever convince the other men that I'm not being
soft on you, sparing you the rough duty because we're lovers.
That is going to destroy morale and undercut my authority.'

"But—But Charles! I can fight! I have! I'm as brave and
as smart as any man, braver and smarter than most of them!
And I love you. I can't *help* it, Charles! I do!"

"I know," Charles answered, so softly Comfort could
hardly hear him. "But you have to understand, there are big
differences between men and women. I don't mean that men
are stronger and more warlike or anything like that. But
Comfort, there's a—a 'chemistry' that works between the
sexes, and it gets in the way of *everything* if you can't control
it, and the younger you are, the harder it is to control. And
here we are now, all of us thrown together into small groups,
working together day in and day out, relationships are bound
to form and somebody's got to keep an eye on that or when a
crisis comes, someone will not make that single most important sacrifice to save the rest of us from disaster. Do you
know what I'm saying to you?"

Comfort leaned forward in the dark, kissed him again,
turned and ran off toward the village. Charles could hear her
crying all the way back down the ridge. He sighed, slung the
shot rifle over his shoulder and took her post. When Reuben
Stoughton came by an hour later, he explained that Comfort
had taken ill and he'd relieved her.

"Women!" was all Reuben said, and moved on about his
rounds.

Charles stayed on watch the rest of the night.

\* \* \*

*"Comfort!"* Charles bellowed as he came through the front door of the Brattles' home the next morning. "Front and center, girl!"

Consort Brattle emerged from the kitchen, wiping her hands on her apron. "Charles, whatever is the matter?"

"Where is Comfort?"

"In her room, I think. But Charles—"

"Get Zechariah, will you?"

Zechariah Brattle came out of his room, cinching his belt about his waist. "What is it, Charles? Are you forming up for training?"

"Not quite yet, Zechariah. I want Comfort out here. Now." He walked back to her room and pounded on her door. After a few moments it opened and Comfort, eyes puffy from weeping, peered out at him. Charles reached inside, caught her arm, and dragged her into the living room, where her parents stood goggle-eyed with astonishment.

"How dare you handle my daughter that way, Charles!" Consort shouted, and started forward.

"What is the matter?" Zechariah asked, laying a restraining hand on his wife. He *did* understand.

"Comfort deserted her post last night. I will have no one on the defense force who can't follow orders and do his or her duty. She is relieved." He let go of her arm. "I wouldn't be alive today if it weren't for your daughter. She took care of me like my mother would have. But that was then. This is now. You find other duties for her, Zechariah, but she is not serving with my force anymore."

"She's a young woman, Charles! You can't expect her to act like a soldier!" Consort protested.

"It's hard enough as it is to keep your people attentive to their duties without someone just walking off her post be-cause—because—" Charles left the thought unfinished.

"Daughter?" Zechariah turned to Comfort.

"Yes, Father, I understand. May I return to my room now?" Comfort looked very small and frail, standing there, child-like, totally devastated. Charles felt a surge of pity so strong he almost cried out, *I'm sorry! I take it all back!* but he suppressed it and kept the stony visage, cruel and harsh, that overlay the utter remorse he felt at having hurt her. How can I ever make this up to her? he asked himself, and then mentally kicked his own behind for even thinking he had anything to apologize for.

"No, you may not," Zechariah told her. "All of us are going to the meetinghouse. The black woman wishes to speak to us."

The black woman, Emwanna Haramu, stood demurely at the pulpit in the meetinghouse, looking completely restored after her ordeal in the desert.

When everyone except the watchers was present, Zechariah Brattle called for order. "Friends, our guest from far away has something important to tell us." He gestured toward Emwanna and indicated she should speak.

Emwanna cleared her throat nervously. "I thank you," she began haltingly, "for taking my son and me into your home and saving us." Her voice was low and well-modulated, but people had to lean forward to hear her words. As she continued, her voice became stronger. "I know we see gods different. Mrs. Flood"—she pronounced the name *Floood*—"she tell me much about your God and how you have suffered from the *things* that destroyed our villages and kill many of our people." Hannah Flood had told her how the Skinks had descended upon their land and devastated it, how the survivors had fled to the mountains for safety and a chance to recover their lives.

"Our gods do not protect us from *things*," Emwanna continued. "We pray, sacrifice, do all to seek their help. No good. But *things* they leave. We think we are safe. Then *men* from the city come." Here she was overcome with emotion and tears coursed down her brown cheeks. She wiped them away with a sleeve. The meetinghouse was engulfed in a dead silence as everyone waited for her to continue. "All dead now," she whispered. Then in a stronger voice she told them what had happened. "One man, he find us, Chisi and me, in cave.

He give us food and drink and let us live. All men from the city not bad." She paused. "I speak to you to thank you and to warn you." She caught Hannah Flood's eyes, and Hannah nodded. "God bless you all," Emwanna said, concluding her speech. She stepped out of the pulpit. The people arose then and surged forward to embrace her.

Charles called Zechariah aside. "*Things* or men, Zechariah, we have to be ready at an instant's notice to react. Our position is now even more perilous. We may have to abandon New Salem."

"Those men were obviously from the Army of the Lord, Charles. I've told you about them. The devils were at war with them and winning, the last we knew. But since we escaped from the great slaughter, we've had no word from the outside world. Now we know the Army of the Lord is still intact. Possibly they won the war. Or maybe those off-worlders, the Confederation Marines, turned the tide. Whoever comes here from now on, we must assume they're hostile. We shall seriously consider moving, but our livelihoods are here, and we are just beginning to get back on our feet. It will not be easy convincing the people to move again."

Charles placed his hand on Zechariah's arm. "I know what you people have been through, my friend, but your trials are not over yet, not by a damned sight. We *must* survive and we *will* survive. You and I are going to have to keep these people motivated."

# CHAPTER
# NINE

All the Marines disembarked when the *Grandar Bay* went into orbit around Thorsfinni's World—34th FIST because it was home, 26th FIST to give its Marines shore liberty before continuing to their home base. As the Marines of 26th FIST boarded the Dragons waiting in Essays for the landing, the Marines of 34th FIST impatiently waited their turn.

"They're going to have all the Reindeer Ale in Bronnys drunk by the time we get there," Corporal Joe Dean groused.

"There won't be anything left for us to wash down our reindeer steaks," Lance Corporal "Wolfman" MacIlargie complained.

Corporal Rachman Claypoole snorted. "No problem. There won't be any reindeer steaks left by the time we get to Bronnys."

"All the girls at Big Barb's will be busy when we get there," Corporal Chan groused. "We'll have to wait a week for a chance at them."

Lance Corporal "Izzy" Godenov looked horrified at the prospect. "No ale? No steak? No *girls*? Then why are we bothering to make planetfall at all? They might as well send us right out on another deployment!"

Corporal Raoul Pasquin reached out and smacked Godenov on the back of his head. "Wash your mouth, you say shit like that, you turd!" he snarled.

"Hey!" Godenov shouted, rubbing the back of his head and glaring at Pasquin.

"Wait just a minute there!" Dean shouted at Pasquin. "Don't

you hit Izzy. He's mine. If he needs to be hit, *I* hit him." He rapped Godenov on the crown of his head.

"Hey, what are you hitting me for?" Godenov leaned away from the two corporals and plopped his helmet on his head to protect it from further blows.

"Because you deserve it," snarled Sergeant "Rabbit" Ratliff. He shook his head. "Why do I get stuck with the gung-ho one who wants to go right out on another deployment? Hit him one for me Dean."

"I don't want to—"

Dean punched Godenov's shoulder hard enough for the *smack* to echo off the walls of the small hold where third platoon, Company L, waited its turn to board Essays. "If you don't want it, then don't say it."

"But—"

Godenov was saved when Staff Sergeant Wang Hyakowa roared, "Attention on deck!" as Lieutenant Rokmonov, the assault platoon commander, entered the hold. Rokmonov had been given temporary command of third platoon on Kingdom after the regular platoon commander, Gunnery Sergeant Charlie Bass, was killed in a Skink ambush. Now he was back with his own platoon and Hyakowa was acting platoon commander as well as platoon sergeant.

There was a brief clatter and clanking as the Marines came to attention.

"At ease!" Rokmonov said loudly. The men relaxed and looked at him attentively. "First," Rokmonov said when they were at ease, "I want to give all you Marines of third platoon a hearty 'well done' for your performance in the face of the enemy on Kingdom. You were a credit to the company, to the battalion, to the FIST, and to the Corps. I was honored to command you. No matter where I go or what I do in the Corps, I will be proud to serve with any of you again." He paused to allow the buzz that ran through the platoon to run down.

"You weren't too bad yourself," someone said.

"Now, I've got some news." Rokmonov was doing his best to ignore the swelling that remark caused in his chest—he knew full well what a challenge he faced following Gunny Bass as platoon commander. "I know there's some, ah, consternation in the ranks because 26th FIST is going planetside first, and there's a suspicion that there won't be anything left to eat or drink in Bronnys by the time we make it down." He raised his voice to ride over the murmurs of complaint. "Don't worry. Twenty-sixth FIST isn't going to Bronnys, they're pulling liberty at the navy HQ, so they'll be drinking up the squids' beer, not yours." He held up his hands to hold down the cheers.

"There's more. Right before the *Grandar Bay* left orbit around Kingdom, Brigadier Sturgeon sent a message via drone to Camp Ellis to let them know we were on our way back and when to expect us. We just got word, the base stocked up on food and drink and they're throwing a big party for us beginning tonight. Enough ale and steak for everybody."

This time he let the cheering continue for a moment before raising his hands and patting the air. "As you were! As you were!" he shouted, to be heard over the cheers.

"Belay that!" Hyakowa roared loud enough for everyone to hear. It took another moment, but the Marines quieted down.

"There's more yet," Rokmonov continued with a broad grin when the hubbub was finished. "Base is ferrying in a lot of girls from Bronnys and other nearby towns to serve and to socialize with us." He had to shout for anyone to hear him over the roar of excitement and pleasure. "Including all of Big Barb's girls!"

After that there was no point in trying to announce anything else. Lieutenant Rokmonov was beaming as he left the hold.

Essays finally brought 34th FIST planetside, in the combat assault approach Marines always used when making planetfall, and deposited the Dragons they carried just over the horizon from the great island Niflheim. The Dragons formed up and raced toward the fjord that led to the town of

Bronnysund. Just short of the town, they roared ashore and sped overland to Camp Ellis, home of 34th FIST, and disgorged their passengers at the FIST parade ground, where the thousand Marines formed up in FIST formation for a welcoming speech from Brigadier Sturgeon. His remarks were blessedly brief; they knew there'd be a more formal formation later. And the men were all anxious to get to the barracks and prepare for the evening's party.

Less than two minutes after he began to speak, Sturgeon handed command of the FIST over to his subordinate commanders, who in turn gave command of their individual units to their subordinate commanders. The Marines then marched to their barracks. Built of native stone and clapboard, the H-shaped barracks were grouped by major subordinate unit throughout Camp Ellis. They had already been cleaned and aired out by base personnel in preparation for the return of 34th FIST.

Behind Company L's barracks, Captain Conorado instructed his Marines to retrieve their gear and personal belongings from the company supply room where they'd been stored during the deployment, and to get themselves unpacked and cleaned up. Preparty formation was to be in two hours. Then he dismissed the men, to roars of approval. He wisely stood aside while his men stampeded.

The barracks quickly filled with the clatter of running feet, opening doors, and storage drawers yanked open, filled, and slammed shut. Yells and catcalls filled the two-story buildings' corridors.

"Make a hole, wide load coming through!" yelled a Marine who'd retrieved his locker box from the company storage room and was hauling it to his platoon area.

"What do you mean, you can't find my locker box? It's got my name and number all over it!" shouted another, whose box didn't appear instantly because it was out of sight behind others.

"Shoup, in here!" Corporal Pasquin yelled to the Marine who'd joined his fire team on Kingdom and didn't know what room they were in, which was repeated by other corporals guiding their newest men to quarters.

"Luxury!" Corporal Claypoole exclaimed as he threw himself onto his rack. "Why, if I could just ignore you," he said to Lance Corporal MacIlargie, "I could believe I've got a private room!" Second squad's third fire team was the only one in third platoon that didn't have three men.

"Nobody can ignore me," MacIlargie replied. "I won't let them."

"Unfortunately, you're right. You smell bad and you make too much noise. And if that's not enough, you're ugly."

"I do not!" MacIlargie yelped.

"Okay. You don't smell any worse than any Marine coming in from a month in the field, and you don't make more noise than a farting kwangduk. But you're still ugly."

"You keep picking on me, I'm gonna tell Sergeant Linsman on you!"

Claypoole was momentarily overcome with laughter. When he got it more or less under control, he said, "Sergeant Linsman will hand me a scrubber and tell me to give you a shower. No, no, no. You complain to him, then I get in trouble for letting you get so smelly in the first place. I think I'll just wait until everybody's got their lockers from the supply room, then go check out a scrubber and take care of the problem my ownself." That set him off again.

"You and what army?" MacIlargie gasped between peals of laughter.

"I'm a Marine corporal. Ain't nothing an army can do I can't do by my lonesome." He doubled up with laughter and kicked his legs in the air.

"Yep, like I said," a voice cut through the laughter. Claypoole and MacIlargie looked to the doorway and saw Sergeant Linsman, arms folded over his chest, leaning on the jamb. "All my problem children in one place, where I can keep an eye on them." Linsman watched them for a moment with not quite concealed amusement, then said, "What say you two clowns get unpacked and get your gear stowed. Uniform of the day for the party is civvies."

"Right, Sergeant Linsman. We'll get right on it," Claypoole said. But neither he nor MacIlargie made a move to begin unpacking.

Linsman turned to leave, paused to say over his shoulder, "By the way, scuttlebutt has it Gunny Thatcher wants to leave one man from each platoon behind for security—make sure the base pogues don't come in and steal anything while we're partying. When company formation is called, he's going to assign the last man in formation from each platoon to that security."

*"Say what?"* The two burst into activity. No way were either of *them* going to get tapped for security duty!

Linsman chuckled as he walked to the squad leaders' room at the end of the corridor.

In fact, when the company formation was called, Gunny Thatcher didn't assign anybody to security. The base military police platoon had canceled all liberty and leave for the night and assigned MPs to security at the parties and the barracks areas.

Corporals Claypoole, Dean, Kerr, Chan, Pasquin, Dornhofer, Barber, and Taylor sat together in a broken circle of lawn chairs, leaving enough of a gap for people to move in and out of the group to get more food and drink, or to respond to nature's call. All of them had eaten enough to swell their stomachs, and they were happily imbibing vast quantities of Reindeer Ale to fill any and all gaps in their digestive tracts. Claypoole and Pasquin puffed away on Fidels, and Dean contented himself with a Clinton.

"Home," Dean murmured.

Carlala, a skinny, large-bosomed young woman from Big Barb's, was the only one who heard. She snuggled closer, thinking he meant the feel of her on his lap, and sighed. She had one arm looped around his shoulders, and her other hand held his stein so he could quaff whenever he wished. His free hand rested possessively on her hip.

Erika, Dean's former main squeeze at Big Barb's, saw the movement. She briefly glared at Carlala, quickly changed her look to an alluring smile, and wiggled her bottom more deeply into Pasquin's lap.

"My brave Marine," she said in a deep, low voice just loud enough for Dean to hear, and ran a hand over Pasquin's visible wound scars. His shirt was open and hanging outside his shorts.

Pasquin belched and grinned at her. He gave her ear a nip and whispered, "Let's give my chow a chance to settle, then go find some privacy."

Erika giggled, and gave her bottom a more meaningful wiggle. She shot another glare at Carlala.

Dean was nuzzling Carlala's breasts and didn't notice.

Claypoole kept his Fidel clamped between his teeth because both hands were busy. One held his stein, the other toyed with Jente's locks, where her head rested on his lap. She's facing the wrong way, he thought, but couldn't ask her to face into him.

Jente wasn't one of Big Barb's girls, and wasn't from Bronnysund, the local liberty town; she was one of the contingent from Brystholde, a village forty kilometers down the coast. Gunny Thatcher had firmly told the Marines of Company L that the young women from Brystholde and the other remote villages were nice girls, and woe to the manjack who didn't treat them the way they'd want their sisters to be treated.

Jente was happy. This Corporal Claypoole wasn't only a very brave Marine, he was more of a gentleman than the rough-hewn fishermen and herders she was accustomed to at home. She rolled her head and lightly kissed his thigh where it emerged from the bottom of his shorts. She smiled when she felt his involuntary reaction against the back of her head. She was twenty-four, time she started looking for a husband— or at least a steady man.

Corporal Dornhofer, the second oldest and second most experienced of third platoon's eight corporals, had more work to do than the others back at the barracks because both of his men were new to Thorsfinni's World. He'd had to see to it that they got all their gear from the *Grandar Bay* and then got their issue from Sergeant Souavi, Company L's supply sergeant. He was tired and all the food and ale put him to sleep. His girl, Klauda, chattered at him anyway and held his hand so it wouldn't slip off its comfortable perch on the swell of her lower belly.

Chan, Barber, and Taylor were much more animated in chatting up the young women who'd paired off with them. What would happen with them before the night was out was anybody's guess, as only one of the women was from Bronnys, and that one wasn't a tavern girl.

Only Kerr was without a comely lass on his lap or seated on the ground next to him. He didn't mind; it was from lack of trying. He'd lost too many friends, on Kingdom, men he'd served with for a long time, to feel like doing any serious partying. Sure, he'd eaten and drunk more than his fill right along with everybody else, but trying to get a girl for the night seemed to him too much of an affirmation of life, and he didn't feel very much alive.

The time Kerr had almost been killed never stopped playing on his psyche. Now and then he wasn't aware of it, but it was never far away, and often it was only severely imposed self-discipline that kept it from overwhelming him. The wound he'd suffered during the first phase of the Kingdom campaign, when his friends were being killed or crippled, had brought it back full force, though he hid it well enough that only he knew it was bothering him at all.

Heavy hands clamped on Kerr's shoulders from behind and a huge voice boomed out, "Corporal Kerr, wad's wrong wid you? You sidding here all alone brooding like a chicken just lost all her eggs to a fox, when there's all these beautiful girls all aroun' jus' vaiting for a strong man like you to take them to heaven?"

The voice startled Dornhofer and he dove for cover, tumbling his girl into an awkward sprawl on the ground. He'd been half asleep, and now he scrabbled about, groping for a weapon. The sound of the other corporals' laughing reminded him of where he was. He flushed and pushed himself up, glaring at Big Barb.

"Allah's pointed teeth, Big Barb! You should know better than to startle a man this soon after he's been in combat!" he roared.

"Dorny, you sid back down and go back to sleep," Big Barb said, ignoring his words. "But first you help dat poor girl Klauda back to her feet. You apologize to her for trowin' her down like dat, den you check her for bruises. If you vind any, you kiss dem and make dem bedder!" She gripped Kerr's shoulders more firmly and pulled him to his feet, turning him around to face her. Dornhofer was already dismissed from her awareness.

"Timmy, it's no gut you sidding dere like dat. Here, I got wad you needs." She let go of his shoulders and reached around to pull two beautiful young women, one blond and fair, the other brunette and swarthy, from where they'd been hidden behind her massive bulk. "Dis iss Frieda and Gotta. Take yer pick, eider one of dem'll take goot care of you, make you wanna live again."

"Thanks, Big Barb, but—"

"What, you tink one's not goot enough? All right den, take bot'!" She let go of the young women's arms and planted a hand on each one's back. They both moved forward before she pushed. She squinted at him threateningly. "And don' you sen' dem avay, neider!"

Big Barb waved at the group and ponderously wandered off in search of other Marines who might need encouragement.

Kerr didn't send the two beautiful young women away. Instead, after his dinner had time to settle, they led him to someplace private.

In time, all of the junior enlisted and junior NCOs who hadn't drunk too much to be functional wandered off with someone. They weren't allowed to take women back to the barracks, but that barely slowed anyone down. Some were fortunate enough to head into Bronnysund to a private room. The rest found other private places. The officers and more senior NCOs mostly had wives or other things to do and left the party earlier.

\* \* \*

Top Myer belched contentedly around the Fidel chomped between his teeth as he finished setting the places around the table and stood back to admire his work. He glanced at the time. The others should show up momentarily, all fed just as well as he was. That had been a good party. Probably still was—when he'd left, most of the enlisted and junior NCOs were still eating, drinking, and chasing. With any luck, the crew coming to play cards would have had more to drink than he had, or started drinking before they had enough food in their guts to absorb the alcohol. In either event, they'd leave their money with him when the game ended.

"Lessee, here," he said to himself. "One, two, three— right, seven places set." A butt tray with a freshly clipped Fidel at each place, munchies bowls alongside the butt trays, and a cooler with half a dozen Reindeer Ales at the side of each chair, with lots more in the refrigerator. Two side tables laden with finger food that wasn't greasy enough to mark the cards too fast, steaks and bakers in the food servo in case anybody got hungry. An unopened deck of cards in the middle of the table, a dozen more unopened decks, and trays of varicolored chips on the shelf.

He looked around, satisfied. After living in the bachelor NCO quarters for a couple of years after his most recent marriage had dissolved, Myer opted for a small bungalow in a housing area not far from the infantry barracks. It wasn't much, the small living room crowded with the paraphernalia for the card game, but it had a bedroom big enough to entertain a lady when the occasion arose, and a small kitchen. Only one bath, though. Hell, if the line got too long later on, anyone who couldn't hold it could damn well go outside and water the neighbors' flowers.

He belched again, puffed away to keep his Fidel going, and reached for an ale. But he put the bottle back before opening it—it wouldn't do for him to be tipsier than any of his victims, er, guests. Not if he wanted to clean them out.

After three wives had left him, he'd decided to do without— at least for the remainder of his Marine career. All three had professed to love him, but claimed they couldn't deal with the stresses of the constant deployments and the uncertainty of whether he would live to come home to them.

As if a first sergeant faced much danger, he thought.

Maybe after he retired he'd get married again. Maybe one of his former wives would want to come back. He told himself he'd have to think about that.

Knuckles rapping sharply on the door brought Myer back to the present. "Come!"

The door opened to reveal the battalion sergeant major, Parant. He looked around, saw only Myer, said, "Oops, sorry to bother you, Top. Someone told me there was a party here," and started to close the door.

"Get in here, Bernie," Myer growled. "You're early, that's all. Have a seat." He got a Reindeer Ale from the kitchen and opened it for Parant. "Have a brew."

There was another knock on the door. It was Company L's gunnery sergeant, Gunny Thatcher, and Staff Sergeant Hyakowa.

"Come on in," Myer growled at them, and got out ales.

Moments later the FIST sergeant major, Shiro, and newly promoted Chief Hospitalman Horner arrived. After he gave them their first drinks, Myer briskly rubbed his hands together and sat down at the table.

"All right, now that we're all here, let the games begin!"

There was a moment of shuffling and scraping as the others took their places and rearranged their settings to their own taste.

"Wait a minute," Parant said. "There's six of us and seven places. Who's missing?"

Myer slapped the unopened deck in front of Hyakowa. "Open them, Wang. You're too junior here to try a fast one on us." He looked at Parant. "Charlie Bass. But you know him, he'd be late for his own funeral."

After a few seconds, Shiro broke the silence that had slammed over the group. "Charlie's dead, Goldie."

"No he ain't. Charlie Bass is too damn dumb to get killed in some silly-assed ambush."

"He's dead," Horner and Thatcher said simultaneously. Hyakowa was too choked up to speak.

"These are my quarters," Myer rasped, giving a gimlet eye to each of them. "This is my table, my game. As long as I'm in 34th FIST, there's a place set at my table for Charlie Bass. Anybody who don't like it can get up and leave."

Parant had to clear his throat before he could speak. "You got that deck open yet, Wang? Let's cut. High card deals."

# CHAPTER
# TEN

It was the darkest time of the night, just before dawn. Charles and a select group of men had been working all night to prepare a defensive position in a draw half a kilometer south of the village. Although he was fast recovering his strength, Charles felt his endurance lagging and decided to return to New Salem for a short rest in the meetinghouse. He wanted to be fresh and on hand for the changing of the watch; the men working in the draw could finish what they were doing before sunrise and get under cover.

Charles had decided to reduce daytime outdoor activity as much as possible from now on, to lessen the chance that anyone might spot movement in the village and come to investigate. In fact, the villagers had partially dismantled some of the unoccupied buildings in New Salem to give the place an uninhabited look, the watch was mounted just before sunrise and just after sunset, and the only foot traffic permitted out of doors at New Salem nowadays when the sun was up was limited to essential requirements, such as communications required by the people on watch. Everyone else slept during the daytime or attended to their domestic chores.

They all knew of infrared sensors and how they worked in the dark, but keeping under cover psychologically increased the feeling that they were doing everything they could to protect themselves. Just like the "fort" they were building in the draw. Everyone knew if the Army of the Lord, much less the devils, attacked them, it would be useless for any long-term effective defensive measures. But the work kept them occupied.

However, the draw proved to have some advantages as a possible refuge and rallying point. It was thickly wooded, and a spring bubbled in the center of the position, which backed up to a vast complex of limestone caverns. It could be reached quickly, and best of all, if it had to be abandoned, the caverns provided an ideal series of escape routes that led to hidden exits away from New Salem. Every centimeter of this cave complex was familiar to the people of New Salem, all of whom had been through them on youthful sprees, family picnics and outings, and lovers' trysts over the years.

Several paths led from the village to the draw, all conveniently camouflaged by undergrowth that flourished throughout the area. Charles chose the one that led most directly back to New Salem. The fronds that brushed against him as he walked were heavy with morning dew. Overhead, the stars glittered in wild profusion. It was utterly quiet; not even a breeze stirred the vegetation.

Charles wondered idly who he was. He knew at one time in his life he'd been some sort of soldier, but not in the Army of the Lord. Zechariah had often pointed out that he was too profane and not quite arrogant enough to have belonged to *that* army! Charles's dreams, when he could remember them at all, were full of military images, barracks scenes, what he took to be maneuvers, weapons, the faces of men he knew and respected. But he could never put names to the faces. The man named Chet, who had come with him from the prison cages, could now remember that he'd been a teacher or educator of some sort, but he couldn't recall where. And Colleen—Charles smiled when he thought of the redhead— could remember things out of her past too, but she was deliberately vague about them, and Charles wondered what she was trying to hide.

Someone stepped out from behind a bush and struck him a heavy blow across his shoulders. Charles fell to his knees, temporarily stunned. Someone whispered, "Hit him again!" and another blow fell across his back, which sent him sprawling into the path. He saw a pair of feet in front of him, and the name "Dupont" flashed into his mind. He grabbed the feet and yanked. With a cry of surprise, the man fell with a thud. Charles crawled up over his legs and landed a heavy blow on the man's face. Then everything went black.

Zechariah Brattle sat alone in the kitchen of his home, staring at his last bottle of beer, left over from their reconnaissance to the destroyed camp in the heights above the Sea of Gerizim. He had been among the survivors who'd made their way to some caves a considerable distance from the heights, and later returned to see what could be salvaged, always with the fear that the attackers would return and finish them off.

On rare occasions since then he had privately consumed the beer, one at a time, the remaining bottles carefully stored at the bottom of the well out back. Like Charles, he had been up all night, constantly on the move between the watchers and the draw, observing, supervising, conferring, letting everyone see him. He'd even found time to drop in on the families of the men on duty. These were all his people, and he felt responsible for them.

It would be light soon—"first light," Charles called it, that time of day when you could read the Bible without the aid of artificial illumination. The watch would have to be posted before then and operations shut down. He looked at his timepiece. He had half an hour to himself. Comfort and Consort were already in bed. They'd worked all night too, preparing emergency stores to take with them into the fort if an alarm came. Three times that week Charles had called alarms, to test everyone's reaction. Zechariah had been pleased with the results. It took no more than five minutes to evacuate everyone to the draw. Charles, however, wanted it done in three minutes, and he promised to keep the drills up until they could do it in that time.

Zechariah's thoughts wandered to the Sea of Gerizim, the turning point in all their fortunes. It had been there that the City of God was destroyed, and with it, all their hopes for the survival of the community of the Lord. He sometimes agreed with the other survivors that it had been the will of

God, just punishment for the evil plot the elders of their sect had put into effect to destroy that cargo ship. He sighed. It is hard to keep your faith in the Lord when all around you is fear and desolation, he reflected. In meeting, where he often preached because he was the leader of New Salem, he never admitted to this weakness. But alone, at the end of a hard day, sometimes his faith wavered and he wondered what God's plan for his people could possibly be. His Bible lay open before him. He'd been reading the Book of Job again.

Zechariah's thoughts turned now to Samuel. At times, when he was alone, he mourned the loss of his son. He'd had such hopes for the lad, just as they'd all had hopes for the City of God, before evil destroyed it, the same evil that had killed Samuel. He was sure that Sam was with the Lord, and to all outward appearances he had accepted that fact. But inwardly he still felt his son's loss as keenly as on the day Samuel was killed. He shrugged. Those thoughts were not good. He was responsible for a lot of other people. As Charles kept telling them, the leader's duty must always be to the job and his people; personal feelings had no place in the world of commanders.

Zechariah opened the bottle and poured half its contents into an empty glass. It frothed pleasantly. His nose wrinkled at the malty aroma of the brew. He sipped cautiously and sighed. He'd never much cared for beer before the Sea of Gerizim, and now he wondered how all those years he could have been so ignorant of such a wonderful pleasure.

*Charles.* Zechariah had come to think of him almost as a son, although he was only a few years older than the stranger. But if Samuel had lived, Zechariah would have wanted him to be the kind of man Charles appeared to be—a strong-willed man, but not without heart. Zechariah knew Comfort was infatuated with him. When the image of the two of them together came into his mind, which it did often these days, he thought of—grandchildren.

But Zechariah was worried about his daughter, who moped around the house all day long, dutiful, as always, but taking little joy in helping her mother or the other women with their domestic chores. Whenever Charles came into the house, she would look at him with mournful eyes that said volumes she dared not speak. So Charles had moved in with Haman and Maria Dunmore, who had no children. Yet when he did visit the Brattles—which was frequently, because he and Zechariah often needed to confer—the tension between the former soldier, for that was how Zechariah had come to think of the man, and his daughter was palpable and distracting.

Everywhere he turned, Zechariah thought, there were problems. But problems were the lot of mankind. He lifted the glass to his lips.

"Zechariah?"

He whirled in surprise. "Why, Charles! Please, sit down. Share this beer with me."

Charles entered the dim circle of light that illuminated the kitchen table.

"My God, Charles! What happened to you?" Zechariah stood and moved to help him into a vacant chair. "Consort! Comfort! Come here!" he yelled.

Both women appeared, still in their nightclothes. "Charles, what happened to you?" Consort asked. He only shook his head. She put Comfort to heating water and carefully took Charles's bloodstained shirt off. He groaned. "I think you have broken ribs, Charles. I'll bind them up, but you'll have to take it easy for a few days."

"No. I'm going to be at formation tonight."

Consort stood back, looked sternly down at Charles and said, "You are in no condition to be at formation."

Charles nodded. "But I've got to show up tonight, Consort."

"Here." Zechariah handed Charles the half-full beer bottle. "Drink up! You need this a lot more than I do."

Consort made a wry face at her husband. "Into that stuff again, Zechariah?"

He shrugged. "It's the last of its breed, Connie, and I've come to learn, in the wisdom of time and with the guidance of God, that a man and his beer should never be separated."

"When we're safe at last," Charles said, "I'm bringing a

Dragonload of cold beer down here and we're going to drink it all by ourselves, Zechariah."

"What's a Dragon?" Consort asked, setting a steaming pan of water and some rags on the table. She was perspiring, and a strand of loose hair hung down one side of her face. She smelled fresh in her white undergown.

"I don't know," Charles answered, then yelled "Owww!" as Comfort began washing the clotted blood off the side of his head.

"More important, where's the 'back' from which you are bringing the beer here?" Zechariah chuckled.

"Elneal!" Charles said sharply and groaned at the pain it caused in his head. "I remember I had beer on a place called Elneal." It came back to him: he'd killed a man on Elneal, wherever that was.

"You'll need a dozen or more stitches to sew up this hole in your head, Charles," Consort said, not paying attention to his ramblings. "I'll give you some analgesic tea. That will relax you and dull the pain. Comfort, would you mix it up for me, dear? Next, get the poultices ready. The poultices will prevent infection, Charles, and aid healing."

"What happened, Charles?" Zechariah asked.

Charles finished the beer in one long gulp and burped loudly. " 'Scuse me, ladies. Someone jumped me. Two of them. I don't know who they were or why they did it."

Zechariah did not believe Charles didn't know who'd attacked him or why, but *he* certainly knew why they did it. Some of the younger men were jealous of Charles and Comfort, and some thought he was a spy. But he kept that to himself. Like all the members of the City of God sect, his people were wary of strangers.

"Ugh," Charles muttered as he sipped the tea, "this stuff tastes positively awful." But he drank it all anyway. "Now what?" He looked at the Brattles and burped again. "Damned good beer, Zechariah!"

The next thing Charlie knew, he was dreaming. He was standing outside a complex of some sort consisting of wooden buildings. The day was overcast, cool and windy, and there was the smell of fish in the air. Before him stood rank after rank of young men in uniform. Their faces were hard, but some, he could see, had tears in their eyes. Strange, very strange, he thought. But they kept their gaze straight ahead, staring right through him. In the closer ranks he recognized the faces and tried to call out their names, but nothing would come. He turned around, and behind him stood several more men dressed in resplendent uniforms, standing on a low dais. "Dress reds!" he tried to say. He recognized them too, and his heart soared with joy, but he could not get their names out either. He tried, but it was as if his throat were stuffed with sand; no sound would emerge. One of the men on the dais, someone Charles realized he'd known for a long time, stared at him in astonishment and said, "Charlie! We thought you were dead!" Then the men in ranks began to chant, "Charlie! Charlie! Charlie!"

"Charles? Charles?" Comfort shook him gently awake. She put a cool, soft hand on the side of his face.

"Comfy? I was dreaming," he gasped as he tried to roll on his side to see her better.

"Lie still, Charles. Mother sewed up the laceration in your head and I put on the poultices. Your ribs will heal in a few weeks."

"What time is it?"

"An hour after sunrise."

Charles lay back on the pillows. "Let me lie here for a while, Comfy? I *have* to make the muster tonight. Ohhh, that potion your mother gave me really works!" He took Comfort's hand in his own. "Seems we just can't stay away from each other, doesn't it? You're always there when I need you the most, young lady."

"I always will be, Charles," she said softly. She glanced at the doorway and added, "Charles, you have visitors." He looked, and saw Colleen and Hannah Flood, both with worried expressions on their faces. They came in and knelt beside Comfort.

"We were worried about you, Charles," Hannah clucked.

Colleen put her hand on Charles's arm and rubbed it affectionately.

"I'll marry you all," Charles chuckled, but it came out sounding more like a croak.

At first none of the women made any response, and then they all laughed.

"The sound of women laughing is the best medicine for a man," Zechariah said from the doorway, "as long as they didn't cause his injuries. Well, how's our wounded soldier?"

"The womenfolk of this household should open their own health maintenance organization, Zechariah." Charles grinned.

Zechariah nodded. "Ladies, leave us for a moment, would you?" When the women had repaired to the kitchen, Zechariah sat at the foot of the bed. "We are making progress on our defenses, Charles. Consort wishes you to remain here under her care for a couple of days. I can supervise the men. They know what to do anyway. But you know, the growing season is upon us. We can't subsist forever on beef and potatoes, and our cattle herd is shrinking every day. We must soon resume farming in the daylight."

"I know. When the time's ready, let's do it. Who knows, Zechariah, maybe we're safe now. Maybe the threat has gone away. We've been living here for weeks and nobody's come this way except the black woman and her child."

Zechariah nodded. "You know, Charles, this world of ours was never heavily settled, not much beyond this continent—Paradise, we call it. The other places," he shrugged, "nobody had much contact with the people in Eden and Nirvana. At some point, Charles, we should try to make contact with the government in Haven, despite what the black woman has told us about what the soldiers did to her people. Also, the Confederation of Human Worlds has—or had—an embassy in Interstellar City. We need to find out what's going on in the rest of the world."

"I agree, but discreetly, Zechariah, very discreetly. Now, tonight I'm making muster. I want to be there when the guard is changed, and I want to see the other men before they go off to the fort. I may not be able to last all night long, but

I'm going to be there. No one is going to stop me. I have my reasons. Agreed?"

"Very well, you hard-headed old soldier."

The watchers who assembled after dusk in the meeting-house consisted of the Rowley family—Paul, the watch master, and his four daughters, Amana, Leah, Adah, and Timna, all of them over the age of fifty. Charles greeted them warmly but perfunctorily. It was his impression that mature women given an important job took it seriously. Paul, he knew, was more than capable of posting the guard and keeping them on their toes.

It was the fort detail he most wanted to inspect. After the night watch had been sent out to relieve the day shift, he addressed the men sitting in the pews before him. By then everyone had heard about him being assaulted. With considerable effort, he suppressed the pain he felt at every movement. The poultice over the wound on the side of his head was kept in place by a white bandage Comfort had prepared for him, so he looked to the men very much like the valiant wounded soldier they thought him to be.

The meetinghouse was dimly lit with small oil lamps, and heavy drapes had been pulled tight over the windows to black the place out. Charles paced back and forth, his shadow looming enormously above the pulpit, telling them what a good job they'd all done and how it was nearly complete. He mentioned the discussion he'd had with Zechariah that morning, about sending someone to Haven to make contact with any survivors there, that the mission would be dangerous, and that he would lead it. While he spoke, he looked very carefully at each man. He stopped in front of Spencer Maynard, who concentrated on the back of the man in the pew in front of him as Charles continued looking at him while speaking.

"So when we go to Haven, men, I'm going to pick only the stoutest hearts among you. Spencer, I think I'd like to have you go along with me. What do you say? By the way, that's a pretty nasty-looking shiner you got there. How did it happen?"

"I, ah, ran into a door in the dark, Charles," Spencer muttered.

"Must have been a damned nasty door, Spence."

"Ah, it surely was," Spencer muttered, grinning sheepishly at the floor. Some of the men laughed, but almost instantly it dawned on them what Charles was intimating, and as a group they turned and looked hard at Spencer Maynard, whose neck flared brick red.

"Well, Spence, count yourself in, then. And by the way, old buddy, old friend, stay away from those 'doors' from now on. They come in pairs, know what I mean?"

From that day forward Spencer Maynard gave Charlie no more trouble, and whenever the projected expedition to Haven came up in conversations, he blurted out proudly that *he,* Spencer Maynard, was the first man Charles had picked to go along with him on that dangerous mission.

Dominic de Tomas had been right, every man has his price. For some, like Spencer Maynard, that consists only in being recognized as a man.

# CHAPTER
# ELEVEN

Brigadier Sturgeon stood front and center on the reviewing stand facing out, looking over the Marines of 34th FIST. Rear Admiral Blankenvoort, commander of the Confederation Supply Facility and the ranking Confederation military officer on Thorsfinni's World, stood immediately to his right. The FIST's six senior staff officers and the FIST sergeant major stood in a single row extending from Sturgeon's left rear. Blankenvoort's six most senior were in a corresponding line to his right rear. From the front, the red-tunic-over-gold trousers, chests adorned with rows of rainbow ribbons suspending medals worn by the Marine officers, outsplendored the medals and gold-insignia-on-blue uniforms of the navy officers.

Forty paces directly to the front, Commander Van Winkle, the infantry battalion commander, faced the reviewing stand. Behind him was the battalion, nearly half of the FIST's strength, in company ranks. To the right, the composite squadron was arrayed in its sections. On the left stood the artillery battery, the transportation company, and the FIST headquarters company.

An icy hand gripped Sturgeon's heart as he looked out at his command and so graphically saw how many Marines he'd lost. Those men who had made planetfall on Kingdom at the beginning of the campaign, on that early, innocent day when they thought they were going in to put down a peasant revolt, wore their dress scarlets. Scarlet-over-gold for the officers, scarlet-over-blue trousers for enlisted. Every one of them wore at least one medal on his chest, and a few

116

had as many or more medals and decorations than Sturgeon.
Far more than at the last formal FIST pass-in-review had
wound stripes on their sleeves. The ranks of scarlet-tunicked
Marines were studded with men in a less formal, rarely worn
uniform—dress blues. Each of them also had at least one
medal on his chest; many had more than one row of medals
and decorations. Each of the Marines in blue had joined the
FIST during the Kingdom Campaign as replacements for
Marines killed in the campaign's first phase. As far as Sturgeon was concerned, far too many of 34th FIST's Marines
wore blue.

There were holes in the formation, especially in the composite squadron. They represented Marines who had been
killed on Kingdom and not yet been replaced. Sturgeon
couldn't tell whether the plethora of blue uniforms or the
scattering of holes hurt more.

Well, when men fought, some men died, he told himself. A
commander had to accept that; if he couldn't accept losses,
he'd make mistakes that would cost more lives. What a commander had to strive for was to keep his own losses to a minimum while causing the greatest number of losses possible
to the enemy—or at least more losses than the enemy was
willing to accept. Sturgeon had to admit that he and his FIST
had accomplished that on Kingdom.

He looked out over his command, saw the losses 34th
FIST had suffered, and knew the Skinks had suffered far
greater. It didn't make him feel any better about the Marines
who had died, but it told him those deaths had not been in
vain. "Now" wasn't the time to suffer those deaths, "now"
was the time to honor the dead.

The Skink commanders were willing to accept more losses
than almost any human commander in all of history. A Skink
unit had to suffer so many casualties that it was ineffective as
a combat unit before it was ready to stop fighting and withdraw from the field of battle. Even then, if they couldn't retreat, they kept fighting until all were dead. Surrender was
not an option. In the entire campaign on Kingdom, the Marines had only captured prisoners once. And another Skink

unit had tracked the Skink prisoners down and killed them. What kind of beings would do that? Sturgeon wondered.

"Marines!" he said in a voice that barely needed amplification to reach everyone in the ranks before him. "In recent months we have lost many comrades in conflict with an implacable foe. Some of those Marines died in the commission of acts that saved the lives of their buddies, some when they refused to quit against impossible odds. Others simply fell in Aries' eternal quest for blood. Whatever the particular circumstances of any one of their deaths, every one of them fell in defense of his fellow man. They may be dead, but they are not gone forever, never to be thought of again. They were Marines. As Marines take care of our own, we remember our comrades who precede us to whatever may come next. Their bodies are no longer among us, but they live on in our memories."

He faced to his left. "FIST Sergeant Major! Read the roll."

"Sir!" Sergeant Major Shiro barked, and lifted a hand in salute. "Aye aye, sir!" Sturgeon returned the salute and took a single step backward. Shiro stepped forward and to his right, to stand to Sturgeon's right front. In his left hand he held a rolled parchment. An unseen drum began to beat a tattoo. Shiro unrolled the parchment and began to read from it.

"Corporal Alvetserati . . ." He paused a beat. "PFC Awatard . . ." Another beat. "Gunnery Sergeant Charles Bass . . ." Only the discipline of a lifetime as a Marine kept his voice from breaking on that name. "Lance Corporal Bhendri . . . PFC Blipstein . . . Sergeant Bunderbust . . . Ensign Chokwatami . . ."

The calling of the roll went on for a long time. When it finally ended, Shiro rerolled the parchment and tucked it under his left arm like a swagger stick. The drum ceased its tattoo and a lone bugle sounded with the ancient, haunting notes of Taps, in final farewell to fallen comrades.

"Sir, the roll is called," Shiro reported after the last note died. He couldn't keep the thickness out of his voice. "All Marines are accounted for."

"All Marines are accounted for, aye," Sturgeon replied. He paused a moment to ensure his composure, then said, "Sergeant Major, you may resume your place."

"Aye aye, sir." Shiro turned sharply and marched back to his position at the end of the rank behind Sturgeon.

"They were our comrades," the brigadier said when Shiro was back in his place. "They live on within us." He raised his right hand in salute.

"Present, arms!" shouted Colonel Ramadan, the FIST Chief of Staff.

"Present, arms!" repeated Commander Van Winkle, Commander Foss, and the other subordinate unit commanders.

The thousand-man formation rippled as Marines brought blasters to the "Present arms" position; those who didn't carry blasters raised their right hands in salute to their fallen comrades.

Sturgeon swallowed, then cut his salute.

"Order, arms!" Colonel Ramadan commanded.

"Order, arms!" the subordinate commanders echoed.

The formation rippled again as the Marines cut their salutes and brought their blasters back down.

"Pass in review!" Ramadan shouted.

"Battalion, right shoulder, arms!" Van Winkle ordered. The Marines of the infantry battalion sharply lifted their blasters to rest on their shoulders.

"By companies, pass in review!"

On the company commander's command, Kilo Company stepped forward, pivoted right, marched to the end of the formation, turned left, left again, and marched past the reviewing stand. Company L followed ten meters behind. M Company, with almost as many blue uniforms as red, trailed. Next came the composite squadron, then the artillery battery and the Dragon company. FIST Headquarters Company brought up the rear.

As each company reached the reviewing stand, the commander cried out, *"Eyes right!"* and saluted. The heads of the marching Marines snapped to the right, except for the right-hand column, whose men kept watching their front.

Brigadier Sturgeon, Admiral Blankenvoort, and their staffs returned the salutes, and the company commanders cried out, *"Eyes front!"* as they cut their salutes.

The entire FIST passed by in only a few moments. The Marines shook hands with the navy officers who'd joined them for the solemn ceremony; the admiral and his staff murmured condolences. They adjourned to the officers' club.

There was no ceremony at the Stones; there never was. The Stones were in a remote corner of Camp Ellis, almost never seen by anyone who didn't go out of the way to visit them. They seldom had visitors and were almost never mentioned except by visitors. But they were there, reverently maintained by civilian workers. They were also, unhappily, updated frequently.

There were five of them, almost identical igneous boulders laboriously collected from all over the island of Niflheim and brought to stand their silent vigil. Each Stone, nearly two meters wide, towered more than three meters above the ground, with an additional meter or more anchoring it below the surface. A dense grove of firlike trees blanketed the hillsides that wrapped around the Stones, sheltering them from the prevailing winds. A broad flagstone walkway led along the front of the boulders. It extended beyond the last one, making room for more to be added to the line. A matching face of each of the boulders had been cut flat just a few degrees off vertical, and the flat face polished until it gleamed. The morning sun reflected blindingly from the polished faces. The faces of the two boulders on the left had engraved upon them the names of the Marines of 34th FIST who had died in combat before the FIST was stationed on Thorsfinni's World. The third Stone's face and three-quarters of the fourth Stone's were engraved with the names of FIST Marines who had been killed in action since the FIST began calling Camp Ellis home.

Much more than half of 34th FIST's existence was before it moved to Thorsfinni's World.

The day after the Farewell-to-Brothers Pass in Review, a

crew of stonemasons engraved the new names on the face of the fourth Stone. It was a brisk morning, and an easy breeze lightly rustled the grove. The air smelled of fish, but nobody noticed; the air always smelled of fish.

The stonemasons could have done the engravings the quick and easy way, using the rock welders that vaporized stone to the desired depth and angle of cut. But they weren't engraving a cornerstone date, or a classical quote on a lintel, or a corporate name or slogan on the face of a building, or even the headstones of ordinary people. These engravings were the names of Marines who had lived and died and now lived eternally in the hearts of the Marines who survived them. These names had to be engraved with a reverence modern methods simply didn't allow. Even if the Marines hadn't told them they wanted the engravings done the old-fashioned way, with hammers and chisels, the stonemasons would have used their ancient tools. They knew that when names are engraved in stone by hand, they had a connection to real people that machine-carved names could not.

Sergeant Major Shiro was at the Stones. Nominally, he was there to supervise the stonemasons and make sure they didn't miss any names, and that all of them had the right rank and were spelled correctly. The stonemasons didn't need the supervision; they had too much pride in their craftsmanship and too much respect for the work to make such errors. So Shiro stayed out of their way and made sure none of the Marines who attended the engraving got in their way. It was an easy job. Few Marines of 34th FIST ever visited the Stones. Even fewer came when new names were being engraved—most found it entirely too easy to imagine their own names being carved on the Stones.

Shiro wasn't surprised, however, that First Sergeant Myer was present. They nodded to each other. Myer offered a Fidel, Shiro accepted, then they lit up and quietly puffed away while they watched the stonemasons.

The Fidels were more than half gone before Myer broke the silence.

"What do they do when they have to take a name off the Stones?"

Shiro considered the question for a long moment, then pointed at the fourth Stone. "See there, a couple of fingers above his left shoulder?"

Myer looked at the stonemason working on the left side of the fourth Stone, two fingers of space above the man's shoulder. The shine on the Stone's face at that point rippled, not quite in sync with the rest of the reflected glow.

"Got it," Myer said.

"That was before either of us were assigned here. The FIST was on a campaign on a world with large carnivores that preyed on people. They gobbled a few Marines. One got his left arm chomped off but managed to get away. His ID bracelet was found in the carnivore's scat, and it was presumed he was dead. He wasn't. He managed to tie off the stump, but then he got lost in the jungle and wasn't found until after the deployment. His name was already on the Stone by the time the FIST was notified. That's the only time a name ever had to come off one of the Stones. That's what it looks like."

"A blank space that isn't level with the rest of the face."

"That's right," Shiro said.

"That's the only one?"

"Yes."

"There's going to be two," Myer said.

Shiro sighed. "He's dead, Goldie. We've got his bracelet, we've got his DNA, we've got enough blood and tissue to know he was pulverized when that rail gun hit him."

"They had that Marine's ID bracelet and the carnivore's scat too."

Shiro slowly shook his head but didn't bother saying anything more. They resumed silently watching the stonemasons at their work.

At noon the masons put their tools aside and broke for lunch. Myer slowly walked to the fourth stone and squatted until the newest names were at eye level. He lightly brushed his fingertips over the freshly carved third new name and wondered why the names were so blurry when they should be sharp.

"I'll see you again, Charlie," he said softly.

He stood back up, stepped two paces back, and came to attention. He snapped the sharpest salute he'd made in years, then about-faced and marched away. Good thing there were so few Marines present, he thought. Something in the air must have gotten into his eyes. He could hardly see where he was going.

# CHAPTER
## TWELVE

Dominic de Tomas was used to being feared, hated, and despised. He was also used to maintaining a very low profile. While millions knew of him by reputation, few would have recognized him in public. He had preferred life that way, being the power behind the scenes, manipulating, planning, plotting, exercising the power of life and death in the shadows.

But now, with those long-deferred plans having come to fruition, all that had changed.

He was about to receive a special public obeisance simulcast on television hookups all across the continent. It was to be presented to him formally by members of the Young Folk League. To a cynic, that would have meant nothing because, as everyone knew, the youth of the organization de Tomas had created and nurtured over the years as a recruiting organ for the Special Group loved their leader. They loved him totally, without reservation, and few parents dared argue with their children about that. But they really did love the man, and what they were about to do that day, in front of the entire world, was a sincere tribute to Dominic de Tomas, the Leader.

The children, all dressed neatly in the simple black and silver uniform of the Young Folk, stood in three rows in the center of the Great Hall at Wayvelsberg, their faces freshly scrubbed, eyes shining brightly with all the enthusiasm one might expect of youth being admitted to the presence of their god.

Balthazar Shearer, Minister for Youth in de Tomas's new

government, stepped forward smartly and saluted the Leader. Shearer, a fortyish, immaculately groomed, but portly man, had directed the Young Folk program for years. He had a talent for organizing and inspiring young people.

A huge brass plaque covered with a velvet drop sheet had been placed on a tripod in the center of the Great Hall. Two young boys stood on either side at rigid attention, waiting for the signal to remove the cover.

"My leader," Shearer began, "the young people assembled here today represent every chapter of the Young Folk League on Kingdom. They have come by express invitation to honor you, our beloved leader." He signaled the two boys, and they pulled the cover off the plaque. On it was a poem entitled, "Honor to Our Leader." Shearer turned to the assembled Young Folk and, like an orchestral conductor, led them in a recitation of the poem, which began, "We live only to hear your ringing voice that strikes deep into our very souls, plunging us into wordless admiration, our very hands tremble in an ecstasy of adoration at every word," and on and on. It was a large plaque.

Gorman, standing beside de Tomas, whispered, "It's from a poem Shearer wrote called 'The Song of the Loyal Ones.' The Minister of Propaganda has had it published numerous times in the media and on thousands of broadsides which he's posted all over the country. It's a bit . . . saccharine, wouldn't you say, my leader?"

"Well, *I* like it, Herten," de Tomas whispered back.

Gorman flinched. "Well, I am told by respected authorities that it does have great artistic merit, my leader, but what do I, a simple soldier, know of art?"

"What's next, Herten?" de Tomas whispered, trying not to move his lips.

"Labor Service parade at Mars Field, and then lunch with Jayben Spears."

"Spears? Ah, lunch with that dour ambassadorial personage is like dining with the Commendatore in *Don Giovanni*—Death and Retribution at the dinner table!"

Gorman permitted himself a brief smile. He was familiar

with the image from Mozart's opera, the ghost of the murdered man sent to seek the don's repentance. "But after that, I've found a new candidate for you to interview, my leader," Gorman whispered excitedly. "I think you shall find her quite satisfactory."

"Bring this one up on the elevator, Herten. Damned stairs tires them all out. Even those in the best shape arrive cranky and sweaty. Besides, I don't want too many people knowing about that stairway."

The recitation, of which de Tomas did not hear another word, finished at last. Shearer bowed to de Tomas and came to the position of attention. De Tomas stepped forward and held out his arms as if to embrace all the children.

"My dear ones, I thank you most respectfully and most humbly on behalf of the people of Kingdom for this singularly significant testament you have so graciously presented to me on this most auspicious occasion! It shall remain on display here always, as a monument to your love and unfailing loyalty, which I promise to return to you tenfold. The future of Kingdom is here this morning, and that future is *you*," he continued sonorously.

Gorman, standing respectfully a few paces behind de Tomas, was impressed. The Leader's voice actually did seem to ring throughout the Great Hall. It was the acoustics, of course. Cameras recorded every word, and the ceremony would be the main news of the day, replayed at five, six, seven, and eleven.

De Tomas talked to the children for ten minutes. He had discovered recently that he liked being loved.

The Confederation Kingdom consulate at Interstellar City monitored every newscast—and every other communication they could intercept—on a regular basis. All this information was analyzed by experts, and reports on events were forwarded to Ambassador Spears. He used them, in combination with his own observations and information gathered from a variety of sources, to prepare his own reports to the President of the Confederation Council, which were forwarded through diplomatic channels. His reports were notoriously acerbic.

Ambassador Spears was putting the finishing touches on another report when his secretary informed him of the live feed from Wayvelsberg Castle. "Sir, you've got to see this!" she advised.

He turned on his video monitor just in time to see the boys removing the cover from the plaque. "Look at the sonofabitch!" he blurted. "He and that Gorman aren't even listening to the kids! They're blabbing away back there!" He lapsed into silence, pulling angrily on his beard throughout the rest of the ceremony, both fascinated by the brilliance of the presentation and disgusted because he knew it was all show.

Spears turned the screen off and returned to his report. Before the interruption, he'd been contemplating just the right tone to use. How direct dared he be? He was known throughout the Diplomatic Corps for his lack of diplomacy and the directness of his language, but even for him there were limits. The image of de Tomas cynically ignoring the children and then addressing them in such flatulent language still fresh in his mind, he changed the word he'd originally written to "claptrap," and sat back in his chair.

"What else on the schedule today, besides lunch with that bastard?" Spears asked his secretary.

"General Lambsblood wants to see you at ten, sir. Then you're free until lunch, and nothing after that."

"Well, have something prepared for my lunch here, after lunch with de Tomas. I won't be able to eat much in his presence, especially not in that medieval torture chamber he calls Wayvelsberg Castle. Where the hell did he ever come up with a name like that?" he muttered.

"Yessir."

"What's Prentiss up to today?"

"He's representing you at Mars Field at ten, sir."

"Better him than me. I'll be ready when the general arrives."

\* \* \*

Mars Field, formerly the Field of Martyrs and Saints, was where de Tomas had decreed party rallies should take place. The first one, just the week before, had drawn 100,000, despite the fact that Haven had hardly recovered from the destruction wrought upon it during the Skink invasion. In fact, the Kingdom Labor Service had been formed partly in response to the need to rebuild the cities of Kingdom. Every young man between the ages of eighteen and thirty-five was required to join the KLS, to be ready for construction work whenever called upon. The term of service was set at two years. The motto of the KLS was "Work Ennobles," and its emblem was a spade blade embossed with a silver goshawk, wings spread, under two laurel leaves. The men of the KLS called each other "comrade."

But the real reason the KLS had been formed, under the direction of the Minister of the Interior, was to militarize the young men of Kingdom and to bring them under the control of the party. So far, thousands had eagerly volunteered because, in reality, the KLS did significant public service rebuilding roads and buildings that had been destroyed. And the training and discipline the young men received under the leadership of specially selected officers and noncoms of the Special Group was challenging and gave them a sense of purpose and accomplishment. It was just the kind of program young men are attracted to, a rite of passage tantamount to actual military service, which most of them would see once their term of duty with the KLS had expired.

That morning, ten thousand men paraded on the huge field. Prentiss Carlisle, sitting in a place of honor on the reviewing stands, was impressed. The ranks were perfectly aligned. Over each man's right shoulder, carried like a rifle, was the ubiquitous emblem of the KLS—a spade. Their field-gray uniforms with green facings and hobnailed black boots looked at once smart, comfortable, and utilitarian.

An officer gave a command that carried to even the farthest reaches of the enormous field: "Order, *spades!*" And as one the ten thousand smartly plunged their spades between their feet with a unanimous *klang!* then spread their legs shoulderwide, hands folded comfortably in front of them, resting on the spade handles.

Prentiss glanced at his watch. The Leader was late. The dignitaries relaxed on the reviewing stand and chatted in low voices among themselves. A car pulled up, and a stir ran across the stands. At once the waiting dignitaries stood, and up the steps came the Leader. He nodded at this man, shook hands with another, spoke a few quick words to a third, and strode to the dais that had been prepared for him.

"A-ten-*shun*!" an officer shouted. As one, ten thousand men slammed their heels together and plunged their spades into the ground two inches to the left of their right foot in a precise one-two movement. The sound echoed over the vast parade ground.

De Tomas stood immobile until the echo faded at last and total silence prevailed. He stood silent for a long moment, head bowed, as if collecting his thoughts. Twice he stepped to the podium and raised his head as if about to speak, but each time he stepped back and nodded his head at the assembled men before stepping up again. At last he put both hands firmly on each side of the lectern and shouted:

"KINGDOM AWAKE!"

The amplified words engulfed the assembled thousands in a tidal wave of sound.

*"Kingdom has awoken! Kingdom is awake! You are the awareness of our awakened people!"*

Then de Tomas spoke for an impassioned thirty minutes. Prentiss Carlisle sat entranced. He knew that every word the man said was a lie, but he listened and marveled at how de Tomas manipulated the language and the emotions of the thousands of young men standing before him. He saw in their rapt expressions that de Tomas was reaching out to touch something that had lain long dormant in them. He was promising them freedom at last from the oppressive restrictions of religious custom and dogma. All those men had lived their lives under the sects, where everyday conduct had been regulated by myriad rules of tradition and taboo. He was telling them *that* was over, now and forever.

When at last, covered in perspiration, de Tomas ended his speech, an officer shouted, "Hail the future!" and from ten thousand throats, over and over until the effect was stunning, they shouted, "Hail! Hail! Hail!" Tears of joy glistened on the cheeks of many of the men on Mars Field.

Prentiss Carlisle, even knowing far more dangerous rules were soon to impinge on the lives of these young men, could not help feeling moved by the display, so brilliant was de Tomas's rhetoric, so overwhelming the response. Now he came to realize fully the genius and the true danger of the man, who had remained hidden, underrated, in the shadows for so many years. De Tomas had the power to move millions. Those men *believed* in him, and worse, *they took him at his word.*

"General." Jayben Spears rose and took General Lambsblood's hand in his. "If at any time I can be of help to you, just let me know. General Banks is my personal representative. Feel free to relay any request to me through him. But General, if at any time you wish to speak to me personally, call me. Any time, day or night." And if you don't, you bloody fool, Spears thought, you're a dead man!

"Mr. Ambassador." General Lambsblood bowed deeply. "I shall do that. Thank you for allowing me the time, and for the excellent coffee as well."

After the general left, Spears reflected on their meeting. Several times during their talk about the operation to discover any remaining Skinks, and while discussing other, more mundane, military matters, Spears had hinted broadly that Lambsblood's future might not be secure under the new regime and perhaps the Confederation could help offset that in some way. He wasn't sure that the general had caught on.

"Well, can't be helped if he didn't," Spears said aloud now. "Time for lunch."

The table de Tomas had laid out in his private rooms at Wayvelsberg was spread with sumptuous viands. Herten Gorman sat there as the third luncheon guest, and he was availing himself of every dish. Spears noted with contempt that the so-called "Deputy Leader" had gained considerable weight. He could see why. Spears dallied with a small salad and ice water, hardly touching either. De Tomas, not to be outdone, sipped occasionally at a beef consommé.

"Mr. Ambassador, you simply *must* sample this paté!" Gorman gushed.

"Thank you, Deputy Leader, no. I suffer from a very delicate stomach."

Gorman shrugged and spooned a liberal amount of the paté onto a cracker, which he shoved entire into his mouth.

"So we are informed," de Tomas said. "I must tell you, Mr. Ambassador, I am very sorry for that, uh, little 'misunderstanding' of ours recently. I do hope your wrist is fully recovered?"

De Tomas was referring to the incident at Mount Temple the day he executed the Convocation of Ecumenical Leaders and bruised Spears's wrist while restraining him. The memory rankled Spears, but he said, "I am fine now. We were all under a bit of strain that day. I believe I'm far better off than the families of the Ecumenical Leaders, which you also executed?"

De Tomas shrugged. "That was a matter of state, Mr. Ambassador, nothing personal in it at all, not on my part anyway. Surely you understand that after years of religious oppression and fiscal improprieties, my long-suffering people could not be restrained." Spears grimaced at the bald-faced lie. The Special Group had summarily murdered the Ecumenical Leaders, and de Tomas had justified the executions by trumped-up charges of malfeasance. The trouble was, many people believed the charges and did not mourn the deaths of the clergymen.

"But under my new government, we on Kingdom no longer conduct government that way." De Tomas continued. "We are very anxious to establish good relations with the Confederation. I wish to ask that you recommend your government formally recognize mine."

"We must have certain assurances," Spears answered stiffly.

"And you shall have them! My Minister of Interstellar Affairs is preparing a formal petition to the President of the Confederation of Worlds that he put before the Congress a proposal to grant us official recognition. You shall have it within the next few days. I sincerely hope you will endorse it."

Spears knew he would not do that. His recommendation would most strongly advise against legitimizing de Tomas's regime. But he knew the Congress would approve it even over the President's recommendation. All he could do was delay it and build a case against de Tomas based on his massive human rights violations.

De Tomas stood. "Thank you for coming, Mr. Ambassador." He bowed from the waist. Spears stood and returned the bow. He was delighted to be released from the disgusting farce. At a signal from de Tomas, an aide entered and escorted Spears out of the room.

De Tomas snorted and sat down. He reached for a chocolate eclair and gobbled it hungrily. "Parsimonious, stingy-assed old bastard," he muttered between mouthfuls. "He's going to recommend against recognition, Herten." He licked the chocolate frosting off his fingers and washed what was left of the eclair down with some wine.

"Won't do him any good," Herten replied around the remains of a salami sandwich.

"Well, who's the girl you've set up for the interview?" de Tomas asked.

Gorman swallowed quickly. "Ah, a very comely lass, late of the Order of St. Suplicia. You'll like her, I'm sure."

"Wasn't that nunnery attacked by the invaders? I thought all the nuns had been slaughtered?"

"Yes, my leader, they did us that favor. But some survived. They were an order of the Fathers of Padua, Cardinal O'Lanners's sect. This particular lady, now that the order is defunct, wishes to return to secular life."

"Herten," de Tomas began, setting his wineglass down with a bang. Herten started. The Leader was angry. "Am I going to have to do this myself? I do not want to see this religious fanatic. Once a fanatic, always a fanatic. Send her away. Give her some money and get rid of her. I'll tell you one more time: I want a woman in her early twenties, blond, blue eyes, perhaps a sprinkling—but just a sprinkling—of freckles on her face. Good teeth. Mark that, Herten, good teeth. Comely figure, of course, athletic, sturdy, breasts—um, this size." He made cups out of his hands. "I think a country girl might fit those requirements. But Herten, no cow, you understand? This woman must be *intelligent* and have a will of her own! But I do not want a whore, some woman who'd sell herself for power. No, no, no! She must have *scruples*. She must present *me* with a challenge, Herten. Are you familiar with Shakespeare?"

"Uh, no, I confess not, my leader."

De Tomas rose and took a book off the shelf. "You must read *The Tragedy of King Richard the Third* sometime, Herten! Very instructive." He flipped through the book. "Here it is, on page 669 of Bevington's edition. It's Richard's wooing of Lady Anne, widow of Edward, Prince of Wales, son of King Edward VI, both of whom Richard has murdered. Fascinating stuff, Herten! Richard marries Anne despite the frank admission he's murdered her very own husband. The wily bastard says he did it out of love for her. Incredible! He gets her through her vanity, Herten, her vanity! No threats, no promises, he beguiles her most artfully. *That* is the challenge I am looking for in my consort, Herten.

"Go out and find me a woman who hates me, Herten, and I will do the rest!"

# CHAPTER
# THIRTEEN

She had survived for weeks now on the edible aquatic plants and invertebrate creatures she'd found in the streams and bogs as she worked her way gradually southward. She'd been left for dead as her people evacuated the underground bunker in panic. Stunned by an exploding bomb, she awoke to find herself completely alone and defenseless in that hostile alien landscape. Since then she'd traveled mostly at night, and lay quietly in the water during the daylight hours, using her gills to breathe. She had conducted some forays onto land in the night, to reconnoiter, and once had been sent scuttling back into the water by the sudden flashing and banging of weapons. Otherwise, she encountered no threats on her silent odyssey. She had no idea if any of the other True People had survived the final assault on their refuge.

Bred to serve her masters, she knew nothing of the world where she was lost and abandoned, neither of its climate nor of the sentient creatures who inhabited it, except that they had defeated her people and, she assumed, were hunting her kind to death.

Her own survival was of no importance to her. It was the female's duty to sacrifice her life, without question, without remorse, when called upon to do so. But her condition was worsening each day. Soon she would have no choice but to stop, seek refuge, and rest.

Toward dawn one morning after many days travel, she found a streamlet emptying into a creek. It looked inviting. The streamlet was protected on both sides by high limestone walls and was heavily vegetated, so it would be protected from the weather and inquisitive eyes. Near where it emptied into the creek it became marshy and overgrown with water plants, an ideal spot to take refuge. The creek flowed slowly south, a full meter in depth, offering her both cover and forage. She would stay there for a while. She burrowed deep into the comforting mud and rested.

Later in the night she froze in terror at noises coming from farther up the small canyon. The noisy creatures did not come down to where she lay hidden, and as the sky began to lighten, they left. An acrid smell came to her along the surface of the water flowing nearby. She guessed it was the result of the creatures' vacating their bowels into the streamlet. It soon dissipated, and as the sun climbed higher, she was at last all alone and undisturbed in the little delta at the canyon mouth. She burrowed into the mud and lay on her side with her arms stretched out before her so that only the gill slits under one arm projected, slightly, above the mud's surface.

She sighed. Her fate was in the hands of the gods. She had no choice but to stay where she was. Her time had come. She could not leave until her child had been birthed.

"The growing season is well-advanced, Charles. We have to get in some crops and later prepare for the harvest or we won't have food for ourselves or feed for our cattle. We have to take a chance and start farming in the daylight."

"I understand, Zechariah. As long as our people remain alert while they're exposed and go to ground if anything is spotted—well, we have no choice, we'll have to chance it. I'll cut back a bit on the training, and we can adjust the watch schedules to give the farmers a break. It's been weeks now since Emwanna came here, and so far no alarm. Maybe we'll be left alone. Maybe the Army of the Lord and those monsters are too busy fighting it out."

"Damn them both," Zechariah muttered.

"Zechariah, today I'll take some of the women down to the draw and let them dry-fire our weapons. And another thing. We've been on constant alert now for weeks, and the edge is beginning to wear off our alertness. Nobody's fault, but you can't stay a hundred percent alert all the time."

"I know. Some of the watchers are beginning to doze off on duty."

"So let's cut back on the watches. Let's maintain full watch at night but keep only one station during the day. We can put someone up on that ridge to the north of town where he'll have a 360-degree surveillance arc. Releasing the day-time watch shifts will also give you more help in the fields. We want to be sure when they're out there in the open that they remain alert for any threat. If something does develop and they can't make it back here, they should go to ground and stay there." Zechariah nodded in agreement. "And one final thing," Charles continued. "I'll also take Spencer Maynard to assist. Spencer's turning into a good soldier."

Zechariah smiled. "He's infatuated with Comfort, you know."

"Infatuation? Yeah, lot of that going around." Charles grinned. "Zechariah, I have no designs on your daughter—"

"I know, I know." But Zechariah Brattle also knew he would not object to having Charles as his son-in-law.

"Speaking of Comfort, Zechariah, let me take her with us today too. She's experienced on the shot rifle and can teach the other women how it operates. It'll give her back some of her confidence. You know, Zechariah, I *had* to relieve her of her duties after she deserted her post that night on watch."

"I would not have asked you to be my military deputy, Charles, if I didn't have every confidence in your ability. I have supported all your decisions because they were the right ones. Very well, then. Today I will work in my own fields. I'll give orders for those who stay in the village to keep movement outside to a minimum."

When Charles had conducted an inventory of the ammunition supply for the shot rifles, he'd found they had only a hundred rounds per weapon. That did not leave much for practice. He had designated four reliable men as alternate riflemen, in case he or Amen Judah became casualties or couldn't use the rifles for some other reason. He'd allowed the four men five rounds each for live fire exercises, just enough to familiarize them with the weapons' operation in actual firing. Everyone else in New Salem, men and women and children over the age of twelve, were taught the weapons drill in dry-fire exercises.

As to the two acid-throwers, as near as anyone could figure, the tanks were more than half full of liquid. But since nobody knew how much of the stuff the tanks held or how quickly they'd be depleted in actual use, Charles had decided that except for occasional testing to see if they still worked, they would not practice with them. The men who'd taken them from the enemy dead were allowed to keep the devices. Charles merely assigned each an alternate to train with the primaries.

How to arm the remaining men and women was a question unanswerable until Zechariah came up with the solution: spears and bows and arrows. "The Israelites of old used them with great effectiveness," he argued, "and as children we all played with light bows and arrows, so construction is not beyond our capability. There's a tree that grows in this vicinity whose wood is ideal for shaping bows, and we have plenty of sheet metal for arrowheads and light plastic we can use for fletching."

They made the bowstrings of ultrastrong filaments found in the abandoned electrical shop. Under Zechariah's instruction— since Charles knew nothing about bows and arrows—even the smallest person on the defense force proved capable of burying an arrowhead in a tree trunk from a distance of a hundred meters. They also made well-balanced spears a trained man could throw with accuracy and make deadly impact from a distance of nearly fifty meters.

"These are weapons made for close-quarter fighting," Charles remarked, "effective enough when backed up by the acid-throwers and our three firearms in an ambush situation, providing the enemy gives us a chance to ambush him. But if we come under a serious, concerted attack, our best defense will be in flight through the caves."

* * *

Charles had been in the caves often enough to know the main passages, but he was unfamiliar with the myriad grottoes and side tunnels that honeycombed the vast complex. In fact, despite nearly two centuries of visiting the caves, the people of New Salem had never bothered to map them accurately. Even so, as an emergency escape route from the village, the caves were ideal. No enemy could track the refugees through them, and even with their slight firepower, the people of New Salem could easily defend themselves against pursuers long enough to be well-hidden within the caverns' depths.

The fort Charles had constructed in the canyon was more a series of traps, obstacles, and defensive positions blocking the north end of the canyon than a structure designed to withstand a siege. He had trained the villagers to defend the approaches to the caves from those defensive positions. The lighter weapons—bows and spears—would be closer to the town, and the more deadly weapons at the rear of the complex, so as an infiltrator progressed into them, the resistance would become stronger and take longer to overcome. The men in the forward positions were trained to fall back through the strong points behind them. The maneuvers were designed to delay an enemy, not to stop him; to give the villagers enough time to get into the caves and disperse.

But Charles felt they had already drilled enough in the defensive mode. The day was hot and oppressive, especially under the heavy tree cover, and most of the people were tired, so he called for a long break after lunch.

"Spence, you and Comfort stay with the group here. Rest or resume training, as you see fit, but Colleen and I are going exploring for a while."

Comfort made a wry face, but Spencer grinned widely. He couldn't think of anything more pleasant than an afternoon around Comfort.

"Don't you worry, Charles," Hannah Flood said, "I'll keep my eye on these two so they don't do their own explorations." She winked at Charles, telling him she didn't believe that he and the redhead were going to do any personal exploring. But Comfort glared after the pair as they clambered up a short slope into the mouth of one of the openings.

Just inside the mouth of the cave entrance, Charles and Colleen paused to rest. Both had recovered from the ordeal of their trek from the prison pens, but neither had yet completely recovered their endurance. "Being laid up so long and sick on top of that knocked the stuffing out of me," Charles remarked, wiping perspiration off his brow.

"Me too," Colleen agreed. She popped a glow ball. The cave there was ten meters high, the floor covered with a thick layer of dust in which could be seen the occasional footprints no doubt made by generations of New Salem's youth. The ceiling and walls were stained black from years of campfires. A thin cloud of fine dust rose about their knees as they trudged farther back into the cave. After a few meters the floor rose and the going got tougher as they picked their way slowly over centuries of rockfalls from the roof above them. Their footfalls echoed hollowly as the tunnel widened into a vast cavern.

Several side tunnels led off from the chamber. Arrows pointing the correct way had been chiseled into the walls. "Let's take this one," Charles said, and led Colleen into a branching tunnel that was clearly off the main path. She followed him in, breathing heavily, and put her hand on his shoulder. The tunnel widened after a few meters. "Let's rest here for a bit. Cool, isn't it?"

She seated herself beside him on a rock ledge. "We've been through a lot together, Charles," she said.

"Yep. You're a good soldier, Colleen." He sighed and stretched out his legs.

"Is that *all* I am to you, Charles?" She put the glow ball on a rock projecting out from the opposite wall. It cast a mellow orange glow over them.

"That's a lot."

She moved closer to him. He put his arm around her shoulders. They sat silently. "Goddamn," Charles whispered at last.

"Charles . . ." At first the stones on the floor stuck painfully into Colleen's back but after a few moments she didn't notice them anymore. They forgot everything—where they were, what they'd been through, their worries about the future, and even their frustration at not being able to remember much of their former lives.

Suddenly Colleen gasped. Frantically, she extricated herself from under Charles and scuttled up against the wall. She drew her knees tightly to her chest, eyes firmly closed, and began to scream.

"Jesus! What is it?" Charles asked.

Colleen pointed to the wall behind him. Charles whirled and stared. In the dim light projected by the glow ball, a tiny, lizardlike creature clung to the wall, head up, huge eyes staring at the pair of humans on the tunnel floor.

"It's only one of those crawly things, Colleen. It's harmless."

*"I—I remember now, Charles, I remember!"* She broke into tears and began to shake violently.

Charles moved to her, put his arms around her and held her head close to his chest, murmuring soothing words. Gradually, her shaking subsided and Colleen began to get control of herself. The little creature scuttled up the wall and disappeared in the shadows above them.

"That little thing reminded me of *them*," she said. "I'm sorry, Charles, but . . . but . . ." she shook her head sorrowfully.

"Tell me about it." He held her tight.

The devils attacked the convent in the early morning hours, before matins, she told him. The nuns shrieked in fear as they were dragged from their cells. The devils lined up the terrified women, who were shivering half naked in the courtyard, and examined each roughly. When the Mother Superior tried to intervene, a devil sprayed her with acid. As she flopped about in agony, her flesh dissolving, the nuns begged God to save them, and meanwhile the creatures' inspection continued. Then Colleen was dragged out of the lineup—she could never figure out why, unless it was because of her red hair—

and the other women were liberally doused with acid and left where they lay, their dissolving flesh staining the flagstones. Two other nuns hid themselves in the septic pool beneath an outbuilding adjacent to the living quarters. The devils took Colleen with them when they left.

"I was a novice in the Order of St. Sulpicia," Colleen continued. "My name is Colleen Starbuck; my confirmation name was Helena. I was elated to be giving myself body and soul to Christ. Now that's all over with. I can never go back there."

Charles did not know what to say. "You're safe now, Colleen. Look, those things are flesh and blood. They aren't 'devils,' they're not supernatural beings. They die when attacked. Look at how Zechariah and the others slaughtered them in the stream on their way here. If they come back, we're ready for them this time. I promise you they will never touch you again!"

"I don't give a damn, Charles, I just want to kill one if I can," Colleen replied. "I was so happy at the convent," she continued in a softer tone. "But now look at me."

"I'm sorry—I didn't know—" Charles said, confused. He started to stand up, but Colleen held him back.

"Charles . . . ?" She pulled him back onto the floor.

His legs were a bit wobbly by the time they'd straightened out their clothes and brushed the dust off. He picked up the glow ball and led the way back to the main chamber.

"Charles, why does God allow bad things to happen to the innocent?"

"You'll have to ask Zechariah, Colleen. He's the Bible man. Around here I'm not very well thought of on questions of religion. Zechariah's been telling me about this Book of Job in that Bible of his. It says God punished Job on a *bet* with the devil. Can you imagine that? Nobody could, unless there's some meaning hidden in the story, so deep the average guy can't figure it out. But if that's the case, what good is a story like that? So God wipes the floor with this poor bastard, Job. When I ask Zechariah if he believes that, he says, 'Oh, yes, it's the literal word of God!' But I know he doesn't, not literally. Nah, I don't think God has anything to do with what happens to us. I think life is like a card game, the only luck is on the deal. It's up to you how you play out your hand, and if God's got this plan Zechariah keeps talking about, that's it. But don't take that as criticism of Zechariah or any of the other people here. They sincerely believe what they say they believe, and nobody's tried to force me to think the way they do."

"But in the end God rewards Job for his faithfulness, Charles. The story actually has a happy ending."

"I know. But Colleen, if God were a human employer, nobody could work for him under those circumstances." They paused in the entrance and looked out at the bright sunlight. "I wonder why it is you and Chet have been able to remember so much while I can't?" Charles said.

"You said you resisted them, Charles. I think that's why. They had to use more power on you to subdue your will. Your memory will come back, don't worry."

"Maybe I'll turn out to have been an ax murderer." Charles grinned.

"Well, as a former acolyte in the Order of St. Sulpicia of the Fathers of Padua, may I say, Charles, God can forgive any sin, if repentance is sincere? But even if you don't repent and God doesn't forgive you, I still like you, and I just won't give a damn."

Charles laughed outright. "By the crabs on Moses's hairy balls, woman, spoken like a true soldier!"

While the others lay under the trees, taking a postprandial snooze, Spencer Maynard persuaded Comfort to accompany him a bit farther down the arroyo to a secluded spot not far from the stream that flowed by its mouth. "Careful, it's a bit muddy here," he warned. They sat on a log and stretched out their legs.

"Hot," Spencer remarked. He wanted to put his arm around Comfort's shoulders; instead he put his hands demurely between his knees as he watched her out of the corner of his eye. "Well . . ." he began, but left the thought unfinished. He was elated but very nervous to be alone with Comfort Brattle, whom he'd loved since she was a nubile fifteen-year-old. He picked up a rock and tossed it into a muddy pool. It splashed with a dull *thuck!* A slight quiver ran through the mud. "Submerged log," Spencer muttered.

Comfort picked up a rock, somewhat larger than the one Spencer had just thrown, and tossed it into the same spot. The splash was bigger and the quiver more pronounced.

"Comfort, don't think I'm being forward or anything, but have you thought much about your future? I mean, once the danger we're in has passed, you know?"

"I want an older man," she answered hastily, aware of the direction Spencer wanted the conversation to take.

"I *am* older, Comfort! I'm twenty-five!"

"I mean older and more experienced, Spencer."

"Aw *hell*! You mean a man like Charles, don't you? He's got *everything*. But he's twice your age, Comfort. And once he remembers who he is and we get through this emergency, he'll be going back to wherever he came from. Hell's bells, for all you know, he might even be married and with a bunch of kids to support!"

"Spencer, vulgarities do not become you," Comfort sniffed. Secretly, she was delighted that at least one of Charles's habits was influencing the men of New Salem; she found his earthy language exciting. She picked up a stick lying nearby and poked at the log in the mud. "Big *damned* log," she muttered, and they both laughed. Charles was rubbing off on everyone, it seemed.

"So *there* you two are!" Hannah Flood exclaimed, emerging from the bulrushes.

The pair scrambled to their feet in surprise and embarrassment. "Oh, hi," Spencer mumbled. He shifted uneasily from foot to foot as Comfort dropped her stick. She looked guiltily at the ground. It was an unwritten but rigidly enforced rule among the City of God that unmarried couples were never to be left unchaperoned.

"We, uh, we're just talking, Mrs. Flood," Spencer said.

Hannah looked at the two closely. Their clothes were in order and they had not even been holding hands when she came upon them. "Well," she said, "Mr. Charles is back, so our break's over. Let's get back under the trees. More snapping-in exercises this afternoon." She glared after them as they trudged by her. Shaking her head, she turned and followed the pair back under the trees.

The log submerged in the mud moved slightly and sighed.

# CHAPTER
# FOURTEEN

"My leader," Herten Gorman began, "reports from the field indicate that some soldiers are refusing to take the new Oath of Loyalty."

De Tomas stiffened and his face took on a hard but eager expression, as it used to when, as Dean of the Collegium, he'd consign someone to the flames. "Religious or political scruples?"

"Religious, my leader. The army divides along sectarian lines."

"There will be no exceptions! Have the refusers shot. Shoot the entire army if you have to. We'll recruit new soldiers."

Gorman grinned. *That* was the old Dominic de Tomas!

This was to be the most elaborate awards ceremony ever staged on Kingdom, the first of many planned.

The Special Group honor guard, dressed in stunning black and silver uniforms, marched smartly into the Great Hall of Wayvelsberg Castle to the stirring notes of "Raise the Flag." The music and lyrics, adapted from an old hymn, were now the signature of the Socialist Party of Kingdom, and by default, Kingdom's anthem. Everyone stood as the black and silver flag of the SPK passed down the hall.

The honor guards' boot heels clacked in sharp cadence on the flagstones as the men marched to the center of the Great Hall and came to a halt facing Heinrich the Fowler's statue, just below a dais that had been erected in front of the sculpture. De Tomas, Herten Gorman, General Lambsblood, and the ministers of de Tomas's cabinet stood at rigid attention on the dais. When the last notes of "Raise the Flag" had faded away into the vast shadowed recesses of the Great Hall, the assembled honorees, their families and guests, lesser government officials, the media, and carefully selected members of the public resumed their seats.

The susurration arising from hundreds of people shifting in their seats in anticipation, clearing their throats, and rustling programs filled the hall. Herten Gorman stepped to the microphones. "Comrades! Countrymen! We are one people united under one government guided by one leader. I give you our leader!" His voice resounded throughout the hall, and immediately the vast crowd went completely silent.

Dominic de Tomas—no longer Dominic de Tomas but *the Leader*!—stepped to the podium, exercising the now familiar but highly effective mannerisms of the accomplished speaker. He stood silently, arms braced on the podium as if gathering his thoughts. He stepped back, as if to begin his speech, hesitated, bowed his head, folded his arms, rocked back and forth on his feet, and then, arms raised as if to embrace the throng, began:

"Citizens of Kingdom!" He paused for several long seconds, taking in the assemblage before him. "Welcome! Your presence here this morning does great honor to your countrymen who will soon be recognized for their service to our community. In every great age of human history, ordinary people have come forward to do extraordinary deeds in service to their fellows. The men and women who will soon stand beside me on this platform are no exception. And you here today and those watching and listening outside this Great Hall are living representatives of our people, embodying the transcendent ideals of honor, loyalty, and sacrifice, the foundation stones of our new and regenerated society."

De Tomas's voice rang throughout the hall and across the continent like a clarion call. For years the people of Kingdom had lived under the divisive and tenuous control of the religious sects, never knowing from one minute to the next when dreadful conflict might break out, their individuality stifled by the oppressive rules and traditions of sectarian bigots. So debilitated had their society become that off-worlders had to be asked to come to their aid during the demon invasion. That invasion had destroyed their cities, towns, farms, and businesses, visited death and grievous wounds upon their families and friends, and left their lives in ruin. Now someone was promising them a chance to start over again, and something better.

A man near the front row—not a plant either—leaped to his feet and bellowed, "Hail the Leader!" and as if that were the signal, all the people rose simultaneously, roaring out "Hail! Hail! Hail the Leader!" over and over until the Great Hall rang with voices raised in ecstasy. They had been swept up in that rapturous state of being outside oneself, overcome by a sense of being lifted up by a larger force.

De Tomas and his cabinet stood basking in the enthusiasm of the roaring crowd. Eventually de Tomas raised his arms and the shouting subsided, but no sooner had it died down enough that he was able to speak, than someone took up the cry again and the hall shook with their shouted adulation. This went on for many minutes before de Tomas succeeded at last in getting them to take their seats.

Jayben Spears, as a special guest of the Leader, sat near the front of the audience with his secretary, Felicia Coombs-d'Merten. "I thought I knew that man," he whispered into Felicia's ear, "but this"—he gestured at the dais—"even I almost started shouting." Spears was fascinated by the performance, because in private de Tomas's manner of speech was quiet and reserved.

"I don't think this demonstration was planned, sir," Felicia whispered.

"That's what scares me," Spears answered. The pair had stood with the rest of the cheering crowd, albeit reluctantly, but those sitting nearby had noted angrily the ambassador's sour expression and his evident hesitation to rise and participate in the spontaneous adulation.

"Shhh!" a nattily attired man sitting on Spears's immediate left whispered harshly.

Spears leaned toward the man and said in his normal voice, through a cupped hand, "*Fuck* you!"

Shortly after seizing power, de Tomas had created a "pyramid of honor," a series of awards to recognize valor and meritorious service by government, military personnel, and citizens who had performed outstanding acts of bravery or service to the community. Outwardly, the ceremony was no different than one any other government might host to honor its outstanding people, but de Tomas had two objectives he wanted the events to accomplish. First, he needed a "pantheon" of heroes to call his own. Once recognized formally and publicly for their deeds and accomplishments, those people would be bound to him. They would become icons of the conduct and self-sacrifice he expected of everyone under his new government, role models for the rest of the citizens. Second, involving as many people as possible publicly in the affairs of the SPK bound them to the political and moral tenets of the party and opened the door for the party to further intrude itself into their lives, and thereby control them under the umbrella of shared community service.

De Tomas signaled to his adjutant, who came forward to make the official presentations.

The highest decoration in the SPK's pyramid of honor was the valor award called the "Knight's Cross with Diamonds." It was a beautiful decoration, crafted by one of the most skilled jewelers in the city of Haven. It consisted of a solid gold cross pattee in a silver frame, surmounted by a cluster of oak leaves under crossed swords studded with real diamonds. It was designed to be worn suspended around the wearer's neck by a black and silver ribbon. Lesser orders of the same award existed in silver and bronze but without the diamonds.

The adjutant opened the award binder. It was encased in genuine leather and printed on a vellum sheet embossed with a full-color representation of the Knight's Cross.

"Private Kater Rumia, First Company, Second Regiment, Third Brigade of the First Division, Army Group A, come forward!" A young man in the dress uniform of the Army of the Lord sitting in the front row came to attention and marched briskly up onto the platform. Sitting next to him were his parents, his company officers, and several of his close comrades, all of whom beamed with pride as they watched him receive his award. The cameras did not fail to catch the tears in his mother's eyes, whether from pride in her son's achievement or relief that he had survived to receive the award, but in any case it was just what the Minister of Propaganda and Popular Culture had hoped for when he set up the elaborate spectacle.

De Tomas and General Lambsblood stepped forward and stood beside Private Rumia. "In the name of the people of Kingdom, I bestow upon Private Kater Rumia, in recognition of bravery above and beyond the call of duty, the Knight's Cross in Gold with Diamonds, given this sixth day of the third month in the city of Haven, signed Dominic de Tomas, the Leader and Supreme Commander of the Kingdom Armed Forces." The adjutant then read the accompanying citation. Private Rumia had indeed performed a deed of considerable valor in a counterattack against the demons. But left unmentioned was the sacrifice of the Marine corporal who'd actually led the counterattack. He had been awarded the Bronze Star medal—posthumously.

Reverently, de Tomas lifted the medal from its velvet-lined case and draped it carefully around the soldier's neck. Both he and General Lambsblood shook the young man's hand.

The next honoree was a surprise: General Lambsblood. De Tomas presented him with the Order of the Kingdom Eagle, the highest decoration for meritorious service. The ribbon for this award was a sash designed to be worn diagonally, slung from the wearer's left shoulder. The medal itself was a heavy Maltese cross in solid silver with golden eagles between each arm, the eyes of the eagles set in rubies.

"The kiss of death," Spears whispered as de Tomas draped the sash over the general's shoulder.

The awards went on. There were awards for achievement in culture and science, in sports, and one even for motherhood: the Mother's Cross of Honor, a blue-enameled cross pattee outlined in silver, the centerpiece a goshawk set upon a Greek shield edged with the words in gold, "Honor Cross of the Kingdom Mother." The reverse of each cross was engraved with the date of presentation and Dominic de Tomas's signature. There were three orders of the award designated by the composition of the shield: gold for mothers who had borne eight children or more, silver for women who'd had five, six, or seven offspring, and bronze for families of up to four children. The children did not have to be alive for a woman to receive the award, and their gender was of no consequence.

The first woman so honored had borne thirteen children during her lifetime. Now retired, a widow, and living quietly in one of Haven's distant suburbs, she had overnight been turned into a national heroine. The award carried a small stipend, but the widow was grateful for it. Ten of her children were dead, six sons killed in the recent war against the demons. In presenting the award, de Tomas said: "God has declared that the mother's heart is the sacrificial vessel of this great age. Your cup, dearest mother of our people, runneth over."

As he bent down to place the award around the old woman's neck, he saw an image of his own mother, as she was when he was a young man struggling to make a go of his poultry business. She'd said to him, "Dominic, why don't you come to see me more often? Oh, well, I know you're busy, I know you have responsibilities, I know you don't have time to call. Don't worry. I'll be all right. Don't bother about this old woman. I'll just sit here alone in the dark. See to your important affairs, sonny, don't worry about me, I can take care of myself."

The tears in his eyes as de Tomas suspended the cross about the aged mother's neck were genuine.

Spears turned to his secretary and whispered, "They get that thing just for having kids! Not for bearing sons who've died in combat or done anything really significant, just for bearing children! Can you believe it? I bet the dumb bitches have got to be loyal party members before they qualify, though. Hamadryad's halitosis, this bastard's got every angle figured out!"

There were also presentations for achievement in sports, science, and culture. To the youth of Kingdom, de Tomas encouraged physical fitness and sports competition, and there was a medal for young men and women who had passed a rigorous physical fitness test that included running, swimming, obstacle courses, and marksmanship. In presenting those awards, de Tomas had said:

"The future of our world depends on the young, those who will replace us and who will create the children who will carry on, in their turn, the great work I have begun. The young must be strong in spirit and body to attain their goals. They must be hard, physically and mentally, for life is a constant struggle, and only those tested in strength and hardness will endure in its great competition."

The medal for achievement in culture went to an operatic impresario named Itzahk Rivera. De Tomas considered music a vital adjunct to his socialist agenda. Music was the emotional glue that bound his followers together. Aside from military marches and soldier songs essential to the esprit of the army, he encouraged "serious" music for the morale of the citizenry of Kingdom. He rejected traditionalists such as Bach, "Sickeningly obsequious!"; Handel, "Badly in need of an enema!"; Vivaldi, "Master of repetition!"; the Haydn brothers, "About as exciting as clockwork!"; Mozart, "Effeminate little snob!"; Beethoven, "Homoerotic capitalist!"; Wagner, "More constipated than Handel!"; and Ravel, "As soporific and exciting as malaria!" Modern composers such as Hock Vinces's nuevo rhythm and blues and Kwame O'Leary's neoprogressive jazz he characterized as "Paleolithic syncopates." Rivera was recognized that day for his revival of the works of the obscure twentieth century German composer

Hans Pfitzner, particularly his staging of Pfitzner's opera, *Palestrina,* which had always enthralled de Tomas with what he saw as its "unrelenting and passionate sincerity."

To de Tomas, Pfitzner's music was particularly compatible with the SPK's political philosophy because it represented the "stern ethos of conquest." The music critic who had earlier called the performance "sublimely silly" and "without a moment of musical epiphany," disappeared the following day and was never heard from again. Subsequently, Rivera's presentations of Pfitzner's music enjoyed laudatory critical reviews.

The prize for literature, on which subject de Tomas considered himself an expert, went to a retired librarian named Paoli St. Vincent Rhode, who'd taken up writing children's literature late in life. His books consisted of tales about young boys and girls who sacrificed themselves for family and community. Upon seizing power, de Tomas had ordered the destruction of all books he considered dangerous to good order and discipline, particularly antiwar novels such as the classics *Knives in the Night* and *The Soldier's Prize.* Copies of the proscribed volumes remained intact in his own private library, of course.

The Staff Judge Advocate stood before the men of the 2nd Regiment's Reconnaissance Company, formerly called the Burning Bush and said, "Raise your right hands and repeat after me: 'I—state your name and rank—swear to you, Dominic de Tomas, as Leader of my government—' "

*"Wait!"* Stormleader Mugabe shouted. "You! Second man on the left, third rank! Fall out!"

The legal officer glanced apprehensively at Mugabe. *"His lips were not moving!"* Mugabe roared. The soldier stepped from the ranks and came to attention in front of Mugabe. "Why were you not reciting the oath?" the stormleader demanded.

"Sir! I am a Quaker and we do not believe in the taking of oaths!"

"Well, then, how did you manage to take your original oath, the one you swore when you enlisted in the army?"

"Sir! I did not move my lips then either!"

Mugabe drew his sidearm in one fluid motion and ventilated the young man's head. Blood, brains, fragments of bone, and hair sprayed all over the men in the first rank, but they stood fast. The young man's body stood upright for a few seconds before collapsing.

"Please proceed." Mugabe nodded at the SJA.

The SJA swallowed and finished the oath. Everyone's lips moved smartly, whether they actually pronounced the words or not. "Captain, you may dismiss the formation, and have the men come up here and sign their oaths—" The legal officer's voice broke on the last words. All he wanted to do was get away from the Special Group detachment and the madman who was its leader and return to churning out courts-martial, nonjudicial punishments, and wills and codicils for indigent soldiers.

Standing in the second rank, a glob of the dead man's brains on his sleeve, Staff Sergeant—formerly Senior Sword—Raipur, waited for his company commander to dismiss him. Once the command was given and he'd signed his oath, he headed for his vehicle, to wash up. He looked at his timepiece. He had forty-five minutes before meeting with his company commander, Captain Sepp Dieter. The battalion had been operating in the N'ra Range for a week, searching for demons, and it was only the night before that Raipur's platoon had come back into the base camp for the oath-taking ceremony. They were scheduled to return to the field after refitting and resupplying. Raipur wanted to see the captain before they left.

Lieutenant Ben Loman caught Raipur's eye as he walked toward the company commander's tent. If looks could kill, Raipur thought, but the lieutenant had nothing to fear, he had no intention of reporting him for war crimes. Carefully, he straightened his uniform before ducking under the flap into the captain's tent.

Captain Dieter, a heavyset older man, sat at a field desk, writing. He was still livid over the execution, and preparing a message of protest to battalion, not that it would do any good; it might just put the finishing touch to his career. He looked up. Raipur advanced to within three paces of the CO's desk, came to attention and saluted. "Senior—er, I mean Staff Sergeant Raipur has the first sergeant's permission to speak to the company commander."

"At ease, Sword." Dieter shook his head. "Sword, these new ranks'll take some getting used to." He grinned. "You wanted to see me? Well, I wanted to see you. You first; your shekel."

"Sir! I respectfully request a transfer to another platoon in the company."

Dieter nodded. "Yes. I understand. Well, Lieutenant Ben Loman—ah-ha, got it right that time!—has already asked me to transfer you to another platoon. I asked him why, and he said you were not aggressive enough in battle, Sergeant. Care to tell me why?"

Raipur hesitated briefly. "Well, we don't see eye-to-eye on some important things, sir. I just think it would be better for the company if I was in a different platoon."

"The other platoons all have their senior sergeants, and the platoon commanders are quite satisfied with them." He thought for a moment. "Maybe I could use you in the company CP."

"That would be fine, sir."

Dieter was silent a moment. "Sword, do you want to tell me why you *really* want out of your platoon?"

"I just don't get along with Lieutenant Ben Loman, sir." Technically that was true enough. The sergeant balked at murdering innocent civilians, while the lieutenant didn't.

"All right, I'll consider yours and the lieutenant's request. But understand this: we are in the field, maneuvering against the enemy. I am *not* going to make any personnel changes in the platoons because you two can't 'get along.' Once we're back in garrison, I'll talk to you two about it again."

Dieter leaned back and regarded Raipur thoughtfully for a long moment. Then he leaned forward, as if he'd decided to say something important. "In case you haven't figured it out, morale in this army is at an all-time low. We had our asses kicked by those demons, and the Marines had to bail us out, and now everything's changed, our ranks, our names, our leadership. I liked being a member of the Burning Bush Regiment, Sword. I learned my profession in that regiment. Now what are we? Numbers, plain numbers. 'Second Regiment, Fourth Division, Army Group B.' " He sneered. He hesitated and an angry flush came to his cheeks. "I do not appreciate either that the leaders of my sect were *murdered*." He spit the word out in a whisper. "Like that boy who wouldn't swear that filthy 'oath'!" He paused. "But we follow our orders," he continued, his voice hard, rasping, "because we're professionals and because we don't want our brains all over the parade field."

Dieter lifted up a sheaf of papers. "See this pile of toilet paper? These are the 'oaths' you men just swore and signed your names to." He threw them on the floor in disgust. "You know what *that man* was before he murdered our legal government and took over this world. How do *you* feel, bound to him by your oath, Sword?" Raipur was not supposed to give an answer to that question. "You know, our 'Glorious Leader' and I have something in common: we've both reached the highest rank we're ever going to hold. As soon as we're back in garrison, Sword, I'm resigning my commission."

Raipur had known Dieter for years. They'd been through the Skink invasion together, and the sergeant was aware that his company commander respected him and would never believe anything Ben Loman might have said about him. But he began to perspire as he stood there. He understood that Dieter had just put his life into his hands. It was safe there. If he wouldn't rat on his useless platoon commander, he was not about to turn on a soldier like Captain Sepp Dieter. Besides, he agreed with every word the captain had said.

Dieter bent to pick up the papers. He motioned for Raipur to step closer to his desk. "I'll tell you something, Sergeant," he whispered. "Much more of this shit and that asshole and his praetorian guard will be in for a very big surprise." He straightened and said in his normal tone of voice, "We'll talk later. For now, dismissed!"

Raipur came to attention, saluted smartly, about-faced and walked out into the heat of the day.

# CHAPTER
# FIFTEEN

The spot she'd picked to birth her young—she was overdue—
the place that she thought would give her security when she
most needed it, was turning into a meeting place for Earthman couples. First the two who'd bombarded her with stones
and then jabbed her with sticks, and now these two. They lay
on the stream bank, grunting and groaning and rolling around.
The dark one emitted muffled squeals while the white one
grunted continuously until at last it emitted a low, protracted
groan and lay still. They both lay motionless for some time,
breathing heavily.

She peered at the Earthmen through the brush and debris
behind which she was hiding, her body stretched out in the
sluggish stream and submerged in the viscous mud. She had
seen it all. It was a curious performance and, frankly, she had
been fascinated. At last she concluded they might be repro-
ducing; the ritual had been similar to what the True People
did. If so, the performance represented a strange kinship between her own people and the alien Earthmen. She was at
once repelled and attracted to the pair; repelled because they
were strangely similar but dangerous natural enemies of the
True People and must be destroyed—as the Great Master told
them, and the Great Master was never wrong—and attracted
because they seemed now to have that very important thing
in common.

She resolved to think about this. While the Earthmen lay
still, apparently communicating in whispers, she recalled the
Large One whose offspring she was carrying. It had been her
duty to serve the Large One, and she had done so enthusias-

tically. She wondered what had happened to him. So many had been killed by the Earthmen before the Great Master gave the order to evacuate. She supposed he lived only in the child she was carrying, hopefully a male.

Spencer helped Emwanna to a sitting position and offered her a drink from the water bottle he'd brought along. He was supposed to be out in the fields that morning, working with the other men, but at first break he'd pretended to wander off, and met Emwanna along one of the trails that led to the fort. No training was scheduled, so they knew the spot would be empty.

During the weeks since Spencer had finally realized Comfort was not interested in him, he'd taken a casual interest in Emwanna, who was friendly and a hard worker, two qualities the New Salemites appreciated. The interest had deepened gradually into something more serious, and one night while on guard, she came to him, in violation of Zechariah's iron-clad rule about no distractions while on watch. They hadn't been discovered, and afterward Spencer began thinking about a permanent relationship with Emwanna.

For her part, Emwanna was looking for a man, any man, to replace the husband she'd lost. She left Chisi in the care of one of the other women and went to meet Spencer at the fort, their prearranged rendezvous.

"You've gained some weight," Spencer observed.

"You feed me good."

"Least we could do for a guest."

"Maybe you make me with baby, Spence-ter." She was improving her Standard English quickly but sometimes had difficulty with pronunciation.

"Ahh . . ." Spencer said vaguely, but let the sentence trail off. It was better he didn't comment at all on that subject.

"Miz Hannah, she teach me lots about your god. She say he is everywhere, in everything, know everything, see everything. Think he sees us now, Spence-ter?"

"Yeah, Emwanna, sure," Spencer replied, starting to put his clothes back on, embarrassed. *Of course* God saw everything, but no normal person went around thinking He was looking over your shoulder all the time. Well, He was, but—

"Among my people, when a woman lose her husband or a wife die, the one is okay to take another mate. All my people, they are dead, I think. Just Chisi, me, now." Spencer helped her to her feet. "You, me, we marry, Spence-ter."

"You are not of our faith," Spencer answered lamely, because he couldn't think of anything else to say in response to such a forward suggestion. After all, the *man* was supposed to make the marriage proposal.

"You like me," Emwanna said. It was a statement of fact, not an accusation.

"Well, yes, but you must accept Jesus Christ as your personal savior and the Holy Bible as the Word of God. You have to do that at meeting, in front of everyone, and people will ask you questions about the truth of your faith."

"Yes."

"You will?" Spencer was astonished at how readily she had agreed.

"Yes. I do not know your god, Spence-ter, but I know your people. You good people. You give Emwanna home. So you good, your god good too. I will follow him."

"Okaaay," Spencer replied tentatively, then: "Okay! Right! Emwanna, I won't go back to the fields this afternoon. We'll go see Zechariah and ask him to help us. Sure, I'll marry you!" He seized her about the waist and they kissed.

Samuel Sewall, at 102 the oldest resident of New Salem even before the massacre, and an elder in the City of God sect, had been called to Zechariah's home for a consultation when Spencer Maynard and Emwanna knocked on the Brattles' door. Consort Brattle answered the knock, and when she saw the two standing there, knew what they wanted. As the premassacre and present mayor of New Salem, and by default the leader of what remained of the City of God sect, Zechariah Brattle possessed all the authority of both a clergyman and a notary. He led the faithful at meeting, but theirs would be his first marriage ceremony.

Consort ushered the pair into Zechariah's study. Samuel, frail but still hardy, kept his seat.

"Sir, we wish you to marry us," Spencer said without preamble.

Zechariah glanced at Samuel, who rolled his eyes. "She is a heathen," Samuel said, not accusatorially, but as a simple statement of fact. "She has not been baptized. You know better than that. You know we cannot condone a union between someone who has been baptized and someone who has not."

"But I thought *because* of her status, we could be married, and then afterward—"

"Spencer, you are not thinking," Zechariah said. "Samuel is making a valid point of church doctrine and discipline. She is not of our faith, and I shall not marry you with her until she is. If you have relations with this woman without the benefit of marriage, you are in danger of hellfire. You know what St. Paul has written on that subject. Now," he held up his hand to forestall a protest, "Emwanna is a decent and hardworking woman, and in her temporal life she lives as cleanly as any of us, but until she is baptized, she cannot be saved."

"Emwanna wishes to embrace Christ and join us."

"Is that so, child?" Zechariah asked.

"Yes, Father Zechariah."

"Ah, just call me Zechariah. Well . . . ?" He turned to Samuel.

"She is not of our race," Samuel said.

"That is true, Brother Sewall. But all souls are equal before God. Anyone who truly wishes to walk in the way of Christ can qualify for membership and participate in the church covenant." He spoke directly to Emwanna: "That's the reciprocal promise we make to Christ as a result of His presence in our church."

"We've been doing that since 1648, child." Old Samuel nodded as he spoke. "Why do you want to marry this woman, Spencer?" Samuel asked. "Is it your passion that drives you two to marriage? Spencer, I have known you all your life, and your father and grandfather before him. You Maynards have *always* been a headstrong clan. Why, your grandfather, when he was in the army—"

"No need to go into *that*," Zechariah said quickly. "But Brother Sewall has asked a good question, Spencer. You are a young man, twenty-four, twenty-five? Miss Emwanna is an attractive and healthy woman. In making this request, are you speaking with your heart or some other organ?"

"Both," Spencer answered immediately.

The two older men looked at one another again and then burst out laughing. "Well," Samuel said, "the boy's quick, I'll give him that, and honest too." He turned to Emwanna. "You will have to undergo a period of instruction, child, and then appear before all of us at meeting and be examined rigorously to satisfy us that your conversion is genuine. A full church member must vouch for you, that you are a virtuous and serious candidate for membership in our church. I believe Zechariah or I would be willing to do that. You have lain with Spencer, I know that, child. But I am convinced your virtue is intact and we shall not speak of that again." He looked at Zechariah for confirmation. Zechariah nodded in agreement. "Then," he continued, "we will vote on your acceptance into the church. Used to be, in the old days, that only the men could vote, but long ago we extended that right to every adult. Once you are baptized, you can take communion with us. At that point, child, you will be one of us. Well, Spencer, Emwanna, do you agree?"

They both answered yes immediately. "Spencer, she already has a child by her deceased husband. Would you take this child as your own and raise him in our faith?"

"Yessir!" Spencer looked at Emwanna, and she nodded her assent.

"Very well, then," Zechariah announced, putting on his invisible ecclesiastical robes. "I will talk to Hannah Flood and ask her and Samuel, here, to guide your intended through a course of instruction. Can you read, child?"

"Not in your language, Father Zechariah." She excused herself immediately by adding, "Among my people the elders are all addressed as Father or Mother. I mean no bad thing when I call you that."

Zechariah smiled. "Good, so long as you haven't confused me with some Popish minister." When he saw the look of confusion on her face, he added, "Just an ecumenical joke, miss, forget it. Spencer, you will teach her how to read English. She must be able to read and understand the Bible before we will accept her into the City of God, and you will be married only after that. You are excused from work in the fields—but not watch—to take care of that and to assist in her religious education. Meanwhile, I charge you—listen carefully, young man!—not to have sexual relations with Emwanna until after you are married. As the chief magistrate of this town and the elder of our church, as elected by its members, I have the authority to solemnize your vows, but shall do so only after you have satisfied all these requirements. Do you understand? Do both of you understand?"

They both answered yes immediately. Spencer grinned. "Well, that only means I'll have to give her a crash course in English!"

"Get out of here, you rascal!" Zechariah shouted, pointing imperiously at the doorway, "and sin no more!" After the two had left, he turned to Samuel and laughed. "Well, I never expected *that*."

"Interesting start to our afternoon," Samuel agreed. "But now on to serious business?" By that he meant an interview with Comfort Brattle. Zechariah felt the time had come at last to talk to her frankly—and officially, not as her father, those talks had gone nowhere—about Charles, and he wanted Samuel Sewall there as a respected elder adviser when he did.

Comfort came in when summoned and sat demurely in front of the two men. "Daughter, I have asked Brother Sewall to join me this afternoon. We wish to talk to you about your future."

"I am in love with Charles, Father, even if he does not love me," she said, anticipating the subject of the interview. She cast her eyes down at the floor as she spoke.

"This love is barren, child," Samuel said. "Charles has assured your father he does not return it, has no intention of returning it. He is a man of his word, child, and your father and I wish you to get a grip on yourself. You are causing Charles distraction."

"No!" Comfort protested, "I would *never* do that! I know Charles does not love me, Father, but that does not change how I feel about him. I cannot help myself." She was almost in tears.

"Daughter, Charles has heavy responsibilities," Zechariah said. "I believe he was sent here by the Lord to save our church, even though he is not a believer himself. The Lord works in strange ways. Besides, I think Charles is in love with the Colleen woman, who endured a horrid captivity with him and is closer to his own age. He is my age, daughter, far too old for a woman of your years. It is unseemly among us for anyone to entertain the thought of such an uneven union."

"And he is not of the faith, child," Samuel added. "That is most important. He is a good man, with a great heart and great courage, but he does not *believe*."

"He does not even know where he comes from," Zechariah continued. "For all he or anyone knows, he is *already* married, with children your own age! Would you be a partner to adultery?"

Comfort Brattle had never felt so alone and abandoned in her young life. She knew everything her father and Mr. Sewall said was true, and she also knew that Charles would never love her the way she loved him. She was disgraced, her removal from watch duties had hurt her self-respect profoundly, and Charles had done it to her, but she still loved him. And in the back of her mind she knew Charles had been right to relieve her that night. She *was* acting like a child, but she could not help herself. She sat there downcast and miserable, and the two old men took pity on her.

"Comfort," Samuel began, his voice gentle, "listen to me. I have lived a long life. You will too, God willing. This will pass, I assure you. You must get on with your life, child. You are strong and brave. It is women like you who hold this community together. Do not disappoint us."

"Daughter, you know I love you," Zechariah said. "Since your brother was killed you have been your mother's and my only hope to continue our line. We want you to marry well, Comfort, to live long and prosper. You are obligated as a member of this church to propagate and ensure the survival of our faith. If you were to go away with this Charles, our family would be destroyed. Do you understand that?"

Comfort looked at him, tears blurring her vision.

"Comfort, young Benjamin Stoughton has formally asked me for your hand in marriage. He is exactly your age. You played together as children. I have invited him to dine with us this afternoon. I only ask that you be polite to him and consider his proposal."

Comfort anticipated that the lunch would be a disaster, and it was, but for reasons no one anticipated.

Consort Brattle had prepared beef and vegetables, needlessly apologizing to her guest for the simplicity of the fare.

Zechariah said grace. His method was to ask the Lord's blessing in as few words as possible. Since he'd been leading the meetings and delivering sermons, everyone appreciated that quality, especially since the seats in the meetinghouse were very hard.

"We are, after all, a simple, plain people, Benjamin," Zechariah said as he passed the potatoes, "so plain food suits us well. Plain food, hard work, and a healthy fear of the Lord, Benjamin, those are the staples of life, all any man needs to prosper in body and spirit. Of course," he grinned, "I would very much like to have a cold bottle of ale to chase this hearty fare."

"A good library too," Consort added. " 'Good books, good friends and a conscience clear, those are the best things we have here,' " she recited.

"Beer and books! Heaven help us, Connie, we're becoming virtual hedonists!"

Benjamin had always liked Zechariah, whose reputation

as a leader of the community was one of fairness in all things moderated by a wry sense of humor. "Your cooking is justly famous, ma'am," he said.

He was a handsome lad, strapping, with coal-black hair. His bright blue eyes fastened on Comfort, and she found it difficult to concentrate on her food, which was all she wanted to concentrate on, handsome as Benjamin was. The two had known each other since childhood, and Comfort in her teens had thought it most likely that of all the boys her age—most dead by then—Benjamin or Spencer would someday be her husband. Now, having met a man of the world, she wondered how she could have been so naive.

"I think the crisis may be over, Benjamin," Zechariah said as he cut his meat. "Charles will lead an expedition to Haven soon, reestablish contact with the outside world. I think it's fair to assume the devils have been thwarted."

"It was not devils, sir, who destroyed the black woman's people," Benjamin remarked.

"Indeed, indeed. That is a troublesome affair now, but in wartime mistakes do happen. I'd want to know more about the situation before I'd accuse the Army of the Lord of criminal acts. That they are still operating is actually a good sign. You are on watch tonight, Benjamin?"

"Yessir. At dark."

"Well, plenty of time for us to finish the meal and—and visit."

Zechariah glanced at his daughter, then continued.

"I have heard good reports about you, Benjamin. Is your father getting his crops in?" He knew every detail of what was going on at New Salem, but wanted to make conversation and get Benjamin to talk more.

"Yessir. Well, with so few cultivating machines and so little fuel, we've had to share, and that has slowed everyone down. And since Charles has forbidden us to cultivate the gardens behind our houses . . ."

At the mention of Charles's name, Comfort's neck reddened.

"Well, sharing is the bond of this community, Benjamin,"

Zechariah said. "This crisis has strengthened that age-old bond. Marriage is another bond. Have you thought of your future in that regard?"

"Yessir!" Now the back of Benjamin's neck colored. "I have thought about it very seriously. After we've finished at table, sir, I would like very much to talk to you about—my future." He grinned at Comfort, his face turning a bright red, his blue eyes sparkling.

"Daughter, you are quiet this evening. Please, engage us. Have you thought of your future recently?"

"Father, I—"

*Klang, klang, klang!* The warning signal for an approaching aircraft echoed through the settlement.

"Dear God, it's an air raid," Zechariah shouted, and bolted for the door.

Amen Judah, the only other person to carry a shot rifle besides Charles, was at lunch with his family when the alarm sounded. Moments later, before they could retreat to the interior of the house, a reconnaissance drone hummed by the kitchen window. The Judahs froze in fear as the machine cruised slowly by, its optics gleaming in the afternoon sunlight. It was small, about the size of a small dog or a chicken, with stubby wings and a whirring rotor. It teetered along, seemingly unsteady in flight as its operator, sitting at his console far away, maneuvered the device between the houses. Then it sped off in the direction of the clanging alarm. As one, the family took refuge underneath the kitchen table.

"Did it see us?" Abigail asked nervously.

"I don't think so," Amen whispered.

For long minutes they crouched beneath the table while their food grew cold. Finally, Judah stood and stretched. "I think it's gone. Let's finish eating." He jacked a round into the chamber of his shot rifle and moved to the window to close the blinds when suddenly the tiny machine was back again, this time hanging suspended in air, *looking through the window directly into his eyes!* Slowly, it edged closer to the window as Amen stood there, mouth open, gaping at the thing. If I only stand completely still, maybe it won't see me, he thought. The device resembled an enormous metallic bumblebee.

Without thinking, he threw his rifle to his shoulder and fired.

"Well," Charles said, examining the wreckage, "this thing was made by men. Look at the patent marks on this fragment." He held up a piece of shredded metal so the small crowd could see the marks: *Patent Pending, No. 4437-A-563, July 2049.* "We're in for trouble now, folks," he added. He turned to Amen. "Why in *hell* did you shoot the thing down?"

Amen shrugged apologetically. "I—just—well, the god-damned thing interrupted my lunch, and that just pissed me off, Charles!"

Someone in the crowd gasped and another muttered, "He's talking like Charles now!"

"Well," Charles replied, laying a hand on Amen's shoulder, "nothing we can do about that now. Everyone into the fort! We're due some visitors, and mighty soon, unless I miss my guess. By the way, Amen, damned good shooting!"

# CHAPTER
# SIXTEEN

The first Seventh Day afternoon after 34th FIST's return from Kingdom finally came. Lance Corporal Zumwald and PFCs Shoup, Gray, Fisher, Little, and Tischler were more or less integrated into third platoon's barracks life routine—Zumwald, Shoup, and Gray, having joined new units a couple of times before, more than the others. Officially, they'd been on liberty since the evening before. Unofficially, everyone in the FIST was still busy squaring themselves away and nobody left the barracks except to go to the mess hall.

Sergeant Ratliff, third platoon's first squad leader, got the silent signal he was waiting for. "That's it," he said as he looked around the squad leaders' quarters. "I'm as squared away as I'm getting. All this garrison mickeymouse has given me a thirst." He looked at Sergeants Linsman and Kelly. "Are you two about ready or what?"

Linsman, the second squad leader, looked at him, then at Kelly. "We've been sitting on our duffs waiting for him to get his shit together, and he wants to know if *we're* ready."

Kelly, the gun squad leader, shook his head sadly. "Do you ever get the impression the wrong man is next in line for platoon sergeant?"

Linsman nodded sagely. "I think you're right. Rabbit must be bucking for a rocker. Either that or he's getting dumb in his old age." He ducked out of the way as Ratliff swung the flat of his hand at his head.

"Getting slow too," Kelly observed. "If that was me swung at you, you couldn't have gotten out of the way in time."

Linsman jabbed at Kelly, who dodged the blow.

"It's all in the reflexes," Kelly said.

Ratliff took advantage of their distraction to step in and smack both upside the head. "If you two are through grabassing, let's get out of here."

Linsman and Kelly bounded to their feet and poked Ratliff on his shoulders.

"You're senior, you go first," Linsman said. "We've just been waiting for you."

"Age before beauty." Kelly opened the door to the corridor and bowed Ratliff through.

Ratliff snorted as he strode out. "First squad!" he bellowed. "If you love the barracks so much, I know where there's some brightwork that can use some polishing!"

Linsman shouldered past him. "Second squad!" he boomed. "I'm heading for Big Barb's. Last man there pays for my reindeer steak!"

Kelly roared louder than either of them. "Guns! What are you doing cluttering my squad bay? Drop 'em and get your asses out of here! I don't want to see any of you in this barracks until morning formation on Second Day!"

All along the corridor doors popped open and Marines looked out.

"You mean we can go outside and play?" someone shouted back.

"We're not grounded anymore, Dad?" someone else yelled.

"Mother, may I?"

"Can I have the car keys, Pop?"

"All I want to see is elbows and assholes," Ratliff roared. "Last man out stays for fire watch!"

Instantly, the heads looking into the corridor vanished and a racket erupted as the Marines of third platoon jumped into their civvies and grabbed whatever they needed to head into Bronnysund for the night. In less than a minute they began streaming out, headed for the stairway to the first floor, bouncing off walls, caroming off each other.

"Now that's the clearest demonstration of Brownian motion I've ever seen," Linsman said. The other two laughed.

Elsewhere in the barracks other platoons were also scrambling to leave on liberty. When the last of their men had left, the squad leaders followed at a more dignified pace. The clatter and yelling of Marines happy to be on their way off base diminished and stopped by the time the three were halfway down the stairs. Only Ratliff had any idea why. He was right. The other two found out when they exited the barracks to the company assembly area and found the company standing in formation before Gunnery Sergeant Thatcher. It was an odd sight, a Marine company in civilian clothes standing at attention in front of the company gunny, who was also in civvies.

"Nice of you gentlemen to join us," Thatcher said dryly. "If you will take your places, please."

The squad leaders glanced at each other, wondering what was going on, and hurried to their places in the formation. In a couple of minutes the last of the stragglers came out and took their places.

Bent forward, his hands clasped behind his back, Thatcher paced back and forth in front of the company. No expression appeared on his face as he looked each man in the eye. He turned at a sound from the barracks and came to attention— Captain Conorado, the other officers, and Top Myer were marching toward him. They also were dressed in civilian clothes.

"Sir!" Thatcher barked in his parade ground voice. "Company L, all present and accounted for." He wasn't in uniform and remembered not to salute.

"Thank you, Gunnery Sergeant," Conorado said. "I have the company. You may take your place."

"You have the company. Aye aye, sir." Thatcher about-faced and marched to his position two paces to the front of the far end of first platoon. Top Myer and the officers took their places behind Conorado.

The company commander quickly looked over the company, then said, "At ease," in a voice that easily carried to the ends of the rear rank. The Marines, uncertain about what was happening, shifted to parade rest but didn't quite go into full ease.

"I've been in this man's Marine Corps longer than most men in this company," Conorado said in the same voice he'd told them to stand at ease. "You know I've seen my share of action." They'd all seen the rows of campaign and expeditionary medals he had, which indicated a full career's worth of campaigns for an infantryman. "Some of the toughest campaigns I've been on were right here, with Company L, 34th FIST. Many of you were on those campaigns with me, so you know what I'm talking about.

"The one we just came off of wasn't the biggest—that was the war on Diamunde, which probably still gives some of you nightmares. But the war on Kingdom was the widest spread, the campaign that demanded the most versatility from you. You functioned as members of a line company, as trainers for a thoroughly demoralized and poorly led army, and as officers and NCOs in a foreign army. You fought on plains, forests, mountains, and caves. You encountered an implacable enemy who fought fanatically with unfamiliar tactics and weapons. And you bested him.

"You have earned the biggest blowout you can get. The brigadier and Mayor Evdal of Bronnysund met yesterday. The entire FIST has seven days' liberty, beginning at eighteen hours today. All food, drink, and lodging in Bronnysund are paid for this week. Women," he cracked a smile, "well, you're on your own there. You don't have to pay for anything else, so go ahead and splurge on the ladies. If you want to go somewhere else, it's on your money."

He had to pause while the Marines cheered. Elsewhere in Camp Ellis, other units of the FIST could also be heard cheering.

"COMP-ney, ten-HUT!" he bellowed after a moment. The Marines in their ranks stopped yelling and snapped to. Conorado turned his head toward Top Myer, who stood with his fingertips pressed to his ear.

Myer nodded and said, "They're coming, sir."

Conorado faced front again. "In a few minutes transportation will be here to take you into Bronnysund. Now . . ." He looked from one end of the company to the other. "What are you doing standing in formation? You're on liberty." He had to raise his voice to be heard over the hubbub as he added, "Platoon sergeants, keep your people together until transportation gets here!" He was grinning when he turned around and swept an arm toward the back of the barracks. The officers and top NCOs were grinning as well as they joined him in his return indoors.

"What are you doing for the next week, Skipper?" Myer asked as they walked side by side.

"Marta and I are heading for New Oslo. I booked a room at the Royal Viking. What about you?"

"Maybe we can have dinner together some evening this week. I know this lady in New Oslo. She told me she got very lonely while we were on Kingdom." Just because he had every intention of remaining single until he retired from the Marine Corps didn't mean he couldn't have a lady friend.

"We're back!" Sergeant Linsman shouted as he bounded through the entrance of Big Barb's.

"Home away from home!" Sergeant Kelly cried out as he entered on Linsman's heels.

The local sailors and fishermen who bought their supplies and did their drinking at Big Barb's combination ship's chandler, bar, and bordello looked up from their drinking, eating, and flirting and raised schooners in salute to the Marines of third platoon who were crowding their way through the door and spreading throughout the main room. Both groups shouted greetings. Big Barb's girls—those who weren't otherwise occupied—squealed and sped to fling their arms around the Marines, welcoming them back from their long absence as though they hadn't seen them at the big party in Camp Ellis just a few days earlier.

"You come home! Velcome! Velcome home!" Big Barb's voice boomed over everyone else's as she waded through the mass of locals like a bulldozer through a landfill to envelop between her massive arms and humongous bosom any Marines she could reach. "It has been so qviet here mitout you." She stopped hugging Marines and turned to her girls. "Vat you standink dere for? Der Marines thirsty, gid dem Reindeer Ale!" Turning back to the Marines, she added, sotto voce, "Price de same, ain't raised it vile you gone for so long. But you don' vorry aboud dat, you don' pay dis veek any-vay."

In moments, every Marine had a liter-size schooner of ale and the girls were guiding them to tables.

"Vait, vait!" Big Barb yelled when she saw some of the girls trying to move sailors and fishermen from their tables to make room for the Marines. "Is der whole platoon here? You vant upstairs room? I got you upstairs room all for tird platoon. Vinnie, Hildegard, Asara! You run upstairs, make sure der banquet room is ready."

The three young women broke away from the Marines, eeled their way through the now crowded main room, and raced upstairs to check on the private banquet room. A moment later one of them reappeared at the head of the stairs and called out, "It's ready!"

"Upstairs, upstairs vit you!" Big Barb shouted at the Marines. She spread her arms and urged them toward the stairs, looking like nothing so much as a sheepdog herding a flock of lambs.

The Marines laughed and joked and exchanged individual greetings with the locals as they let themselves be funneled upstairs. Nearly half of the people who climbed the stairs were women. The room they went to was considerably smaller than the main downstairs room, but it was large enough to hold six tables that could each easily seat eight, and had enough space left over for a small dance floor. Pitchers already set on the tables kept more ale cool, and dishes with small-food were within easy reach of every chair. A bar with spigots, bottles, and glasses was at one end of the room, and a table piled with covered hot-trays ran the length of one side.

The Marines didn't at all mind the close contact with the young women who pulled up chairs and crowded their way between them.

Not all the young women sat with the Marines at first.

About half of them busied themselves refilling schooners from the bar spigots before they found seats.

"Hi, Marine. You look lonely. Mind if I join you?"

Corporal Claypoole was hardly lonely. Most of second squad was at his table with him, as were six of Big Barb's girls. He turned his head and looked up.

"Jente?"

The young woman from Brystholde he'd met at the party smiled down at him.

"Jente! Sure, sure." He pushed his chair back and scrambled to his feet. "Please, join us." He looked around for a chair but she already had one. He helped her sit, then wedged his own chair back in.

"What are you doing here?" Unless something had happened in the days since the first party, Jente was one of the nice girls Top Myer had warned them to treat the way they'd want their sisters treated. She definitely wasn't one of Big Barb's girls.

She raised an eyebrow at him. "Oh? I'm not welcome? Aren't you happy to see me?"

Claypoole blushed furiously. "Of—of course I'm glad to see you. It's just that I didn't expect to see you," he vaguely waved a hand, *"here."*

She raised both eyebrows and pinched her lips together to keep from smiling at his embarrassment. "But we agreed to see each other again."

"Yes, I know we did. But this is the first time I've been off base. I planned to come to Brystholde this week, just like I said I would." They had spoken a couple of times since the party, and arranged for him to visit her as soon as he could get a couple of days' liberty.

"Do you want me to leave you," she vaguely waved a hand, "here, and wait for you to come to visit me?" She made to push her chair back.

"No—no!" He clamped a hand on her thigh to keep her from rising. "Please stay. It's just that I'm surprised to see you—" He again made a vague wave.

Jente could no longer restrain herself and laughter pealed out.

She leaned toward him until their foreheads touched. "I know what this place is and who—what—Big Barb's girls are. Barb saw us together at the party. So when this affair was set up, she called me and invited me to come and keep you company." She pulled back a little and cocked her head at him, but decided not to add, *I'm here protecting my interests*.

Claypoole grinned. "I'm glad you came." He leaned in and lightly kissed her lips. He didn't notice the roars of laughter from the other Marines until he saw Jente blush.

He looked indignantly at his tablemates. Corporal Chan was senior to him, and so was Corporal Doyle. But Claypoole was a fire team leader and Doyle wasn't. He outranked everybody else.

"As you were, people!" he said haughtily when the laughter ebbed. "I'll thank you to behave yourselves. There's a lady present."

That set off another roar of laughter, this time punctuated by the higher pitched laughter of the women. Claypoole turned redder than he already was.

Sigfreid, who had paired off with Chan at the FIST party, leaned across him and put her hand on Jente's arm. Jente leaned close to hear what Sigfreid whispered into her ear. She laughed, then whispered something back. Both women laughed loudly.

"What was that about?" Claypoole asked.

Jente covered her blush with her hands and shook her head.

Claypoole looked at Chan, who spread his hands and shrugged; even he hadn't been able to make out what the two young women were saying just below his chin.

"But—" Claypoole objected. If Chan hadn't heard and Jente wouldn't say, he had no way of knowing. He thought he should know, because he was pretty sure it had something to do with him—and why Jente was there.

He was right, and Jente wasn't about to repeat to her quarry what Sigfreid said, about how many of Big Barb's girls had married men they'd met on the job—or what she'd replied, that Jente'd become one of Big Barb's girls, if that's what it took to land Claypoole.

Jente wasn't the only woman present who didn't work at Big Barb's. Kona, a widow in her late thirties from Hryggu-randlit, sat close to Sergeant Ratliff at the table the squad leaders shared with Corporals Kerr and Dornhofer and Lance Corporal Schultz. Their table wasn't as crowded as the others. The more junior men generally preferred to party away from the sergeants, and most of them were wary of Schultz. No one at their table drank as much or laughed as long or as hard as everybody else; the men and most of the women were older and ruled less by their hormones.

Stulka, who was one of Big Barb's girls, was the youngest and most flirtatious. She was fascinated by the quiet threat that radiated from Schultz no matter how relaxed he was, and her hand flitted from his thigh to his shoulder to his cheek to his back in an endless round of contacts. Schultz didn't seem to notice. Gotta, the brunette from the party, sat primly next to Kerr. Blond Frieda, who had helped Gotta break Kerr's foul mood, was with Dornhofer. Klauda hadn't forgiven Kerr for the way he'd dumped her onto the ground when Big Barb startled him, so she paired off with Sergeant Linsman. Linsman didn't say anything, but he thought there might be something unmilitary—certainly un-Marine—in a sergeant having a girl who'd been dumped by a corporal. But he decided to overcome his scruples in the spirit of the liberty. Sergeant Kelly neither knew nor cared to know the name of the woman who propped her leg over his knee. She was pretty, friendly, and available, which was all he cared about that night. He wasn't even aware that she was one of the "nice girls" Top Myer had warned them about. She certainly wasn't acting like a "nice girl," not the way she levered herself onto his lap and allowed him to kiss her.

Ratliff wasn't known for being reflective—in that group, Kerr was the reflective one, though Schultz sometimes surprised people with his perceptiveness and analytic abilities—but he was the one reflecting.

"Look at them," he said. "They seem so happy, so carefree. No one who didn't know would guess the hell they've just returned from."

Kerr looked up from idly twining a lock of Gotta's hair around his finger. "The return from hell is *exactly* why they're so happy," he said. "On some level, just about every one of them believes he should be dead. So they celebrate the life they aren't sure they deserve."

Ratliff nodded. "Party hard, just in case the universe realizes it made a mistake and takes them."

"Right."

"Hell of a way to make a living."

Linsman snorted. "Do you think anybody does this to make a living?"

Nobody said anything for a while. Kona almost imperceptibly increased the distance between Ratliff and herself.

Ratliff couldn't let it go for long. "I keep looking and not seeing faces I saw the last time we were here. And I see faces I've never seen here before. It makes me wonder how many faces will be different after our next deployment. If one of the missing faces will be mine."

"Get out," Schultz said.

Ratliff grunted. He knew Schultz wasn't *telling* him to get out, but had asked if he was thinking about it. Kona lifted a hand to his shoulder and moved a shade closer.

"He can't," Linsman said. "We're quarantined. All transfers, retirements, and resignations have been canceled for the duration."

Kerr laughed bitterly. "Are they going to quarantine 26th FIST? The *Grandar Bay*? Kingdom?"

Schultz nodded. "A little while."

"And knowledge of the Skinks will still get out," Kerr said.

"Someone will notice," Linsman agreed. "It'll come bit by bit, but it will come."

"Skinks?" Kona asked. "What are you talking about?"

Linsman closed his eyes.

Ratliff shook his head. "Nothing," he told Kona. "Forget we said anything."

"We may have just condemned ourselves to Darkside," Kerr said.

The existence of the Skinks, the sentience they'd fought on Kingdom, was of course a tightly kept state secret. It had been made very clear to the Marines of 34th FIST that any man who let the secret out would be sentenced, without trial, to Darkside, the penal world from which there was no parole. That had been conveyed to them when nobody outside 34th FIST except a few individuals very high in government and the military knew about the Skinks. How few? Not even the Commandant of the Marine Corps was cleared for that information.

"Only if someone tells," Schultz said.

"Tells what?" Kona asked.

"Nothing," Ratliff said. "There's nothing to tell."

Stulka, Frieda, Gotta, and Klauda looked confused. Kelly and his girl were otherwise occupied and hadn't heard a word.

"ATTENTION ON DECK!" a commanding voice boomed out.

Chair legs scraped and falling chairs clattered on the floor as the Marines reflexively rose and stood at attention. Male voices ceased instantly. Only the higher voices of the women continued for a moment as they looked at the entrance to see what was happening.

Staff Sergeant Hyakowa stood just within, sideways to the entrance. Captain Conorado marched past him and through the room to the bar, followed by Top Myer and Gunny Thatcher. Conorado and Myer stood in front of the bar, facing into the room, while Thatcher went behind it. Conorado took a step forward.

"At ease, sit down," he said. "Ladies," with a nod and a smile, "please excuse the military formality. We aren't here to interrupt the party. Thank you," he said to Top Myer, who handed him a filled schooner. Then back to the room, "I want to tell everybody to have a good time. Enjoy yourselves, just don't get into any trouble that will force me to take action. Ladies, these Marines have just been through a very rough time. Be patient, and be nice to them. *But!*" His voice cut through the whoops at that. "But! Don't take any guff off them either. You don't have to do anything you don't want to. If anyone tries that, he has to answer to me."

"*After* he answers to me," Myer growled. He looked pointedly at the women he recognized as being from the neighboring towns and villages.

Many of the women tittered, and several playfully slapped at their Marines.

"Now, if everyone will rise for a toast." He waited a moment for everyone to stand, then raised his schooner. "To our fallen comrades, all of them true Marines." He put the schooner to his mouth and took a sip of the Reindeer Ale. "Good stuff," he murmured, and put it on the bar. "That's it. Have a good time. I'll see you at morning formation in one week."

"ATTENTION ON DECK!" Myer roared, and the Marines snapped to attention as the three left the room.

Hyakowa was the last to leave, but had something of his own to say before he left.

"They're off to New Oslo or wherever," he said, "but I'm staying here in Bronnys. Don't make me waste my liberty playing mother hen." Then he waved a hand at them and left.

# CHAPTER
# SEVENTEEN

"Sir! I lost the Fly!" the surveillance technician shouted.

"You don't just lose a Fly, what are you talking about?" The lieutenant looked up from the RPV console he'd been trying to repair. Everything in the RPV section was breaking down these days. In fact, everything everywhere in the Army of the Lord seemed to be breaking down. He got up and leaned over the technician's shoulder. The screen was blank.

"It just disappeared," the technician confessed. "There was this flash and it was gone. Someone shot it down, that's what I think."

"What sector were you searching?"

"X-Ray Romeo 546371, an abandoned village named New Salem, sir. In support of 2nd Regiment's reconnaissance platoon."

The lieutenant thought for a second and remembered that the platoon was commanded by Lieutenant Ben Loman. His upper lip twitched; he had no use for Loman.

"What is the position of the village relative to the platoon?" he asked.

"It's about forty klicks to the south of the platoon's last reported position, sir. Heh heh, guess New Salem ain't so abandoned after all, eh, sir?" The lieutenant gave him a hard look. "The platoon is preparing to fort-up there for the night," the technician continued quickly. "The lieutenant asked me to use the rest of the daylight to extend my surveillance area."

"Play it back." He turned to his sergeant, who was also busily trying to repair something. "Sword, get Battalion. I think we've found a hot one here. Tell the duty officer to hang on, I'll be with him in a minute. And get a message through to Ben Loman to hold where he is until further orders." He turned to the technician. "Play it back," he said again.

"This is where I first got suspicious," the technician said as the trid played back on the monitor. The remotely piloted vehicle was poised before a window in what looked to be an unoccupied dwelling. "The people who lived here were members of the City of God sect that was wiped out by the demons out by the Sea of Gerizim," the technician volunteered. "Look! I thought I saw movement in there! Can't be sure, the way the light plays tricks on the Fly's optics."

"This equipment is obsolete," the lieutenant muttered behind the technician's shoulder. "Maybe our Glorious Leader will 'reform' our procurement system so we can get something that works." Then in a normal voice, "Hmm, yes, something sure moved inside there."

"I thought it was just the optics, sir, so I zoomed off down the main street. That's what you're seeing now. Place looks deserted, doesn't it?"

"Hold it! Back up the image," the officer said. "There! Freeze it." He stared intensely at the image on the monitor. "Look here." He placed a finger on the monitor. The technician looked. The lieutenant removed his finger.

The technician automatically wiped the officer's smudgy fingerprint off the screen. "I don't see anything, sir."

"I think that's a footprint there. Can't tell if it's human or one of *them*. Look again."

The technician stared hard. He still couldn't recognize a footprint in the dust of the street. But what the heck. "Yessir, maybe it is. Smudged, sort of. I must have missed that. Hmmm. Well," he continued, "I got to thinking, and returned to that house. *Now* see what happens." The drone was looking back through the window when suddenly there was a bright flash and the screen went dead.

The lieutenant glanced at the bottom of the screen: elapsed time from shootdown, three minutes. He picked up the handset his sergeant was holding for him and briefed the battalion staff duty officer. Lord, wouldn't it be something if his section was the first to find some demons? "Request an Avenging Angel overflight, sir, and prep of the area before I inform my recon platoon. *I think we've found them.*"

There was a slight pause over the communicator, and then, "Roger that. I will have a flight airborne in zero-five. Time-on-target at coords you gave me, twelve plus five. Tell recon to move out now. If they can make it before dark, go in and do a bomb-damage assessment, otherwise first light. Hold this line open." The duty officer contacted his air liaison officer and gave him a verbal frag order to strike New Salem. He came back on the line. "Birds on the way. Uh, Surveillance, problem with tactical troop airlift assets here. Lot of birds down for maintenance. Ground support will have to come overland. I will start them now, but tell Recon he won't be reinforced until late tomorrow at the earliest. Who'd you say was in command? Ben Loman? He's an aggressive one. Tell him don't—repeat, don't—engage the enemy, if anyone's left after the Angels make their passes. Keep me informed. Out."

The lieutenant looked up at his sergeant and grinned. "*Yes!* Time to rock and roll!"

Charles and Spencer Maynard were the last ones out of the village. They had brought up the rear to make sure nobody was left behind. As they jogged down the path toward the fort, Charles in the rear, they heard the first aircraft approaching from behind them. "Take cover!" Charles shouted to Maynard as he threw himself into some nearby bushes.

They proved to have sharp thorns, but Charles hardly noticed as he crashed to the ground. The aircraft, two of them, roared so low over where they lay that the ground beneath them shook. They circled off to the south and came back a second time, west to east, and on the third pass they unleashed their fury upon the village of New Salem.

Charles was suddenly someone else, somewhere else, no longer clutching the ground, staring through the thorns at

Spencer's feet. He shouted at the top of his voice to be heard, "Dupont! Dupont! Get those goddamned pilots on the horn and tell them this is a goddamned *friendly* position down here!" Despite the danger from the predatory aircraft lazily circling the village, Charles grinned. Something like this had happened to him before! Wonderful!

His full name was Charlie Bass and he'd been in the armed forces of the Confederation of Human Worlds.

"Give me the list." De Tomas held his hand out as his Minister of Justice passed it to him. De Tomas glanced at it briefly and smiled. "Have these people been taken into custody?" He handed the list back to the minister.

"As of three A.M., my leader."

"Good, good. You have some rather talented people on that list. How will you employ them?"

"We require skilled hands in our industries, my leader. I'm sure some of these individuals can be trained to work in our porcelain factories."

Soon after taking power, de Tomas had begun arresting various prominent individuals—churchmen, preachers, theologians, writers, artists—people who for various reasons he felt might oppose his regime. The arrests were not called that. In view of the rampant "corruption" that had "infested" the theocracy, and the arrested persons' alleged involvement in that corruption, de Tomas had been taking those people into custody to "protect" them from the righteous wrath of the people. No specific charges had been preferred. Several hundred were being held in a prison compound in a remote suburb of Haven until the Ministry of Justice felt they could be released. Meanwhile, the prisoners were being subjected to hard labor. Many had already succumbed.

While the man in the street on Kingdom was being encouraged to show his emotions and express his opinion—within limits—the natural leaders of each community were being quietly rounded up and disposed of as insurance against the development of any organized resistance to the new regime.

"Keep developing the lists, Minister. Please excuse me now. I have another engagement." The Minister of Justice bowed and let himself out of the office.

The "other engagement" was with Miss Rauber, the cosmetician. She entered de Tomas's private office wheeling her instruments in a cart, a huge smile on her pretty face. "I am pleased to serve you, my leader." She curtsied. "Massage? Manicure? Pedicure, my leader?"

"Sit down beside me and do my nails, Andrea." De Tomas held out his left hand. Andrea dutifully took it and began cleaning the nails with a small file. They made small talk. Andrea Rauber came from a small village a few kilometers outside of Haven that had been destroyed in the Skink invasion. She was taken in as an apprentice by Gelli Alois and had worked for her for several years before de Tomas seized power on Kingdom.

"I wish I could see you more often," she whispered at last. She was consumed by a religious awe of de Tomas. He was the finest thing ever to come into her short life, a life she would gladly give if he asked her to.

"Alas, my dear, running the world takes up so much of my time."

"Your speeches are divine, my leader," she sighed.

De Tomas smiled. "I believe God has given me the mission of saving this world, Andrea."

Andrea hummed contentedly as she worked. She was not only an intimate of a great man, but a man whom God Himself had recognized as His disciple.

"Running a government is very hard work, Andrea. I feel like Sisyphus."

Andrea looked up at de Tomas. "Do I know him?"

"Sisyphus? No, my dear." De Tomas laughed. "He was a Greek, in ancient times, who never could get his work done."

"Oh, I knew a Greek once!" Andrea crowed. "They never sit down in church. I'm finished, my leader. May I please have your right hand now?"

"Let's go back into the private room now," de Tomas said, rising abruptly from the chair.

"Oh, yes!" The "private room" was de Tomas's bedchamber. Very few people knew where it was. "But my leader, I haven't even started on your right hand yet!"

"No matter, Andrea. It'll be there when we're done." Poor Andrea, de Tomas thought. If Gorman ever succeeded in finding him a consort worthy of a man of his stature, he would have to do something with Andrea. He had preached to the men of the Special Group many times that *hardness* was essential to success. A man had to steel himself to do unpleasant things for the greater good of his people. De Tomas was not running a harem, and besides, it was essential the people did not know about Andrea. When the time came, she would just have to be retired—without a pension.

The only complaint Andrea had about her hero was that he liked doing it on the floor while still wearing his boots.

General Lambsblood and Major Devi were sitting in the command post of the 2d Regiment of the 2d Brigade, 2d Division, Army Group B, when the word came through that a reconnaissance patrol had spotted some demons in the abandoned village of New Salem. Lambsblood had been in the field for several days, visiting units and observing operations. The general had also been conferring hastily and in private with his commanders, feeling out their attitude toward the new government and the reforms that had been imposed by it on the army.

"Do you have an aircraft that can get me out to the reconnaissance company CP?" Lambsblood asked the regimental commander.

"I'm afraid, right now, sir, all our Hoppers are down. It's this confounded weather and the incessant dust storms. Been hard on maintenance, and we just don't have the spare parts we need. I've sent a request up to Division for the parts, but, my S4 tells me we won't have them here until tomorrow at the earliest. It's the same for the other units, sir. We're all in need of parts and equipment and the depots are nearly empty." The colonel spread his hands helplessly.

"That's all right, Colonel," Lambsblood said with a barely concealed sigh. "It's not your fault. Keep me informed."

After the colonel had left, Lambsblood turned to his aide. "Maintenance and spare parts, the lack of them is killing this army, Devi. We have *got* to get the Confederation to kick in so we can replenish our depots. Having all the army's maneuver elements in the field at the same time is wearing us down. By the time we're through with this wild goose chase, the Army of the Lord will have broken its back."

"You don't think there are any of the demons left, sir?"

Lambsblood shook his head. "Even if there are, they can't be much of a threat, and we don't need the whole army in the field to deal with them. No, Major, there's only one reason we're out here, and that's so we'll be out of the way."

"You think . . . ?" Devi lowered his voice to a whisper.

"I'm dead meat, Major. You too, our whole command staff. Do you think that bauble our Great Leader gave me at the ceremony actually *means* anything?" Lambsblood sighed and hung his head in his hands for a long time. "I have been a fool," he whispered sadly. "And a coward."

"Sir, I don't think—"

"No, no, Major," Lambsblood said. "I can admit that now. I actually *resented* Sturgeon's presence here during the war with the Skinks. God, do I wish the man and his lovely Marines were still with us!" He leaned back in his chair. "And I stood by meekly when that man murdered our legal government. Stood by. Too scared to do anything, and God forgive me, consumed with ambition." He paused again, then leaned forward before he spoke. "Major Devi, I appreciate your loyalty. I am afraid that loyalty will soon be put to a severe test."

"What can we do, sir?" Devi asked. He was frightened that General Lambsblood himself had given words to what he had been thinking privately for some time.

Lambsblood shook his head in resignation and said, "Give me that overlay, the one that shows our dispositions in the vicinity of Haven." The general unrolled the overlay and studied it for a moment. "Major Devi, as soon as they have an aircraft available, I want you to fly to Army Group B HQ—no message traffic on this, purely person-to-person—and have a top secret meeting with General Bhoddavista. You are authorized to tell him—*and him only,* no staff should be in on this—that his very life depends on secrecy and speed." He put a forefinger on the overlay.

Major Devi leaned over and looked at it. The finger rested squarely on the military map symbol for an armored infantry battalion.

"I want him to move that battalion to the maintenance depot in the outskirts of Haven, you know the one, and stay there on full alert until I personally give them the order to stand down or deploy." He straightened up and looked Devi right in the eye. "The future of our world may depend on this move. And I want you to make sure those men in that battalion are alert and combat ready. You stay with them, as my personal representative. If we have to call on them, they must be ready to fight the Special Group." He whispered the last words into Devi's ear.

"Sir? General Banks has offered us help."

"So has Ambassador Spears. I'll meet with him when I get back."

"Sir? *What are we doing?*" Devi whispered.

General Lambsblood leaned very close to his aide and whispered directly into his ear: "That oath we took to that madman? It's worthless and illegal. We are planning a coup."

Major Devi stepped back a pace, then grinned and saluted. "Yessir!" he said.

As soon as the sound of the aircraft had faded into the distance, Bass jumped to his feet. *Dupont!* He remembered now! Dupont was a Marine and he'd been killed in an attack, the same attack that had wounded him and caused him to be taken prisoner. Was he a Marine? He'd been told the Marines had left Kingdom a long time ago. *They left him behind!* How could that have happened? The Marines didn't leave their own behind—he'd always heard that. Well, no time for that now. "Spencer!" he shouted. "To the caves! Quick!"

To Bass's utter dismay, he found the strong points unmanned. The people of New Salem were clustered about behind the barricades, some weeping, others shouting in rage.

Even Zechariah was beside himself. "Our homes, our farms! Destroyed, destroyed!" he shouted over and over, clenching and unclenching his fists in frustration and rage.

"Goddamnit!" Bass bellowed. "You people get a grip on yourselves!" He began seizing the men who were supposed to be manning the barricades and shoving them into their positions, none too gently either. "The rest of you people, get your asses into the caves! Come on! Get moving! There'll be a ground probe anytime now! Move, move, move!"

Those not assigned to the barricades headed slowly toward the caves. Behind them, huge clouds of smoke billowed up from the burning buildings.

"Look!" someone shouted. "The meetinghouse is still standing! The Lord has protected it. So are some other buildings. Zechariah, your house is untouched!"

"Damnit, get under cover!" Bass shouted. "You can't rebuild New Salem if you're dead!"

"Charles is right," Zechariah said, getting a grip on himself. His assignment was to remain with the people in the caves; Charles would command the defense.

"Before anybody goes," Bass said, "I remember the rest of my name. Charlie Bass. I was in the Confederation military," he said excitedly.

Zechariah nodded sagely. "I knew you were military, Charles. Do you remember anything else?"

"I remember the attack where I got wounded and captured. There was a Confederation Marine with me. He got killed."

"Were you a Marine?"

Bass's face screwed up in pain as he tried to remember. "I don't know," he finally croaked. "Maybe. I was with a Marine."

"You must have been a Marine, Charles. The Marines were here, but not the army."

"The navy has people with the Marines," Colleen interjected.

"They do?" Bass asked, surprised at the thought that he might have been a squid—where had that word come from?—in the navy. "Maybe I was," he admitted. "I don't know."

Zechariah clapped him on the shoulder. "It is good that you are remembering, Charles. You will remember more."

"Yes." Bass nodded. "It's good." He looked at the burning village. "But we don't have time for that now. Anyone who has a position to take, get to it. Everyone else, back to the caves. Now!"

The people scattered and Bass took up his position behind the first barricade. "You men keep down," he told the two villagers beside him. The men were armed with shot rifles. If the position was discovered, the men would fire one magazine each and, Charlie hoped, lure the enemy into the defile. Then they would abandon that position. Meanwhile, Bass and two men armed with acid guns would take them under fire from concealed positions above as they tried to break through the earth and rock barricade. If there were too many of them or if they had armor, it'd be all over for the defenders, but Zechariah and the surviving villagers would have time to flee into the caves.

"Okay." Bass patted each man on the back. "You know what to do. Can you hold here?"

The two faces coursed in perspiration nodded grimly.

"Fire your four rounds and get out of here. If they try to come through, I'll get them from topside. It'll be dark in a few hours, and if they don't come by then we'll be all right. They may never find us down here."

"Pray God you're right, Charles," one of the men said. He grinned briefly through the sweaty dirt on his face.

"You look and talk like a Marine," Bass said with a grin. He ran back behind the barricades and picked up his men with the acid guns. "Come on, we've got to get up there and under cover before they come back."

"H-How long will we be up there, Charles?" one of the men asked.

"Until dark. Let's go."

They ran back down the ravine, sloshing in and out of the muddy stream as they went. One of the men lost his footing and fell on his bottom into the mud. Bass reached down, pulled him to his feet, and they continued on almost to the river, where the walls weren't so steep. They scrambled up and ran back up the ravine to their positions above the first barricade, Bass and one rifleman on one side, the other alone across from them.

Panting from the run, they checked their weapons. The acid tanks were at least half full. The hand-blaster he'd gotten from Zechariah had a full charge. "Now we wait," he said, loud enough for the man across the ravine to hear him. "You men relax. I'll keep watch." He lay prone beneath some branches camouflaging his position and looked back at New Salem. He had selected the position and sited the barricades below it because from there he had excellent observation. In the distance, the buildings continued to burn. If anyone came toward them, he would see them in plenty of time.

He stiffened. Damnit! *The trails!* The trails they'd used to go back and forth snaked down from the outskirts of the village like huge fingers pointing straight at them! They hadn't appeared that way before now. Bass snorted. Jesus, typical goddamned military screwup—if something could go wrong, it sure would! If a recon patrol got to the near edge of the village, they'd see the trails for sure. Well, can't do anything about that now. So come on, you dirty bastards, come on!, he said to himself, We aren't some poor unarmed tribesmen! We are gonna kick your asses!

She had to get out of this place! First it was the Earthmen tossing things at her, and just now one of them had actually *stepped* on her back! It hurt where the Earthman's filthy foot had fallen on her. She'd almost lost her child, the shock was so great. *But they hadn't discovered her!* What a miracle!

The Earthmen were having a war among themselves, she realized, so they weren't too interested just then in what lay underfoot. Good! She'd heard the aircraft and then the explosions. She knew they weren't her own people come back to take their revenge. She'd heard the Earthmen's aircraft often enough to know the difference. Good! Maybe they would all kill themselves. But she couldn't stay there any longer. She was almost due, and when the baby did come, she'd be helpless to protect it in that altogether too-well-traveled spot. She cursed the ill luck that had brought her to that place.

As soon as night fell she would ease out into the river. If the baby came while she was in deep water, she'd have to manage as best she could, until she could find a safe place to burrow in.

Her only thought was to preserve the life inside her. She had been bred to serve unquestioningly and never to dishonor herself or the True People. She had been privileged to serve warriors all her life, and she hoped the child inside her was a male so it too could be a warrior. If it hadn't been for the child, she would have committed suicide already rather than live abandoned among the Earthmen. But a primal instinct drove her, overriding years of training and discipline.

Her people called her Chichi.

# CHAPTER
# EIGHTEEN

It was nearly dusk by the time the reconnaissance platoon reached the hills overlooking New Salem. Lieutenant Ben Loman parked his vehicle just behind the crest of a ridge and crawled carefully to the top. Most of the buildings that had been hit by the Avenging Angels were still smoldering, even though the attack occurred several hours earlier. The ridge sloped down to an open field about half a kilometer from the outlying structures of New Salem. Sergeant Raipur crawled up beside him. They focused on the village through their optics.

"Doesn't look like anything could be alive down there," the sergeant muttered.

Ben Loman only grunted in response. Raipur shrugged. He was getting used to the officer's cold shoulder. He hadn't exchanged more than a few words with his lieutenant since the raid on the savages. For his part, Loman was incensed that the company commander hadn't yet reassigned the sergeant. He had expected the NCO to file charges against him for what had happened during the raid on the Pilipili Magna, and was surprised that Raipur evidently hadn't yet said anything to Captain Dieter. In anticipation, he was quietly collecting statements from the other men to show that he had conducted himself properly during the attack.

Raipur, meanwhile, knew about the statements the officer was collecting; he just didn't care. He wasn't going to file charges. He was only interested in keeping himself in one piece and away from a court-martial until they were out of the field and he could assume the duties of Captain Dieter's operations sergeant. It amused him that the lieutenant was going to all that trouble to defend himself against a charge that would never be filed.

"I suggest one vehicle, Lieutenant, in case there's an ambush waiting for us down there. The rest of us can support from up here or reinforce if the probe runs into trouble. *We* can't be reinforced until tomorrow sometime. We're on our own until then."

"I know all that. Do you think I'm an idiot? Get the vehicles on line behind this ridge. We're going in all at the same time."

"Lieutenant, this isn't a bunch of primitives here! Surveillance and Battalion think it may be demons! We go charging in there across that field, and whoever's under cover in there can pick us all off. They shot down the Fly, sir. Whoever they are, they're armed. Besides, I heard the order from Battalion not to engage."

"We're better armed, and Battalion is not here—I am. Now *get the vehicles on line, Sergeant*!"

Raipur switched to the command net and ordered the drivers to pull up beside the lieutenant's scout vehicle. All he got was static. He tried several times with the same result. He switched to the frequency assigned to his own vehicle. Nothing but static.

"Lieutenant, my communicator is on the fritz. I'll have to go back down and tell them in person." He scuttled backward, then thought better of it. "Sir, can you raise them on your set?"

Loman cast a look of total exasperation at his sergeant, but he tried and couldn't raise the rest of his platoon either. "*Nothing* in this army works anymore," he muttered, slapping his helmet with the palm of his hand. That only caused the static to get worse. He tried raising the company CP. Nothing! What the hell . . . ? Was someone blocking his tactical frequencies? Probably not. It was not the first time their comm had failed recently. Loman suppressed a pang of fear. They would be out of touch until the reinforcements arrived or until they could laager up somewhere and tinker with the radios. Well, if anybody was down in that village, he was going to kick their asses good, radios or no radios.

"Sir, we go in there without tactical comm and—"

*"Get the vehicles on line!"* Ben Loman shouted, "I will not tell you again. We'll communicate through hand signals!"

*Hand signals?* Raipur gritted his teeth. "Lieutenant, I protest! I swear to you now and by all the gods of my fathers, if this goes bad you will take the blame for it." The two glared at each other for an instant, then Raipur obediently scuttled back down the ridge to the vehicles.

Each recon platoon consisted of five scout cars carrying a driver, a commander, and a gunner. The cars were designed for optimum off-road performance and could go almost anywhere. When they could go at all. They were very old models and spare parts were hard to find, their high-performance engines generating minimal heat signatures, rendering them virtually silent. They had covered the forty kilometers from their last position, some of it over improved road, to be sure, in less than thirty minutes. So far none had broken down. Raipur prayed that none would now.

The scout cars rolled slowly into line. Raipur glanced at the sun and estimated they had forty-five minutes of good daylight left. If they met no resistance, they could be in and out in that time. But if something went wrong . . .

Bass scanned the ridge on the far side of the village. The main road to Haven ran down from there, and that was the most likely direction any probe would come from.

"Why are they doing this to us, Charles?" young Nehemiah Sewall whispered beside Bass.

Bass shrugged. "I don't know. This is really your world, Nehemiah, not mine. I'm convinced of that now. From what I've been told about the way things work here, even in good times everyone hates everyone else. But I think they sent those aircraft because they're scared stiff the devils might be here. And for all we know, they're still around and the war with them is still going on. Uh-oh."

Atop the ridge, five low-silhouette vehicles were rolling into sight. They paused in a line and sat there for some moments. Taking stock, Bass thought. "They're here," he called down to the men in the ravine. "Five reconnaissance vehicles. Everyone remain calm and under cover. We'll let you know if they come this way." As if thinking out loud, he whispered, "They'll send one of those vehicles down into the village while the others cover it from the ridge. No sweat, Nehemiah, they'll never spot us here. The commander of that vehicle will want to get in and out of New Salem as quickly as possible."

Bass waved his hand at young Levi Stoughton on the opposite side of the ravine. "Okay over there?" Levi nodded. "Follow my lead, Levi."

Beside Bass, Nehemiah stiffened. "They're *all* coming!" he shouted.

"Aw, hell!" Bass groaned.

Ben Loman stood in the cupola of his command car. "All right, men! There's our objective! At my command, proceed at speed! Numbers one and five, you drive around the outskirts right and left. The rest of us will go straight through and meet you on the other side. Open fire on anything that moves! Men, we have a chance here to *avenge* our comrades, let's not fail them now! We are the cutting edge of the Lord's sword! *Are you ready?*"

He was answered by an affirming chorus of shouts.

He raised his right arm and held it above his head so all could see it, then pointed his hand at the village. *"Forward!"*

Bass and his two companions watched them from cover. The vehicles made no noise as they rushed forward, though they left long clouds of dust behind them. Two broke off from the other three and circled around the village, while the remaining trio headed straight into New Salem. Then, clearly heard on the cooling evening air, came the sound of gunfire, the high-pitched whine of hypersonic fléchette guns punctuated by the distinctive *bang-hiss* of the individual soldiers' fléchette rifles.

"What are they shooting at?" Nehemiah asked.

"Ghosts, shadows, maybe some of your loose cattle. All right, men," Bass shouted, "get ready! They'll be through the village and on our side very soon now. Hold steady."

New Salem was shrouded in smoke from the fighter attack, so the three vehicles that maneuvered between the ruins were forced to slow down as they moved forward into the center of the village. Raipur's driver pulled out onto the main street. The way was strewn with wreckage, but at the far end of the street stood an intact and imposing wooden building. To both sides, structures had escaped significant damage. "Watch those houses," he told his gunner. The gunner swung his weapon left and right as the vehicle crept down the street. From somewhere, another gunner fired at a target. Raipur's gunner opened up. *"What are you shooting at?"* Raipur shouted. The onboard communications system was out too, forcing him to give his commands by voice. The gunner did not answer, but continued shooting. Clouds of acrid wood smoke drifted down the street, obscuring the spaces between buildings.

Something moved off to their right front! The gunner laid into the target. Raipur had seen the demons before today, and to his clouded vision what moved behind the cloud of wood smoke looked just like one. The smoke cleared for an instant and he could clearly see the projectiles hitting something and the blood and flesh gouting into the air. The thing bellowed. "Stop!" he shouted into his driver's ear. He reached back and grabbed the gunner's leg, giving it a hard pull. "Cease fire!"

The gunner, a triumphant grin on his face, leaned down into the cab and shouted, "I got him, Sword! I got him!"

"Stay here and keep alert," Raipur told his driver. "Come on," he called back to his gunner, "we're going to take a look." They dismounted and, personal weapons at the ready, ran back between two houses to where the creature had been hit.

Raipur's heart was in his throat as he walked between the

buildings. What if this was an ambush? "Keep alert," he gasped. The building on the left was still burning, but the one on the right was intact, though already embers from the fire had drifted onto its roof. The heat from the burning structure was intense. They shielded their faces from the heat and smoke as they advanced.

"You sure got him," Raipur muttered as they came upon a large pool of blood. He looked around. "He must have crawled off somewhere."

"I blasted him!" the gunner enthused. "Over there!" he shouted, pointing over to his right.

They approached the target cautiously, weapons at the ready. At first Raipur thought the man had shot a tent, because all he saw was something flat on the ground colored red, white, and black. He moved closer. Horns and a long face? "Congratulations, buddy," Raipur said, "you just killed somebody's cow."

Eventually the platoon rallied on the far side of the village. The vehicle commanders dismounted and gathered under the cover of their cars to confer with Ben Loman, whose face was flushed beneath a thick layer of soot. All the men were breathing heavily from the excitement and exertion—and relief that apparently the village was deserted.

"We'll withdraw to the ridge where we started from," Loman began, "and fort-up there for the night, until reinforcements arrive tomorrow. The village may be empty now, but—"

One of the gunners called down something from his cupola.

*"What is it?"* Loman answered, annoyed at the interruption.

"Sir . . ." He nodded his head toward the thickets that spread outward from their positions. "There are well-beaten paths leading away from the village in this direction."

Loman paused, then he nodded and climbed up into the nearest vehicle, motioning for Raipur to accompany him. "How much time to sundown?" he asked his sergeant.

"I'd say about twenty minutes, sir," Raipur answered, a sinking feeling in the pit of his stomach.

"Hmm." The lieutenant looked in the direction the gunner had pointed. "Yes, definitely a path leading down there. Okay, here's what we're going to do. Sergeant, I want you to take your vehicle and one of the others and perform a reconnaissance down this path. See where it leads. You should be able to plow through these bushes without any trouble."

"Yessir," Raipur answered. It wouldn't do any good to argue with the officer, so he'd go down as quickly as possible and get it over with.

"Make it quick, Sergeant. We'll cover you from here."

Raipur dismounted and picked one of the vehicle commanders to follow him down the path. "Stay fifty meters behind me," he said. "If we run into an obstacle, offset a few meters to either side of my vehicle, to give supporting fire and an escape route. I don't want you shooting into my back, understand?"

"Got you covered, Sword!" The man grinned fiercely and gave Raipur the thumbs-up sign. He was one of the two men who had accompanied him to the caves the night they slaughtered the Pilipili Magna. The man liked to kill.

"Okay," Raipur sighed, "let's mount up. We don't have much time until sunset, and I sure don't want to be down in there after dark."

The width of the reconnaissance cars was considerably broader than the trail, but Raipur's vehicle rolled forward without resistance, crushing the bushes and shrubs beneath it. Dust drifted up from the broken vegetation and caused Raipur to sneeze violently, but the pleasantly tangy odor of crushed fiber filled the air around them. It reminded Raipur of the freshly cut lawn about his father's house. He'd joined the army to get away from the dead-end backwater where he was born. *Stop daydreaming!* a voice shouted inside his head.

Gradually the trail steepened. Soon it was joined by other trails, all of which looked heavily and recently traveled. Raipur told his driver to stop. They were at the top of a wash or ravine that descended into a steep-sided arroyo. The entrance was blocked by what appeared to be thick foliage and a rock fall. That struck him as strange. A series of well-traveled trails leading into a dead end?

"Open fire on that barricade!" Raipur screamed at his gunner. "Get us closer!" he shouted at his driver. The concussive *whirr* of the high speed fléchette gun pummeled the top of Raipur's head as his driver inched the vehicle closer to the barrier. The man's face had turned white as he concentrated intently on steering the car forward. "Closer!" Raipur screamed, to be heard over the gun.

The topside gun abruptly stopped firing. "Jam!" the gunner shouted, followed by a string of foul curses as he tried to clear the malfunction. Raipur leaned out his window and opened fire on the barricade with his personal weapon. Foliage was splintering and turning to dust and wood chips. He could see clearly as it flew away that it wasn't growing there. It'd been piled up to camouflage a barricade.

The vehicle suddenly shook violently from the impact of the second car's hypersonic fléchettes. The dumb sonofabitch was firing into *him*! "Move to the flank!" Raipur said into his mike before he remembered their comm was out. "Get us out of here!" he shouted at his driver.

"I can't, I can't!" the man screamed, almost in tears. "The reverse is shot out!" He tried desperately to shift. "He shot the engine out!"

The gunner screamed in agony and dropped back down inside the car, writhing and clawing at his clothing. Then a viscous green stream of liquid washed over the vehicle's windscreen and it began to melt. With gripping horror, Raipur knew instantly what the stuff was. So did his driver, who howled in fear and leaped out of the car. A bright flash winked at Raipur from the barricade, and the windshield disintegrated in front of him, though miraculously, he was not hit by the single 9mm pellet that penetrated the windscreen. The four remaining pellets of the round hit his driver, who flopped to the ground, blood spurting from the buckshot wounds.

A man appeared on top of the ravine, a tank of some sort strapped to his back. *A man!* It wasn't a demon! Instinctively, years of training taking over, Raipur leveled his weapon at the figure and squeezed off a burst. The fléchettes struck the tank on the figure's back and it ruptured. Raipur could hear the man screeching hideously. His gunner lay behind him, quiet now, dead, his face eaten away by the acid. Raipur felt a rush of elation that the man on the ridge had died the same way. He was familiar with the Skink acid throwers, for that's what the man up there had used, but he did not stop to wonder how a human would have come to have one. He dove out the door, scrambled underneath the vehicle and lay there panting. They were *men,* he could deal with that! Where the hell is my backup? he wondered.

It was totally silent except for the hissing from the ruptured engine. It seemed a long time passed as he lay there, but it couldn't have been more than a few minutes because it was still light when finally a commanding voice shouted, "Come out from under there and no weapons! Let's see your hands! You have ten seconds!"

Raipur crawled out from under the car and raised his arms. A man stepped up and struck him in the side of his head with the butt of his shot rifle. "That's for Levi!" the man snarled. Levi Stoughton, only seventeen, was the man Raipur had shot atop the ravine.

"Kill him!" someone shouted. Men began to kick and pummel the sergeant as he lay curled into a ball.

"Stop!" another man shouted. Raipur heard him approaching, grabbing the other men and pushing them aside. "None of that! This man is our prisoner."

"But he killed Levi!" someone protested.

"Look inside the vehicle. Levi got his licks in first and you killed this other man over here. It was a fair fight. You will not hurt this man. Get him to his feet. Tie his arms behind him. Get back to your positions. We sleep on our weapons tonight, men. Now you," he turned to Raipur, "you're coming with me." The man who spoke was of medium height but solidly built. He was strong. Raipur realized as much when the man grabbed his arm and shoved him toward the barricade. In the fading light it was hard to make out the color of his hair, but it was dark. His face seemed craggy in the bad light, and scarred—the face of a fighter, a man who'd been in more than one desperate scrape with other powerful men. The way he spoke, he seemed used to command. He sure commands *here,* Raipur realized.

The men around him scampered at his captor's orders and resumed their defensive positions. He was pushed through a narrow opening in the first barrier and through the next two, all of which were manned with determined-looking men armed with, he was surprised to see, bows and spears. The two who'd fired on his recon vehicle had projectile weapons; he'd seen them. They were used extensively for hunting where Raipur came from.

"My name is Charlie Bass," the man said.

"Sergeant Sudra Raipur," Raipur answered. His bruises were beginning to bother him and he had some difficulty speaking clearly from the blow to the side of his head.

"What's your unit?"

Raipur did not answer, and the man called Bass just shrugged and shoved him up a slope and into a large cave. They walked back into the recesses of the cave. Women and young men were gathered in there.

"You killed my son!" a woman screamed, and lunged at the sergeant.

"He killed my gunner and he tried to kill me, madam," Raipur answered.

Bass stepped between Raipur and Mehetabel Stoughton. "This man is my prisoner and he shall be treated humanely." He looked at Mehetabel while he spoke but he addressed everyone in the group.

"That is right." Zechariah stepped forward. "He's wounded, Charles, I'll have someone tend to his injuries."

Bass took Raipur to a spot some distance removed from the group, who accepted his orders, but with very bad grace.

"Sit." Raipur sat, awkwardly, with his hands bound behind him.

Bass squatted in front of Raipur. "Tell me your unit, where the main force is, its strength, weapons, intentions, and I'll untie you."

"No," Raipur answered.

Bass smiled. "Didn't think you would. Look, we don't mean anybody harm. We built these defenses against the devils or whatever they are. They had me in a cage. They tortured me. They killed all the people in the City of God sect except those who are here with me now. They killed your people too, from what I know. Why did you people attack us? Aircraft—your aircraft—came and bombed our homes, for no reason. What are you people up to?"

Emwanna, carrying a pan of water and some clean rags, came and squatted beside Bass. She started when she saw the sergeant and spilled some of the water. *"It is him!"* she whispered. She reached out a hand tentatively and touched Raipur's face.

"Who?" Bass held a glow ball close to Raipur's face, and it also illuminated Emwanna's features.

The two stared intently at each other in disbelief. It *couldn't* be her! Raipur thought. Then he smiled.

"He is the one who spared our lives when these men killed my people," Emwanna said. "Let him go, Charles."

Bass looked at the two of them. "Well, I'll be go to hell," he said as he cut Raipur loose.

# CHAPTER
# NINETEEN

Dominic de Tomas sat at his desk, reviewing marriage applications submitted by the men of the Special Group. Every man of the SG who wished to marry had to obtain the personal approval of the leader of the SPK—Dominic de Tomas. Marriage was encouraged for the men of the Special Group, after a certain age, to ensure that future generations of recruits would be produced who would carry on the values of their fathers. It was also intended to provide the stability of family life for the older members of the organization.

But marriage notwithstanding, the men of the Special Group were encouraged to father children, providing the mothers were women of sound genetic material. Any offspring born out of wedlock were raised by the Fountain of Life, a special institution devoted to the care of such children. The program had been in effect long enough that now some of the male children, devoted to the black uniform, were willing recruits for the Special Group. The females, likewise thoroughly indoctrinated and devoted to the party, were eager to marry SG men or to have their children. The offer the Fountain of Life held out to young single women—"that every unmarried woman who longs for a child can confidently turn to the Fountain of Life, which will supply her with a 'breeding helper' "—had been eagerly accepted by women throughout Kingdom.

De Tomas looked at the holograms of the young couple in the file before him. They were a handsome pair. The prospective groom, a shooter—the equivalent of private—was the son of an SG man; that counted for a lot. The future bride's background check revealed only a casual religious affiliation; that was excellent. But he wrote in the appropriate space, "Rejected." They were too young. The groom was but twenty, and his intended twenty-one. De Tomas wanted his men to have at least eight years of service before marrying. No one was accepted into the SG who was already married. He added something to the remarks section: "Get the girl pregnant." That was an order.

The next file was that of a much older man, a storm man, a sergeant. He was thirty, she twenty-nine; excellent. Long ago both had been members of the Fathers of Padua, but they had formally renounced their affiliation, describing themselves simply as "Believers in God," the strongest religious affiliation permitted to members of the Special Group. Gods of any stripe simply did not play a part in the philosophy of Dominic de Tomas.

He wrote "Approved" on the application and reached for the next one.

The intercom on his desk squawked. "Minister Oldhouse is here to see you, my leader."

De Tomas considered. He had another of those receptions in a short while. Well, he could always cut Oldhouse short if he ran longer than a few minutes. "Send him in."

Joseph Oldhouse, Minister of Propaganda and Public Enlightenment, bustled into de Tomas's office. He'd put on weight in the months since his appointment to the government, not that he had ever been slim. But the man was full of energy and ideas, evidently highly pleased with his new duties—and with himself. But most important, so far as de Tomas was concerned, he had so far proved completely devoted to de Tomas. Under one arm he carried a large leather portfolio. "I have some *wonderful* posters here for you to approve, my leader!" he said with enthusiasm.

De Tomas gestured toward the coffee table. Oldhouse opened the portfolio, took out a wad of small, multicolored posters, and spread them across the table. "These I am calling 'Weekly Paroles.' Each week, my leader, the party central press will issue posters like these in the thousands, to be distributed all over Kingdom and placed in public places for everyone to see. They will help to keep the philosophy of the party constantly before the public's attention in an eye-catching format that will be easy for ordinary people to understand and to remember."

De Tomas picked one out of the display. It showed a sturdy farmer with his implements standing arm in arm with a soldier in full battle dress. It read: " 'The farmer and the soldier stand hand in hand together to guarantee the people of Kingdom their daily bread and their security'—Our Leader." De Tomas smiled. The quote was from a speech he had made to the Kingdom Agricultural League the previous month.

"Excellent propaganda for production and military service, two pillars of the state," Oldhouse gushed. "We'll have others for all walks of life—simple, dramatic, graphic statements that appeal to the eye and are in plain language." De Tomas nodded as he flipped through the collection. "I have military recruiting posters too, my leader," Oldhouse said, digging inside the portfolio. He took out a large rolled poster and opened it up. "Since so many of our people live in poverty due to their exploitation by the previous regime, life in the army will offer otherwise potentially fractious young men a focus to their lives while keeping them under control and off our streets."

"Hmmm." De Tomas admired the artwork, two handsome young shooters in black dress uniforms. The black of the uniforms contrasted brilliantly with their silver badges and trimming, and the lettering, in bright red, leaped off the paper, shouting, COME JOIN US, YOUNG MEN, SEVENTEEN AND UP! "Damned impressive," de Tomas muttered. "Almost makes me want to sign up. But you know, Minister Oldhouse, impressive as all this is," he gestured at the posters spread out on the table, "isn't it, um, well, a bit superficial? Not much depth to any of it, is there?" The question was rhetorical; de Tomas knew the answer he was looking for.

"Ah-ha, my leader! If you will permit me?" Oldhouse selected one of the "parole" posters. He held it up. It was intended for the upcoming Mother's Day and showed a huge heart with a rose growing out of it. The inscription read: "GOD HAS MADE THE MOTHER'S HEART THE SACRIFICIAL VESSEL OF THIS GREAT AGE." "Poster art does not lie in the scientific training of the individual but in calling his attention to certain facts, processes, necessities, and so on, whose significance is placed within his field of vision!" Oldhouse grinned.

"Go on."

"Well, you see, my leader, the *art* consists in doing this so skillfully that everyone will be *convinced* that the fact is real, the process necessary, the necessity correct, and so on! My leader, all propaganda must be popular and its intellectual level must be adjusted to the most limited intelligence among us. The greater the masses it is intended to reach, the lower its purely intellectual level will have to be. The more modest it is, the more exclusively it takes into consideration the emotions of the masses, and then the more effective it will be!"

De Tomas smiled. " 'The art of propaganda lies in understanding the emotional ideas of the great masses and finding, through a psychologically correct form, the way to the attention and thence to the heart of the broad masses.' Does that sum it up, Mr. Minister?" De Tomas was grinning broadly now.

"Yes! Yes, my leader! That is it! Are those your words, my leader? Brilliant!"

"No, Mr. Minister, not mine. I'm quoting a past master of the art. But there we have it, eh? How did you learn so much about the art of propaganda?"

Oldhouse shrugged. "I was a preacher," he said, and laughed.

"Your plan is approved, Mr. Propaganda Minister. I want you next to start building the morale of the army. See me in, say, a week's time, with a plan to achieve that end. I might suggest, among other things which I think your fertile mind will come up with, entertainments for the troops in the field, variety shows, things like that."

Grinning happily, Oldhouse gathered up his posters. "Yes, my leader! You will be delighted to know that my staff is already working on that project! I have in fact recruited some of the finest dancers in the world to entertain the men!"

De Tomas glanced at the time. He was running late for the reception. No matter, Oldhouse's ingenious poster program had put him in an excellent mood. "You will accompany me now to the reception," de Tomas said. "If you please, Mr. Minister, wait for me in the outer office and we'll go down together."

Oldhouse, still grinning broadly, bowed and left.

The reception was being held in the Great Hall of Wayvelsberg Castle, in honor of the members of the Haven Women's Auxiliary, the largest chapter of the organization on Kingdom. De Tomas had ordered the hall to be redecorated for this purpose, to dispel the somber atmosphere that usually was obtained there in favor of lots of natural light and an abundance of flowers. Even the imposing statue of Heinrich the Fowler had been garlanded in fresh bouquets. This was to be an informal affair, no great speeches, just the Leader himself, relaxed and congenial, circulating among the dames and matrons, many of whom had come from afar just to attend their leader on that occasion.

Herten Gorman was already there when de Tomas and Minister Oldhouse stepped out of the elevators. Immediately, the guests ceased their conversations and turned their attention to the Leader as he walked amiably through the little groups of chatting women, kissing hands here, bowing there, making small talk, letting the women see him up close. Wet-eyed middle-aged matrons, their cheeks flushed with joy, listened attentively to every word their leader spoke. Many begged for his autograph. Several of the ladies actually swooned and had to be dragged off into corners to recover their composure. Enlisted men of the Special Group circulated among the crowd, offering serving trays laden with drinks and hors d'oeuvres. Oldhouse excused himself and circulated among the members of the media who had been invited.

At one point in their voyage between clusters of admiring females, de Tomas turned to Gorman and whispered, "Do any of these bitches have daughters I might be interested in?"

"Possibly, my leader. Shall I make inquiries?"

*"Of course, you idiot!"* de Tomas hissed. He couldn't believe Gorman hadn't already done that simple thing. You want a good candidate for a Great Man's consort, go to society's elite.

Gorman's ears reddened. De Tomas had lately taken to insulting him too often for the Deputy Leader's satisfaction. He was tiring of being his leader's pimp. He bit back a sharp response. "I shall do so at once, my leader. Surely some of the families represented here have daughters who'd be a credit to you, sir."

Several large-busted ladies in their fifties rushed up to de Tomas. "Ohhh," one gushed, "I did *so* much *love* your speech at the awards ceremony, my leader!" Another said, "I was so *honored* to receive my Mother's Cross in Silver, my leader! Thank you and God bless you!" Another: "My daughter simply *worships* the ground you walk on, my leader! We pray for you every night!"

"Madame, I do so sincerely appreciate your thoughts," de Tomas said to the last speaker, "and would you convey to your daughter my best wishes for her future happiness? You understand, ladies," he snatched a glass of wine from a passing server, "that the Lord's blessing is all I wish for the work I am trying to do for the good of our people."

Another woman rushed into de Tomas's presence. "My leader! My daughter is *here,* in the Great Hall! It would be such an honor if you would speak to her!"

De Tomas bowed gracefully. "Take us to see the dear child, then." He held out his arm and, totally enchanted, radiant with joy, the matron accepted it. She could already see herself in the society pages. She floated across the hall, the Leader of all the people of Kingdom at her side, and called a young lady away from a cluster of young women admiring an officer of the Special Group. The officer came to rigid attention as de Tomas approached, and the girl curtsied respectfully before the Great Man.

"Her name is Joy," the girl's mother announced breathlessly. The girl was fat, with a bad complexion.

Taking the girl by her elbow, de Tomas gently brushed his lips over the back of her hand as he murmured, "What a joy, miss." Joy almost fainted on the spot. "Your mother tells me wonderful things about you. All you young people," he took in the group of girls who'd been talking to the SG man, "are the hope and the future of Kingdom. Well," he turned back to Joy and her mother, "I must spread my charm about, ladies." He bowed and, taking Gorman by the elbow, steered him toward another group. Behind him the ladies stood transfixed, following de Tomas with their eyes.

"Shall I arrange for Miss Joy to have a private interview, my leader?" Gorman asked in a whisper. Inwardly he smiled. That'll teach him, he thought.

De Tomas looked up at his deputy sharply. Does this idiot really mean that? he wondered. "I was thinking, Herten, she might prove just the girl for *you*. Find me young ladies whose faces won't turn into a pustule pie whenever they eat a candy bar. Understood? God's guts, you know what I want, Herten! You keep putting me off and I'll just grab that little doxy of yours and fuck her ears off."

Herten almost gasped outright at the remark. Why that sonofabitch! he thought, but he said, "What is mine is yours, my leader. I shall find you the woman of your dreams. It is just that your requirements are difficult to fill."

But de Tomas had already moved off to talk to another group. Herten stood looking after him, thinking, You bastard, don't forget you're as mortal as the next man. Outwardly, however, he remained the Great Man's calm and obedient servant.

"Your position here is, ah, let's say, delicate, Sergeant Raipur," Bass said. "You people attacked us without provocation, and you personally killed one of our young men. And now we know that it was your outfit that wiped out Miss Emwanna's people. *What in the hell are you people up to?*"

They were sitting in the back of the cave entrance. Emwanna had gone to fetch some food and drink for Raipur, who rubbed his wrists. "I did what I could to stop the slaughter of the savages," he said, "but when the acolyte"—he shook his head—"the *lieutenant* gave the order to open fire, well, I couldn't stop the men." He shrugged helplessly.

"I know, I know, it happens. But why did you attack us here?"

"We thought demons were here, and when I saw it was men shooting at us, I shot back. I did what I'm trained to do."

"You could have buttoned up and told the vehicle behind you we're men, not devils. You could've told your officer. We could've gotten a cease-fire."

Raipur shook his head. "Our communications system is down and I guess the commander of the vehicle behind me only saw the acid guns in operation. Believe me, we know what those things can do."

Bass nodded. "What can you tell me about your army's intentions?"

Raipur paused before answering. "Look, I didn't make the decision to bomb your town, but if it had been up to me, yes, under the circumstances, I'd have used whatever I had at my disposal to soften this place up. Those men who came in here with me, they're *my* men, poorly led, maybe, and a bit wild because of that, but I'd have killed everything here before taking a chance on losing one of my men to an ambush. I won't tell you anything that might endanger them. What happened to the vehicle that was my backup?"

"It took off like a big bird. A few minutes later the remaining four beat it back over the ridge on the other side of the village. Listen, I was held in interrogation too, much worse than anything you'll get here. I respect your silence on military matters. But understand that we don't want to fight anyone. Surely you know what happened to these people? Almost the entire sect, thousands of innocent victims, was wiped out by the devils. We thought the devils were still out there. These people are scared, is all. We never would have opened fire on you unless you fired first, and that's what you did."

"I thought we were about to be ambushed. I gave the order to open fire. So would anybody."

A figure approached. It was Spencer Maynard. He held out his hand. "Emwanna told me about you. Thanks." They shook.

"How's the child?" Raipur asked.

"Fine, thanks to you."

"Spencer, stick around, I'll be needing you in a little while." Bass nodded toward the knot of villagers gathered about the cave entrance. They were casting nasty looks back at Raipur. There was big trouble brewing there. Bass knew he couldn't exactly blame the Stoughtons, but the law of warfare regarding prisoners would be observed. And this man might come in very handy tomorrow.

Emwanna came with dried beef and cold water. Raipur ate ravenously, thanking her profusely between bites. She kissed the sergeant's hand, then withdrew and left the two men alone.

"Reinforcements won't be here until sometime tomorrow," Raipur offered. "They will come in overwhelming force. You won't have a chance."

"We might not be here tomorrow morning. But if they're left alone, these people want to rebuild their village, take back their lives. Will your commanders listen to us? Will you go to them under a flag of truce?"

"I will," Raipur answered with confidence. He knew that Lieutenant Ben Loman, left to himself, would have gladly wiped out the survivors of New Salem, but he would stay under cover now, until the reinforcing column arrived, then cooler heads would be in command and Raipur was sure he could prevail upon those commanders to hold their fire and avoid another massacre.

Lieutenant Ben Loman raced as far away from New Salem as fast as he could. Raipur and his men had been killed by demons—the sergeant's backup had seen the whole thing. There was a nest of them, heavily armed, back in that draw, and he was not about to stick around and take them on.

Loman and the rest of his platoon got fifteen kilometers beyond New Salem before darkness closed in. The men were in a panic. They forted for the night when it got too dark to proceed any farther. Fortunately, they got one of the radios working again and contacted their company commander, reporting Skinks "in force and heavily armed" at New Salem. Captain Dieter informed Battalion, and the message was passed up to the regiment, brigade, and then division army group, which passed it up to General Lambsblood's headquarters. Nobody at a lower echelon wanted to take the initiative to attack a "heavily armed" and aggressive "nest" of demons without orders from higher command. The reinforcements Ben Loman's battalion was about to dispatch to New Salem were held back waiting for clearance.

General Lambsblood requested guidance from Dominic de Tomas.

# CHAPTER
# TWENTY

Midnight. Flaring torches cast pale wavering light over the men of the Special Group assembled in the Great Hall at Wayvelsberg Castle. Utter darkness filled the distant recesses of the hall and the assembled faithful. In the flickering torchlight, the graven image of Heinrich the Fowler, the warrior-king who unified the ancient German states and whose statue many thought resembled Dominic de Tomas, seemed to come to life as it gazed down on the rites with baleful solemnity.

De Tomas stepped forward and stood before the dozen men standing at rigid attention in the center of the Great Hall. As he did, the clear, soaring notes of a single trumpet sounded "Attention!" The notes echoed throughout the vastness of the hall, and when they died away, a band struck up "Raise the Flag!" the anthem of the Special Group and the SPK. All the hundreds of men present stood in ranks around the hall, singing the stirring words.

"Raise the flag! Our ranks are tightly closed . . ."

When the last note and the roar of the voices had vanished into the stygian corners of the great darkened hall, two shooters—one bearing a velvet-lined case studded with a dozen silver rings, the other holding richly engraved leather binders containing certificates printed on vellum—stepped into position to de Tomas's left and right rear. The only sound in the hall was the fluttering of the torches as de Tomas silently looked into the faces of the dozen men standing before him. They were about to receive the highest honor a man of the Special Group could aspire to, an honor given only at

213

midnight on the sixth day of the week, and only in the Great Hall. No matter where a man was when selected to receive this accolade, he was called back to Haven for the ceremony. Each occasion was presided over personally by de Tomas; no one was ever permitted to stand in for him.

The twelve men assembled that night at Wayvelsberg were about to receive the Special Group Death's Head Honor Ring.

When de Tomas had taken over as the Dean of the Collegium, he realized that it was necessary that the men who enforced its authority should see themselves as standing apart from the rest of humanity. Their special uniforms, their rigorous selection and training, the sense of belonging to an elite corps that was fostered by their leaders and fellows every waking hour of every day, all were vital ingredients in a process carefully designed to bind each recruit to the mystique of the Special Group. The Honor Ring, given only after a man had proven himself, was the final step required to induct him forever into the sacred companionship of his comrades.

At last de Tomas signaled the man to his left, who handed him one of the leather binders. "Shooter Camarines Ambos, Special Group Number 42,678!" de Tomas read in a voice that reached every corner of the Great Hall. The single trumpet once again sounded "Attention!" as Shooter Ambos took one step forward and came to attention.

"I hereby decorate you with the Honor Ring of the Special Group," de Tomas intoned. He did not have to look at the certificate. He'd done this so many times over the years, he had the text memorized. "It is a symbol of our loyalty to each other, our unmitigated obedience to our superiors, and our everlasting faith in our comrades. The Death's Head is an admonition to be prepared at any time to sacrifice one's life for the life of the collective whole. The Death's Head is surrounded by the goshawks that symbolize the unshakable faith in the rightness of our mission in the service of justice and in the victory of our worldview. This ring may never be allowed to fall into the hands of anyone who is not one of us!

When you leave this life, this ring will be returned to your leader. Like your spirit, it will live on in our community, to one day honor other men who have earned the right to wear it. Wear it in honor!"

The shooter to de Tomas's right presented the case of rings, and he took one. Again the trumpet sounded, this time accompanied by a quick drum roll. The rings had been sized a long time ago, and this one slid perfectly onto the middle finger of Shooter Ambos's right hand. He accepted a brief handshake from the Leader, took his certificate, saluted smartly, and stepped back into the rank.

Herten Gorman stood in the shadows. He was remembering the time when de Tomas had presented him with his own Honor Ring. He glanced at it now. The silver skull inlaid in black opal and surrounded by spread-winged goshawks was his prize possession. His heart swelled within his chest the night de Tomas had slipped this ring onto his finger. Well, that had been a long time ago, he thought, and the world had changed drastically since then. And so had Dominic de Tomas. Oh, he is in great form tonight, Gorman reflected; nobody can outdo him in public. He recalled the night only recently when they'd had the reception for the Auxiliaries in that very hall, when the great Leader had kissed hands and sweet-talked the ladies, bowing, scraping, ingratiating himself, and how he, Herten Gorman, had been relegated once again to the despicable role of the Leader's pimp.

Worse, far worse, was when he, Deputy Leader and technically the man responsible for running de Tomas's government, had recently been frozen out of all the major decisions, hardly even consulted, reduced to a figurehead.

In all the time that Gorman had served in the SG, de Tomas had been the distant, ruthless, and ascetic power behind the Collegium. In those days, except on ceremonial occasions, most men of the SG never saw their leader. But they all respected him—and feared him. But since the seizure of power, de Tomas had taken on a new personality, presenting himself as a "man of the people." The last executions he'd ordered had been of the professors at the university. Since then, even those who explicitly opposed his rule or posed a threat to it, instead of facing summary execution, were placed in "protective custody." No picnic, to be sure, but they were still alive. Gorman believed that a serious mistake. He thought back to the students who'd been caught distributing leaflets on campus. Gorman would have fed them into the furnaces and executed their entire families, stamped out the treason at its source. But de Tomas had let them go!

Where everyone else in the Great Hall of Wayvelsberg Castle that night smelled only the aromatic bouquet of the flaring torches, Herten Gorman smelled the seeds of disaster. He placed his right hand, and the finger bearing the ring, behind his back.

Now that it was full dark outside, someone had carefully erected a screen across the entrance to the cavern. Bass and Raipur stepped into the circle of lamplight that illuminated the small group of villagers assembled there. Everyone was present except for the men detailed to watch the approaches to the ravine.

The Stoughton family—Esau and Mehetabel, the parents, their daughters Lela and Tamar, and sons Reuben, Benjamin, and Elon—stood apart from the others in a small cluster. As Raipur came into the light, Reuben, the oldest son, stepped forward and leveled his finger at him. "You murdered my brother!" he accused. Behind him, his mother wailed her grief, and as Esau held her in his arms, he cast a murderous glance at the sergeant.

Bass held up a hand. "Listen to me!" he began.

"We are tired of listening to you!" Reuben shouted. "That— That *man* there killed Levi, and I—we—demand retribution!" Several others nodded and murmured assent.

Knowing how these people loved to vote on community issues, Bass took stock. He could count on Zechariah and his family to support him; probably Hannah Flood, and possibly the Maynards, especially Spencer; Amen Judah and his family too. Colleen and Chet would support him. How many adults was that? He counted them up mentally. Counting himself, that would be fourteen. Discounting the seven Stoughtons, there were fourteen others he could not be sure of if this situation came to a vote.

Then it couldn't be left to a vote.

"This man is our prisoner and he will be treated—"

"Damn you, Charles!" Mehetabel Stoughton screamed.

"Mehetabel!" Zechariah exclaimed.

"Damn you, Charles!" she screamed again. She strained to break loose from her husband's grip. "May God damn that man's soul to eternal hellfire!" she shouted, eyes blazing and spittle flying from her lips. She pointed at Raipur as she cursed. "And you too, you damned *foreigner*!" she raged at Bass.

"He is not even a believer," Esau Stoughton added, meaning Bass.

"Put him on trial now!" Tamar, the Stoughton's forty-year-old daughter shouted, pointing at Raipur.

"He's even untied him!" someone else cried, noticing for the first time that Raipur's arms were unbound.

"Friends!" Zechariah held up his arms. "Friends, this animosity must pass. This is not our way, we live in the spirit of Christ!"

*"I want that man dead like my son,"* Mehetabel croaked. Her voice, like an icy curse from the tomb, froze the tableau into shocked silence.

Zechariah worked his lips soundlessly, searching for words.

Bass broke the silence. "Now you people listen up—" he grated, his voice just above a whisper.

"We don't have to listen to you!" Reuben Stoughton shouted.

"Reuben, you interrupt me one more time like that and you will not live much longer," Bass rasped. He placed his right hand on the blaster holstered at his side and glared at Reuben, who tried staring back but after a moment cast his eyes downward and stepped back with his parents and siblings.

Zechariah cleared his throat nervously. "You have the floor, Charles," he said, returning to where Consort and Comfort were standing.

"Now listen up and nobody give me any shit," Bass began. "I've been busting my ass for months, trying to whip you yokels into a force that could protect itself. And you did today, you did fine. Young Levi did his duty like a soldier, Mrs. Stoughton, and we should all be proud of him for that. But I am *not*—repeat, *not*—going to let you degenerate into a godforsaken mob! I'm in charge of the defense of this village and you *will* obey my orders, is that understood?"

Nobody moved or said a word. In the dim lamplight Bass cast a huge shadow over the rear wall of the cave, and to the people gathered about him, he looked physically bigger now than they remembered him in the daylight. His right hand rested easily on the blaster at his side.

"This man is our prisoner, and if anyone here—man, woman, or child—touches a hair on his head, I will kill you." The word "you" echoed off the cavern walls. Still nobody moved a muscle. Bass looked into the eyes of each person gathered about the smoking lamp. "Tomorrow," he continued, "this man," he laid a hand on Raipur's shoulder, "will go out under a flag of truce and end this foolishness.

"Yes, Mrs. Stoughton," Bass's voice softened as he looked at the Stoughtons, "I am a foreigner. You people saved my life, and you saved the lives of Emwanna, Colleen, and Chet. And because of that we're in this with you up to our eyes. You people have come through a lot because you stayed together and worked together and prayed together. And I haven't come this far with you to let it all degenerate, as I said, into a godless mob action. I only have one question to ask of you: What would have happened today if you'd been attacked and you didn't have a plan to defend yourselves?" Nobody ventured an answer. Bass nodded. "Well, I'll tell you—you'd all be dead, and any of you who might have survived would be wishing they were dead too.

"Now here's what we're going to do. Those who want can go back to the village while it's still dark and there's enough light from the fires to salvage what you can from your homes. No matter what happens to our peace mission tomorrow, we'll be living in this cave complex for a while, so we might as well get as comfortable as possible." He turned to Raipur. "You stay right beside me for the rest of this night."

The staff duty officer, an overstorm leader, considered the dispatch he had just received from General Lambsblood's headquarters. Should he disturb the Leader? It was late. Perhaps he should call the Deputy Leader and pass the information on to him for a decision? That was the chain of command. No. The dispatch was an opportunity for him to have direct contact with the Leader, and he wasn't going to pass it up because of the chain of command. If the demons were still active on Kingdom, that was news of the utmost importance.

But first—the overstorm leader checked the daily Special Group order of battle. Yes. There was an airmobile company on standby. He made a quick calculation. They could be there in forty minutes, by 0130 hours local time. The men of the Special Group had never engaged the demons during the recent invasion. His heart raced. *Yes!* The chance of a lifetime! He picked up the communicator and entered the code that would connect him directly with the Leader in his private suite at Wayvelsberg.

"What the hell do you want?" de Tomas snarled. "It better be nothing short of total war," he added ominously.

"My leader, we have just received an urgent dispatch from General Lambsblood's headquarters. It is of the utmost importance."

"Nothing that idiot could tell me could ever be of any urgency," de Tomas replied sourly. "Well, what is it?"

"A reconnaissance unit has engaged demons in strength at a village called New Salem, my leader. Our forces inflicted heavy casualties before withdrawing to await reinforcement. General Lambsblood wishes you to know about this before he takes steps to close with them in force and annihilate them."

What! de Tomas thought. That fool has actually managed to find some surviving demons? Will wonders never cease? " 'Inflicted heavy casualties,' Overstorm Leader?" he said.

"In the parlance of Lambsblood's so-called army, that means they got their asses kicked."

"Yes, my leader! Precisely. My leader? May I suggest we take this matter out of the army's incompetent hands and handle it with our own troops?" The overstorm leader tried to keep his voice even, though his heart was pounding as he spoke.

"What? Do we have the forces?"

"Yes, my leader! There is an airmobile special weapons and tactics team standing by. They are specially qualified in city fighting and night operations, my leader. Their mission is to be on hand if it becomes necessary to restore order in Haven, but they have never needed to do that, and when this operation is over, they can be back here quickly. In the interim, I can call another team to stand by."

De Tomas hesitated, thinking. "You recommend a *night* operation, Overstorm Leader?"

"Yes, my leader, before the demons have a chance to consolidate their position and strengthen their defenses."

"Very well. Give the order."

"Yes, my leader. One more thing, my leader, I don't think you should leave this matter to a junior officer." He hesitated briefly before plunging ahead. "I request the honor of leading the operation."

"Who the hell are you again?"

"Overstorm Leader Martins, my leader. I commanded the Hesperus Special Group Detachment in Radak for five years, and before that I was—"

"No need to recite your service record, Overstorm Leader. You have my verbal permission to command this operation. Report to me directly when it's over. Oh, by the way, why did you not report this situation to Deputy Leader Gorman instead of calling me directly?"

"I considered it of too great importance, my leader, to trust with anyone but yourself."

"Good, very good. What's your name again?"

"Overstorm Leader Martins, my leader."

"I'll remember that. Hop to it."

\* \* \*

"Do you know what time it is?" Ambassador Jayben Spears gasped as he looked unbelievingly into the receiver of his communicator.

"It is time, Mr. Ambassador, that we talked," his caller replied smoothly. There was a tone of amusement in the voice, and that angered Spears even more than the lateness of the hour.

*"Right goddamned now?"* Spears asked. "Are you out of your mind, Gorman?"

"I'm out of patience, Mr. Ambassador," Gorman answered patiently. "Let us say seven hours, at the consulate? It is better I come there than you come here."

"Yeah." Well, there goes breakfast, Spears thought. "Gorman, is this to be an *official* visit or are you just eager for intelligent conversation?"

"I will explain when we meet." The comm unit went dead.

*Well well well. . . . First General Lambsblood intimates to General Banks that he's not entirely satisfied with the new Maximum Leader on Kingdom, and now the number two man in the hierarchy calls in the middle of the night for a private meeting, the purpose of which he is unwilling to discuss openly.*

Spears put his arms behind his head and lay back. Something was beginning to unravel on Kingdom. One thing for sure, though, Mr. Herten Gorman was the last man on Kingdom he was about to trust. No, correction, the *second* to last man.

Things were beginning to get interesting.

Silently, slowly, she pulled herself out of the mud. The pains were coming very quickly now. The baby would be out soon. She simply could not birth it here, with those noisy Earthmen only a few meters away from her hiding place. It had been a mistake to think the streamlet was a safe refuge. Painfully, she inched her way down to it. She was weak from lack of a proper diet. She had been living off the carbohydrates stored up in her body because of the danger posed by foraging so close to the Earthman camp. Well, after the baby came, she would feast and hunt enough for the two of them.

She plopped at last, almost soundlessly, into the stream. A great weight seemed to be lifted from her body as the water buoyed her up. She sighed as the caked mud washed off her skin in the swift, cool current. She used her gills and just drifted along with the current, floating that way for some distance until the water became too shallow. Then she found a mud bank and crawled out under some water plants that she hoped would shield her. There, the baby came.

It was a healthy male.

# CHAPTER
# TWENTY-ONE

The Brattles' house, along with that of the Rowley family, was one of the few left relatively undamaged in the bombing, so Zechariah invited the Judahs—Amen and Abigail—and their three children—Deuteronomy, Ruth, and Aaron—to come with them and salvage whatever they could use from the place. The Judahs had lost everything in the bombing. "I want my linen," Consort Brattle had said, "so at least we have clean sheets to sleep on!"

"We'll take everything we can back to the caves to share with the others," Zechariah said. "But let's get a move on. The fires are dying and we need the light to see by."

"I'll go with you," Bass said. He turned to Spencer Maynard and handed him his sidearm. "You stick with Raipur here until I get back." He glared at the Stoughtons as he spoke. "Don't let anyone near him."

"I won't, Charles." Spencer eagerly accepted the weapon and strapped it on.

"I stay too," Emwanna volunteered. Chet and Colleen stepped forward and stood beside Spencer.

"You don't need to worry, Charles, I'll keep order here while you and Zechariah are gone," Hannah Flood announced as she moved her large frame into the lamplight.

"Very well," Zechariah said. "You are all welcome to come along if you want," he told the others. "We'll salvage everything we can and be back here before sunrise." He paused, expecting everyone to go, but only the Rowleys moved toward the cave entrance. The others stood sullen and silent. They were the ones who'd lost everything in the bombing, or thought they had. That they were not even willing to go back to check on their property was a bad sign. "After all we've been through together, all you people can do is stand there and stare at me?" Zechariah looked each one of the adults in the eye, but no one was willing to hold it. Zechariah sighed. "Very well. We'll be back in a couple of hours, then."

The windows in the Brattles' house had all been blown out and there were holes in the roof, but otherwise the structure was sound and intact. "I wish," Zechariah muttered as he went in the front door, "there was still some of that beer left."

"Zechariah, when this is over I promise you, we'll lay in a year's supply and I'll help you drink it," Bass said from behind him. Consort snorted but Comfort laughed.

"Beer? I didn't know you had beer, Zechariah!" Amen Judah exclaimed.

"You're a good shot with that rifle of yours, there, Judah," Zechariah replied, "but stay away from my beer supply." He felt like reminding Judah that if he hadn't shot down that spy device, they would not be in this position, but dismissed the thought as unworthy of a Christian.

After a few trips inside, they managed to collect a pile of things to take back to the cave. "Charles, there's a wheelbarrow out back in the shed. Would you mind fetching it so we can load these goods?" Zechariah asked. "I want to take some of these things back to the cave right now, though." He hefted two sacks of vegetables he'd gotten out of the root cellar. He'd stuffed them into pillowcases, which he tied together so he could sling them over his neck and shoulders. "These might help lighten the mood back there, and besides, I want to be sure our prisoner is still safe."

"Zechariah," Bass said, "I can do that for you."

"No, Charles, these are my people. Besides, I want to check in person, make sure they all know I'm behind you."

The fire in the house next door had almost burned itself out, so the light out behind the Brattle house was very poor. Once he got the door to the shed open, Bass had difficulty finding the wheelbarrow. The tools were mostly old-fashioned implements intended for minor carpentry jobs around the

house and for working in the flower and truck gardens the
Brattles kept. Consort was fond of gardening. He had to
search essentially by feel. He brushed something hanging on
a peg in the wall and it fell with a crash.

"Goddamnit!" Bass swore.

"Charles, you shouldn't talk like that," a woman said from
behind him.

Bass whirled. Comfort stood outlined in the dim firelight
against the doorsill. He knew her by her voice and the outline
of her head against the flames. He didn't know what to say,
so he said the only thing he could think of, "Give me a hand,
will you?" then turned back to what he was doing.

She stepped inside and laid a hand on Bass's shoulder. It
was not a helping hand. He straightened up and faced her.
She put her arms around him and rested her head on his
chest. *"Charles,"* she whispered.

At first Bass held his own arms out at his sides, awkwardly
wondering how he—should he? could he?—get loose of her
embrace. Then he put his arms around her. Comfort Brattle—
what an appropriate name!—was a beautiful, healthy, ener-
getic young woman who'd never asked anyone for anything
for herself. And she had nursed him back to health like a latter day Florence Nightingale. The devils had ruined Charlie
Bass's memory, but the rest of him worked quite well. Numerous times he'd thought if only Comfort were just a few years
older . . . Now, he rested his head against hers. "Comfy . . ."
He was pleasantly aware of her young body pressed close
against his. "Comfort, this'll never do."

"I know. I don't care." She sighed. "Just let me stay like
this awhile. Please?"

They stood there for a while. "Comfy," Bass began, "I'm
sorry for the way I talked to you that night on guard duty—"

"I acted like a child that night. I'm sorry I let you down."

Bass could feel her arms tightly about him. He smiled in
the dark. "Let's have a seat."

"There's nowhere to sit in here, Charles."

"Sit on the floor with me, Comfy." They sat on the floor
and Comfort rested her head on his chest. He felt her warm

breath against his neck. Her hair smelled of earth and wood smoke. He lifted her chin and kissed her lips. Her teeth scraped against his. "Ah, *goddamn*," Bass whispered, but this time it wasn't meant as a curse.

Later they dug out the wheelbarrow. "Get in, little girl," Bass said laughing, "and I'll give you a ride!"

He wheeled her around to the front of the house, where Comfort's mother was busily sorting linen and utensils into separate piles. "I'm so very happy someone's enjoying the evening," Consort Brattle said. "What took you so long? Father's probably halfway back to the cave by now."

"Mother!" Comfort leaped out of the wheelbarrow. "Let me help you!"

"What has come over you?" Consort stared at her daughter. She was radiant, even in the dim firelight. She hadn't appeared this happy since ... when? Consort looked up at Bass, who studiously avoided her eyes. *"Comfort!"*

Amen Judah, followed by his wife and children, all laden with goods, emerged from the house.

From somewhere came a strange sound, a *hooosh-hooosh-hoosh*ing noise. Then Hoppers swooped in at rooftop level using infras to mark their targets. Judah and his family, since they were moving, stood out from the lingering fires. The pilot in the lead machine fired.

A rocket decapitated Judah in a spray of blood and exploded at Abigail Judah's feet, shredding her body and killing both Ruth and Aaron instantly. Fifteen-year-old Deuteronomy was thrown bodily back into the house by the blast and knocked unconscious. He would not survive the night.

The second projectile, fired from a hovering Hopper, hit the piles Consort Brattle had assembled in the street. The blast knocked her, Comfort, and Bass to the ground. Men in black body armor were suddenly swarming everywhere over what was left of the village of New Salem, firing at everything that moved or looked like it might.

Consort Brattle lay in the dust, her left arm gone at the

elbow, and stared up at the hulking goliath in body armor who loomed over her, his rifle in her face. He fired. Comfort jumped to her feet and ran to where Amen Judah's body lay. The man swung his rifle in her direction and fired again but missed. Comfort snatched the shot rifle Amen had been carrying, unconsciously checked that the safety was off, and fired from the hip. The man's body armor was designed to defeat high-energy weapons, not projectile weapons, and the shot ripped through his chest. Comfort fired again at another man and he went down too.

From where he lay, Bass shouted for Comfort to take cover. Another rocket detonated between them. The last thing Bass remembered was the flash.

Comfort was thrown to the ground by the blast but did not lose her grip on the shot rifle. She fired twice more from a sitting position, both times hitting men, though she couldn't tell how seriously. But she'd been unconsciously counting her rounds, and realized after the third that she had only one round left. A big man was almost on top of her. She fired. At less than one meter, the buckshot load from a standard shot rifle dispersed less than twenty-five millimeters. The shot passed between the man's legs. He grabbed Comfort by the front of her shirt and drove his fist into her face.

"Your breakfast is getting cold, Mr. Ambassador," Herten Gorman murmured around a mouthful of ham and eggs. Smacking his lips noisily, he reached for the coffeepot and refilled his cup. "Excellent coffee, Mr. Ambassador. You keep a hearty table, I must say." He burped and, smiling, patted his stomach. "Where I was brought up, a burp at the table is a compliment to the host." He leaned back and belched loudly. "Ahhh! Makes room for more!" he wheezed. "Good thing it didn't come out the other end, eh?" He laughed enormously and stuffed a piece of toast into his mouth.

Jayben Spears glowered balefully at his unwanted breakfast guest. Gorman's table manners were atrocious, and knowing that, Spears had hoped he wouldn't arrive until after he'd eaten. But Gorman arrived just as the servomech was laying out the table, so he had to invite the portly criminal to join him.

"Not hungry this morning?" Gorman asked, pretending to be solicitous. "In this season in Haven, colds are quite common, Mr. Ambassador. Never could abide food in the morning when I had a cold. You know, nose all stuffed up, can't taste a thing, constantly hawking and blowing the snot out of my sinuses." He shook his head. "Astonishing! Medical science can regrow lost limbs, regenerate failed organs, and has eliminated nearly all diseases that used to keep people from living their full four score and seventeen standard years. Yet we are still plagued by the common cold.

"Do you mind?" He gestured with his fork at the platter of ham in the center of the table, and when Spears shook his head, he speared himself another helping.

"You've gained weight, Gorman," Spears observed sourly. He hadn't even touched his breakfast, and wouldn't, so long as Gorman remained at the table.

Gorman patted his midriff. "Damned desk job, Mr. Ambassador! Weakens a man faster than a blowjob." Again he laughed uproariously.

"Spare me any anatomical descriptions, please," Spears muttered.

"Har har har," Gorman laughed, gesturing happily at Spears with his fork, bobbing his head up and down vigorously until he choked on a fragment of ham. He began to cough. Spittle flew into his napkin and his face turned almost purple as he tried to dislodge the meat. Spears brightened for the first time since Gorman arrived. Maybe he'd strangle. No chance of him performing a Heimlich maneuver if he did. But no such luck. At last, with a profound heave of his entire body, the errant piece of ham shot out into his napkin.

"Damn!" Gorman picked the meat out of the napkin and regarded it carefully before popping it back into his mouth. "Missed me that time, you old bastard," he said, dramatically raising his eyes heavenward. "Besides, untold millions in Human Space would give their left nuts for food like this, Mr. Ambassador. It would be a sin to waste it." He smiled contentedly as he chewed on the fragment. He swallowed. He sighed and forked more food into his mouth.

Spears's face turned a shade of beige and his stomach lurched uncomfortably. "Why are you here, Gorman?"

"Ah!" Gorman gulped down the rest of the ham he'd been chewing, sipped his coffee noisily, and daintily patted his lips with his napkin. He tossed the napkin into the center of the table and sat back in his chair. Raising his chin up, he regarded Spears through his left eye, like a bird reconnoitering a worm. "I'm going to assassinate Dominic de Tomas," he said.

Spears did not comment at once. Instead he carefully rearranged his silverware. Then: "Why should I care? You're both murderers and despots. The best thing for Kingdom would be for someone to kill you both."

"My my, Mr. Ambassador," Gorman replied mildly. "What happened to the obligatory diplomatic sangfroid?"

"I don't use it with people like you, Gorman. Why are you telling me this?"

"If I get rid of him, I want you to get me out of here safely."

Spears did not expect this. "You mean you aren't going to assassinate your head of state because you want to take over the government yourself?"

Gorman smiled. "You call this a government? No, I want off this world. But I want de Tomas dead for my own personal reasons. After I do that, I can't count on the loyalty of the Special Group. They're devoted to him to a man. Once I get out of here, I've got a place to go where I can live comfortably for the rest of my life."

"Well, why do you need me? Just kill him and take the next ship outward bound from here."

Gorman shook his head. "No, no. I can't chance it. Too many people love that bastard. I don't know how he did it, but he's convinced a lot of us that he's Kingdom's savior. Never suspected he had that talent, Mr. Ambassador. Sooo, I've got to have a guaranteed escape plan. I don't want to end up like some latter-day Mussolini, hanging upside down from a lamp post, eh? I need safe conduct to Interstellar City and passage on one of your naval vessels. Just get me to its next planet of call, is all I ask, and I'll be on my way. I'll have some 'baggage,' but you can arrange for that."

"Your 'baggage'—it wouldn't consist of anything from the party's treasury, would it?"

Gorman only smiled cryptically. "If we plan this carefully, Mr. Ambassador, you can call the shots as to whom the next ruler of this world might be. But I need one more thing—I need total and exclusive immunity from prosecution for anything I might have done while I was Deputy Leader of the Kingdom Socialist Party and a member of the Special Group. I am not asking for anything that is not within your power to grant."

"I will not be an accessory to murder, even the murder of a swine like your boss."

"Mr. Ambassador, this is your chance to—"

"Gorman, you may leave now," Spears rasped, and stood up, his knees jostling the table and spilling Gorman's coffee.

"Sir, you should consider my proposal very carefully! Your embassy exists here only at the pleasure of my government, and—"

"Gorman, you are on Confederation property! If you don't get your fat ass out of here right now, I will have you arrested. I will then inform de Tomas of what you have just told me and *you* will be fed feet first into those goddamned furnaces you keep lighted at Wayvelsberg! Yes," Spears nodded, "I know what goes on up there. Now get out of here, you sonofabitch!"

Gorman, shaking, his face white with rage, stood. "You will regret this, Spears," he whispered.

"Yes yes, whatever. But let me tell you something, mister: *don't you ever come back here again.*"

Gorman stomped out, almost knocking Prentiss Carlisle over as he barged through the door. Carlisle took in the disarray of the breakfast table and the look on Spears's face. "Is everything all right, sir?"

"Prentiss! Why, yes, everything is just absolutely peachy. What's for breakfast in the cafeteria this morning?"

"Why, ham and eggs, I expect," Prentiss answered, somewhat befuddled at the question. From where he stood, he could plainly see the untouched food on the ambassador's plate.

"Well, come on, let's you and me go down and have some. What do you say?"

"Why, thank you, sir. I'd enjoy that."

"Good. Let's get General Banks to join us there. And when we're done, let's take a little trip out to General Lambsblood's headquarters. Prentiss, my lad, we have a busy day ahead of us!"

"General, since the weather is so fine this morning, could we talk outside?" Jayben Spears asked General Lambsblood.

"But . . . ? Why, certainly, Mr. Ambassador!" the general answered, but he was perplexed. The weather was awful, damp and foggy, as it usually was in Haven at this time of the year, the cold season. Another reason the general did not like walking outside his headquarters complex was because he'd have to return dozens of salutes from passing soldiers. But Spears had something important to say, so he would have to be indulged. Besides, the visit could not have come at a better time for Lambsblood, who had something of his own to tell the Confederation's ambassador to Kingdom.

"I didn't see Major Devi this morning, General," Spears commented as they stepped alone into the headquarters courtyard. Brigadier General Banks and Prentiss Carlisle, both to their amazement and pleasure, had been told to remain behind to finish their coffee.

"Nossir, he's on, ah . . . well, detached duty for a while. I'll tell you more about that later."

The fog outside had turned incredibly thick. The men's footsteps echoed dully as they slowly made their way over the cobblestones of the courtyard, thick with condensation.

Spears laughed. "I wouldn't know how to find my way back to your office in this fog."

"Don't worry, I know the way, sir."

Spears turned serious and said in a low voice, "We've found several eavesdropping bugs in the consulate, General, so I'm sure de Tomas has you bugged here as well. I doubt his agents can overhear us out here, which was why I asked you to go walking with me."

Lambsblood nodded. "I understand. I suspected as much myself, though I'm surprised even he would have the temerity to bug the Confederation embassy."

"Earlier this morning Herten Gorman visited me. He wants to assassinate de Tomas." Despite the fact that so far they appeared to be alone in the courtyard, Spears spoke just above a whisper. In the fog, he could just make out Lambsblood nodding, as if this weren't news to him. Or as if he were agreeing it was a good idea to assassinate de Tomas.

They walked along in silence for a few paces as Spears waited for some reaction from the general.

"He wanted your help, I assume?" Lambsblood eventually asked.

"Of course."

"Did you agree to give it to him, Mr. Ambassador?"

"Not only did I say no, General, I said '*Hell,* no!' "

Lambsblood smiled. "You asked after Major Devi. He is temporarily on duty with an armored battalion at the local depot. I have put the unit on full combat alert and it is standing by, awaiting orders." Someone approached them. A young soldier, obviously an enlisted orderly, emerged from the fog.

"Good morning, sir!" he said as soon as he recognized the commanding general. He was carrying pots of tea or coffee on a tray so he couldn't be encumbered with a salute. Lambsblood nodded and smiled and the soldier quickly passed on.

"Are you expecting trouble?" Spears asked.

"Yes."

"What kind?"

"Wayvelsberg," Lambsblood whispered.

"On your own?"

"If I have to, yes. De Tomas is only keeping me around until he's totally hamstrung my army, and then I'm history. I won't wait for that to happen. And I don't like what he is doing to this world of ours."

"You're not alone, General. But this unit, General, who knows it's on standby alert? Do you think de Tomas might suspect something? And are the soldiers loyal to you?"

"The soldiers are loyal. You should realize how low morale is in this army of mine right now, due mostly to de Tomas's 'reforms,' and his total lack of support. He is deliberately wearing us down while he builds up the Special Group, and everyone in uniform knows it. The armored unit was put on standby ostensibly to reinforce elements in the field. You know that yesterday a reconnaissance unit thought they encountered Skinks and were attacked by them?"

*"No!"*

"I pressed the panic button—on purpose. I passed the decision of what to do to de Tomas, and he sent a Special Group air assault unit to the scene. They took off after midnight and returned before dawn this morning. I haven't received an afteraction report yet and, as arrogant as those SG guys are, probably won't. But that the force came back, apparently intact, is proof to me that they weren't up against Skinks. I made it very clear that I put that armored unit on alert in anticipation of just this sort of thing, though. De Tomas doesn't believe I have the guts to pull off a coup against him, you can bet on that."

Lambsblood paused before asking, "I can count on you, then? The Confederation will back me?"

"Yes." Spears was nonplussed that his intelligence people had missed the report about the Skinks. But he felt a deep sense of relief that apparently whomever the SG men attacked, it probably hadn't been Skinks.

"What kind of help can you give me?"

Spears shrugged. "My endorsement for the government you will head when de Tomas is removed. In a few days a Confederation Navy starship is making a port call here. You will have her armaments to back your tanks and soldiers."

"Accepted, with thanks. I have one condition, though."

"What is that?"

"If this coup succeeds and I survive, I don't want *anything* more to do with government! I want a guaranteed retirement. Let someone else run this world."

"Agreed. And General, that says volumes for your personal integrity. I have my own condition, though."

"Yessir?"

"De Tomas must be taken alive and placed on public trial. Too many of your people have come to love him. I don't know how in the hell he managed that, but he has. The only way a truly honest and representative government can succeed him is if his crimes are aired and the people realize at last what a monster he is. If you can guarantee Gorman immunity, he'll sing like a canary. That's all I ask. Can you guarantee me that?"

"I'll do my best, Mr. Ambassador."

Spears held out his hand. They shook.

"General," Spears said in his normal voice, "let's go back to your office and have some more of that excellent army coffee!"

# CHAPTER
## TWENTY-TWO

Yamagata Shannon grinned up at Prisoner 9639, revealing the gaps in his rotten teeth. "This'll hurt *you* a lot more than it will me," he said, giggling. The bright lamplight glinting off his spectacles gave the impression he had no eyes, only huge white holes on either side of his bulbous nose. Prisoner 9639 shivered as he took her forearm and put it firmly into his tattooing device. "The laser does all the work," he explained happily. "In the old days here at Castle Hurse, when all we had were criminals and religious crazies, before you politicals flooded in, we just photographed each new prisoner. But, ah, this laser technology marks a prisoner forever as one of ours, and it's much more fun!" he cackled.

He held up a forefinger. "But first, the obligatory photo! The higher-ups want to see what our ladies look like, dearie! That bruise on your jaw doesn't look so pretty, my pretty, but yes, you are buxom, quite buxom. They shall be pleased. Look into the camera, please!" A bright flash, and a few seconds later 9639's digital image printed out of the computer. Shannon slipped it into her dossier. "And now," he crowed happily, "the *zapper*!" Shannon fiddled with the controls, double-checking the prisoner's number against the number on her dossier, and then, smiling, hit Enter.

Prisoner 9639 screamed shrilly as the laser burned the numbers 9639 into the flesh of her left forearm. Shannon giggled and pretended to sniff eagerly at the odor of singed flesh that filled the little room. "You get used to it," he said to no one in particular. "When hairy-armed men come through here, whew!" He handed one of the SG guards 9639's dossier and called out, "Next!"

Supporting 9639 by her armpits, two SG guards hustled her out of the little room and down a long corridor. She tried to walk, but her guards were moving too quickly so she was simply dragged along the corridor to a door at one end. One of the guards knocked respectfully.

"Come," a soft voice called from the other side. The room was bare except for a single folding table, a chair, and a lamp suspended from the ceiling. Behind the table sat a man in the uniform of the Special Group. He had the rank insignia of an overstormer, the equivalent of a captain. One of the guards handed him 9639's dossier. "Sit," he commanded. He opened the dossier and glanced at the single sheet of paper inside. "If you do not answer my questions, or if I find you have lied or exaggerated in any detail, your guards will discipline you immediately." He nodded, and one of the men grabbed 9639 between her neck and shoulder and squeezed. She screamed. "See? Are we ready to proceed?"

Tears of agony streaming down her cheeks, 9639 nodded numbly.

"Good," the overstormer said. His voice was soft and pleasant. He appeared to be a man in his middle years, a slight fringe of gray about the edges of his closely cropped hair. "I like for these interrogation sessions to go smoothly and pleasantly. First, I am Overstormer Rudolf, commandant of Castle Hurse. You will address me—and every member of my staff—by their rank. You will assume the position of attention when addressing one of us. You are Prisoner 9639, the only name that you will have here. That is how you will be addressed, and that is the only name you will answer to while you are here. Is that understood?"

Prisoner 9639 tried to rise out of the chair to stand at attention, but Rudolf waved her back down. "That rule will only apply when you leave this room. Do you understand?"

"Y-Yes," 9639 answered, "M-Mister Over—"

"Overstormer. Now. Tell me about yourself. Do you have

any special training or skills? Be honest, 9639. Don't tell me you're a scientist when all you really are is a peasant."

Prisoner 9639 admitted to being a member of the City of God and said her father was a farmer at New Salem and that they had miraculously survived the attack at the Sea of Gerizim. "I have no particular skills. I helped my mother and sometimes worked on the farm with my father."

"You know how to shoot."

She thought quickly. "We used those rifles for hunting. My father taught me the skill."

"Are you married?"

"No, Overstormer."

"Boyfriend?" Rudolf grinned.

"No, Overstormer."

"Hmmm. A pretty young girl like you? Hard to believe."

"Overstormer, how—how long will I b-be here?"

Rudolf smiled. "You will never leave here, 9639. You killed a man of the Special Group while he was acting in his official capacity and wounded several others, one seriously. You are lucky they did not kill you on the scene. Your case will be reviewed at the highest level. A decision will be pending shortly. Life?" He held up his right hand. "Or death?" He held up his left hand and made the motion of weighing her fate. "The best you can hope for is life."

"But—But those men attacked us! They killed my mother. I was only defending—"

One of the guards gripped 9639 behind her right ear and pulled upward. The pain was so intense she quickly rose to her feet, then struggled to catch her breath when he let go of her.

"You forgot to ask my permission to speak, 9639." Rudolf smiled. "Now. You will be assigned to a barracks with other female prisoners. Each barracks is under the direct control of a prisoner who has been specially designated as barracks chief. She will assign you a place to sleep and explain the other rules of Castle Hurse to you. You will obey her as you obey the members of my staff. Do you have any questions, 9639?"

Prisoner 9639, white-faced, cheeks tearstained, glared at Overstormer Rudolf for a moment and then shouted, "May God damn your soul to eternal hellfire! May God damn all of you! Hear me, Lord! Damn these monsters, damn—"

When Prisoner 9639 regained consciousness, she was lying in a bunk in one of the women's barracks.

Back in his office, Overstormer Rudolf entered a note in her file. Good-looking girl, he thought, shame to kill someone so pretty. He thought of his own daughters and his lovely wife. They were having staff over tonight for a dinner party. He would arrange for some talented prisoners to provide the music. There were two former concert violinists among the prisoners at Castle Hurse just now. They would be delighted to play for an extra ration. It was important to maintain the attributes of civilization in a place like this, separate the official world from the private world.

Overstormer Rudolf lit a cigarette. Back to work. Well, he was only a jailer. He initialed the sheet and closed the file. In the morning he would send it to Wayvelsberg with the others.

In the file he had written: "Plucky girl. Break her."

Prisoner 9639 awoke on her bunk. A hulking, short-haired woman loomed over her. "Rise and shine, my beauty," she rumbled.

"Please . . . ?"

"My name is Munglo Patti, chief of Barracks Ten. When I say 'shit,' you shit. Now get your pretty ass out of that bunk and stand at attention!"

Painfully, Prisoner 9639 staggered to her feet. Munglo Patti carefully inspected her. She carried a thick, leaden truncheon with which she prodded 9639, not particularly looking for anything, just toying with her. "You're a real mess," Patti snorted. She nodded at a woman who stood with a pile of clothes in her arms. "Strip," she told 9639. Slowly, 9639 began to take her clothes off. "Underwear too." Patti stood by impatiently, tapping a booted foot on the floorboards. "Change into these clothes."

The other woman, a mousy type with furtive eyes, quickly deposited the clothing on 9639's bunk and stepped back out of the way. It was then that 9639 noticed she was wearing a green brassard on her right arm.

"Hurry!" Patti urged impatiently. "The others will be back from their work shifts in a few minutes, and then we'll have evening roll call."

Prisoner 9639 slipped into a loose-fitting gray smock that reached down to just below her knees and sealed up the front. She slipped her feet into ankle boots a size too large for her, then looked at the yellow armband and slipped it over her right sleeve. "Good!" Patti exclaimed. "You're a political. You get yellow. We crooks get green." She laughed. "And the religious crazies wear pink. You'll see them, but at a distance. They're quarantined."

A shapeless duffel coat with a hood completed the outfit. "Slip the armband on the *outside* of the coat, idiot!" Patti said. Awkwardly, 9639 did as she was told. "Okay, beautiful, here're the rules in one quick lesson. We have roll call three times each day—dawn, noon, and dusk. Be there. Only excuses are sick call, work, the commandant's order, or death. When I call out your number, answer, '9639 present, Barracks Chief!' No ad-libbing, no stuttering, hear me?

"We eat twice a day, after morning and evening roll call. You won't get fat on the food they give you here. If they don't execute you and you get to learn the ropes, there are ways to get good food and other things you might need. The doctor will inspect you tomorrow. He'll decide if you're able to work, and then the commandant will assign your work detail.

"Whenever a staff officer passes by, you are to come to attention. Never speak to a member of the staff without permission, and use that person's rank when addressing him or her. There's a chart of Special Group and penal service ranks on the wall by the latrine. Memorize it. If you slip up, you'll be beaten. Punishment at Castle Hurse ranges from a verbal admonition to death. Believe me, sweetie, the latter is the preferred method around here, makes for fewer mouths to feed. None of us will ever get out of here alive, and the commandant, who is responsible to no one but his superiors in the Special Group, does not care if we live or die. Here, we are all enemies of the state. And let me tell you, sweetie, you politicals are on the lowest rung of the ladder, even below the religious crazies. So keep your mouth shut, follow the rules, don't cause any trouble, and you might live awhile longer. Otherwise, it's Suburbia for you for sure."

Munglo's face became animated when she lectured. Her black, squinty eyes glistened, her face reddened, and saliva flecked her lips. Her high cheekbones turned her eyes into narrow slits when she was angry, and she was always angry. She had a stocky, very well-muscled body. As barracks chief, she was solely responsible for discipline in her barracks, and for performing the job well she received preferential treatment from the commandant and his staff. She was ruthless, and more than once had beaten a transgressor to death with her truncheon. She had to, to maintain her position. Otherwise she knew she'd be relieved and go before the firing squad.

Munglo Patti had been a prisoner at Castle Hurse for five years. Her crime was murder.

A whistle shrilled. "That's it. Roll call. Out into the street!"

It was overcast, damp, and misty. A cool wind blew down the street between the barracks buildings. About a hundred women in four ranks stood in front of 9639's barracks. All along the street other women were also standing in ranks. Farther off, in another compound surrounded by a high, apparently electrified fence, was the men's compound, and hundreds of them were also standing rigidly in ranks. Ten-meter-high guard towers were spaced at intervals along the fence.

A stormleader stood huddled in his greatcoat, a voice projector in one hand. He raised it. "Barracks Chiefs! Begin the count!"

Slowly, Munglo Patti walked down the ranks, checking

each prisoner off her roster as she called out her number. Several times Patti used her truncheon, leaving unfortunate women doubled over and retching. Prisoner 9639 began to perspire. *How did Patti tell her to respond at roll call? Dear God, she couldn't remember! Was it . . . ? No! Should she request permission first before responding? Oh, dear God, what am I doing in this terrible place?* She thought of her family, her friends, her home, and tears flowed down her cheeks.

"Stop whining like a snuffling little mama's girl," Patti grated. She nudged 9639 with her truncheon, and shouted, "9639!"

"Prisoner 9639 present, Barracks Chief!" she croaked. Patti checked her off her list and passed on down the rank.

"Easy, girl," an older woman standing to 9639's right whispered without moving her lips. "The bitch ain't so bad if you stay out of her way."

Patti whirled and stomped back to stand in front of 9639. "I have *very* sensitive hearing, ladies! What the hell did you say? I heard somebody whispering! Who was it? You, 9639? You'll do. Goddamnit, no talking in ranks!" She slammed her truncheon into 9639's left shoulder, glared at the women standing rigidly in the rank, then went on with her count.

"Sorry," the woman to her right whispered.

Eyes blurry with tears, holding her left shoulder with her free hand, 9639 nodded. "It's okay," she whispered.

Finished with her count, Patti took up her place four paces to the front center of the first rank. "Report!" the stormleader shouted. Each barracks chief reported her count. There were twenty barracks buildings in that section of the prison compound.

"Barracks Ten! All present and accounted for!" Patti shouted when her turn came.

But still the roll call went on, as recounts were demanded to resolve discrepancies and the stormleader's questions about absences were answered. Several times he stopped the reports to hold whispered conversations with his sergeant.

It began to rain and dusk closed in. Still, the hundreds of women stood there at attention. The men, they could see, had long since been dismissed.

"Barracks Chiefs!" the stormleader announced as the last vestiges of daylight faded. "Dismiss your prisoners!" By now they were drenched, shivering in the cold.

"Follow me," the woman who'd been standing to 9639's right said. Prisoner 9639 noted she was a green-armband inmate. The woman took her elbow and guided her between the barracks buildings toward a huge wooden structure into which long lines of women were disappearing. "Time to eat," the older woman announced.

Inside the dining hall each woman took a tin bowl, a spoon, and a tin cup out of bins and stood in the serving line. Indifferent cooks, also prisoners, handed each person in line a slice of black bread and ladled out soup and a weak concoction called coffee as the cups and bowls were held out. The two found seats on a bench at a long trestle table and sat down. "My name is 9606," the woman announced as she spooned the soup into her mouth.

Prisoner 9639 did not realize how hungry she was, even though the "soup"—a greasy concoction of tepid water, thin strips of tasteless meat, and soggy "vegetables"—was sickening. The "coffee" tasted like swamp water. But 9639 consumed it all in under a minute. "What's your name?" she asked 9606.

"*Never* ask a prisoner that! The only person who has a name among us is our barracks chief. That's a privilege they get for taking the job, and one reason she's killed to keep it. And if you find out someone's real name, never use it. If you are overheard, you will be beaten senseless. We exist here only by the numbers they've given us. We have no other identity. You get used to it. You may wonder why 9606 is standing next to 9639. That's because the women with the intervening numbers are all dead. They never reissue numbers."

All around them women ate their meal amid loud conversations. Several fights started—over what, nobody knew—

and the combatants, rolling on the floor and pulling each other's hair, were objects of high amusement. The fights ended as quickly as they started. "May I ask why you are here, 9606? You seem to be a decent person," the newcomer said.

Prisoner 9606 shrugged and slurped the last of her soup. "Embezzlement, 9639. I worked in the administrative offices of the Fathers of Padua sect. I skimmed quite a bit off their accounts for myself. They gave me life." Prisoner 9639 mouthed the word "life" in astonishment. "Yeah, life," 9606 confirmed. "That was ten years ago. That's right, *ten years* in this hole. That was before even our Great and Wonderful Leader appeared on the scene to 'free' us from the clutches of the sects." She laughed cynically and lowered her voice. "These sonsabitches are all alike, 9639. All alike." She paused and regarded the bottom of her soup bowl. "Take that stormleader this evening. Whenever that bastard is duty officer, he loves to hold us in formation until way after dark, just inventing reasons to keep us in ranks. The worse the weather, the more he enjoys himself. Someday I'm going to cut his goddamned balls off for him."

"You'll have to stand in line, dearie," a painfully thin woman sitting next to 9606 said. "I'm 9432." She held out her hand to 9639.

"You'll like 9432, 9639," 9606 said. "She's in here for manslaughter. Cut her husband's equipment off and fed it to him." Then 9606 laughed so hard she started coughing. The coughing brought up spittle flecked with black and red. "What I wouldn't give for a cigarette now," she gasped.

"He didn't die," 9432 added, "but they gave me life for it anyway."

"I love my husband," 9606 offered after she'd gotten her breath back. "We were a team. He's over on the men's side. I think. Maybe he died. He got life, same time I did. What did you do, 9639? You don't look 'political' to me."

Briefly, 9639 explained what had happened back at New Salem. "Whew!" 9432 exclaimed, "*killed* one of them, huh? Honey, it's Suburbia for you for sure!"

"What's Suburbia? Patti said I might go there. Is it like—like solitary confinement or something?"

Prisoner 9606 glared at 9432. "That's a remote section of the prison compound," she answered after a brief hesitation. "It's where the executions are held. We call it 'Suburbia' because that sounds better than calling the place what it really is—you know, like 'kicked the bucket,' 'bought the farm.' When someone says, 'She's gone to Suburbia,' well, you know what that means. But honey, if they were gonna execute you, they'd have done that already. At least not until your case can be reviewed. You know that within the last few months the dossiers of all new female prisoners are personally reviewed by someone at Wayvelsberg Castle?"

"What, or where, is Wayvelsberg Castle?"

"It's the Leader's headquarters."

"Why?"

"Who the hell knows—or cares? Maybe they're looking to get laid up there," 9432 cackled. "But hell, old hags like me and 9606, we've got nothing to worry about!"

"What do we do now?" 9639 asked.

"We turn in our utensils and go back to our barracks and they lock us in," 9432 said. "And remember, never, but *never,* keep the flatware! They inventory it after every meal, and if they find any missing, the guards tear the barracks apart until it's found. You can take a spoon and turn it into a weapon if you work at it hard enough. Remember this too: terrible things are done to people here, but nothing, *nothing,* is permitted that is not authorized specifically by either the commandant or the duty officer. So if a guard rapes someone or beats someone up on his own, he's in trouble. And suicide is against prison regulations."

"At twenty-two hours sharp the lights go out," 9606 added. "Between now and then we can do what we like, provided we do it inside our barracks. What is your work assignment, 9639?"

"I don't know yet. Munglo told me I'll get that after I see the doctor tomorrow."

"Can you do anything special? Workwise?"

"N-No. I helped a bit with the farming—"

"We have a farm here. You could go there," 9606 said.

"Try to get into the kitchen," 9432 volunteered. "It's indoors and you get better rations. I'm on the compound beautification detail myself. I'm outdoors a lot but the work is easy."

"The porcelain factory isn't bad either, especially if you can get into the offices," 9606 informed her. "I worked there for several years. I was a glazer, put high-fire glazes on things. We used calcium or barium as flux, you know? 'Feldspathic' glazes, they were called, since we used feldspar as a source of alumina and silica. I kept the kiln at 1250 degrees centigrade. Hard-paste porcelain, is what it was. I think that's where I picked up this goddamned cough." She smiled wistfully. "Now I'm in the laundry." She sighed. "The best thing about the factory," she brightened, "is that you get to meet some of the men and people from outside. The contacts you can make at the factory can get you stuff you need in here."

"*Don't* get assigned to the clay quarries," 9432 advised. "You ride there in a closed van and they work you in all weather. Mostly that's for the male prisoners, and they don't last long out there."

"What about our barracks chief?"

"Patti?" 9432 responded. "She's not a bad sort. She has to be hard to keep her position, and we all respect that. Stay on her good side and she'll look out for you."

"How do I do that?" 9639 asked.

The two older women exchanged glances. "Just obey her orders."

Sleep did not come easily to 9639 that first night at Castle Hurse. Her fellow inmates continued whispered conversations until well after lights out. It was after midnight before she finally dozed off.

She was awakened by someone's hands on her. At first she didn't realize where she was. "Don't say anything," Munglo Patti whispered in her ear. So this was what "looking out" for a fellow inmate meant? She fastened her teeth on Patti's ear-lobe and bit down as hard as she could. "Aarrgghh! Bitch! Bitch!" the barracks chief shrieked, and broke off her contact. "You're dead! You're dead!" Patti screamed, holding a hand to her bleeding ear.

"Good!" 9639 shouted back. "Kill me! I don't care! I've killed real men, and devils, *devils* in armed combat, you monster. Do you think I'm afraid of *you*? Put your hands on me again and you're out of a job around here!" She wiped Patti's blood off her lips and spit.

"You're dead! You're dead!" Patti screamed again, then turned and ran for the latrines.

Someone began to laugh. "Good work, girl," an inmate whispered.

"You'll be gone in the morning, new girl," someone else said, "but by God, we won't forget you very soon!" Someone at the far end of the room began to applaud softly, and then all the women joined in.

Prisoner 9639 lay in her bunk, shivering with anger, fear, and despair. Dear God in heaven, help me! she prayed. Why am I here? What kind of world is this? She began to weep. She drew her thin blanket over her face and stuffed it into her mouth to stifle her sobs. Mother! Father! she called silently. Ah, they were dead! Gone! *"Charles,"* she groaned aloud, but he was dead too. She was alone. And lost. She had only the Lord to stand by her now. *Oh, Death, where is thy sting?*

The overstormer in charge of morning roll call noticed Barracks Chief Munglo Patti's earlobe and called her over. "What happened, Barracks Chief?" he asked.

"I cut myself shaving this morning, Overstormer!" Patti answered immediately.

The overstormer stared at her blankly for a long moment and turned to his sergeant, silently asking, Did I hear her right? The man shrugged. " 'Shaving'?" the overstormer asked, and then his face lighted up and he burst out laughing. "Shaving! She was 'shaving,' storm man! Shaving!" The two almost collapsed with laughter. Tears streaming down his cheeks, the sergeant bellowed, "Let's look and see if she's got scratches on her back!" and that sent the two into further gales of laughter.

Roll call for Barracks Ten went very smoothly that morning.

# CHAPTER
# TWENTY-THREE

Charlie Bass awoke to the sound of someone weeping.

The blast that had knocked him out hadn't injured him seriously, although he did sustain numerous cuts and bruises. The tang of burned wood stung his nostrils. It was almost dawn, first light, that time of day when one can read a newspaper without artificial light. Automatically, he glanced at the ridge on the outside of town. Nothing, at least nothing he could see in the early morning light. Around him lay the shapeless heaps that had once been the members of the Judah family.

Zechariah Brattle cradled Consort's body in his arms. It was he who was weeping.

"Zach—Zechariah," Bass whispered. His throat felt like dried newsprint from the last century. *"Zechariah."* Bass stumbled to his feet and staggered over to where Zechariah sat on the ground. "Wh-Where's Comfort?" Bass croaked. He swallowed and collected more saliva in his mouth. He forced himself to look at Consort. She'd been shot in the chest at point-blank range. He could see the jagged white of her rib cage. What kind of bastard would shoot a wounded woman like that? Bass wondered, but he already knew. Men sometimes went wild in combat and shot everything that moved—until it didn't move anymore. "Where's Comfort?" he asked again.

Zechariah shook his head. "I don't know. Gone. They're all gone now. They're in God's hands."

The thought of Comfort dead cut through Charlie Bass like a red-hot knife blade. "We should look for her, Zechariah," he croaked, laying a comforting hand on the grieving man's shoulder. "Come on, Zechariah, we've got to get a move on. They'll be back as soon as it's light. Come on."

Zechariah shook his head. "No. It's all in God's hands now. I don't care what happens to me. I'm staying with my Consort."

Bass decided not to argue with the man. He walked around the house swiftly and then just as quickly searched the house itself, but no sign of Comfort. That was a relief. The Judah boy lay just inside the front door. His eyes were still open but he was already dead. Bass shook his head sorrowfully and stepped back outside.

"Zechariah, *leave* her. We've got to get under cover. *Now.*"

"I—I *can't* just leave her here like this!" Zechariah whined. The front of his shirt was soaked in his wife's blood.

"We *must,* for now anyway. They'll be back, those men. When they come, we want the bodies where they can see them. Make them think they got us all. Do you understand, Zechariah? When the danger is past, we can give them a decent burial. There was another family came back with us, the Rowleys? Have you seen them?"

"L-Leave Consort here? Like this?" He ignored the question of the Rowleys, and so did Bass. If they'd been killed, so be it. If captured, as he expected Comfort had been, then it might not make much difference what precautions they took. Flight through the caves was the only alternative. They'd know soon enough. Anyway, now there was no time to spare digging graves and conducting funereal obsequies.

"Until they've made their reconnaissance and satisfied themselves we're no longer a threat to them. Yes. Now come on, Zechariah."

"*No!* I can't, Charles! I'm staying here, and if they come back I'll die here."

Bass sighed. "Zechariah, you remember what you did after Samuel was killed? You've told me about it often enough. You went back to your people because they needed your leadership. You refused to let your grief infect them. Remember? Well, you've got to put Consort down now, Zechariah, and come back with me to the caves. Your people still need you. I can't lead them without you."

Zechariah shook his head and groaned, holding Consort's mangled body even closer and tighter.

Bass drove his fist into the side of Zechariah's head and then pulled the stunned man to his feet. He grabbed him by his belt and shoved him bodily toward the caves. "You aren't going to crap out on me now, goddamnit!" Zechariah staggered, and Bass shoved him again. He stumbled in the dust, and Bass picked him up. "Keep moving. Keep moving," Bass urged, looking over his shoulder as he propelled Zechariah forward, his eyes on the sky in the direction the fighters had come from. They were well into the scrub when an Avenging Angel swooped down on the village, flying slowly and very low. Bass pushed Zechariah under some bushes and crawled in after him.

"Why didn't we pretend we were dead and lay out there for them to see us?" Zechariah asked.

Bass smiled. Zechariah was himself again.

"Because if they come back later and we're not there, they'll notice there aren't as many bodies as there were."

"Oh. Charles?"

"Yeah?" Bass warily eyed the sunlight glinting off the aircraft's frame as it cruised in a circle over the ruins of New Salem. Apparently, it was just a reconnaissance flight, not a bombing sortie.

"I'm sorry. I lost control. Thank you. Thank you, Charles."

"Don't mention it, old friend. Look, I'm sorry I hit you like that. I couldn't think of what else to do."

Zechariah rubbed the side of his head where Bass had struck him. "Next time, try bribing me with a cold bottle of beer." He chuckled. Then he groaned. "God forgive me for that. I shouldn't be talking like that with my beloved wife and my beautiful daughter dead."

"I don't think Comfort's dead, Zechariah." The Avenging Angel roared away. "Let's just stay here for a while."

*"Not dead?"*

"No. I think they captured her, Zechariah."

"Oh, thank God! I pray you're right Charles! Alleluia! Praise the Lord!" Zechariah began to weep again, this time tears of joy. Immediately, he got control of himself. "I'm sorry, Charles, it's just so—"

"You don't need to apologize to me. Hell, who could keep a dry eye after what's just happened?" He thought of Comfort and had to exert an effort to control his breathing.

"What do we do now, Charles?"

"Now?" Bass laid a hand on Zechariah's shoulder. "Right now we're going back to the caves and get your people organized. And then, Zechariah, I am going to get Comfort back for you."

The doctor's examination was perfunctory and consisted of asking 9639 routine questions about her medical history. He was an older man, much older than the commandant. His face was thin and narrow and his expression sour. He wore an immaculate white lab coat over his black SG uniform. His black boots shined like mirrors. He was very diffident in his physical exam, such as it was, as if reluctant to get his hands dirty touching his patient.

"You may dress now." Quickly, 9639 slipped back into her prison garb. "You'll do. You can work," he said at last, as he made a note in her dossier, which he handed to the guard. He leaned back, put his hands in the pockets of his lab coat and grinned. "You had a fight with your barracks chief last night? But you have no marks on your body, 9639. Who won?"

She gasped in surprise. *How did he know about that?* "It was nothing, er—" She hesitated because with that lab coat over his uniform she couldn't see his rank. "—*Mister* Doctor."

"I am Understormleader Shirbaz, 9639. I could not care less what happens in the barracks. All I do is patch you up so you can return to work or bury you, whichever occurs first. Ah, 9639, I see you are surprised! You have studied the rank chart in the barracks, haven't you, and you are wondering why an understormleader, who comes between overstormer and overstormleader, is not *himself* the camp commandant?

It is a question that has occurred to many. That is because I am a *medical* officer, and medical officers *never* command anything but a medical unit. So I sit here, day in and day out, looking up your dirty behinds, and take orders from people with half the education and experience I have."

Having had no idea of the doctor's relative rank, she really was surprised now. He was the first staff member so far to talk to her as if she was a real person. Despite the way he'd lewdly gazed at her nakedness during the "exam," she felt a twinge of sympathy for the man. And it was evident to her that this was a sore point with him and that he'd given that speech many times before.

"Well, 9639, good luck. If you learn to fight like an animal, you may be barracks chief someday. Take her to the commandant's office," the doctor ordered.

Once again 9639 stood before the commandant. "Sit," he said, reading her file and not bothering to look up at her. She sat. He looked up. "Now, 9639, the doctor says you are fit to work. Since your ultimate fate has not yet been resolved, I cannot assign you somewhere permanently. All my staff are screaming for prison help. You have no particular skills. So, you will work in the kitchen until ultimate disposition of your case." He slammed her dossier shut. She expected to be dismissed, but he kept her sitting there for a long moment and then reopened her dossier. "I want to go over some things with you."

"Yes, Overstormer."

"During the initial interview with the Special Group personnel who captured you, you stated that you were one of the sole survivors of the demons' attack on your sect at the Sea of Gerizim. You said that, let's see, um, sixteen of you, all told, out of those thousands, survived the attack. Tell me how that came to be. Did you know that the Special Group identified only ten bodies in the ruins of the village after their attack?"

"No, Overstormer, I did not know that. I saw the Judahs killed and—and my mother. I don't know what happened to the Rowleys and my father. My brother, I told them, had been killed earlier. Perhaps the other bodies are in the ruins somewhere?"

"Um. How did you survive all those months?"

She told him about the night the devils attacked and how they managed to get by after that. She omitted everything else that had happened over the last months. She was confident that the rest of the survivors were safely hiding in the caves. She prayed silently this interrogation was not a trick, that she was the only prisoner, that there was no one to contradict the story she had told. Then she thought, So what? What are they going to do if they find out? Send me to jail?

Overstormer Rudolf listened attentively. "How did you kill the soldiers who attacked your village? They reported you were in fortified positions some distance from the village and that you used acid weapons on them." Evidently someone had just passed this information to Rudolf, or he would have asked it earlier.

She thought fast. The interrogation the Special Group men had given her just after her capture had been only perfunctory. She remembered them, highly excited men, slapping each other on the back and laughing as if they'd just come through a tremendous battle safely. They acted like drunks, she thought at the time. She could see that clearly through her fear and pain.

"Many years ago we built a water catchment in a ravine outside the village, to trap runoff for our cattle, and we hid in there during the bombing. It was not a fort, Overstormer. We used shot rifles, old-fashioned things like shotguns that we found in the abandoned camp above the Sea of Gerizim, after the devils attacked it. They were not expecting resistance. It was easy to kill them. I don't know what they mean by acid guns, Overstormer." She paused. "We came out in the night to get things from the homes that were not destroyed. Then these other soldiers came."

"Um. You're lying, 9639." Rudolf slammed her dossier closed with a bang. "I know that. You know that. But who cares about a bunch of ragtag Bible-thumpers? I don't give a good goddamn. I'm a jailer, not an intelligence officer. You

will write down your statement in full. Here is writing material. I am leaving you with your guard. When you finish,
leave your statement on the desk and he will take you to the
kitchen."

"Oh, dear God, have mercy on us!" Hannah Flood groaned
when Zechariah told her about the attack.

"Charles," Spencer Maynard pleaded, "we didn't dare come
out. We heard the shooting and could see the aircraft hovering and we were really scared! We were afraid they'd come
down here to investigate. The reconnaissance car would be
plain to see. I don't know why they didn't come here."

"It was night, Spencer, and there was a lot of shooting—
anyway, they may not even have known about the car," Bass
answered. He surveyed the faces of the people anxiously
gathered inside the cave. They reflected horror, fear, and
anger. They were on the edge of breaking down.

"We thought you were all dead," Samuel Sewall croaked.
He came forward and embraced Zechariah, tears in his
rheumy old eyes. The others crowded around Zechariah and
offered him their condolences.

Bass took Raipur aside. "Those men were wearing black
uniforms, body armor, shooting everything in sight. Who
were they?"

"Special Group men," Raipur answered at once. "Not our
bunch, Charles. Do you know who the Special Group are?"

"Something to do with enforcing orthodoxy, like an inquisition. I haven't had much time to study your culture since
coming here."

Raipur briefly filled him in on recent events.

"They took Comfort—that's Zechariah Brattle's daughter.
They may have captured some of the Rowley family, we
don't know. But if they did, it won't be very long before they
come back for the rest of us."

"If they have the girl, aren't we already done for?"

Bass thought for a moment. "Maybe not. Comfort's a
tough and smart little lady, and she's as brave as any man
among us. I think she could hold up under interrogation."

"Well, if the Special Group comes back out here, I won't be of any help to you, Charles. And I know my platoon commander. He won't be back without heavy reinforcements, and obviously it was decided not to send them. So there goes your peace overture. But Charles, I hate those people as much as you do, and I think most of the men in my army feel the same way about them. But what do we do now?"

"Well, not everything's come back to me yet, but I'm pretty sure I am a citizen of the Confederation and was here as part of its military force. The Confederation has an embassy or something at Haven, right?"

"Yes. At Interstellar City."

"Then that's where I'm headed. I'm going to find out just who the hell I am, and then I'm going to find out where Comfort Brattle is and I'm going to get her back."

"How will you do that?" Raipur asked, astonished. "I mean, how are you going to get there? It's far, far away. And—And what'll you do once you get there, assuming you do?"

"I'll walk. And I'll free Comfort with my bare hands, if I have to."

"By yourself?"

"No, I may need a few good men. Are you with me?"

"Yes, I am, Charles."

The woman in charge of the kitchen was a huge mountain of flesh. When she moved, her several chins jiggled. She was always huffing and puffing and perspiring, and her face was constantly red from exertion. She had a pronounced mustache on her upper lip that she constantly brushed with the back of her hand. A cigarette butt always stuck out one side of her mouth, sometimes lit, sometimes not. And she laughed a lot.

"You are a KP, that's kitchen police, dearie," she told 9639 as soon as the guard dropped her off at the kitchen. She draped one enormous arm around 9639's shoulders. "Everywhere in Human Space machines do all the hard work, dearie. But not here. Everywhere else you press a button, I'm told, and machines wash your clothes; press another set, and they clean your house; a third, and they prepare your food. For all I know they have buttons to make machines do their fucking for them too. But at Castle Hurse we do our work the old-fashioned way, with our hands. Hard work is good for us, 9639. Takes our minds off things like oh, sex, food, escape, the usual.

"We start work here at three hours every morning, seven days a week, and all of us work until after nineteen hours, sometimes even as late as twenty-three or even 01, depending on the availability of rations and the preparation we need to get the following day's stuff ready. But we have it good in here, 9639. It's always warm, we get good rations—hell's bells, how do you think I maintain this girlish figure?" She shook with laughter. "And the work is easy. You work hard for me, show you're willing to learn, and in time I'll teach you how to be a cook. But for now you're a KP and *do I have a job for you*!"

She shuddered. "Yes, 8372?"

"Come on." Prisoner 8372 led her to the back of the kitchen. She stooped and with one enormous hand removed an iron grating in the floor. "Do you know what this is?"

"No, 8372," she answered as she peered cautiously into the floor. An oily substance gleamed back at her.

"It's the grease trap, honey! It has to be cleaned daily. You dip it out and put the stuff in cans out back to be picked up. Over there on the wall are some rubber gloves, a ladle, and a container. The galvanized can out back is marked 'Grease.' If the outside girl is screwing off somewhere, don't get it confused with the 'Edible' and 'Nonedible' garbage cans, okay? When you're done with that, find me and I'll give you something else to do. Maybe pots and pans?" She laughed enormously and waddled off singing a nonsensical ditty, "—and his ghost may be heard, a-singing in the grease trap, 'You come a-peeling potatoes with me, peeling potatoes, peeling potatoes, you come a-peeling potatoes with me!' "

Prisoner 9639 pulled on the gloves and knelt on the floor.

Her stomach churned uncomfortably at the task before her. She got to work.

The next days passed quickly and relatively pleasantly, for life at Castle Hurse. Barracks Chief Patti studiously ignored 9639. "But," 9606 warned her, "she'll get you for what you did to her, so watch your back."

Prisoner 9639 found her companions in the kitchen to be mostly a very tight-knit, hospitable group, reflecting 8372's attitude, which was easygoing. She knew that 8372 was also a "political" prisoner. Her crime had been to join a small protest group that was formed shortly after de Tomas assassinated the Convocation of Ecumenical Ministers. For that she'd gotten life. She said she was lucky—the other members of her group had just disappeared.

Early one morning a few days later, the entire barracks was awakened by 9606's coughing, which had gotten steadily worse. "I'm not long for this world," she confided to 9639 at supper. Prisoner 9639 recalled how she'd coughed up blood into her soup bowl, and then, in the pale moonlight streaming in through the windows, 9606 lay drenched in perspiration and gasping for air. Large quantities of blood stained the bedclothes.

"We must get her to the dispensary," 9639 pleaded with the other women standing around 9606's bunk.

"You idiot," Barracks Chief Patti said. It was the first time she'd addressed 9639 directly in days. She smiled in the wan moonlight, knowing 9606 was friends with 9639. "You don't leave the barracks for any reason after lights out. And sick call is only held between 06 and 08 hours in the mornings! The doctor doesn't make house calls in here!"

"But we can't just stand here and do nothing!" 9639 protested in tears.

Someone laid a hand on 9639's shoulder. "It happens, honey. Get used to it. Nobody is going to get up in the middle of the night for any of us."

She grabbed 9606's hand and began to pray. The sick woman struggled up on her elbow. In the dim light her face looked as pale as the moon that hung in the sky outside. Bubbles of blood formed on her lips as she tried to speak. "I—My name—is Mary Dungarvan. *Mary Dungarvan!*" she shouted. The effort exhausted her and she lay back. A little while later she gave an enormous hacking cough and died.

Prisoner 9639 wept bitterly. Patti, cursing that they'd have to clean up the mess in the morning, stomped back into her room at the end of the barracks.

"Come with me," someone said. She put her hand on 9639's shoulder and gently led her into the washroom. It was pitch-black in there. The woman produced a tiny glow ball. "Get caught with this and you're dead," she whispered. The ball cast a dim light that the woman shielded with her hands. She squatted in one corner and said, "Grab this panel here and pull it up and then out. Come on! Come on! We don't have all night! I think you can be trusted now. I want to show you our secret."

She did as she was told, and after some effort, the panel came loose in her hands. The other woman held the glow ball close to its back side. "See?" The back of the panel was covered with names, hundreds of them! "Mary's is in there somewhere. So am I. So is everyone, from the time this building was first occupied," she whispered.

She handed 9639 a nail. "The panels adjacent to this one are all full, but there's still room on this one. Write small and write so it can be read. We do this so we don't forget who we are. That's a key to survival in this place. The other is that we help each other. Don't believe that nonsense Patti is always telling us, 'Every woman for herself and damn the hindmost!' If you believe that, you'll die. We survive by helping each other, looking out for each other, remembering who we are, and remembering there's a world outside this place and someday we'll all be free again."

"Who are you?" 9639 whispered.

The woman put her lips close to 9639's ear. *"Nong Khai."*

Carefully, Comfort Brattle had scratched her name into the wood.

And then one morning at roll call the duty officer called 9639 out of ranks. "Report to the commandant's office," he said. "You are going for an interview."

Behind her, 9639 could hear Barracks Chief Patti murmuring in a stage whisper, "Suburbia for her! Last we'll see of *that* bitch!"

# CHAPTER
# TWENTY-FOUR

Prisoner 9639 was shackled to the inside of a landcar and driven from Castle Hurse. She couldn't see where they were going since the passenger compartment had neither windows nor vid displays of the outside. She had no way of measuring the passage of time, except she fell asleep for a while and was hungry and needed to relieve herself when she awoke. When the landcar finally stopped and she was let out, she found herself in the huge courtyard of an equally huge castle. Her guards handed her over to two matrons who led her to a chamber with plumbing. They instructed her to disrobe, wash, and void herself. They watched while she did. Afterward they gave her a smock and led her to an opulently appointed office where she was interviewed by a Special Group senior stormleader.

"Welcome to Wayvelsberg Castle, Comfort Brattle," the senior stormleader began. He continued with no other pleasantries. "You are a member of the now defunct City of God sect and your family are all dead?"

"Yes, Senior Stormleader," Comfort answered.

"Do you know why you are here, Miss, um, Brattle, isn't it?"

"No, Senior Stormleader."

He nodded but said nothing. Then, "Have you ever been with child or had sexual relations with a man?"

The question caught Comfort off guard. "No, I have not, Senior Stormleader," she replied after a brief hesitation.

The stormleader looked up suspiciously. "Why did you hesitate with your answer?" he asked sternly.

"I—I was just surprised at the abruptness of the question, Senior Stormleader," Comfort stuttered.

"Yes. Thank you. Now. You are here because someone wishes to interview you for a very special, um, job. You are on the list of interviewees because of, let us say, 'special' qualifications. If you are selected, you will not have the option to refuse, but your selection will mean immediate release from Castle Hurse and, within certain limits, a life of comfort and comparative freedom. Is all this clear to you, miss?"

"Yes, Senior Stormleader," Comfort answered, but thought, What kind of a job?

"You wonder what this employment entails. You will find out during the interview. That will take place in precisely three hours from now, when the candidate before you is finished with her interview. In the meantime,"—the cosmetologists, Gelli Alois and Andrea Rauber, entered at the senior stormleader's signal and stood smiling down at Comfort— "you will accompany these ladies. They will prepare you." He waved the women out of his office with a hand.

Comfort had been impressed with the vastness of Wayvelsberg Castle, the guards snapping to attention, staff rushing about on their business. Now she was ushered into a beauty parlor.

She had heard of such places before, but because her people prided themselves on the simplicity of their lifestyle, no woman of New Salem had ever stepped inside such a place. To the Neo-Puritans, beauty parlors were chambers for the rich and decadent. Now she found herself in one. And she was glad to be there, if only to escape the rigors of Castle Hurse, no matter how temporarily. But she cringed inwardly as Gelli and her assistants applied their washes—she was happy to have them!—and cosmetics, primped and perfumed, then dressed her in expensive silk garments. She longed to wipe the disgusting powders off her face and rip off the false nails they were applying to replace the real ones, scarred and dirty from her work in the kitchen. Her face burned with shame as red as the rouge they were applying. They were turning her into a Babylonian whore!

"You're as skinny as a rail, girl," Gelli exclaimed. She looked at her critically, offering advice and directions to her assistants as they worked over their unwilling customer. "You are in good hands, my dear," Gelli said. "We attend to the beauty needs of the highest party officials' wives and even some of the officials themselves." She laughed. "Your dark brown hair is very beautiful, now that it's been washed. It was filthy. We don't have time to give you a decent bath and still finish all the other things you need, but we'll sponge you off in the proper places and fix you up with deodorants. Take off those clodhoppers." Comfort slipped off her shoes. "Oh, by the Virgin's God-fucked clit, girl!" she exclaimed. "Have you spent your whole life walking through cowshit!" Gelli shook her head in dismay. "Wash her feet—thoroughly! And give her a pedicure," she ordered Andrea Rauber. Comfort's face turned even hotter. Gelli's blasphemy was far worse than her cosmetics. Being in jail with felons was bad enough, but they'd had good reason to use strong language. Those Harpies struck her as just plain indecent.

"We are not undertakers, miss, but we'll come as close as anyone can to putting some *life* back into you!" Gelli sighed and shook her head again. "I see a very nice hairdo coming your way, though. We'll also outfit you with something that'll cover your bones. Despite those bags under your eyes, you have a pretty face, healthy complexion. Open your mouth." Comfort opened her mouth. "No dental work? Your teeth look perfect. Brush them thoroughly and use our special mouthwash before you see him. You'll glow like a spring sunrise before we're through with you. That'll impress him."

"Please, miss," Comfort asked, "just what *is* it you're getting me ready for?"

Gelli looked sympathetically down at Comfort. "We can't tell you. But I can tell you this: better you than me."

"Who knows how to get to Haven?" Bass asked.

"I do," Zechariah answered, "and I'm going with you,

Charles. Comfort is my daughter, and I'm going to get her back and hang anyone who objects."

Bass turned to Raipur. "You haven't changed your mind about coming along?"

"No. And I know where International City is and how to get there," Raipur volunteered. "Besides, I'd be no good to you here," he added, glancing out of the corner of his eye at the Stoughtons.

"How will we get there?" Zechariah asked.

"We walk," Bass replied. "It's what, a hundred fifty, two hundred kilometers? Five, maybe six days on foot?"

"There'll be patrols, Charles, especially if we use main roads."

"We'll use the roads but we'll move at night and rest during the day. If we're stopped, well, that's where you come in, Raipur. We'll ditch our weapons and be refugees, and you'll be leading us to safety, escorting us to civilization. Something. We'll figure it out as we go along. If we run into your folks, I think we'll be all right. Those Special Group people? Well, if we run into them, we'll be in the shit for sure. But I'm going, with company or without."

"I don't think we will run into the SG, Charles. They made their mark. They're mainly enforcers, not combat infantry. But if we do run into them, we'll be able to fight: We can take the individual weapons you got from my recon vehicle."

"Good. Now, I suggest we take Chet and Colleen with us. Any objections?" There were none.

"Who will be in charge back here?" Zechariah asked.

"I'd say you, Zach, but since you're going along, I recommend Spencer Maynard for military matters and Hannah Flood for overall leadership. Will the others accept that?"

"They will. I guarantee they will," Zechariah replied. Bass could tell from the expression on Zach's face that they sure as hell *would* accept the decision.

"It's going to be a rough trip. We can't carry a lot of provisions with us and it won't be easy moving at night, especially if we run into patrols. Let's leave tonight. Zechariah, I promise you one thing."

"Yes, what is that, Charles?"

"When I get in to see the Confederation's ambassador, I'm going to arrange for a lifetime supply of beer, just for you."

"Charles—Lord forgive me for saying this!—but I'd follow you to Hell for a deal like that." The three men shook hands all around.

Comfort had never seen Dominic de Tomas in real life, and the figure that strode into the library did not look very much like his picture. He was handsome. She stood.

"Please, keep your seat." He smiled. "Sit, sit. I want to talk to you for a while." Comfort sat back down, and de Tomas took a seat opposite her at the table. He sat down with an easy grace. He looked at Comfort intently for a few moments, then smiled again. "You think I am a monster, don't you?" he asked, his smile turning sardonic.

Comfort did not know what to say at first, then she decided to be blunt. "Yes. You burned people alive, and you must know what goes on at Castle Hurse where innocent people are tortured and murdered and made to live like animals."

"You killed and wounded some of my men. Tell me about that."

Comfort told the story of her capture. She had gone over the events of that morning so many times that she could now tell the story dry-eyed. As she spoke, de Tomas observed her intensely, watching for any trace of emotion. There was none.

"Your father taught you to shoot like that?"

"Yes."

"What happened to him?"

"I do not know. I think he was killed."

"What went through your mind, when you were shooting up my men?"

Comfort hesitated briefly before answering. "Nothing," she replied at last, shrugging. "I just fired at the men like they were paper targets." She paused. "Oh, I felt satisfied my marksmanship was so good, that I hit every one I shot at except the last one."

"And now? What do you think now?"

"I wish I had shot more of them," Comfort answered without hesitation.

De Tomas smiled. "I appreciate frankness, Miss Brattle. You are 'Miss Brattle' while in this room, not just a prison number. I want to take that number away from you and restore your name."

"You do?"

"Possibly."

"What must I do, then?"

De Tomas shrugged and held out his arms. "Have dinner with me?"

"That is *all*?"

De Tomas nodded. "To begin with."

"And then?"

"We shall see. Serve us," he said, and two SG enlisted men wheeled a cart loaded with steaming dishes into the library. "Are you hungry, miss?"

Comfort nodded. Gnawing hunger had become a constant companion since her incarceration at Castle Hurse, and she hadn't eaten since before she was taken from there, however long ago that was. Her eyes widened at the array of servings on the cart: cooked and cold meats, two kinds of soup, drinks, nuts, fruit, confections, a mouth-watering array of edibles fit for royalty.

"Help yourself, Miss Brattle." De Tomas smiled as he took a thin slice of ham and some vegetables and put them on his plate. He uncorked a bottle of red wine cooling in ice and poured. "Be careful of this wine. Eat something before you taste it. It's a rare vintage. You will like it."

Comfort piled her plate with meat, vegetables, bread. She ignored the soup and other things. At first she tried to eat slowly and delicately, but the food tasted so *good*! She couldn't help herself. Tears streamed down her cheeks as she plunged into the food, devouring it like a starving animal. Then she saw herself as she was at that moment and thought of the other women in Barracks Ten and how they would only get slop for their meal that evening. She stopped eating and wiped her lips with the back of her hand.

"Good, isn't it?" de Tomas asked, smiling over the rim of his wineglass. He had hardly touched his food.

"Y-Yessir. Yes. Very good. Forgive me, I—haven't eaten like this ever before."

"You are no doubt thinking of the vast disparity between life in prison and life here at Wayvelsberg Castle, life anywhere outside Castle Hurse." De Tomas gestured at the unfinished food on Comfort's plate. "That is a fact of life, Miss Brattle. Some live well in this world, some don't; some die young, others die old; and on and on. It is an old story. It is also a fact of life that someone has to make the unpleasant decisions. That lot has fallen to me. I ordered the attack on your village, Miss Brattle. If anyone is responsible for what happened to your family and friends, it is I. I ask you only to understand that I do not make such decisions lightly, and as I am only human, I make mistakes sometimes."

Comfort saw de Tomas's face soften as he spoke and his eyes fill with tears. "I have done things others think were terrible, that's true, Miss Brattle. But I exist only to serve the people of Kingdom, and everything I have ever done was done to that end." He looked down at his plate and toyed with the meat, moving the slices about with his fork. Then he looked up at Comfort. "You haven't touched your wine!"

Comfort looked at the sharp paring knife lying beside the fruit. She saw herself in her mind plunging the blade into de Tomas's throat, the blood spurting. Revenge, she knew, was not a Christian thing, but this one time she would act contrary to God's law. She knew she could do it! Her right hand moved involuntarily toward the fruit. *No, not now,* she told herself, *wait. The time will come.* Her heart raced as she thought of Judith and Holofernes. With her own two hands, like Judith in the Old Testament story she knew so well, she would cut off this monster's head. "Uh, no, sir," she stuttered. "May I have some water?"

De Tomas nodded affably and poured water from a carafe.

"I understand you actually bit off your barracks chief's ear," he said. "Tell me about that." Comfort was no longer surprised that everyone seemed to know the story.

"Well, I didn't actually bite her ear off," she replied, and briefly told him what had happened that night.

De Tomas smiled broadly and nodded. Comfort realized he was enjoying these stories and admired her for what she'd done. It dawned on her, then, that this man was going to choose her as his consort. Good! She would perform any perversion to compromise this monster! She tried to look coy and admiring.

"I want someone I can *talk* to, someone to keep me company in the quiet hours of the night, someone I can rely on body and soul, Miss Brattle. I do not want a whore or a mistress, do you understand? I want a *companion*. I selected you for this interview because you are a fighter, you have spirit, you speak plainly—I know that now—and you are comely. I won't deny that you are attractive. In time, perhaps we can lift the veil between us, who knows?"

"Thank you, sir. I would be honored to pierce that veil."

"I will let you know my decision in due course, Miss Brattle." De Tomas stood. "You will go back under escort to Castle Hurse." He bowed and walked out of the room, leaving Comfort to wonder what her fate would be.

But de Tomas had already decided that.

"My leader, that one's a viper," Herten Gorman warned.

"I know. Did you see her eyeing that knife?" De Tomas laughed.

"I'd best warn you to keep sharp instruments away from her," Gorman said.

"She's the one, Herten," de Tomas said enthusiastically. "Let her sit around Castle Hurse for a day or two, then haul her back up here. Yes, yes, yes! Good work, Herten! She's just the type I want."

"Yes, my leader!" Gorman was excited at the prospect of Comfort alone with de Tomas. First, it meant that Gelli was off the hook as a possible candidate; better still, Gorman had no doubt this violent young woman would cut de Tomas's throat at the first opportunity and save him the trouble.

"Oh, Herten, call off the search. And as for the other candidates, execute them. They're nice girls, but get rid of them."

"Yes, my leader."

"In time, Herten, I'll bring her around. In time, I'll fuck her good."

Yes, Herten Gorman thought, and in time, she'll fuck you good.

Barracks Chief Patti's eyes fairly bulged out of their sockets when she saw Comfort. "Well, 9639," she shouted, tapping her truncheon against a calf, "you smell like a whore, you look like a whore, so you must be one." Comfort had arrived after evening roll call, as the prisoners trooped back listlessly from their evening meal. "Look at her, girls," Patti shouted. "All dolled up! You thought you were somebody special, getting out of here, huh? But you're back now, aren't you? And you're *mine* now, you little bitch!"

Patti was vastly disappointed Comfort had not been executed. Her mangled earlobe was a constant and painful reminder that Comfort had defied her and gotten away with it. It also meant that Comfort was now a possible rival for barracks chief. When Comfort was called away, she'd breathed a sigh of relief. Now . . .

The other women stared at Comfort in disbelief. Never before, even in the memory of the prisoners who'd been at Castle Hurse the longest, had another prisoner ever been treated so generously. Some of the women had had illicit affairs with the guards and other staff members, gotten themselves choice work assignments thereby, but no prisoner had actually made it outside the prison walls to return in such a glorious state.

Patti abruptly lunged forward, grabbed the front of Comfort's dress, and ripped it half off. "Get into your prison rags!" she yelled.

"Leave me alone!" Comfort yelled back. She saw the truncheon coming and hunched over in time to take it on her shoulders. Still, Patti was a big woman and she put all her weight behind the blow. Comfort collapsed to her knees. The next blow struck her in the kidneys, sending her sprawling. Patti jumped on her back and began banging her head on the floor. The last thing that went through Comfort's mind before she lost consciousness was that the other women did nothing to help her.

# CHAPTER
# TWENTY-FIVE

It started to rain on the morning of the second day, making travel very slow and tedious that night. Bass considered that a good thing, however, because the storm gave them additional cover and the assurance that patrols would not be out in the bad weather. But they became more and more miserable as they slogged along. Bass called a halt early so they could get under some cover and avoid hypothermia. "If I'd known it would be this bad," he told Zechariah, "I'd have joined the Marines!"

They found a deep ravine on one side of the highway and camped in some trees high up on the slope to avoid the runoff along the bottom. It was the best cover he could find in the dark and the rain.

It was Colleen who gave their position away. She awoke from a fitful sleep long after daybreak with a powerful demand to relieve herself. Not wanting to bother the others, she eased out from under her ground sheet and quietly worked her way toward the rim of the gorge. Without thinking, she stepped out onto the shoulder of the road. Not fifty meters away Raipur's old platoon was forted-up for the night. They never knew they were there and probably would not have discovered them if it hadn't been for Colleen's carelessness. She froze. A few meters away, just on the other side of the road, Lieutenant Ben Loman stood, calmly relieving himself. His eyes went wide with surprise and his mouth formed into a small black circle as he stood there dumbly holding onto himself.

Colleen scuttled back down into the gorge. Behind her,

Loman was shouting, but in the wind she couldn't make out the words. She didn't have to because seconds later the lieutenant appeared over the rim of the gorge, weapon in hand, followed by his men in various states of disarray, but all armed.

"Halt!" he screamed, leveling his weapon at her. Colleen stopped, turned around and held up her arms. "Don't move!" Loman yelled. "Get up here!" he shouted, contradicting himself.

"You want me to stay here or come up there?" Colleen hollered back.

"Come up here! Keep your hands where I can see them!"

Chet emerged from the bushes, causing Loman to scream even louder. He raised his hands and came to stand beside Colleen. Raipur emerged from the dripping foliage next. Loman gasped. *"You!"* he screamed.

"Good morning, Acolyte." Raipur smiled, raising his hands slowly.

"Gentlemen," Bass said from the roadway behind the small group, "there is no need for those drawn weapons." He had doubled back down the ravine and come up behind Ben Loman and his men. They whirled in astonishment. Bass stood there, his shot rifle casually slung barrel down over one shoulder, a fierce grin on his face. "If we were a threat to you, you'd all be dead now," he said calmly.

Ben Loman glanced fearfully at the four people standing on the slope below him and then back at Bass. *"Who are you?"* he shouted at Bass. Loman's men had lowered their own weapons and stood about their lieutenant nervously, not sure what to do.

"I am Charles Bass of the Confederation embassy in Interstellar City, and these people are refugees. I am accompanying them back to the city of Haven. And who are you, sir?" It was a small, inspired lie but one Bass could live with.

"I-I-I'm supposed to be asking the questions here! And— And, what are *you* doing out here?"

"I was captured by the devils but I escaped. Well, I told you who I am. Now you tell me who you are."

"I'm First Aco— *Lieutenant* Ben Loman," Loman stuttered.

"He's commander of the first platoon of the Recon Company of the Second Regiment, my old outfit," Raipur said, stepping up onto the shoulder of the road. "How you doing, Lieutenant?"

Several of the enlisted men standing around nodded affably at Raipur.

"We thought you were dead!" one of them said.

"Good to see you again, Sword," another volunteered.

"This man is a *deserter*!" Loman shouted, pointing at Raipur.

"No, he is not, Lieutenant," Bass said. "Now, I want you to take us to your company commander. I have important information for your commanding general and the Confederation ambassador."

*"I will do no such thing!"* Loman shouted. "You are my prisoners! Drop your arms! If you resist I will have you all shot!"

"Like you did those villagers, Lieutenant?" Raipur asked mildly. He made no move to divest himself of his weapon.

"Drop your weapons! All of you! Did your hear me?" Loman screamed. "Seize them!" he ordered his men, but none of them made a move.

"He's our sword," one of the men admonished Loman, nodding in Raipur's direction. "What happened, Sword?" He meant during the attack on the New Salem defenses.

"Moron over there put a round into my engine and I lost my gunner and my driver," Raipur answered, nodding at the man who had commanded the second reconnaissance car. It was a small distortion, but just then the literal truth about what had happened that night at New Salem would not have benefited him or his companions.

"Hey, Sword! We were shooting at the demons! That round was just too low!" the commander of the second car protested.

*"Silence!"* Loman shouted. "Arrest these people!"

Bass stepped closer to Loman. "Did you hear me, Lieutenant? I require your assistance to get to the city of Haven. Will you give me your cooperation?"

"No! Now you see here, Mr. Whatsyourname—"

Bass's uppercut struck Loman just under the tip of his jaw so hard that everyone could hear the officer's teeth slam together with a loud *crack!* His eyes rolled back into his head and he collapsed like a wet sack to the ground.

Suddenly, Bass was almost overcome with a rush of déjà vu. He had fought like this once before! In that Elneal place, a desert somewhere, he and another man. They had fought with knives. The memory flooded his consciousness. It had been hot, and they'd gone to the ground, and the other man had cut him but he had—he had *killed* his opponent! Bass could remember plunging the knife into the other man's—

"Charles? Are you all right?" Zechariah asked.

"Uh?" Bass returned to the present. "Oh, yes, yes. I'm fine," he protested. The men of the first platoon were looking at him in shocked silence for striking the lieutenant. Then one of them laughed. "Not very respectful," Bass chided.

"Well, Charles, he's a prize asshole," Raipur said.

Bass just nodded. "I think I may have run across one or two of those in my time. Now men," Bass said, flexing his fist, "you police up your lieutenant and stow him in one of your vehicles. When I see your commanding general I'll get citations for all of you. Now, Sergeant Raipur. You take command. I believe you are the senior ranking man here now? And in the immortal words of someone famous, 'Take me to your leader.' "

"You assaulted one of my officers," Captain Dieter said, but it was not an accusation, just a statement of fact. He had sized Bass up immediately upon his entry into his command post: a man of authority, a man used to exercising that authority and accustomed to being obeyed.

"Well, he gave me a ration of shit, Skipper. I must see the Confederation ambassador. I asked him for his help, he refused, I had to take direct action. I apologize."

*Skipper?* Where had he heard that term before? Dieter wondered. He gestured that Bass should be seated. "Mr. Bass, may I inquire as to the nature of your mission?"

"Yessir. Your Special Group men—I believe that's what they're called—assaulted the village these people—the people who came with me—lived in, and kidnapped a certain young lady, after killing many harmless people. I am going to report this incident to the Confederation ambassador, get that young woman back, and punish the men responsible." He then went on to explain how the assault on New Salem took place, starting with Ben Loman's ill-fated probe. "I am sorry about your men, but they attacked us for no reason, Captain. We had to defend ourselves."

Dieter nodded. "How does Raipur fit into this mission you're on now?"

"Captain, he's a damned good man, a fine NCO. I'd like to ask you to let him come with us. I think I'll be able to use him."

"I never believed Ben Loman's report that he'd run up against demons. And those Special Group people? They aren't 'mine,' Mr. Bass. And anything you can do to bring those *bastards* to justice, I'll help you any way I can. I am going to give Raipur the first platoon and get him commissioned, but yes, sir, he's on loan to you as of right now." He stood and extended his hand. "You're going up against some ruthless men."

"Captain, with all due respect, I don't think they're so tough. I've been told that during your war with the devils they stayed aloof and all they ever did anyway was arrest people and torture them. No wonder you hate them. I think when they run up against some really tough opposition, they'll fold like the bullies they are. And I am going to get that opposition, even if I have to assault their goddamned fortress by myself."

Dieter looked intensely at Bass, then said, "I'll get you to Interstellar City, Mr. Bass. I'll have my operations officer arrange for a Hopper. But first," he turned to the entrance and called, "Lieutenant?"

Dieter's operations officer stepped into the CP. "Yessir?"

"Get Ben Loman in here right away. I want to talk to that sonofabitch."

* * *

"Those are some nasty bumps and scratches you have there," de Tomas observed as Gelli Alois led Comfort into his office.

"She was beaten up by her barracks chief at Castle Hurse, my leader," Gelli volunteered. "We did our best to clean her up." She bowed and left them alone.

"Please be seated, Miss Brattle. Do you wish me to punish the people or the person who beat you up?"

"No."

De Tomas nodded. "I admire you for that. Evidently, among your many sterling qualities, you are not a vengeful person."

"I wouldn't be too sure about that," Comfort replied as she sat down. But de Tomas's tone of voice was solicitous. She appreciated anyone being solicitous of her welfare after Castle Hurse.

De Tomas smiled. "I have decided it is you I want as my companion. Are you feeling well enough to visit with me for a while?"

"Thank you, but I do not want to be your companion. May I return to prison now?"

De Tomas laughed outright. "Not only no, Miss Brattle, but '*Hell* no!' "

"I am already married," she lied.

"I don't care. You will be mine, Miss Brattle, your soul first and then your body."

"Never!" Comfort shouted, half rising out of her chair, face flushed with anger.

"Yes, I assure you," de Tomas answered calmly.

"Never," she repeated, this time calmly but with determination. "You killed my people. I hate you. You are the Antichrist, I recognize you now."

"Tut tut. That's a little beyond my capabilities." He spread his arms. "Look, I am only flesh and blood. Lonely flesh and blood, at that. Being at the top of any pile is a lonely place. I breathe, I eat, I shit just like any other man."

"I will never, *never* give in to you," Comfort whispered. She was verging on tears of anger and frustration.

"Good! That's the spirit! That's just why I picked you. May I offer you some refreshments?"

"No."

De Tomas was so engaging, Comfort found her anger cooling, in spite of the fact that the man who sat opposite her was a cold-blooded murderer. But he was handsome, suave! His years as Dean of the Collegium, all the crimes he'd committed in his rise to ultimate power, had not marked him outwardly. She glanced around the room, at the books, the furniture, the maps and paintings, the rich carpets and drapes. It was the study of an educated, cultured gentleman, a man who loved and appreciated good things. And he was treating her now like—like her *uncle,* not a slobbering beast! She tried hard to steel herself by concentrating on Charles, her mother, her father, the people of New Salem, but all that tragedy seemed so long ago. She realized, deep inside, that in time de Tomas's overpowering will would break down her barriers. As morally strong as she knew she was, he was far more dangerous than anyone she'd ever met, even the vicious inmates and guards who ran Castle Hurse. They would only destroy a person's body. It was her soul de Tomas was after.

"I might like some wine now?" Comfort said in a small voice.

"And you shall have it, my dear." He poured her a glass and she sipped at it. Then de Tomas reached across the table between them. "Give me your hand, please?" She extended her right hand. He took it in his own. His hand was smooth and warm to the touch. Again Comfort was surprised. Was it the hand of a killer? "You have done some hard work with these hands, haven't you? Not just hard work in prison, but hard work at home. I can feel the calluses. Yes, you lived primitively in your village and your people were farmers and artisans. You are no society girl, Miss Brattle. You are like me. I once worked with my hands, when I was much younger." He patted the back of her hand gently and let it go.

"Please, I am very tired. May I rest for a while?"

De Tomas smiled gently. "Yes, you have earned that. I'll have someone show you to your quarters immediately. I'll have you awakened for supper. Miss Brattle—may I call you Comfort? What a delightful name! Your accommodations are ready and you will find them more than adequate. You are my honored guest here at Wayvelsberg Castle. All I want is your complete loyalty. I shall have it! And then, my dear Comfort, you will stand beside me and share my glory."

Her room was luxurious. It even had its own bath. But the door to the hall was locked. Comfort lay on the bed but could not sleep. De Tomas's last words kept ringing through her brain. She wished she were in prison. She had never felt farther from God than she did in these sumptuous surroundings; Wayvelsberg Castle was Hell. She closed her eyes and prayed and prayed, and finally she slept.

The spot she had picked to give birth to her male child proved to be an excellent hiding place. The stream there flowed slowly and deep and the water was full of crustacean-like creatures that were good to eat. There was plenty of foliage for concealment and the mud was deep and comfortable, reminding her of Home. She longed for Home and others of her kind, but she knew she would never see either again. She was on her own, and her only focus in life was the child. He was growing fast on the nourishing food; she had even taught him to swim in the calm, clear water that flowed outside their hiding place.

Best of all, the spot was far away from those Earthmen and the disturbances they caused. She would never understand those strange creatures. Her own people were warlike, yes, but with them the military virtues were an important aspect of their culture, which was also refined and ancient. Besides, it was ordained by the gods that civilization should rule over savagery, and the skinny, ugly Earthmen were little more than animals with deadly technology. The only thing the Earthmen seemed to want to do was destroy everything about them.

She missed the wonderful rituals that governed the lives of her people. Often, when her child slept and homesickness was upon her, she swam in the stream, sometimes following its current several kilometers, drowning her sorrow in the pleasure of exercise before turning back to her lair. When, after several months her child—whom she named Jedo, after his father, a great warrior—had grown sufficiently that he could forage for his own meals, she increased the distance of her explorations. She discovered that the stream emptied eventually into a river, and curious about its destination— river deltas were great places to live—she swam out into the water and allowed herself to drift along on the current. Going back upstream would require some effort, she realized, but she felt strong and confident that morning. Jedo could take care of himself while she was gone.

The sun was bright and warm and the water temperature comfortable. She closed her eyes and drifted along, and eventually she dozed in the pleasant weightlessness of the flowing current. She never sensed the increase in the strength of the current or heard the roar of the falls that spilled a hundred meters onto the rocks in the canyon below.

# CHAPTER
# TWENTY-SIX

Captain Sepp Dieter winced as the mild electric current coursed through a very sensitive part of his anatomy.

"Electricity is a very interesting and useful phenomenon of nature," the interrogator whispered. He was a pudgy, balding man of indeterminate age with ears that stuck out like handles from the sides of his head. His forehead glistened with perspiration—not from the heat, for the interrogation chamber was cold, but from excitement. He grinned a lot and spoke in a soft, intimate voice just above a whisper, as if he were talking to a child—or a lover—and he talked constantly, maintaining a rambling monologue, hardly missing a word even when his victims screamed in agony. When they did scream, he raised his voice slightly as if *insisting* that, even in their pain, they must pay attention.

"I don't know anything," Dieter said. He did not bother to protest his arrest or the torture; he knew it would do him no good, and he was determined not to give the monster the satisfaction of an easy confession. They had come for him not two hours after Bass and the others left for Haven. He now bitterly regretted that he didn't open fire on the SG men who arrested him. They had come in their own Hopper, a dozen of them led by a swaggering officer, barging into his command post, catching him totally by surprise. They arrested him immediately and, weapons at the ready, hustled him into the waiting aircraft. There was nothing his men could do but stand by and watch in startled amazement. The Special Group men had taken him straight to the cellars of Wayvelsberg for questioning.

Lieutenant Ben Loman, as the senior officer left in the reconnaissance company, would have taken command. That was a bitter cup for an old soldier like Sepp Dieter. He wasn't sure whether Loman had informed Battalion, but in any event his ordeal at Wayvelsberg would be over by the time army headquarters could learn of his arrest, too late to protest the action. Not that a protest would do him a bit of good.

"Oh, you know nothing, Captain?" The interrogator smiled. "On the contrary, my dear sir, you *do* know things, yes indeedy, you *do*!" The interrogator chuckled, rubbing his hands together, then flicked a toggle switch on his control panel. A stronger current caused Dieter to grunt. "That was a mere ten milliamps, my dear captain. Did you know that the average man can withstand up to sixteen M.A.'s? Parenthetically, I might add, women can only tolerate about 10.5 M.A.'s, some more, some less; everybody's different, heh heh heh. *Vive* the difference, eh? Those dosages, sixteen and 10.5, respectively, are known as the 'let go' levels? Heh heh heh. You can still let go of a wire at those charges, but any higher, depending on gender . . ." He gave Dieter forty M.A.'s. Dieter gasped and spasmed against his bonds. The interrogator, smiling happily, let the current go for twenty agonizing seconds. When it stopped, Dieter sat gasping for breath, his body covered in cold perspiration.

"This is an old but a tried and true method, Captain, and a lot more fun for me than drugs. I have an interesting formula for the application of electroshock in interrogations. Would you like to hear it? I call it 'forty-sixty-eighty.' By the time we reach eighty milliamps you'll be telling me everything I want to know. At levels of over a hundred, by the way, the subject usually goes into ventricular fibrillation and, unfortunately, dies. I do sincerely hope we don't have to go that route today. Shall we continue?"

Ben Loman sat behind Captain Dieter's field desk in the company command post. He put his feet up and placed his hands behind his head. He mused on how fickle fate could be. One moment a man is cast down, as he had been after the chewing out Dieter had given him, and the next—well, here he was now, *commanding,* and Dieter was . . . well, too bad. Now that he was in command, he'd make some changes around the company. First would be that sergeant, Raipur. Just wait until he came back—*if he came back*—he'd be *Private* Raipur henceforth! Ah, the fickle finger of fate!

The senior stormleader in charge of Intelligence looked dispassionately at the wreck that had been Captain Sepp Dieter. "Will he live?"

The interrogator shrugged.

"What did he tell you?"

"A very interesting story, Senior Stormleader. Those people whose transport to General Lambsblood's headquarters he facilitated were refugees from New Salem, apparently, the last of the City of God sect, I should think. Survivors of our attack on the place. One of them, however, is an off-worlder, a man named Bass. Strange name, isn't it? I think it's a kind of fish. Well, anyway, this Bass is looking for the young woman who was captured during the raid on New Salem. I believe, sir, she is here right now, upstairs with our leader. I also believe that is all this man knows."

The senior stormleader arched an eyebrow. "Who else back there knows anything about this encounter?"

"Our informant. A Lieutenant Ben Loman."

"Bring him up here. Question him. See what he might be holding back. Everyone holds back *something.*" He turned and left the room. Moments later he stood before Herten Gorman. "I have information, Deputy Leader, that I believe you should pass to our leader immediately." He related what the interrogator had learned from Dieter.

Gorman sat silently for a moment, then put his office suite into its security mode so he would not be interrupted. He got to his feet. "Come to the window with me, Senior Stormleader, I have something to tell you." He laid a hand on the senior stormleader's shoulder and guided him toward the window. It was opaque. With the security system engaged, it reflected their images like a mirror. "Who else knows of this, old friend?" Gorman asked.

"Just me, Deputy Leader, and the interrogator, of course. Perhaps our informant with the reconnaissance company in the field too, but I gave orders for his arrest. He should be here in a few hours. I came right up as soon as the interrogation was over."

"Good!" The senior stormleader never saw the dagger Gorman plunged into his neck just below his right ear. Blood spurted all over the window as the man instinctively lurched forward in an attempt to steady himself against the glass, meanwhile trying to stanch the blood with one hand, bracing himself on the windowpane with the other hand to keep his footing. With each contraction of his heart, arterial blood sprayed between his fingers. Bloody handprints smeared down the glass as he slid to the floor, gurgling away his life.

Gorman stood back and looked for something on which to wipe his hands—blood had spattered on his uniform. He snatched up a nearby tablecloth, pulling a lamp to the floor as he did so, and wiped his hands carefully. What a mess! Well, he would wash and clean it all up later. It wasn't as though it was the first time he'd had to dispose of a body. He returned to his desk and activated his communicator. "Heeps?" He spoke to the interrogator in the bowels of the building.

"Yes, Deputy Leader!" Heeps's cherubic face replied from the screen.

"Get rid of that Captain Dieter. Same goes for that lieutenant who's coming back here for questioning. Clear? Keep all of this to yourself, understand? I'm going in to see our leader right now. Then when you're done with those two, come and see me." He switched off the device and grinned. Now all he had to do was give this Comfort woman—what a ridiculous name!—a knife and let her do the rest! He leaned back and put his hands behind his head. How fickle, he mused, is the worm of fate, twisting first this way and then that, putting you on the bottom one minute, lifting you to the top the next! Well, it didn't hurt to give that old worm a little nudge now and then.

In the bowels of Wayvelsberg Castle, Heeps grinned. Captain Dieter was slumped in the chair, unconscious, nasty burns all over his body from the electric shock. Well, the Deputy Leader did not say *when* to kill him, so he would keep him around for a while, try out some technique variations, electrodes *inside* various body cavities, for instance. Yes! Slow death as the innards were gradually crisped! Wonderful! He never imagined when he awoke that morning the day would turn out so pleasantly. And then he'd have that lieutenant to work over. It had been a while since he'd had *two* subjects in one day!

It was the lunch hour. Again Comfort was de Tomas's only guest. They were having a delicious soup made from beta bitula, a beetlike vegetable native to Kingdom. The bloodred liquid was thick, tangy with a slightly salty but pleasant aftertaste. The vegetables were actually one of Comfort's favorite dishes, and in spite of herself, she spooned up the steaming liquid with evident pleasure.

De Tomas smiled, genuinely pleased that his consort was enjoying the soup. "Tasty?" he inquired.

"Yes. They are also good fried, with leeks and tomatoes. My mother," she paused, "used—used to make it that way all the time."

"I shall see that the cook prepares it for you tonight. Tell me, are your quarters comfortable?"

"Yes, as much as any prison cell *can* be comfortable."

"That is merely a precaution, Miss Brattle. Soon you shall be free to roam Wayvelsberg Castle as you please."

"Will that include the infamous torture chambers?"

De Tomas smiled. "Certain areas, of course, are off limits. We still have a police function to perform here. But Miss Brattle, much of what you have heard about this place and my role as former Dean of the Collegium is greatly exaggerated. We never *really* burned people at the stake, for instance." He laughed.

"But people have been executed," Comfort retorted. "There's a place at Castle Hurse the prisoners call 'Suburbia,' where prisoners are shot and the bodies are fed into incinerators."

"Castle Hurse is a prison. Felons are confined there, murderers among them. Of *course* executions take place there, my dear. And Comfort, I can hardly be blamed for the decisions undertaken by the criminal justice system, can I? I follow a strict hands-off policy on those matters. I just let the courts pursue justice according to our laws."

In times past, inmates at Castle Hurse had been executed and buried in mass graves on the prison grounds. After taking power, de Tomas had ordered the bodies disinterred and burned. The inmates had done the work, and then the laborers themselves were executed and their bodies fed into the flames.

"In fact, Comfort," he continued, "as Dean of the Collegium, I used my powers to spare the lives of many people. The power that office carried in the hands of another man could have unleashed genocide in the world, but I used it with restraint." That was pure rubbish. "And when I took power, I abolished the Collegium. Nowhere on Kingdom is anyone investigated or persecuted for his religious beliefs anymore. So you see, my dear, you simply cannot believe everything you may have heard about me." He smiled and poured her another glass of sparkling Katzenwasser '38.

"But I am classified as a political prisoner," Comfort protested, "and so are hundreds of others confined in Castle Hurse!"

"I can see that was a mistake in your case. But Comfort, you must understand that every government has its dissidents, people who oppose its policies, no matter how enlightened. The sects have ruled on this world from the beginning, and their leaders, large and small, were not willing to give up their hold on the people overnight. Those men and women, the ones who have not joined us, are dangerous enemies of the state. Every state has the right to protect itself! Thus, we have 'political' prisoners, as you call them.

"And Comfort, *someone* must be in charge! What is preferable, a government that changes every few years as happens in the so-called 'democracies,' or a government that is stable, run by the same individual for forty years? How would your church operate, for instance, if every two years you had to have a new pastor?

"But enough of this. Tell me about your family."

Comfort thought fast. What was it she had told her interrogators? She couldn't contradict herself now! She played it safe and described the bucolic life of New Salem. De Tomas listened intently. "I am very sorry about your family, Comfort. I think I would have liked to meet your father. If he were still alive, I'd be honored to have him here with us at this meal. I'd invite him here to live with us." He sighed. "Well, I have official business to attend to. Would you like something to read in your room?" He gestured at the book-lined walls.

"May I read the Bible?"

"Of course! Or anything else you see here you like—plays, novels, histories, works of art!"

"B-But I thought these books were banned!"

"Oh, they were, Comfort, they were. By order of the Convocation of Ecumenical Leaders. In their narrow-minded ignorance, they feared any ideas contrary to their own. So I was forced to burn whole libraries. These volumes I rescued from the flames, at great peril to myself, my dear. But I took the chance to preserve them for the future generations of this world. I will soon donate them to the Free University of New Kingdom, which I am in the process of endowing. They will form the nucleus of a great system of learning."

"You will give up all these?" Comfort took in the shelves crammed with books and pamphlets. She had never seen so many books before. The people of the City of God were familiar with books and printed materials, actually preferring printed Bibles to Bibles in electronic form, but they did not have libraries as such.

"Yes, sadly." De Tomas brightened. "But they go for the good of my people. Did you know, Comfort, that I do not even receive a salary for my work? Yes," he nodded, "that's right. Oh, I live well, as you can see, but I am paid nothing. I have no fortune. I have no estate. Were I to die now, I would leave only my good name and my good works." Actually, de Tomas was worth millions from investments he'd made using funds accumulated by the Special Group's business ventures, enterprises that flourished on prisoner labor.

"Thank you, thank you very much." Comfort searched the shelves and pulled down a dog-eared copy of the King James version of the Bible. Her face radiated her happiness. Despite all the lies he had just told her, de Tomas could not help being pleased to see her so joyful.

"Sir—Mr. Bass, if that is your real name—do you really expect me to believe this story?" General Lambsblood scoffed. Bass? He thought. What a strange name! Like that Marine commander, Sturgeon, wasn't that also the name of a *fish*? These off-worlders certainly were different, but as he'd often thought since 34th FIST had departed, he wished the Marines were back on Kingdom again.

Bass looked at Zechariah, who was sitting next to him, then back at the general. "That *is* our story, General, believe it or not. All I ask is your help getting into Interstellar City so I can lay our case before the Confederation ambassador. Captain Dieter said you would help us."

The general's scowl softened. "A good soldier, young Dieter." He drummed his fingers on his desktop. If this rough-looking character sitting before him with his fishy story really was a Confederation Marine—maybe he was, if he'd actually done all the things he'd just related—then he could prove *very* useful in the events that were about to unfold. Dieter believed him, and that counted for something. And that enlisted man, Raipur? Dieter had assigned him to escort these people up here. Well . . .

Lambsblood had the foresight to borrow some of Ambassador Spears's electronic surveillance equipment, so at least he could discuss matters privately in his own office now, instead of walking about out-of-doors. The technicians had discovered a dozen bugs during the first sweep. He regarded his guests, the man called Bass and this Zechariah Brattle, formerly mayor of New Salem. The man had a straightforward honesty about him that Lambsblood respected. He knew almost nothing about the City of God sect, and he didn't want to know anything more. They had kept to themselves mostly, and that was good from Lambsblood's point of view. They'd also been almost wiped out by the Skinks, so this Brattle might be the last of his breed. And, if it was *his* daughter and only child in the custody of the Special Group, well . . .

The communications console on the general's desk bleeped a high-priority message. "Excuse me a moment, would you?" he said to his guests. He read the message.

From where he was sitting, Bass was alarmed at the expression that passed over General Lambsblood's face. Zechariah noticed it too, and they exchanged nervous glances, but neither dared ask him what was the matter.

"Getting into Interstellar City is no easy task," Lambsblood said after a long pause. He spoke almost as if he were talking to himself. "The surveillance there is very tight and constant, everyone going in and out is closely screened. No, I think it'd actually be easier to get the ambassador out here."

"Then you will help us, General?" Zechariah asked, surprised at what he saw as a sudden change of heart.

"They've arrested Captain Dieter," Lambsblood said in a husky voice, "and if I miss my guess, we are next."

"You *will* help us, then?" Bass asked.

"You're damned right I will," the general answered firmly.

# CHAPTER
# TWENTY-SEVEN

The two heavily armed shooters stood on opposite sides of the gate leading into the sprawling compound on the outskirts of Haven known as Interstellar City. One checked foot traffic in and the other harassed the people going out. Other men stood by, ready to check any vehicles that might pass through.

"ID!" one demanded of an elderly woman going in.

"I pass through here every day, sonny!" the woman protested, but she reached for her identification crystal anyway.

"Orders is orders," the man replied, holding out a hand. "Besides, Mrs. Summara, you could be an imposter," he said, laughing at his own wit. "If you'd ever give me a little kiss in the morning we wouldn't have to go through this routine every day. I can always tell a woman by her lips," he said to his companion, winking at the old lady.

"You say that to every girl who comes through here, you beast," the woman groused, but secretly she enjoyed the little game. He took her crystal and popped it into a reader. She was employed as a charwoman. Her ID checked out, as he knew it would, and he waved her on. Passing by, she slapped him playfully on his rear, as she did every morning, and the other sentries roared with laughter.

A young couple emerged, off-worlders. "Identification! State your business!" the sentry demanded.

Each word and every image of each encounter was monitored and recorded by an officer behind protective glass in his control booth. "Ambassadorial personnel," the duty officer said into his throat mike, "give them a hard time."

"Where are you going?" the sentry demanded, holding their ID crystals but making no effort to read them.

"We're just taking a morning walk, soldier," the young man replied affably. The men of the Special Group hated being called "soldiers," and the young man knew that.

"You can't do that in the compound?" the shooter asked. "Wait here." He stepped into the control booth.

"Let them stand out there for a while," the officer said. "Leave their IDs with me until I feel ready to let them go."

"Stand by," the sentry told the couple.

"What's the problem?" the young woman asked.

"The problem is you're here," the sentry answered. "Now stand back, you're in the way of traffic."

"This is absolute nonsense," the young man said at last. "What's your name? I'm going to log a protest when we get back!"

A vehicle flying the ambassador's pennant rolled up to the gate. Two shooters approached. "Good morning, Mr. Ambassador," one said. "May we ask where you are headed this morning, sir?"

"No you may not," Spears replied. "You keep up this nonsense and I'll land a shore party and have you all wiped out." This too was a ritual the sentries were used to—except they didn't know that this morning Spears meant it.

The sentry peered inside the vehicle. "Ambassador Spears, General Banks, and Mr. Carlisle, destination unknown," he reported to the duty officer. "He's making threats, as usual," the man added.

Aha! the stormleader on duty thought. At last, something to report to headquarters! "Let him through." He turned to his noncom. "Track them." He gathered up the young couples' IDs and stepped outside. "You may proceed," he announced with an airy wave of his hand.

"I'm going to report this," the young man said firmly.

"Oh?" The stormleader turned back to the pair. "Well, excuse me, sir," he said with a polite bow, "but obviously you have me confused with someone who really gives a shit," and all the SG men within hearing laughed. "Have a nice day," he said to their backs as they stomped off.

The surveillance operation at Interstellar City was performed by the SG Security Service, a small but well-trained detachment commanded by the equivalent of a colonel. It was good duty.

By treaty agreement, there was only one way in or out of Interstellar City. Before de Tomas seized power, the Convocation of Ministers restricted contact between the diplomats and the faithful of Kingdom because they were afraid of the possible "contamination" of new ideas that they were sure would be spread by the unbelievers of the Confederation. De Tomas continued the strict surveillance while permitting free passage because ideology did not bother him—he just wanted to know what everyone was up to.

"Arrogant bastards," Carlisle muttered as the SG man waved them through the checkpoint.

"Has this vehicle been swept today?" Spears asked the driver.

"Yessir."

"Good. Good, too, that General Lambsblood borrowed one of our technicians to sweep his own office suite. At least we'll be able to talk indoors today instead of walking around on the parade field. Why do you think Lambsblood called for this meeting, Dick?" Spears asked Brigadier General Banks. "Do you think he's ready to make his move?"

"Maybe, sir. Major Devi's been on this detached duty with that armored battalion for some time now. It's the most potent military force he has immediately available. The CNSS *Marne* is in orbit, and the general knows she's up there."

"Prentiss?"

"I agree with Dick, sir."

"I think it's time. I've talked to the captain of the *Marne* and he's ready to lend us whatever support we request. As soon as the action starts, he'll land a shore party. I have the authority to ask for protection from the navy in case of civil disorder here." He pulled back his coat and displayed a compact hand-blaster in a shoulder holster. "Gentlemen, may I introduce my faithful Sig-Walther? I never go to a revolution without it!"

Mugabe lighted a cheroot, sucked in the smoke and exhaled it luxuriously. "These things taste best at a time like this." He smiled at Uma.

"They *never* smell any good to me." She grinned, running a fingernail down the stormleader's chest.

"It's my only bad habit," he said. "Well, one of my only two bad habits." He laughed.

"And the other?" Uma Devi asked playfully.

Mugabe pretended to think about that. After a moment he said quite seriously, "You."

She scowled and grabbed him. "It's not *me,* my dear stormleader, but *this* that's going to get you into trouble!"

"Yiii!" he rolled away from her and sat on the edge of the bed. "Uma, I've been thinking."

"A bad habit for a member of the Special Group."

Mugabe smiled. "Uma, we're a compatible couple. We've known each other for how long now, weeks? That's a long time. We both come from good families. I'm an officer in the Special Group. We're both unattached, never been attached to anyone else, in fact. What do you say we get married, you and me?"

Uma said nothing at first; either from surprise or shock, Mugabe wasn't sure. She rolled over on her side, took the cheroot and inhaled. She blew smoke out through her nostrils. "All right," she said.

Later Uma said, "I guess that day the Leader rejected me as his consort was really my lucky day. I met you. Did he ever find anyone, I wonder?"

"Yes, I've heard he did. Some girl from the provinces, I hear, a really scrappy bitch. He's spending all his time with her, up in his sanctuary. It's a bad thing when a man allows sex to get in the way of his duty. I hate to say it of such a great man."

"A girl from the provinces?" Uma mused.

"Yes. Bottle is her name, or something like that. We arrested her when we attacked her village, New Salem. Thought there were Skinks there but only found these miserable survivors of the City of God sect. She's the only one who survived." He shrugged. "Anyway, our leader picked her as his consort, so now she lives in splendor up in his penthouse."

Later, while Mugabe slept, Uma padded into the toilet. She pulled out her comm. "Krishna?" Her brother answered. "I have something you may want to know. I give it to you with only one condition."

"I think I know that man," Spears muttered as they were ushered into General Lambsblood's private office. The general and his guests stood as the ambassador and his party entered.

"Mr. Ambassador, so good of you to come on such short notice." The general extended his hand. "May I introduce my special guests? You know Major Devi, but here are Mr. Zechariah Brattle and Mr. Charles Bass."

Jayben Spears took Bass's hand and shook it warmly. "Well, Mr. Bass, a pleasure! Have we ever met before?"

"I don't remember, sir," Bass replied, and told him in as few words as possible what had happened to him, as far as he could remember. "I guess we won the war against the Skinks, whoever 'we' are," he concluded.

"Yes, we did," Spears said. He was positive he'd seen this Bass before, but where?

They sat. "We don't have much time," General Lambsblood said. "I am going to launch an attack on Wayvelsberg Castle. I am going to overthrow Dominic de Tomas or die in the attempt. I'll decide when after this meeting, but it'll be today. I need your support, Mr. Ambassador."

"We thought so," Spears said. "You have it, of course. Please continue."

"It will be a tough fight," Prentiss Carlisle offered. "You're going up against the Special Group. They're well-armed and highly motivated, General. Forgive me for saying so, but your men have had a very rough time these last months."

"I don't think so," Bass said. They all looked at him in astonishment.

"They're very tough men," Ambassador Spears said.

"I don't think so, sir," Bass repeated. "Oh, they're tough when it comes to breaking into peoples' homes and arresting them, executing unarmed men, burning villages, torturing people. But remember, in your war with the Skinks," he looked at General Lambsblood, "where were they? *You* fought the aliens, *you* stood with the Marines, *you* took casualties while they hid out in their dungeons or that castle of theirs on the other side of town, doing karaoke to the tune of the 'Horst Wessel Lied.' "

"I think Charles is right, sir," Raipur chimed in. "When they attacked Mr. Brattle's village, they were totally unopposed by any real military force, but they still took casualties. Of course they claim it was a great victory and all that, but so far as I know, that was the first and *only* tactical military operation any of them ever participated in. No wonder they think it was a walkover."

"Gentlemen," Brigadier General Banks spoke up, "we hit them hard in the head, knock out Wayvelsberg, hit them fast and with everything we've got, and I think Mr. Bass is right. They'll fold up like an old field shelter." He was half out of his seat now, pounding one fist into the palm of his hand, eyes flashing, an old war-horse awakened by a distant trumpet.

"Mr. Brattle." Major Devi spoke directly to Zechariah. "I know where your daughter is." He briefly explained what his sister had told him earlier in the morning. "And moreover, she knows how to get into Wayvelsberg."

Zechariah almost jumped out of his seat at the news.

"Gentlemen, gentlemen." Lambsblood held up a hand. "One thing at a time! Let's coordinate our plan now, shall we?"

"Mr. Bass." Spears tapped Bass on the knee. "You look like a military man and you talk like a military man so you must be a military man. Does the name Ted Sturgeon ring a bell with you?"

Often great landslides that rush down upon unsuspecting villages are started when a single boulder on the mountainside is jarred loose. It tumbles away, dislodging somewhat larger cousins as it rolls along, gathering rocks and dirt and trees until it becomes part of a roaring wall of earth rumbling and crashing inexorably to the bottom of the valley.

*Ted Sturgeon.* That name was Charlie Bass's boulder. He sat bolt upright in his chair, eyes staring, face drained white as if he'd seen a ghost or had a vision of his own death. Or as if he were having a heart attack! Zechariah, alarmed that it was the latter, put his arm around Bass's shoulders. "Charles! Charles! *What is wrong with you?*"

Bass could not get any words out, although his lips moved as he tried to form them. For a moment he did not even know where he was as memory after memory crashed in upon him. There was poor Dupont again! Top Myer! The Skipper! Camp Ellis! Big Barb's! Wonderful schooners of sparkling cold Reindeer Ale! Cigars, delicious, divine cigars! All the faces of the men he'd come to love and respect, the living and the dead, danced before his eyes.

"Get him water!" General Lambsblood ordered.

"A medic! We need a medic!" Raipur started for the door.

Bass shook his head vigorously and held up a hand, gasping, chest heaving to get air into his lungs. A thin film of perspiration covered his forehead. And then tears came to his eyes and he grinned. At first he said nothing, could not say anything, he was too choked up, just sat there, looking triumphantly at the people nervously gathered about him. "I am—" he croaked, swallowed and started again:

"I am Gunnery Sergeant Charles Bass, commander of third platoon, Company L, 34th Fleet Initial Strike Team, Confederation Marine Corps!"

Zechariah Brattle hugged Gunny Bass, tears forming in his own eyes, and, looking up toward heaven shouted, "Praise the Lord God Almighty, Lazarus has risen!"

# CHAPTER
# TWENTY-EIGHT

"General," Bass said, the color back in his face, "I'm ready to go again."

"Gunny Bass! I thought I recognized you!" Spears interrupted. "I know Brigadier Sturgeon very well, and I know two men from your platoon also, Lance Corporals Claypoole and Dean. They were with us on Wanderjahr, when we raided Turbat Nguyen-Multan's hideout. So, wouldn't you like me to dispatch a message to Fleet, telling them you're alive and well?"

"Small universe, sir," Bass replied. Claypoole! Dean! My God, how he wanted to be back on Thorsfinni's World, eating a big steak at Big Barb's, a schooner—no, a *battleship!*—of ale at his elbow! But first there was Comfort Brattle. "But not just now, sir. Could we wait until our present business is concluded? I'd like to hear the general's plan."

"Excellent! Gentlemen, Major Devi will brief you."

"Here's what we've worked out. H hour is midnight. The forces involved consist of—"

"Excuse me, General, Major," Zechariah interrupted, "but I came here to rescue my daughter, and this major of yours here said he knows where she is."

"I came here for the same reason, General," Bass said. "Her name is Comfort and we want her back."

"And General, sir, if you have no objection, I would like to go with Gunnery Sergeant Bass," Raipur added.

"Well?" Lambsblood looked at Chet and Colleen, and they nodded. "Very well, then. Major Devi? But be quick, time is of the essence."

Major Devi explained what his sister had told him. "She has been into de Tomas's private quarters and knows how to get into Wayvelsberg Castle. You'll need explosives to get through the doors—small shaped charges should do—and we have them at the depot where the assault force is waiting to move out. I suggest you accompany me there when we're done here, and we'll outfit you. My sister requested one condition, though."

"What's that?" Zechariah asked.

"There's a certain stormleader in de Tomas's Lifeguards Battalion, Mugabe is his name. She wants him spared any harm."

"Why?" Zechariah asked.

"I think they're going to get married. He's my brother-in-law-in-waiting, I guess you'd say." He shrugged and his face turned red with embarrassment, but there it was. As a good staff officer, he just didn't keep things from the boss.

"Well, this day has been *full* of surprises, hasn't it?" General Lambsblood exclaimed.

"Will your sister go along with us?" Bass asked.

"I think so. I think she'll have to go at least as far as the castle grounds."

"Tell her we agree," Bass said, wondering how they would know who this Mugabe was if they saw him, and how to take him down without injuring him if he fought them. "General, can we coordinate your attack with our busting into this place?"

Lambsblood looked at Devi, who nodded. "Yes. Major?"

"Now, here's the plan." Briefly he explained how the operation would work. The armored battalion at the depot consisted of twenty Gabriel fighting vehicles, each with the capacity to carry fully armed infantrymen and a three-man crew. Those men plus the maintenance personnel and the battalion's supporting infantry company, recon, signal, mortar platoons, and the rest gave the unit a combat strength of five hundred men when fully manned. Over the past weeks, however, Lambsblood had secretly reinforced the infantry company with men drawn from field units so that the battalion's fighting strength was closer to six hundred. All the men were loyal to the general and eager to attack.

"There are roughly a thousand men in the Lifeguards Battalion at Wayvelsberg," Major Devi continued. "They're housed in barracks about half a kilometer from the castle itself. We'll have the element of surprise, and we'll be attacking at night, so the garrison at the castle will consist of no more than a hundred men. Half our force will attack the barracks, while the remainder hits the castle; the mortar platoon will take out the airfield that is next to the barracks. Gunny Bass, you go in the back door as we go in the front. We'll be in constant radio contact from the moment we leave here to go to the depot. General Lambsblood will coordinate the operation from here; Ambassador Spears will stand by at Interstellar City.

"Call signs: the general's is 'Wholesaler'; the armored battalion commander's is 'Shipper'; you, Ambassador Spears, will be 'Middleman.' Gunny, we'll call you 'Customer.' And Wayvelsberg is the 'Store,' while the barracks and airfield are the 'Apartment.' The signal to commence the attack will be 'Home.' Use those words in whatever combinations work. We know the Special Group monitors radio communications closely, so only use the radios when it's absolutely necessary."

"I can have the *Marne* jam all electronic communications on command," Spears offered.

"Not a good idea, sir," Lambsblood replied. "We'll need to be able to communicate with our forces to be sure nothing goes wrong, or to let each of the three attack elements know if anything does." He nodded at Devi to continue.

"Everyone will be in position to attack by 2345. We've rehearsed this over and over at the battalion. The streets will be free of traffic at that hour so we'll have a clear route to Wayvelsberg and be there before anyone realizes what's up. Any questions?"

"What if something does go wrong?" Bass asked. "What are the contingency plans?"

Major Devi shifted uneasily in his chair. "We've considered various contingencies, Gunny. Basically, we'll play it by ear. We're flexible. We'll be in constant touch with one another from now until the attack. Our armored battalion is the most potent military force in the city. Remember, the Special Group is spread out in garrisons all over Kingdom, and by the time any of those garrisons can reinforce the Lifeguards, the battle will be over.

"Remember also, we have the strategic initiative. Tactically, we're outnumbered, that's true, but the enemy is dispersed. We will mass our forces to concentrate our firepower to the best advantage. If the forces attacking the barracks do not completely destroy the garrison there, they'll prevent it from reinforcing Wayvelsberg, and the Wayvelsberg defenders will be outnumbered four-to-one."

"What about the city's population?" Carlisle asked. "You know how popular de Tomas is. What are you going to do to secure the channels of public information, so you can explain the revolution, win his supporters over?"

"We don't have the forces to do that," General Lambsblood answered. "We had to keep this operation secret. I could not even bring in my staff, much less civilian counterparts who might be with us. Besides, by two hours tomorrow de Tomas will be in our custody, and once he's out of power, we will fill the vacuum. There may be a short period of instability, but without de Tomas, his government will topple. We'll win the people over during his trial, when we can bring to light all his crimes. Until then, of course, we may have to deal with public demonstrations. But on the other hand, de Tomas has enemies, and once his oppression is at an end, they'll come out of the woodwork. Anyway, the army is with us."

Ambassador Spears spoke up. "Gunny Bass, as soon as the attack has succeeded, I'll issue a de facto recognition of the interim government to be headed by General Lambsblood. If there is any serious armed resistance that the general's forces can't handle, I'll call up the *Marne*. And Charlie, if your attack bogs down, I'm going to dispatch the landing party and put the *Marne*'s batteries on call to support you.

That's against all the rules the Diplomatic Corps lives by, but I'm going to do it anyway." What he did not say, and what Bass knew as well, was that if the *Marne* opened fire on Wayvelsberg Castle, it could not be a "surgical" strike, so nobody's survival would be guaranteed.

And as to that stormleader, Mugabe, Bass had already made up his mind that anyone who got in his way would die, regardless. But Bass nodded his agreement with the plan. He understood its weaknesses: Lambsblood had no air support and the Special Group did. What if the SG were successful in getting Avenging Angels, or even armed Hoppers, into the air? Even one aircraft could be a significant threat. And any military operation inside a populated area like Haven could bog down instantly if the citizens got in the way. But in the time they had left, the plan was as good as it could be.

"When will your sister join us, and how do we get to Wayvelsberg?" Raipur asked Devi.

"I'll call her when we leave here. She'll meet us at the depot. You can use one of the recon vehicles. We'll load you up with enough weapons and explosives to blow the place to Hell."

"One more thing," General Lambsblood said. He reached into a drawer and took out a pair of shoulder straps, each with three silver pips on it, the insignia of a captain in the Army of the Lord. "Sergeant Raipur, Captain Dieter and the senior lieutenant in your company have been arrested. You know what that means. I'm giving you a field promotion to Captain. I'll follow that up with the proper written orders as soon as tonight's operation is over, but as of now, you are Captain Raipur."

After the obligatory congratulations to newly minted Captain Raipur, the discussion over the plan went on for a few more minutes and then General Lambsblood stood. "Lady," he bowed toward Colleen, "gentlemen, it's nearly fourteen hours now, time to get ready. Eight more hours and the tyranny that has gripped this world for so long will be ended." He stepped out from behind his desk and shook each person's hand warmly. "We are on the verge of a historic moment," he said. "Generations yet unborn will look back on this day as the turning point in the history of this world. Friends, comrades, go now to your stations, and may our Lord and Savior be with you in the coming hours." There were tears in his eyes as he spoke these words. Silently, each person in the room saluted him before turning and leaving.

He stood alone at last. He'd been a foolish martinet all his career, he knew that now. But at last he was doing something to make up for that.

But God did not smile on General Lambsblood. Two hours later the Special Group arrested him.

The dinner things were still on the table where they'd left them. De Tomas was too preoccupied to bother calling a mess boy to have them taken away. Besides, he didn't want the mood interrupted. Now, a brandy snifter in one hand and an Anniversario in the other, he sat facing Comfort across a small coffee table. Comfort gingerly sampled her brandy. It was good! She'd finished about half the snifter already. The alcohol had brought a pleasant flush to her cheeks. "You have never looked more beautiful," de Tomas said, and he meant it.

Comfort stuttered, "I—I can't help thinking about all those people back at Castle Hurse—"

De Tomas inhaled and blew out a thick cloud of blue-white cigar smoke. He waved the Anniversario casually in the air. "Give me their names and I shall grant them a pardon. I am a merciful man, especially when my mercy pleases my consort-to-be."

"Thank you, sir! Their names are, um . . ." She frowned. "Ah, yes. Why there's old, er . . ." She wrinkled her brow. It must be the brandy, she realized. She wasn't accustomed to alcohol and it was fuzzing her mind. She laughed and immediately clapped a hand to her mouth. "Ex-Excuse me!" she giggled.

"Forget them for now, my dear. We'll arrange their release in the morning. Tonight, let us put our cares aside and relax." He looked carefully at Comfort as she wrinkled her brow, trying to get the names of her friends out. Good. The chlorpromazine-based tranquilizer—ancient and crude, but still an effective drug—was working. He'd take the bitch now, and when he was done, she wouldn't be of use to anyone else and she'd *have* to remain here, with him. He undressed her with his eyes and his passion rose. "Drink up," he urged.

"Whoooo!" Comfort swallowed the remainder of the brandy. "Oh my." She gasped as it warmed its way into her stomach, where its tendrils crept pleasantly into every fiber of her body. She lolled in her comfortable armchair and stretched her legs out under the table. She wondered why she'd taken that fruit knife at dinner and put it into a pocket. *Aw, who gave a damn?* The room began to swim pleasantly. She sighed. She smiled. She could taste the brandy on her breath.

She did not protest when de Tomas picked her up and carried her to a couch in one corner of the room. She thought of the shed behind her father's house, and could smell the tangy odor of old wood, seed for the garden and feed for the livestock in burlap sacks, the oil on her father's tools, the sweat of the man she loved. The couch was big enough for two. Comfort grinned and rested her head on de Tomas's shoulder as he stretched her out gently. Then he carefully began removing her robe. "Charles," she sighed, and closed her eyes.

"Believe what you will," de Tomas snorted, fumbling with the fasteners, "but it's Dominic who's mounting the assault on your ramparts, my dear, and your defenses are down."

"My dear general," Heeps gurgled, "my fearless over-stormer is away somewhere, obviously out arresting people all over town just now, so I have the privilege of conducting our little interview all on my own, heh heh. I would've seen you some time ago, but we are arresting a lot of people today and it took a while for them to get around to you. I haven't even had time to finish my talks with your other men. That lieutenant of yours, why, he squealed like a baby before I was done with him, but I really don't think he knew very much. I am so pleased we can work together now, you and I. We shall

achieve an understanding this evening, have an intimate
chat, tell each other our most private secrets, bare our souls.
Ready? Here I come, ready or not!"

Lambsblood knew he was referring to Dieter and Ben
Loman, but they knew nothing of his own plans. He gazed in
terror at Heeps. The electrodes attached to his body with
clamps had drawn blood, they were so tight, but that did not
bother him as much as that he knew what was about to come.
Everyone knew about the torture chambers of Wayvelsberg
Castle. He would talk, he knew he would, and the whole operation would be compromised! Oh, God, he thought desperately, why didn't I let my staff know? They would have
warned me and I could have died like a man! But he hadn't
let his staff in on his plans, and they did not resist the Special
Group men when they came for him, and he'd been taken totally by surprise.

Lambsblood needed time. "I'll tell you everything," he
pleaded, "every detail, just unhook me."

"Is that so, General? Well, let's see—"

*"Aiiieee!"* Lambsblood screamed as the current ripped
through him.

"That was forty M.A.'s." Heeps giggled. "Just a sample
of what is to come, my dear, dear boy. You were saying?"
Lambsblood screamed again as Heeps sent another jolt
through him and then a third.

Lambsblood gasped and panted. He fought in vain against
the straps holding him into the chair. "I'll—I'll talk, just,
*Dios! Stop it!* Please stop it!" He was weeping now, and
looked totally unmanned. Through his tears he saw Heeps
smile and caress the switches, but he did not throw any of
them. *If only I could keep him occupied! But until midnight?
Oh, God!* Maybe—just maybe—Devi would realize what
had happened and launch the attack prematurely. "I'll tell
you everything." Lambsblood wept, he sobbed, he begged.
And he talked for an hour, making up things as he went
along, trying desperately to remember the details of the false
information that poured out of him. He knew Heeps would
go over and over the story with him, and he prayed that

would take hours and that he could remember enough of what he was saying to be consistent. Heeps just sat there impassively, nodding every now and then but saying nothing.

"That is enough, General," Heeps barked at last. "I-do-not-believe-a-word-of-what-you-have-just-told-me!" he shouted. He punctuated each word with the toggle of a switch that sent sixty M.A.'s of electrical current into General Lambsblood's body. The general convulsed violently, in time to the jolts, jerking like a marionette under the control of a spastic puppeteer. He vomited and his bowels let loose and he screamed until he lost consciousness.

Lambsblood sat slumped in his chair, unconscious. The room reeked of his waste. Heeps, a wild grin on his face, eyes staring, panted harshly in the still, fetid air of the interrogation chamber. Perspiration rolled off his cheeks. He giggled, hunched over, his own body convulsing with laughter. "Ah, my dear boy," he gasped at last, "let us take a break—this ordeal has been very tiring for me too! And then, well, then, my dear, we'll just have to start all over again!" He chortled and clapped his hands together happily.

They were at the depot going over the attack plan one more time when word came to them that General Lambsblood had been arrested. The shock of the news went through the small group of officers standing around the map board as if they'd suddenly been called to attention. Major Devi's face went white. The battalion commander, a laser pointer in one hand, looked at Devi. "What in the name of the Great Buddha do we do now?"

"We attack, right now," Bass said before anyone else could respond. He shouldered his way through the officers and stood next to the battalion commander. "How long will the general hold out before he spills his guts?" he asked.

"Not very long," someone said.

"Then, gentlemen, we attack *now*!" Bass thumped the map board with a fist.

"It's still daylight! The streets will be filled with farmer's carts heading back out of the city, and tradesmen and mer-

chants going home. The Lifeguards will all be up and alert!"
one of the platoon commanders shouted. The news had put
them on the verge of panic.

"They'll see us coming if they don't already know our
plans," another officer said.

"No!" Bass said loudly enough to cut over the protests.
"Here's how we'll do it." He took the pointer out of the commander's limp hand and began to trace routes on the map.
"You head out of the city, right now, soon as you can mount
up. You get to this point here"—he indicated a highway on
the outskirts of Haven—"and then you go hell for leather
around this way, and attack Wayvelsberg from *this* direction
instead of straight through the city."

"It'll take an hour to get there that way," Devi protested.

Bass shrugged. "Move slowly to the beltway, so people
will think you're just going back out to join the rest of the
army, and then go like hell when you get to the highway.
Shoot anyone who tries to stop you. When you get to your
jump-off point, *here,* debouch into two columns, one straight
to Wayvelsberg and the other to the barracks and the airfield.
It'll be cross-country, but your Gabriels and your personnel
carriers were made for cross-country maneuvers. Yeah, you'll
be in plain sight, but they won't expect an attack from that
direction. Remember, they think your army is demoralized
and inefficient and understrength and underequipped and all
that. And everyone thinks you're buffoons."

"Gunny Bass is right," Major Devi said. "Let's do it!"

"What are our choices anyway?" the battalion commander
said. "We're all dead men if we stay here. At least this way
we'll go down fighting. And when word gets out to the field
army, maybe someone else will take up after us—"

*"No! No! And no again!"* Bass roared, "No fucking
maybes! None of that kind of thinking, Colonel! You will *not*
die, you *will* succeed, you *will* kill them, and you *will* rescue
your general! You start thinking you're going to be defeated
and you sure as hell will be! Goddamnit, men, you're *soldiers,* not a bunch of Special Group *wimps*! You've got right

and honor and whatever gods you want on your side, damnit, now go out there and get some!"

They all stood silently, staring at Bass, who had just become General Lambsblood's de facto replacement.

"All right, men," the battalion commander said, breaking the silence, "you heard the man. Let's move!" The officers sent up a cheer and everyone ran for the doors.

At the agreed-upon time and place, Gunnery Sergeant Bass, Major Devi, along with Zechariah Brattle and the people who accompanied them from New Salem, boarded a military vehicle and picked up Uma Devi.

"Gunny Bass," Devi shouted, "get into position. Stay on the radio. When I give you the word, go in!" He stepped over and hugged his sister. "Oh, Bass, by the way, how in the world did you come up with that plan so quickly, and using a map you'd never seen before?"

Bass shrugged and grinned. "Major, I'm just real good at this military shit."

# CHAPTER
## TWENTY-NINE

"Well, children," Bass said as he started the engine, "are you ready? Uma?"

"Yes, Charles," Uma Devi answered from the back of the vehicle, where she was sitting next to Colleen and Chet. She was a statuesque, athletic woman, very attractive, Bass thought as he guided the vehicle into the empty side street. He'd demonstrated to her how to load and fire the fléchette rifle that she gripped tightly by its forward hand guard. She'd been a quick study.

"Uma, why did you volunteer to come along on this mission?" Colleen asked.

"Because Jaimie is at Wayvelsberg Castle."

"Who's Jaimie?"

"My fiancé," Uma replied. "And my brother will be there too, we hope. We do things together in my family," she said with a nervous smile.

Bass shook his head. "Uma, they threw the mold away when they made you." He clapped Raipur on the shoulder. He was riding shotgun. "Let's go over the plan one more time."

"Turn right at the next cross street," Uma directed.

Bass nodded. "Uma," he continued, "guides us to within half a klick of the castle, where we ditch this car in the woods. We approach on foot to the dirt road and go to ground there until we get word that the battalion force is in position. I set the first charge. When we're inside, Raipur, Zechariah, and I go up the stairs to the top and set the second charge. Chet, Colleen, and Uma—you cover our backs while we're going up. In that narrow stairwell any attacker from outside will never get in if you concentrate your fire."

"Straight ahead four blocks, then right at the next light," Uma said.

"Time?" Bass asked.

"1750."

"Now, if the attack doesn't materialize but I can still get into Wayvelsberg Castle, I'm going in by myself," Bass told them. "The rest of you are excused."

"Not me," Zechariah answered.

"Nor me," Raipur said.

The others, even Uma, also insisted on volunteering.

"Zechariah, yes; Raipur, okay; but Colleen, Chet, Uma, no. You don't have a personal stake in any of this like Zechariah and I do, and Raipur's a professional soldier. So why risk your lives? If there's no attack, you ditch your weapons and get out of here. I mean it. No arguments. I'm going to get Comfort back or die trying. In any event, with or without the armored column, I'm going to kill some of those bastards."

"Straight ahead until the road bends to the right, maybe two kilometers," Uma said. "You can see the roof of Wayvelsberg now, over the tops of the trees, off to the right." The traffic was light, with no pedestrians and only a few of the ubiquitous horse-drawn vehicles driven by civilians going about their normal late afternoon business. "Pull over here," Uma said at last. Bass guided the car off the road and drove it deep into the bushes, beneath low-hanging tree limbs.

"Now we get out and walk," Uma said. "The dirt road to the rear of the castle is about a hundred meters down on our right."

They reached their final point and Bass parked. "We don't know how long it'll take the column to get into position, but let's move out smartly, people," Bass told them. He passed out extra magazines for the weapons and slung the shaped charges over one shoulder. He had four of them, each weighing half a kilo. It never hurt to have a backup.

"What if someone sees us?" Uma asked, slinging her rifle.

"If they don't stop, fine. By the time they can give an alarm, we'll be inside. Otherwise, kill them. I don't care who they are, shoot them. But let's hope nobody comes along until we're down that dirt road."

They trotted along in the slowly lengthening shadows, a little trail of dust rising in the still air behind them.

*1801.*

De Tomas gazed down upon Comfort's supine form. Her robe lay open down the front, exposing her to his gaze. Her eyes were closed. "We can't have this," he said aloud. He shook her by the shoulder. "Comfort! Awake, arise, my love!" She murmured something unintelligible but her eyes stayed closed. "Wake up, damn you to hell!" He shook her harder and swore. The dose had been too large! Now, instead of being just compliant, she lay there like a pillow!

*"Do you need help, there, my leader?"*

De Tomas whirled. "Gorman! What are you doing here? I didn't call for you. Get out!"

Gorman came nearer. "I have important news, my leader." He craned his neck, and seeing Comfort on the couch, his eyebrows arched and his lips twisted into a knowing smile. "Well, well, that little beautician wasn't good enough for you, eh?"

"Get out, you buffoon!"

"You should hear what I have to say," Gorman persisted.

His smile infuriated de Tomas. "I'll tell you one more time, you stupid, useless dog, *get out of here*!" He moved toward Gorman, fists clenched.

Gorman raised his hands. "Calm, my leader, be calm! The Army of the Lord is on the move. There is a column of Gabriels on their way here. I thought you should know."

De Tomas hesitated. Then, "Damnit, Gorman, take care of them! You don't need me for that! Call out the Lifeguards! Now put your tail between your legs and leave us alone! That is an order, Gorman! Scat, scram, screw off. *Now!* You understand, you worthless cur?"

Gorman did not move, only stood there, leering.

De Tomas had never faced such defiance before, and he exploded. "Gorman, I made you and I can break you, and break you I will if you don't leave now!"

Gorman stood his ground, his smile gone now. "I'm a dog, am I? Well, Dominic, this dog just grew teeth." He drew his sidearm and fired from the hip. The bolt took off de Tomas's lower jaw and part of his tongue. He stood there, astonished, not comprehending that he'd just been shot. He tried to speak but the air only wheezed through his windpipe. Then he clapped his hands to his mangled, bleeding throat and staggered toward Gorman. The Deputy Leader sidestepped adroitly, and de Tomas crashed over an armchair onto the coffee table, which collapsed under his weight. He lay there, gurgling and gasping for air.

"Oh, my," Gorman burbled, pleased with himself, "that was easy!" Then solicitously, bending over de Tomas's writhing body, he asked, "How are we doing there, Mr. Leader?" De Tomas only gurgled in reply. "Not so good," Gorman muttered. "Well . . ." He placed the muzzle of his handgun just behind de Tomas's ear and pressed the firing stud. A burst of fléchettes slammed into de Tomas's skull, and blood, brains, and bone splinters sprayed all over the room. Fragments splattered back onto Gorman, clinging to his clothes and face. "Disgusting," he muttered, holstering his sidearm. He wiped a brain fragment off his cheek and diffidently shook other gore off his uniform.

Someone banged on the door to the outer office and an anxious voice asked if there was a problem.

"Stay out of here!" Gorman roared. The banging stopped immediately.

Next he turned his attention to Comfort. It was now 1808.

They crouched in the bushes along the dirt road. Bass could clearly see the loading dock and the door, just as Uma had described it. It was hard to believe no one had spotted them. If Lambsblood had talked, they were walking into an ambush for sure. But there was no movement anywhere and it was very quiet. Bass flicked the Talk button on his radio.

"Shipper, Shipper, this is Customer. We are at the Store. I say again, we are at the Store, over." Nothing but static. "Mohammed's pointed teeth," Bass muttered, shaking the radio. "Try yours," he told Raipur.

Raipur got only static on his set too. "The castle's blocking transmissions. These sets are too weak. We wait, Charles, that's all we can do," Raipur said.

"How long should it take them to get here from the depot?" Colleen asked.

Bass shrugged. "I don't know. Let's see. They were on their way at 1745 and it's now 1809. I guess it's twenty klicks from the depot to the jumping-off spot the way they went. They ought to be about in position by now, don't you think? How fast can one of those damned Gabriels travel over improved roads anyway?"

"Fifty kph, tops," Raipur answered.

"How are the streets around here at this hour?"

"Heavily clogged out that way," Uma answered.

Bass was concerned, for reasons he could not have articulated. But he knew his instincts had never betrayed him before. "I'm not waiting, I'm going in now," he said, then stood and trotted down the road toward the loading dock.

It was 1810.

Gorman bent over Comfort. He pulled her robe aside and admired her body. No wonder de Tomas wanted this little beauty, he thought. Well, every dog has his day, and this day was his. A battle was coming. He'd just stay here and let the Special Group bloody itself. Whoever won, he'd come out on top. He placed his lips over Comfort's and reached between her legs.

From far away he heard a dull thud, as if someone had slammed a door. Gorman paused and cocked an ear toward the secret stairway, where the noise seemed to have come from. And now alarms were sounding in the castle. He'd turned his head toward the door when Comfort drove the fruit knife up under his jaw. The keen blade sliced through his tongue and into the roof of his mouth, and Gorman pitched forward. As he did, she shoved the blade in deeper, using both hands. He grunted and managed to stagger to his feet, meanwhile trying to shriek his agony to the world, but the blade had stapled his tongue firmly into his soft palate. Blood flowed out of his mouth in a torrent, huge red drops splattering everywhere. He grabbed the knife handle and yanked the blade out. It clattered harmlessly to the floor. Holding both hands to his mouth, Gorman lurched into the same armchair over which de Tomas had just fallen and plunked down on top of his erstwhile leader.

Comfort rose to a sitting position, staring at Gorman while clutching her robe about her to hide her nakedness. She felt horrified and triumphant at the same time.

Gorman crawled away from de Tomas and got to his knees. One knee slid out from under him on the blood-slick rug and he pitched forward onto his face—the pain from his wound was so terrible he didn't realize two of his front teeth were knocked out when he hit the floor.

It was now 1815.

The first charge worked perfectly but left the door hanging by a massive hinge. The door itself weighed no less than 120 kilos. Bass physically ripped it away and tossed it over the railing as if it were plywood. He saw stairs covered with debris, which rose into the darkness. Far off, the strident shriek of alarms sounded. He took the steps two at a time for the first five flights. He heard someone following him but did not look back. By the seventh flight his breath was coming in gasps. He hadn't known how out of shape he'd become.

"Give me the bomb!" Uma shouted as she came up beside him. Wordlessly, he handed her one of the charges. He'd shown everyone how to set them. She raced off up the last three flights of stairs as if riding a thermal.

Moments later Bass saw a bright flash, and heard a dull thud! Breathing hard, hand-blaster out and ready, he brushed past a grinning Uma and stepped inside.

The first thing he saw was a room in shambles. The second thing was a man crouching on the floor fumbling with a holster, drawing an ugly-looking fléchette gun. Before he could bring it to bear, Bass fricasseed him.

The traffic that day was heavy on the beltway, but the column forged on at top speed, causing a number of accidents as commuters dodged the heavy fighting vehicles. Eventually the commuters ahead of them caught on and drove helter-skelter for the sides of the road.

"Steady, steady!" the battalion commander cautioned over his command net. "Keep your intervals, keep your intervals!"

"We're almost there!" Major Devi shouted above the roar of the command car's engine. He knew they were making good time. Bass should be in position by now. Just a few more minutes.

"Just ahead," the colonel's voice crackled in Devi's headset.

"All right, men! You know what to do! You men in those Gabriels, hold on, we're going cross-country and it'll be a rocky ride!"

The column of vehicles turned off the main highway, down a steep embankment, and across a farmer's field, bouncing over irrigation ditches, crashing through fences and scattering livestock. A huge cloud of dust rose into the air behind them. If they didn't know we were coming before, Devi thought, they'll sure know it now. They smashed across a secondary road, the Gabriels and APCs leaping a meter or more into the air, sailing over the road and crashing down on the other side. Devi was firmly strapped into his seat but still felt the jar in the fillings in his teeth.

They came to another road, which ran at a right angle to their column of march. This was it! To the left, no more than five hundred meters down the road, loomed Wayvelsberg Castle. Devi marveled at how Bass had understood it all after just a glimpse at the map.

"Good hunting!" the battalion commander said, saluting the element that peeled off and headed toward the barracks. "Form a firing line!" the commander ordered, and his

Gabriels pulled up on each flank of the command car. The vehicles roared into line behind them. Everything was proceeding perfectly.

"Range, 457 meters," a gunner announced laconically.

"Fire one round on my command and then advance in line of battle," the commander ordered.

Major Devi peered through his optics at the main entrance of Wayvelsberg Castle. He could clearly see the look of astonishment on the faces of Special Group troops running for cover. One of the Gabriels fired. He counted 1001, 1002— bright flashes temporarily obscured the main gate, followed by the *thud-thud-thud* of the high-explosive projectiles impacting on and around the front of the building. Sections of the masonry were crumbling but clouds of greasy black smoke hid most of the damage.

"Forward!" the battalion commander ordered. "Fire when ready!"

The Special Group commander at the barracks had alerted his men at the first word of the approaching column, and as a result, they were deploying along the road to Wayvelsberg when the armored column appeared on their flank. The two lead Gabriels burst into flames almost immediately from the antiarmor rounds fired at them by the SG. The driver of the foremost vehicle, knowing he was a dead man as the flames roared all around him, made no attempt to get out, but drove on. Just before the fire seared his lungs, he rammed straight into a truckload of SG men; both vehicles exploded in a fireball, blocking the road and cutting the reinforcement column in half.

The last Gabriel in line, seeing what was happening on the road ahead, dismounted its infantry and drove around the barracks complex and onto the airfield, where its rapid-fire pulse gun wreaked havoc with the parked Hoppers warming up on their pads. The fully loaded aircraft burst into flames as incendiary rounds ripped into them, setting off their fuel tanks and ammo. The exploding air-to-ground rockets on board the burning Hoppers zoomed all over the tarmac, and within seconds the fuel dump went up with an enormous *whoosh!* A huge column of black smoke rose high above the airfield, orange flames licking hungrily skyward, and then *kaboom!*—the ammo dump went up.

The Gabriel commander, a young sergeant, ordered his vehicle to one side of the field and took in the damage. His driver whistled. "We did all *that*?"

"Great Dagon be praised," the sergeant muttered. He looked around. He was alone in the burning waste that had been the airfield. No one had followed him from the column, so he assumed they were all engaged along the road. "Come on." He tapped his driver on the helmet. "Let's drive around this mess and onto the road. We'll come up behind the SG and give them a taste of Hell!"

Meanwhile, back at the road, the supporting infantry, greatly outnumbered by the SG force, dismounted resolutely and returned fire as best they could. Their commander knew they were doomed, but he hoped to delay the reinforcing column long enough so the main body of the battalion could crack Wayvelsberg open.

Then the fire from the Special Group began to slacken. The column commander peered cautiously over a small mound of dirt. Men in black uniforms were streaming back into the barracks complex. They were retreating! They were bottling themselves up in their barracks! He looked at his watch. It was 1829.

Zechariah followed Bass into the room. "My God!" he shouted, seeing Comfort covered with blood. He rushed to his daughter's side.

*"Father!"* She sat up and threw her arms around him.

"Lie still, lie still! You're wounded!"

"No! No, Father! The blood belongs to him." She nodded toward the bodies on the floor. "He shot the Leader, and then I stabbed him, and then—Charles! *Charles!*" Comfort began to laugh and cry at the same time.

"Who are these two?" Bass asked, gesturing toward the dead men.

"Herten Gorman and Dominic de Tomas!" Comfort shouted happily through her tears, "They're dead! They're dead!" She was almost dancing with joy.

Raipur, weapon at the ready, came through the door, followed closely by Uma. He took in the shambles at a glance, then cautiously opened the door to the outer office. "Oops!" He slammed it shut. "There are men with weapons out there!" he warned Bass.

From behind them, down the stairwell, they heard the sharp *crack! crack!* of weapons firing. Seconds later Colleen and Chet stumbled into the room. "Men are coming up the stairs!" Colleen gasped.

"We got two of them," Chet added, "but there are more coming behind them!"

Comfort had thrown her arms around Bass, and now he gently removed them. "Not now," he said, and shoved his rifle at her, then drew his sidearm. "You know how to use this. You did a good job with that knife."

Bass turned to the others. "Chet, Colleen, cover the stairway. Comfort, Uma, you stay as far back from that outer door as you can. Zechariah, Raipur, you come with me. We're going to clear out those guys on the other side." He flicked on his comm. "Shipper, Shipper, this is Customer! We are at Home. I say again, we are at Home. Aw shit, screw this call sign shit! De Tomas and Gorman are dead. I say again, dead. Do you hear me? Over. Goddamnit!" he shouted. "Where the hell are you? We're in! We cut the snake's head off! Where the hell are you people?" Nothing but static. "Damned crap! This high-tech shit *never* works!" He tossed the comm into a corner.

"Wait!" Uma shouted. "These charges. They have time fuses. We can set them for a couple of seconds and toss them down the stairs and out there."

"Good God, woman, good thinking! Quick!" There were two left. "All right, one down the stairs, and I'll toss the other out this door, and then we go through shooting. Then, folks, it's time to fix bayonets!"

"We don't have bayonets!" Raipur gasped.

"Simulate, then. Ready?"

But before they could spring into action there was a series of heavy explosions close by. They could feel the concussions in the floor under their feet. "I believe that is the cavalry," Zechariah said. Raipur looked at him questioningly. "I read that in an old book somewhere," he said, embarrassed.

Both the outer office and the stairwell were empty. It was 1833.

# CHAPTER
# THIRTY

The Great Hall of Wayvelsberg Castle was an utter shambles. Where great speeches had once inspired thousands and mystic ceremonies of initiation had echoed through the darkened recesses, chaos now ruled. The massive likeness of Heinrich the Fowler had sustained a direct hit and lay in fragments all over the hall. Only Heinrich's massive feet stood intact on their pedestal.

Gaping holes in the roof and walls, testaments to the work of the Gabriels' gunners, allowed the morning sun to cast its rays like brilliant golden fingers into the farthest corners of the hall. Discarded weapons, clothing, wreckage, and body parts littered the flagstone floor. A Gabriel armored fighting carrier sat just inside the foyer, where it had come to rest after smashing through the fortress's defenders the night before. The barrel of its high-energy pulse gun jutted toward the roof at an impossible angle, and its armor was pitted and buckled from numerous hits. Its rear ramp was down, bloodied first-aid dressings and items of individual equipment could be seen in the troop compartment, and black pools of blood had coagulated on the floor and walls. A sticky smear of lubricants slowly spread from under the Gabriel's broken chassis, and greasy boot prints fanned out from around the ruined behemoth, viscous evidence of the infantry's victorious and bloody passage through Wayvelsberg Castle's portals.

The smoke of battle hung over the vast emptiness in a hazy pall, most of it concentrated toward the roof, where tendrils gradually filtered out through the holes. The effect of the sunlight casting rays through the smoky veil would have been beautiful were it not for the smell that permeated everything—the reek of high explosive and charred flesh, the dank mustiness of extinguished fires and the fetid odor of ruptured water and sewer lines.

As word of the castle's fall spread throughout Kingdom in the early hours of the morning, army commanders far and wide sent messages of support and loyalty to General Lambsblood. A battalion of military police was flown in just after the battle to assist in processing prisoners, of whom there were hundreds—demoralized Special Group men, bureaucrats, office workers trapped in the building when the battle started, and de Tomas's cabinet officials. They had been assembled into small groups and put under guard at convenient places in and around the fortress. The civilian workers were taken first, and most of them had been released. The Special Group men meanwhile hunkered in disconsolate bunches, awaiting transportation to a proper prisoner of war compound, where they would be thoroughly interrogated.

The members of de Tomas's cabinet who had taken refuge in Wayvelsberg the night before were being held separately under heavy guard. They would be the first of the regime to go on trial, and the commander on the scene was taking no chances that any of them might opt out by suicide.

It took hours to secure Wayvelsberg after its outer defenses were cracked. The infantrymen went room by room, from the dungeons to the roof. What they discovered in the dungeons was shocking, and it went a long way toward explaining why anyone who resisted them afterward was shot without mercy.

"We're staying right where we are," Bass had told his party. They could hear the battle raging outside, and then in other parts of the building. "Worst thing you can do in a situation like this is go wandering the halls."

"Charles," Zechariah Brattle said, extending his hand, "God bless you for all that you've done for us!"

"Hear, hear!" the others shouted. Now that the tension of

Comfort's rescue had been broken, they felt giddy on the effects of adrenaline.

"Charles," Zechariah continued, "God has taken two of the dearest people from me that any man could wish for, but He gave me you, and you saved the one person who can give any meaning to the rest of my life." He hugged Comfort and would have hugged Bass too had the Marine not busied himself with his weapon.

Embarrassed, Bass finally said, "Well, let's cover up these bodies for now, shall we? This guy lived like a prince." He gestured at the room's plush furnishings. "And if I'm not mistaken, there's a wet bar somewhere around here and probably cigars to boot. Let's look."

There were, and they found them and enjoyed them, and when at last a haggard infantryman kicked in the door from the outer office, he was astonished to see seven disheveled survivors propped up in the furniture, toasting two bloody corpses covered with drapes torn from the windows.

At last, Zechariah Brattle drank cold beer.

"First thing we have to do," Jayben Spears said as he picked his way cautiously around the spilled oil and over the piles of disgusting rubbish littering the floor, "is form an interim government."

"Who, sir?" Brigadier General Banks asked.

"That, Ricardo, is the question, isn't it? I haven't seen anything this bad in more years than I care to remember," Spears mused, taking in the ruin and wrinkling his nose at the smell. "Let's find who's in charge and offer him Confederation's services."

"First thing I want to do is get this army some communications equipment that works," Banks muttered. Ambassador Spears had also lost communication with the attacking force during the most critical phase of the action.

A begrimed officer approached them. It was Major Devi. "Mr. Ambassador! General Banks! Prentiss!" He shook hands all around. "I have good news. Dominic de Tomas and Herten Gorman are dead. I've seen the bodies. And Bass and my sister and that Brattle man and the others who went with him are safe! They're upstairs, ah—" He laughed. "—well, frankly, sobering up! But come over here and let me introduce you to someone." He led them to a makeshift aid station in one relatively undestroyed section of the Great Hall.

"General Lambsblood!" Spears exclaimed. He knelt beside the general's litter.

"We're about to put him into a stasis unit, sir," a medical officer said.

"Doctor, I'm Jayben Spears, the Confederation's ambassador to your world." He extended his hand and they shook. "The entire medical suite available on the CNSS *Marne* is at your disposal if you need it," Spears said. "General, we thought for sure you were dead!"

Lambsblood grinned. "I didn't tell them *anything,*" he said. "Not a thing. I think Dieter and Ben Loman are still alive too," he added. "They didn't finish us off. How are my men?" A strange expression came over the general's face, as if he were trying to maintain his train of thought, and then he smiled beatifically and said, "I'd like the cream of onion soup for lunch, steward, and—and . . ." His voice trailed off.

"He's been sedated," the doctor said. "He's sustained severe electrical burns and he's a little out of his head just now. Yes, if you can arrange it, I'd recommend transferring him to the *Marne* as soon as we've stabilized him."

"I'll see to it at once," Carlisle volunteered.

"I *am not* out of my head!" General Lambsblood shouted from the floor, "and I am *not* going anywhere until you get my officers over here. I have something to tell them."

Major Devi ran off to do the general's bidding.

"General, you should listen to the doctor," Spears said.

"Give me a minute." It was clear he was fighting hard to resist the stupefying effects of the painkillers he'd been administered. Soon Devi returned with the armored battalion commander and the commander of the military police battalion.

"Lean close," Lambsblood said. With considerable effort he raised himself on an elbow. "I have time to say this only once. Krishna, Major Devi, I hereby appoint you my deputy and give you the authority to manage our army's affairs while I'm gone. Gentlemen, you will all support him in this. Furthermore, Major, I hereby appoint you to the grade of General and direct that you will cooperate with Ambassador Spears to form an interim government. You are all witnesses to this." He lay back on the litter and sighed. "Never felt better," he muttered, and closed his eyes. The doctor nodded at two medics, who gently lifted him up and placed him into a stasis unit. Before it was sealed he opened his eyes and said in his normal voice, "Would somebody please get me a cheese sandwich?"

Spears and his party stood with now-General Devi and his commanders in a shaft of light shining in through the broken roof. "General, I recommend the first thing you do is get to the media and present your case for the revolution," the ambassador said. "You have the bodies of de Tomas and Gorman. Put them on display with the story of how they died. Don't waste any time. I know, it sounds gruesome, but you have got to act quickly and decisively and then follow up with real reforms."

Devi hesitated. "I don't know, Mr. Ambassador," he answered doubtfully, "propaganda is not my forte."

"Perhaps I may be of assistance?" a voice said from behind them. A pudgy, balding man stepped out of a small knot of prisoners. A hulking military policeman moved to bar his way. "Please," he pleaded, "I can help you."

"Goddamn, it's Oldhouse!" Prentiss Carlisle exclaimed.

"What do you want?" General Devi asked sharply.

"Well, gentlemen, as Minister of Propaganda and Cultural Enlightenment, I created de Tomas's image in the public eye. Very successful I was too, as you all must admit. I would be happy—honored, in fact—to perform the same service for your new and, might I say, enlightened government." He smiled and bowed from the waist.

Devi looked at Spears, who shrugged, obviously leaving the decision to him.

"You were a Judas to your congregation, Oldhouse, and a

Judas to the people of Kingdom," Devi said. "And as a Judas, you will stand trial with the other Judases. Take him away," he ordered the grinning military policeman. Then he turned to Spears. "We'll have no one from that old government in the new one, Mr. Ambassador. Since this place is a mess, I'll be needing a temporary seat for our new government. May I establish it at Interstellar City?"

"Consider it done, General," Spears said, coming to attention and saluting.

"My first decree as the head of the interim government," Devi went on, "will be to declare Interstellar City a suburb of Haven and grant free access to everyone."

Later, all of them—Bass, Zechariah, Comfort, Uma, Colleen, Chet, Raipur, and Ambassador Spears, arms linked, walked proudly out of Wayvelsberg together and into the sunlight of the new day.

"Shall I send the message now, Charlie?" Ambassador Spears asked.

"Yessir, tell my Marines I'm coming home."

"I've asked Fleet to let us keep the *Marne* in orbit here until the new government has its feet on the ground, but I'll book you passage on the first commercial ship that can get you to within walking distance of Thorsfinni's World. How does that suit you?"

"Fine, Mr. Ambassador."

"Is something troubling you, Gunny? You don't look too happy to be leaving us."

"In a way, I'm not."

"Unfinished business?"

Bass sighed and finished his beer. "In a way, yes." He sighed again and nodded. "Yes, definitely unfinished business."

"Well, then, Gunny, finish it," Spears said, and toasted Bass with his glass.

Time for good-byes.

Bass, Raipur, Chet, and Colleen sat in a corner of the officers' club at army headquarters where General Devi had given them honorary memberships, a large collection of empty beer bottles in the center of their table. Bass had insisted they not be removed until the evening was over.

Comfort could not be there, and Uma Devi was off with her fiancé, the former stormleader, Jaimie Mugabe, who'd been temporarily released from confinement to get married. He'd survived the battle at Wayvelsberg Castle and in fact had been one of the first to surrender, thus saving lives on both sides.

In general, the proceedings against the Special Group men and the former members of de Tomas's government were being conducted by the letter of the law. The one exception had been Heeps. After Captain Sepp Dieter had revived enough from his ordeal to describe what had happened to him, a search was initiated to find Heeps, who'd hidden himself in a water closet. He was dragged screaming and weeping to the nearest window and summarily hung. Two days after the fall of the fortress, his rotting body still swung from Wayvelsberg Castle's battlements, a warning to his compatriots of what they might expect after their trials.

The bodies of Dominic de Tomas and his henchman had been put on public display. Every member of de Tomas's government and every party member had been forced to view the corpses, and then the bodies were cremated and the ashes consigned to the sewer system.

Zechariah had returned temporarily to New Salem. General Devi had asked him to help with the civil administration of his interim government. In parting with Bass, the old Puritan had broken into tears. "I never knew a finer man," he said, shaking Bass's hand. "I wish there was something I could do for you, Charles."

"Well, there is, Zach."

"I'll remember you in every prayer I say for the rest of my life."

"I sort of figured you'd do something like that. But do me one favor?"

"Anything! Anything within my power!"

"Just call me 'Charlie' from now on, would you?"

Chet was leaving the next morning for his home and family, and Colleen was determined to refound the Order of St. Sulpicia. She would retake her vows. Besides, she told Bass in private, having lived a little would make her a better servant of God.

"It's getting late," Raipur reminded the others at last. "I have a big day tomorrow."

"One last toast?" Colleen proposed.

"What'll it be to?" Chet asked. "Something to remember all this by. Charles, you propose it and we'll drink to it."

Bass thought for a moment, then stood and raised his glass. "You people are more than just friends, you're comrades. I'm not going to go all weepy on you, but by God, I've never served with a finer bunch, and believe me, I know good people when I see them. So here it is. Are you ready?"

"Shout it out!" Raipur yelled.

A wry grin crossed Bass's face. "Write if you get work," he said, and drank up.

Bass found Comfort in Barracks Number Ten at Castle Hurse, supervising a work crew that was carefully dismantling the wall in the latrine. The barracks was empty. All the politicals had been freed from imprisonment, along with most of the felons sentenced for relatively minor crimes. Only the hard-core criminals were still there, in a remote section of the sprawling grounds, and their sentences were under judicial review. Other work crews were busy tearing down the barbed-wire fences and guard towers and dismantling the unoccupied barracks buildings.

"Who wrote all those names there?" Bass asked as he approached Comfort.

She whirled about in surprise, then threw her arms around his neck. The workmen nodded and smiled knowingly, then continued their work. "Oh, those are the names of all the women who were prisoners in this barracks. I'm having them put into a memorial to be built here, Charles, so we never forget them."

"You're one of a kind, Comfort." Bass smiled. "Can we talk outside?" They walked out into the street. "This is where they put you?" he asked. "Oh, Christ, Comfy, it must have been terrible here."

"It was, Charles, the worst experience of my life. But," she sighed, "these last months, I've learned a lot about myself and other people." She brightened. "You know, General Devi, when he heard my suggestion about a memorial to the martyrs who died here, asked me to chair the commission. That's why I'm having the panels removed."

"He picked the best person for the job. Comfy, I—"

"I know. You have to go back to your Marine Corps."

"Yes. I'm still a Marine, and the Corps is my profession. And I can't take you with me."

"I know."

That was the answer Bass was looking for, but strangely, he was not happy with it. "Comfort, you know, by the time I'm sixty or so and ready to retire and settle down, you'll just be in your prime years."

"I know."

"And, well, you know, life in the Corps for a married woman is pretty hard. I'd be gone on deployments all the time, and company business would keep me busy while in garrison, and, well, you know . . ." he finished lamely.

"I know."

"And your father needs you. And, well," he gestured, "you have important work to do here."

"Yes, I do."

"Well, goddamnit, Comfort, you really *are* one of a kind." He laughed. "Would you come to Thorsfinni's World if I asked you to?"

"Yes, I would."

"Leave all this, your home?"

"Yes, I would."

"And marry me?"

"Yes, I would. But Charles, I'd come even if we didn't

marry. I'd do your washing, sleep under your bunk in the barracks if I had to, or rent a room in town, get a job as a barmaid. I wouldn't care."

"All right—all right." He was holding her hands now. "I have to go back by myself, report back in. It'll be a while, but I'll send for you. Christ on a crutch, what am I getting myself into?"

"Charles, you shouldn't take the Lord's name in vain like that, but goddamn, I'll come, fucking-A I'll come!"

"Oh, no," Bass groaned, "I've rubbed off on her!"

The Flood boys—now the Brattle boys, because their mother had married Zechariah—Joab, twelve, and Samuel, nine, often spent their free time exploring the banks of the stream that ran by the caves just outside New Salem, chasing the harmless water bugs and amphibians that lived there. It was on one such expedition that they made an astonishing discovery: a toddler. He wasn't a lost babe from any of New Salem's families, and they didn't recognize him as being from any of the other villages they knew. The small child was quietly feeding on a large bug he had captured. He squealed in surprise and fright and dived into the shallow water when he saw the boys. They plunged in after him, and in the course of a wet struggle, subdued the little fellow.

"Who is he?" Samuel asked his brother, who was older and should know the answer to such things. The boys held the gasping, shivering little one by his stubby little legs—he was obviously male.

"*What* is he?" Joab asked back. He held the toddler up and showed his brother the strange lines on the little one's sides and his pointed teeth.

Samuel scrambled back to the stream bank and retrieved the rest of the water bug the little fellow had been eating. "Here," he said, holding it out to the strange babe. He snapped up the remains of the bug, swallowed it with an audible gulp, then stared at the boys with his liquid black eyes.

"Jedo," he said.

"Whoever he is, he can talk!" Joab exclaimed.

"Jedo," the toddler repeated.

"Let him go and see if he tries to get away," Samuel suggested.

Joab took off his belt and fastened it like a leash around the little one's chest, under his arms.

"Come on, Jedo, we're taking you home to mama!" He turned to Samuel. "Mama will get mad at us if she finds out we found a baby and left him out here alone."

Hannah Brattle was clearly baffled by the toddler her sons called Jedo. "That is the *oddest* child I've ever seen," she exclaimed. She was more than a little disturbed by the little one's pointed teeth and the strange lines on his sides. He looked at her as if he expected something of her as he stood unsteadily on her lap, looking up at her with a baby's huge eyes. Well, she supposed, a child this small would expect something of a woman. "Why do you call him Jedo?" she asked her sons.

"Because that's what he said," Samuel answered.

"Can we keep him?" Joab asked. "He eats bugs."

"He doesn't seem to have a home," Samuel jumped in.

"I think he's an orphan," Joab added.

"I wonder who you are, little man. Where are your parents?" Hannah asked.

Jedo burbled.

Hannah's boys shrugged.

"I have never seen anything like this," Hannah mused almost to herself. A tiny knot of doubt glowed in her stomach, almost a twinge of fear. The toddler was small and harmless looking, but didn't he resemble those devils that killed Samuel Brattle back in the woods? She had not seen them herself at the time, but Zechariah and the others had described them. And then there were the devils they'd seen at that camp or whatever, on their way back to New Salem. She'd only seen them through the grass and at a distance, and they didn't really look very much like this baby, but . . .

"Mother, Baby Jedo is one of God's creatures, same as we are!" Samuel reminded her.

"Yes, so was the devil, Samuel"—she wondered why she made that connection—"as you should remember from *Paradise Lost,* if either of you ever paid attention when we read it last year. Well, all right, for now, until your father gets back from Haven."

# CHAPTER
# THIRTY-ONE

Colonel Israel Ramadan, deputy commander of 34th FIST, read the message summary from the CNSS *Vicksburg,* a light cruiser that had just arrived in orbit around Thorsfinni's World, then reread "Paragraph 4, Personnel." He linked to "Annex C, Personnel Details," and quickly scanned it before reading it more carefully. Then he reread "Paragraph 1, Navy Transit Order." He quickly tapped out the commands that sent the relevant portions of the summary to Brigadier Sturgeon, then contacted the FIST commander by voice.

"Got a minute, boss?" Ramadan asked.

"Sure, Come on over," Sturgeon replied.

Half a minute later Ramadan swept through Sturgeon's anteroom with barely a nod to the secretary and aide. He hardly paused to knock on the door frame before stepping into the inner office and closing the door behind him. Sturgeon cocked an eyebrow. When his number two closed the door, it meant something important, or something highly unexpected.

"Have a seat, Ram. What do you have for me?" It couldn't possibly be another deployment already, could it? The FIST was still shorthanded from the Kingdom Campaign.

"Take a look at this," Ramadan said. Instead of sitting, he reached over Sturgeon's desk to bring up the *Vicksburg* message on his console. "And then tell me how the hell you managed to pull it off." Only when he saw the message appear did he sit.

Sturgeon read "Paragraph 4, Personnel." A smile briefly

creased his face as he gave "Annex C, Personnel Details" a quick glance.

"It pays to be on first name terms with people in high places," he said, looking at Ramadan.

"Yes?"

"When we stopped at Kingdom on our way back, I sent a back-channel to Andy." Another fleeting smile. "That's Assistant Commandant Aguinaldo, to you. He came through."

Ramadan leaned back and looked at his commander with a mix of disbelief and admiration. "It looks like he rerouted Marines who just graduated from schools and yanked Marines from duty posts on Earth."

"It does indeed," Sturgeon agreed. He looked back at his monitor. "I asked Andy to get us the replacements we need as fast as possible. I was sure he'd come through, but I didn't expect him to get seventy-five new Marines to us so quickly." His brow furrowed. "I wonder how long it'll take for the other forty-three to reach us?"

Ramadan accepted the question as rhetorical and ignored it. "Call up 'Paragraph 1.'"

Sturgeon did and cocked an eyebrow again as he read it. He looked back at Ramadan but his eyes didn't focus on him. "It would appear that the assistant commandant is also on first name terms with people in *very* high places." The paragraph, a Navy Transit Order, instructed the captain of the *Vicksburg* to head to Thorsfinni's World by the most expedient route and delay his previously given cruise orders until after he delivered his Marine charges to 34th FIST.

Ramadan nodded. There was no hint of a deployment for 34th FIST in the message summary or any of its annexes. A major deployment was the only reason he could think of for the Chief of Naval Operations to so abruptly alter cruise orders. The Combined Chiefs wouldn't overrule the CNO on such a matter. That meant Aguinaldo had pulled strings with either the Minister of War or the President of the Confederation of Human Worlds.

A light on Sturgeon's desk began blinking. He touched a button next to it. "Speak," he said.

"Sir," came the voice of his aide, Lieutenant Quaticatl, "the *Vicksburg* has launched six Essays. ETA at Boynton Field, fifteen minutes."

"Thank you. Get my vehicle, I'll meet them. I want the sergeant major to come with me." He cut the intercom before Quaticatl finished saying, "Aye aye, sir" and told Ramadan, "That must be our replacements. Let's go meet them."

The first man off the first Essay to make planetfall at Camp Ellis's landing field was the light cruiser's captain, followed immediately by his chief of ship. A ground crewman ushered the two into a landcar, which whisked them the hundred meters to the waiting Marines.

The captain dismounted, came to attention two paces in front of Sturgeon and saluted. "Sir, I'm Commander Egerhazi, captain of the *Vicksburg*. This is my chief of ship, Senior Chief Bosun Penya."

Sturgeon returned the salute. "Welcome to Camp Ellis, Commander, Chief." He introduced the members of his party, and hands were shaken all around. "I'm surprised to see you. I wasn't expecting to get replacements so fast."

"I'm surprised to be here myself, sir."

"I understand you've got seventy-five Marines for me."

"Ninety-two, sir."

"Annex C only showed seventy-five."

"Yessir, that's how many I brought from Earth. We had a stop along the way to deliver a diplomatic pouch to the embassy on St. Brendan's. A drone from HQMC arrived just a few hours ahead of us. When we broke orbit, we had half of the embassy's Marine guards added to those we already had for you. Something else wasn't in the message summary I transmitted to your headquarters." He made a sour face. "I'm also turning over half the *Vicksburg*'s Marine contingent.

"Sir, I'm normally the last man to leave the ship when we make planetfall. But with all due respect, I just had to meet the Marine commander who swings enough weight to delay the start of a warship's cruise, and strip both an embassy and that warship of half their Marine contingents."

"You were delayed leaving Earth?"

The *Vicksburg's* commander nodded. "We were less than an hour from breaking orbit when the CNO himself ordered us to stand by for new orders and passengers."

Egerhazi also delivered a sealed communication to Sturgeon.

The clerical work to put the new men in their units was complete by the next afternoon, but Brigadier Sturgeon held them isolated in the FIST HQ area for two more weeks. The sealed communication Commander Egerhazi had delivered was from Assistant Commandant Aguinaldo:

Ted,

Thanks for your reports. They gave me a much clearer picture of what happened on Kingdom and Quagmire than the official reports did. Be assured that I was able to use all of it to good effect.

I'd like to tell you more, but there are things I won't entrust to a written communication. Besides, most of your replacements are boarding the CNSS *Vicksburg* right now and I have to get this up there before she sails. Expect the rest of your replacements within two or three weeks. Be patient, I'll fill you in when I see you—which will be sooner than you expect.

Andy

When he sees me? Sturgeon wondered. Which will be sooner than I expect? Am I being called back to Earth? He shook his head. Not likely. Is he coming here? He knew that when the ACMC visited posts, it was announced well in advance, and "Sooner than I expect" wasn't well in advance.

His thoughts weren't productive, so he put them aside for the time being and devoted his energies to directing his staff to develop new tactics to use against the Skinks—he was positive 34th FIST would fight them again, and probably sooner than later—and to training his Marines to fight that enemy more effectively. In odd moments he tried to figure out why the Skinks simply attacked, and resisted every attempt at communication.

Aguinaldo surprised him again. The remaining twenty-six replacements, to bring the total up to 118, arrived within two weeks. Sturgeon ordered all the newly assigned Marines assembled in the base theater for a "greetings from the commander" message. He didn't always bother with such things, and when he did he usually let FIST Sergeant Major Shiro deliver it. But he gave this one himself.

The newly arrived Marines, ranging in rank from PFC to lieutenant, sat in the center-front rows of the theater built to hold two thousand people. The first sergeants of every company in the FIST sat behind them, keeping close watch on everyone. There was a buzz of anticipation as the new men speculated on whether Brigadier Sturgeon was going to explain why their orders had been changed so abruptly, or why they had been yanked out of their duty stations before normal rotation and sent to a very active FIST located on a hardship world. The Marines who had already been through a change of permanent duty station knew how unusual it was, and that such changes were usually made for disciplinary reasons—not that they'd done anything to merit disciplinary action. In comparing notes with each other, only a few of them noticed that almost none of them had families, or at least no family they were close to. Those few thought there was something more ominous than simple disciplinary action behind their transfers—but they didn't share their concerns with the other Marines.

Sergeant Major Shiro, in his dress reds, marched onto the stage. His heels clicked loudly enough on the wooden boards to draw all eyes to him and cut off most conversation. The left breast of his tunic bore more decorations and medals than most of the replacements had ever seen on one Marine before.

"Attention on deck!" Shiro bellowed.

The 118 replacements and the company first sergeants jumped to their feet and snapped to attention.

Brigadier Sturgeon, also in dress reds, marched onto the stage and took his place front and center. There was a lectern, but he didn't hide behind it. He stood at ease at the front of the stage, his feet spread to shoulder width, hands clasped loosely behind his back. His scarlet tunic had at least as many decorations and medals as the sergeant major's, maybe more. He looked over his new men for a long moment before speaking.

"Good morning, Marines," he finally said.

"Good morning, sir," they all said back.

"At ease." There was a brief rumble as the Marines sat.

Sturgeon looked at them for a moment longer, then resumed.

"You're probably wondering what's going on," he said. "Most of you are now in your second or third unit since enlisting—some of you have been around for a good deal longer than that. So you know that once orders have been cut and issued, they're graven in stone for anything short of a major deployment. You also know how unusual it is for Marines to be transferred in the middle of an assignment for anything other than disciplinary reasons—which isn't the case for any of you. I'm about to clarify matters for you."

The house lights dimmed and a hologram popped up to rotate next to Sturgeon. It was a curious figure, not much more than a meter and a half tall clad in a tan field uniform none of the replacements had ever seen before. The figure had a three-tank arrangement on its back, and a hose ran from the tanks to a nozzle held in his hands. His face was convex, his skin a dry-looking tan, like old parchment, and there was something peculiar about his eyes.

"I know he doesn't look like much, Marines, but he's the fiercest opponent I've ever encountered on the battlefield. He is what we call a 'Skink.' " He paused to observe the men's reactions, which he could still see in the darkened theater. Some showed none, some looked puzzled, and some were merely curious. A few opened their eyes wide as they caught the implication of "what we call."

"He's not human," Sturgeon said bluntly. He ignored the

subdued gasp that met his announcement. "I know you've always been told *Homo sapiens* is the only sentient species in the known universe. Other than the Marines of 34th and 26th FISTS, who just fought a major campaign against them, and the residents of Kingdom, where that campaign was fought, almost nobody knows about the Skinks. The top level of the Confederation government has made the determination that their existence will be kept secret.

"Since you are now in on the secret, you are quarantined. Until such time as new orders come in—if they come—you are in 34th FIST for the duration. You will not be transferred to another unit. All retirements and other releases from active duty are canceled. You may not go on off-world leave. You are not to speak of these matters to anyone outside of 34th FIST, or anyplace where anyone outside of 34th FIST might overhear. You will not, in any way, shape, or form, communicate any of this information to anyone off-world. The penalty if you violate any of these strictures is Darkside. Yes, Darkside does exist, it is not just a boogeyman parents use to scare their children into behaving.

"This isn't as bad as it might sound at first. Thirty-fourth FIST has been quarantined for over a year now. No one has gone to Darkside. We are all living our lives, we are all carrying on. You will adjust.

"Welcome to the Confederation's unofficial First Contact military unit.

"Now, Sergeant Major Shiro will release you to your company first sergeants." He turned to march off the stage.

"ATTENTION ON DECK!" Shiro roared. Everyone jumped, up, stunned by what they'd just been told, and stood rigidly at attention until Shiro ordered "AT EASE!" Then he handed them over to their first sergeants.

How are they taking what I just told them? Sturgeon wondered as he left the stage. He knew it was a hell of a thing to be told, especially when they were already confused and concerned about the way they'd been transferred.

Well, he thought as he straightened his shoulders even more than they already were, they're Marines. Marines go where we are sent and do what we are told. Nobody says we have to like it. They'll deal with it.

Third platoon met outdoors, along the sunny side of the barracks. It was a mild summer day at this latitude of Thorsfinni's World, with temperatures not much over fifteen degrees centigrade. The gusty breeze smelled of fish, but the Marines didn't notice; Thorsfinni's World always smelled of fish. Three Marines they didn't know, a lance corporal and two PFCs, stood at a corner of the wall. They were obviously new men, replacements for the Marines they'd lost on Kingdom, but they didn't have the slightly nervous look of Marines joining a new platoon.

Corporal Dean murmured to Corporal Claypoole, "They look like they just came off a major campaign."

"Yeah," Claypoole agreed. "Someone must have told them about us."

"Hell of a way to wake up in the morning," Corporal Pasquin said.

"You've got that right," Corporal Chan chimed in.

Corporal Dornhofer looked at the three Marines. "I'll bet they're put off by the fishy smell," he said.

"Do you smell fish?" Claypoole asked. "I don't smell fish." The others laughed.

Corporal Kerr wondered if he was going to be given one of the new men. If he didn't get one, he'd have to talk to Staff Sergeant Hyakowa and find out why not. When he hadn't been given one of the six replacements the platoon received midway through the Kingdom Campaign, he'd wondered if that was because Hyakowa and Lieutenant Rokmonov, who had taken over as platoon commander after Gunny Bass was killed, didn't trust him to break in a new man. He knew he was capable. Or thought he was. He shook his head sharply. Stop that! he ordered himself. He was probably better than anyone else in the platoon at teaching a new man. If he hadn't been away for so long after being almost killed on Elneal, he'd probably be a squad leader now. I'd better get one of the new men, he thought.

Corporals Barber and Taylor from the gun squad looked at the new men and tried to figure out which of them was a gunner. They figured the gun squad would be reorganized and Barber would get the new man—he was both senior and more experienced.

Staff Sergeant Hyakowa strode out of the barracks and took a position facing the members of third platoon.

"All right," he said. "We've got new Marines for the platoon, but you already figured that out." He nodded toward the new men. "The platoon's getting a reorganization," he went on, addressing the older Marines. "I'll give the basic assignments to the squad leaders, then you reorganize your squads and report to me how you did it." This was the normal way new men were integrated into the platoon. Hyakowa crooked a finger at the new men. They stepped out from the corner of the barracks and walked over to the platoon sergeant.

"Lance Corporal Groth just graduated from Marine Corp communications school on Earth. Yeah, that's right, he's way overqualified to be a platoon comm man. Someone must have pulled some heavy duty strings to get us replacements as fast as possible.

"PFC Dickson, show yourself." A tall Marine with a scar on his left cheek took half a step forward. "He comes to us directly from the CNSS *Vicksburg,* where he was ship's complement. That's right, one day he's a spacegoing bellhop, the next day he's in the mud with us. This is his first assignment to a FIST. He's got a primary MOS of guns. Hound, he's yours."

Sergeant Kelly gave Dickson a wave, and the new man joined him.

"That leaves us PFC Summers. He has a tour with 39th FIST behind him, but he joins us directly from embassy duty on Carhart's World. Rat, you've got him."

Sergeant Linsman, second squad's leader, nodded. Summers joined him.

"That's it. I'm not going to muck about anymore with

squad assignments right now. We've got a new platoon commander coming in and he might have other ideas."

"Do we know who the new ensign is yet?" Sergeant Ratliff asked.

"All I know is his name's Bestwick. He's meeting with the Skipper now and gets command tomorrow at morning formation. Any other questions?" There weren't any. "Squad leaders, do your things. Groth, come with me." He headed back into the barracks, trailed by Groth.

"Second squad, gather 'round," Linsman said. His men formed a tight semicircle in front of him and Summers. He looked at his squad for a long moment, pondering how he was going to plug Summers in.

The easiest thing would be to give him to Claypoole, who was missing a man. But Claypoole was his most junior fire team leader and simply didn't have the experience. Chan could do it; he'd proved that on Kingdom when he got two new men. But the best man for the job was Kerr. Hell, Kerr should be squad leader, not him, Linsman thought. But he already had Kerr running herd on Corporal Doyle, and Kerr was probably the man in the platoon best qualified to handle Lance Corporal Schultz. So what was he to do? He didn't want to give Claypoole a new man until he had more experience or there were so many replacements at once that he had no way to avoid it. Neither did he want to make Chan the squad's official breaker-inner of new men. That meant he had to give Summers to Kerr. Besides, he'd gotten the impression that Kerr had his nose bent out of joint on Kingdom when he wasn't given one of the new men there.

He had to move one of Kerr's Marines to one of the other fire teams, but which one? And to whom? He couldn't give Corporal Doyle to Chan or Claypoole; even though he was filling a lance corporal's slot, Doyle had time in grade over both Chan and Claypoole, so technically he was senior to both of them. And Schultz, who seemed to live and breathe combat, was very capable of scaring the shit out of anybody given command over him.

Well, he was a Marine, and like the Marines always said, "When in doubt, act decisively."

"Tim, you get the new guy. Rock, I'm moving Hammer over to you."

Kerr simply nodded. He'd rather have lost Doyle than Schultz, but he'd already thought along the same lines Linsman had and understood why he made the choice he did.

Claypoole grinned as he said to Schultz, "Welcome to my home, Hammer," but he looked a bit sickly. Linsman expected *him* to handle Schultz? Was the man out of his flipping gourd? *Nobody* could handle Schultz, except Gunny Bass and Corporal Kerr.

Linsman looked at Claypoole, Schultz, and Lance Corporal MacIlargie. "I've got you where I want you," he said. "All my problem children and troublemakers together in one fire team, right where I can keep an eye on you." He managed not to quail when Schultz looked at him.

Ensign Bestwick had mixed emotions. He'd been a staff sergeant, a platoon sergeant, and became acting platoon commander when his platoon's commander was badly wounded on a deployment a year earlier. He performed well enough that when his FIST returned to its base he was offered a commission and was sent to Officer Training School on Arsenault. But the day before graduation, he was put aboard a fast frigate and sent to Thorsfinni's World to join 34th FIST. He wasn't happy about missing the graduation ceremony or about losing his assignment to 11th FIST. On the other hand, 34th FIST had a reputation for being hardcharging, and a deployment and combat record to back up the reputation, where 11th FIST was almost a ceremonial unit rather than a combat unit. So he felt good about that. Then there was that shocking news Brigadier Sturgeon dropped on them less than an hour ago. He still hadn't gotten over that, and doubted he would in the immediate future.

Sentient, spacefaring aliens who only wanted to fight and kill humans? That was the first he'd ever heard of sentient aliens, except for rumors. And 34th FIST was the designated military First Contact unit—and was quarantined to keep the secret safe? He might never go home again? Not that he had a real "home" to go to, but still . . . And never get transferred or be allowed to retire? If those "Skinks" really were as bad as he'd been told, living long enough to retire was problematic anyway.

If all that wasn't bad enough, here he was, facing his new company commander, Captain Conorado, and Company L's other officers and senior NCOs, and they weren't doing a very friendly job of welcoming him aboard. Instead of the captain and other officers taking him to the officers' club, the eight of them were all crammed into the Skipper's office. Conorado was leaning back in his swivel chair, playing with a stylus and not doing a lot more than eagle-eyeing him until he became uncomfortable. The others were doing their best to keep a distance from him, and not one of them looked in the least bit happy about his presence.

Conorado finally leaned forward and placed the stylus at a precise angle near the corner of his small desk.

"Mr. Bestwick," he said, "you are in a very difficult position. And I don't mean simply being so unceremoniously dumped into a situation none of us signed up for. Tomorrow morning you are going to take over third platoon, and that's a tough job for anyone who hasn't already proved himself." He held up a hand to forestall anything Bestwick might want to say about a need to prove himself. "Yes, I know you've performed well through your entire Marine career. It's all right there in your record and in the letters of recommendation from your former commanders up to FIST.

"But you haven't proven yourself to the Marines of third platoon. They're going to be judging you against one of the harshest scales I can imagine. Every step of the way they're going to be comparing you to their former platoon commander, Gunnery Sergeant Charlie Bass, who was killed by the Skinks on our most recent deployment.

"There's hardly a man in this company, up to the rank of staff sergeant, who wouldn't have wanted to be in Charlie's platoon. Probably a majority of the men in the infantry bat-

talion would have liked it. That's who you have to follow."
Something must have shown in Bestwick's face, because
Conorado rushed right on with, "Don't labor under the mis-
conception that popular commanders are necessarily poor
commanders. I know, we all know, that history is replete with
commanders who were very popular with their men but
wound up getting them killed and losing battles and even
wars because they were poor commanders.

"Charlie Bass wasn't one of them. Charlie Bass's platoon
won their battles, all of them. His platoon won battles for the
entire company. If he'd been willing to accept a commission
and go up through the officer ranks, he could have been an
outstanding FIST commander. But he didn't want to be more
than a platoon commander.

"Mr. Bestwick, in effect, you're following a legend. That's
a tough act to follow. I don't envy you."

He stood abruptly. "Gentlemen, I believe the sun has
passed the yardarm. Let's retire to the O Club and give Mr.
Bestwick a proper welcome aboard before we throw him to
the wolves."

# EPILOGUE

The air scrubber in First Sergeant Myer's little cottage was fighting a losing battle with the Fidels. Sergeants Major Shiro and Parant both risked burned lips from the stubs they managed to keep burning in the corner of their mouths. Gunnery Sergeant Thatcher gnawed more than puffed his and had to frequently relight it. Chief Hospitalman Horner puffed more sedately and still had three inches of Fidel between the fingers of his left hand. Staff Sergeant Hyakowa had just snubbed out the stub of his and looked at the humidor, wondering if he should take a second without a specific invitation from their host. Myer himself was on his second, a full twenty centimeters of stogie jutting from his mouth. The thoroughly masticated end of his first lay soggy in the ashtray that sat near his wrist.

"You're showing part of a busted straight and you're staying in, Bernie?" Thatcher snarled. "You think I came in with the kwangduks, I can't tell a bluff when I see one?" He was showing a pair of deuces. "I'm in."

Parant removed the cigar stub from his mouth and turned up the edge of his hole card as though looking at it for the first time. Then he regarded Thatcher blandly. "Goldie," he said as he dropped his stub in his ashtray and reached for a fresh Fidel.

Myer *harumphed* and looked at his hole card again. He showed a trey, seven, and ten of spades. "Who dealt this garbage?" he groused.

"You did," Horner said.

"Oh. Well, in that case, dealer's in." He tossed a kroner

into the pot. He looked around the table. "Nobody's out. I'm surprised. Wang, stop mooning and take another Fidel before Fred gets the last good one."

Hyakowa's poker face slipped for a second, then he reached for the humidor and barely managed to beat Shiro to it. The FIST sergeant major glowered but let the junior man have his choice.

"Six, got a pair showing, Frigga high," Myer said as he dealt Hyakowa his fifth card. "Frigga, no help," to Horner. "Odin, there goes Bernie's straight." He tossed the card to Shiro. "Nope, busted straight's still alive." He glanced at the open place, then dealt Parant a seven to go along with the eight, ten, and Thor showing. "Ten, no help," to Thatcher. "Dealer gets a . . ." He flipped the top card over. "Shit. Dealer's out." He turned his cards facedown. "Wang, it's up to you."

Hyakowa finished lighting his fresh Fidel and studied his four up cards. "Two." He tossed two kroner into the pot and looked at Horner.

"I'm out," the infantry battalion's second-ranking corpsman said, and flipped his cards facedown.

Shiro studied his cards, peeled up the corner of his hole card, and drummed his fingers on the tabletop.

"Your choices are see, raise, or fold," Myer said. "You're showing garbage."

"But you don't know what this is," Shiro said, and plunked a finger down on his hole card.

Thatcher snorted. "Garbage is garbage, your hole card doesn't matter."

Shiro shrugged and tossed two coins into the pot. "I want to see if you've got that third deuce."

"See, raise." Parant shoved three kroner into the pot. His face showed nothing, not even awareness of how close the coal of his Fidel was to his lips.

Thatcher leaned back and stared at Parant. "You *do* think I just came in with the kwangduks. A busted straight is garbage. See." He put three kroner into the pot.

"You still in, Wang?" Myer asked. "Your pair of sixes beats

the deuces, but there's a possible flush and a possible straight showing."

Hyakowa leaned back and thought. His hole card was another Frigga, which meant he beat anything Thatcher could have unless his hole card was another deuce. But what were the odds of Shiro or Parant filling their flush or straight? He began to extend a hand, but nobody but him ever knew whether it was to ante up or turn his cards over because the door suddenly slammed open.

"Good, you saved a place for me," Gunnery Sergeant Charlie Bass said. He dropped a small duffel on the floor. "Where's the beer? I'm thirsty."

"In the cooler next to your chair."

That was the last thing anybody heard clearly for the next several minutes. The six men jumped to their feet and rushed to greet Bass back to the living; they knocked over chairs and jarred the table, scattering cards and coins. Two ashtrays thudded to the floor.

Finally things calmed down enough for Bass to tell them, "I made planetfall less than twenty minutes ago. I don't know if someone else is in my quarters in the barracks, so I couldn't go there. It's late enough that the mess hall is closed. I'm hungry and thirsty. What do you have to eat and drink?"

Parant used his arm to sweep a clear space at the table while Myer ordered his food servo to cook up a reindeer steak with all the trimmings. It was ready before Bass half finished the bottle of ale Horner pressed into his hand.

Myer resumed his place and asked, "How the hell did you survive? That site was spattered with gore. Other than your helmet and ID bracelet, all we found of you was a few strands of DNA. We figured their rail gun zeroed in and vaporized you."

The mention of the rail gun caused a digression while Shiro explained how the navy engineers figured out what the Skinks' new weapon systems were.

Bass whistled when Shiro finished. "Damn," he said around a mouthful of steak and trimmings, "I'm just glad they haven't figured out how to turn that into personal weapons."

"Shut your mouth, Charlie," Thatcher snapped, and knuckled him in the short ribs. "We don't want to give those things new ideas. And what were they doing capturing you? Everyone was convinced they never took prisoners."

"I don't know." Bass shook his head and took another bite. He didn't answer until he swallowed his food. "They used drugs to mess with our memories. Mine is still mostly blank on what happened when I was a POW."

"So you just woke up one day and everybody was gone?"

Bass nodded, using a piece of bread to push the last crumbs of his meal onto his fork. "That's about right. Except there were four of us."

That set off so many questions he had to let out a parade ground roar to get them to shut up.

"How about if you just let me tell you what happened and hold your questions until I'm finished?"

They grumbled, but agreed. They grumbled even more when they noticed how the cards and money had been messed up.

"I'll put the pot aside, we'll use it to enrich the next hand," Myer said. That was greeted with more complaints, but nobody said not to.

Bass told his story, and his audience listened enrapt for half an hour.

"I always thought those theocrats should be overthrown," Myer mused at the end, "but not that way."

Horner nodded. "Got rid of one bad government for another just as bad."

"All it took was one good Marine with a wild hair up his ass to fix matters," Hyakowa said.

Everybody laughed. Not too loudly, though. In their self-image, it was well within the capabilities of "one good Marine" to overthrow a planetary government. And it wasn't as though Charlie Bass had done it single-handed. He'd merely led one small faction and coordinated its final activities with a larger faction. Besides, he hadn't even had a direct hand in the demise of Dominic de Tomas or his chief henchman.

"So what happened on the campaign after I was captured?" Bass asked when the polite laughter ebbed. Everybody began talking at once, and he popped another brew while he patiently waited for them to sort themselves out to tell the story.

At the end of the telling, he breathed a sigh of relief. "No more dead in third platoon, that's good. The only new names I'll have to learn are the replacements for the men who died before I was captured."

Silence thudded over the group.

Bass looked warily around the table. "What haven't you told me?"

"Ah, Charlie," Myer said, "some of the replacements that we got are officers. An ensign got assigned to Company L. He's getting third platoon."

Bass fell back in his chair, stunned by the news. He was losing his platoon! "Damn! What's going to happen next, do I get assigned to issuing sports equipment for the FIST?"

"There is one out, Charlie," Shiro said.

Bass looked at him like the "out" might be worse than losing command of third platoon. "Tell me."

"I can get the brigadier to offer you a commission tomorrow. If you accept it, he can find another position for that ensign and let you keep your platoon."

"Damn," Hyakowa muttered. "Isn't it bad enough I have to take orders from him, you mean I'll have to salute and call him 'sir' too?"

Read on for an exciting preview of
**STARFIST: WORLD OF HURT**
by David Sherman and Dan Cragg
Published by Del Rey Books in
December 2004.

Gunnery Sergeant Charlie Bass woke with a groan on the first morning after his return to Thorsfinni's World. His head hurt and his stomach began lecturing him on the need to mend his evil ways. He cracked an eyelid to see where he was, and immediately slammed it shut to block the murderous sunlight that stabbed into his brain. He groaned again, and lay unmoving while he tried to reconstruct what he'd done the night before, in hope that would give him a clue to where he was.

Right. It had been evening and he'd gone straight to First Sergeant Myer's quarters, where he'd found the Top, Gunny Thatcher, Staff Sergeant Hyakowa, Doc Horner, and both the FIST and battalion sergeant majors eating reindeer steaks, drinking Reindeer Ale, and playing cards. They'd all been shocked to see him—except for the first sergeant, who acted like he was expecting him. Bass had joined them for an evening of eating, drinking, and general revelry. He smiled at the memory, but quickly stopped because the effort hurt too much. He vaguely remembered being taken very late to the transient barracks, where newly arrived Marines were quartered when they joined 34th FIST, before being assigned to units.

He listened, but didn't hear any of the normal sounds of Marines performing their duties in Camp Major Pete Ellis. Then he remembered: last night was Fifth Day on Thorsfinni's World. Which meant this must be Sixth Day morning, and nearly everybody was off base on liberty.

He shifted into a more comfortable position—well, a less uncomfortable position—and assayed another smile; that one didn't hurt as much, so he let it linger. It was such a comfort to wake up without immediately worrying about fending off an attack from the Skinks, or the army of Dominic de Tomas.

*Comfort.* He sighed as he remembered the young daughter of Zachariah Brattle. Well, not *that* young—she was a full-grown woman, after all, which she'd demonstrated to him beyond all doubt. That woman would make a wonderful wife for a warrior. He sighed again. But Comfort was still on Kingdom, probably holding down some important government post, and he was back where he belonged, with 34th FIST on Thorsfinni's World, and he'd never see her again.

Back where he belonged.

He swore, comfort and Comfort forgotten, and rolled up to sit on his rack with his legs over its side.

*Right. Back where I belong.* He'd been commander of Company L's third platoon for three or four years, ever since Ensign vanden Hoyt was killed in action on Diamunde. But he was a gunnery sergeant, a company level noncommissioned officer; a platoon commander was supposed to be an officer. And last night he'd been told that during the time he was thought dead, an ensign had been assigned to take command of his platoon.

Shit.

He *liked* being commander of Company L's third platoon. Of course, he could get command of another platoon easily enough—all he had to do was accept a commission.

Charlie Bass liked having his own platoon, but had refused a commission every time one was offered to him. In his opinion, officers had to do too much crap. They had to have fancy mess uniforms, act like proper "gentlemen," and not "fraternize" with their subordinates.

Well, senior NCOs weren't supposed to socialize with junior NCOs and enlisted men either, but he'd never let that stop him from playing cards or getting drunk with any Marine he felt like.

And to be an officer he'd have to go back to Arsenault, where he'd gone through Boot Camp so long ago, to that damn finishing school the Confederation Marine Corps called the Officer Training College, and learn which fork to use and how to hold his pinky out while he drank tea from a china cup. He already knew everything a Marine platoon commander needed to know to fight and win a battle and bring his men back alive, with the mission accomplished. Hell, the only fork a fighting Marine needed to know how to use was the one in his mess kit. And holding a pinky out in combat was a good way to lose it.

But there was no way he'd get third platoon back even if he accepted a commission. It was Marine Corps policy that when a Marine completed officer training and got commissioned, he was assigned to a unit he'd never served with before. Charlie Bass knew his only alternative was to accept whatever gunnery sergeant billet in 34th FIST he was assigned to, wait for a platoon commander in the FIST's infantry battalion to get killed, then hope for a reshuffling of officers that would open his job back up.

He grimaced. Marines died, more often in 34th FIST than in almost any other unit, but he couldn't wish death on another Marine, not for his own benefit.

Groaning and huffing with the effort of moving, he set aside his sour mood and struggled out of the rack to go to the head for his morning shitshowershave.

A lance corporal wearing the armband of the duty NCO stopped him on his way back to his room.

"Gunny Bass? Some people want to see you. They're in the office," the Duty NCO said. Awe was audible in his voice and visible on his face. He'd heard about Charlie Bass. He didn't have much trouble accepting that Gunny Bass had somehow survived being captured by the Skinks and managed to escape from them. But to single-handedly overthrow a planetary government! Well, that went a bit beyond what he thought a Marine capable of—even if the Marine in question was *the* Gunnery Sergeant Charlie Bass he'd heard so many stories about, and he had the assistance of a rebel army and a rebellious army general.

"Thanks, Lance Corporal," Bass said. "Any idea what's up?"

"Nossir— I mean, no, Gunny."

Bass shot him a look. Enlisted men "sirred" sergeants major, but all other enlisted addressed each other by rank or the title "Marine." He saw how nervous the unknown lance corporal was and took pity on him. "Thanks," he said, and clapped him on the shoulder. "Keep up the good work, Marine."

"Aye aye, Gunny. Thanks, Gunny."

Bass was wearing only a towel wrapped around his waist. He decided that wasn't appropriate dress for reporting to the transient barracks office, so he stepped into his room and, so as not to jar his aching head and queasy stomach, cautiously pulled on a set of drab-green garrison utilities.

The office was a few steps away. Bass opened the door and entered. Top Myer and Gunny Thatcher were sitting on two unoccupied desks. It was indecent how chipper they looked. Then he saw Captain Conorado, Company L's commanding officer, and Lieutenant Humphrey, the company executive officer. He pulled himself to attention.

"Gunnery Sergeant Bass reporting as ordered, sir," he said to Conorado.

"Relax, Charlie," Conorado said, stepping forward to shake his hand. "Welcome back."

"Thank you, sir. It's good to be back." He repeated the greeting with Humphrey. Only then did he notice that all four men were in undress reds, a much more formal uniform than they normally wore, certainly more formal than they wore on the weekend—much less the one he was wearing. "Undress reds" was a bit of a misnomer, as only the uniform's tunic was scarlet; enlisted men's dress uniform trousers were navy blue and officers wore gold.

"About time you decided to show up!" Thatcher snarled. But he smiled, so Bass knew he was just putting on an act.

"Actually, we aren't the ones who want to see your dumb ass," Top Myer growled. He picked up a garment bag and handed it to Bass. "This is your undress reds. Go back to your room and change into the appropriate uniform."

Bass looked at him, wondering what was going on.

"Here," Thatcher said. "Doc Horner said to give this to you, though I'm damned if I know why he'd want to cure your hangover after your behavior last night."

Bass took the thing Thatcher held out, a tiny box with a hangover pill. He wondered what Thatcher meant. He didn't remember doing anything more outrageous than anyone else the night before.

"Aye aye, Top. Thanks, Gunny." He turned to Conorado. "By your leave, sir?"

Conorado, blank-faced, pointed a finger at the office door.

What the hell? Bass wondered as he headed back to his room to change. The only reason he could imagine for them to wear their undress reds was an award ceremony. But decorations were always handed out at full-FIST assemblies— and those ceremonies called for full dress reds. Besides, he hadn't done anything to rate another medal. His part in overthrowing Dominic de Tomas didn't count, since he hadn't done that in his capacity as a Marine. He dry-swallowed the hangover pill on his way back to his room and was already beginning to feel better by the time he started changing into his undress reds.

They were waiting outside the office when he returned.

"Let's go," Conorado said. He led the way out the front door of the barracks to where a landcar waited for them. "Go," he said to the driver as soon as they were in, and the landcar smoothly moved out.

"Where are we going?" Bass asked. Everybody looked away, but he wasn't left in suspense for long; the landcar took them to the headquarters building of 34th Fleet Initial Strike Team, only a few minutes' drive from the transient barracks.

Conorado again took the lead, and in moments they were in the outer office of Brigadier Sturgeon, 34th FIST's commander. Colonel Ramadan, the FIST executive officer, waited for them. Ramadan was also in undress reds. He rapped on the door frame to the inner office and announced, "They're here, sir."

"Bring them in," Brigadier Sturgeon said. He was on his feet at the side of his desk as they came in. FIST Sergeant Major Shiro stood to the side of a row of visitor's chairs in front of Sturgeon's desk. The infantry battalion CO, Commander van Winkle, and the infantry battalion's senior enlisted man, Sergeant Major Parant, were also there.

Conorado came to attention in front of the brigadier and said, "Sir, Company L detachment reporting as ordered!"

"At ease, gentlemen," Sturgeon said. His lips quirked in a cut-off smile and he added, "I'm tempted to say, 'and you too, Charlie,' but that wouldn't be very decorous."

Every reply Bass could think of was even less decorous, so he didn't say anything.

Still looking at Bass, Sturgeon went on, "Everybody but you knows why we're here, Charlie. And you're smart enough, I'm sure you figured it out even before you got here."

Actually, he hadn't until just now, but he wasn't about to admit to the slightest bit of vincibility. So he said, "Ground I believe we've covered in the past, sir."

"Indeed we have, Charlie," Sturgeon said, "and you made me bend Marine Corps regulations every step of the way in order to keep you as a platoon commander." He went behind his desk to sit. "Seats, gentlemen, please." He cocked an eyebrow and added, "You too, Charlie."

Conorado, Lieutenant Rokmonov, and Myer sat on the sofa against the office's side wall, Thatcher sat on the sofa's arm. When Bass began to move to the sofa's other arm, Parant grabbed his arm and pointed at the chair between him and Shiro. Bass's lips pursed, since that chair put him dead center on Sturgeon's desk, directly across from the brigadier.

Gunnery Sergeant Charlie Bass felt more seriously outnumbered than he had when he faced Dominic de Tomas's Special Group.

"Gunnery Sergeant Bass, when you disappeared on Kingdom, we all thought you were dead," Sturgeon said. "Since our return to Camp Ellis, 34th FIST has received enough replacements to fill every vacant billet. One of those vacant billets is—was—commander of third platoon, Company L of the infantry battalion. One of the replacements is an ensign who I can plug into that slot.

"Then you had to come back and complicate matters. Captain Conorado," he nodded toward Company L's commander, "wants you to resume command of third platoon. So does Commander van Winkle," he nodded at the infantry battalion commander. "I concur. That platoon has been outstanding under your command.

"But the billet is supposed to be filled by an officer, and I have an officer to fill it." Bass opened his mouth to say something, but Sturgeon raised his hand to cut him off. "I know, it's within my prerogative as commander of a remote FIST to assign a senior noncommissioned officer to permanently fill a platoon commander's billet. In the past I've done that through the simple expedient of never having an extra officer who would go to waste. But this time, believing that you were dead, I requisitioned an ensign to fill that slot.

"Well, we all want you in command of that platoon, but you've created a problem for me. So this time I'm making you an officer and that's that." He nodded to Bass, giving him permission to speak.

"You can't do that, sir."

"I don't care what you say, Charlie. I'm doing it."

"Sir, with all due respect, you can't. As you said, sir, Marine Corps regulations allow for the commander of a forward FIST to permanently assign a senior NCO as a platoon commander, but they don't allow for a Marine to be assigned to the Officer Training College against his will. Besides, the last I heard, 34th FIST was quarantined and nobody is allowed to be transferred, so I couldn't go to Arsenault even if I wanted to."

"You're absolutely right, Charlie. I can't make you go to Arsenault against your will, and I wouldn't if I could—if I did, I wouldn't get you back after you received your commission. And we *are* still under quarantine, so Arsenault is a moot point."

"Sir?" Bass said, confused. "How can you make me an officer if I don't go to the finishing school?" The pill Doc Horner had provided may have eradicated most of Bass's pain, but his neural pathways weren't quite up to snuff yet, otherwise he wouldn't have called OTC "finishing school" in front of the brigadier.

Shiro and Parant both sharply elbowed him in the ribs, and he bit off a grunt.

Sturgeon bowed his head to hide a smile. Stone-faced again, he looked up. "Gunnery Sergeant, yes, there is some etiquette instruction at OTC, but more than ninety-five percent of it is in matters such as leadership, tactics, weapons, combined arms—courses you're well qualified to teach. Frankly, sending you to OTC would be a waste.

"Do you know what an Executive Order is, Charlie?"

Bass was startled by the abrupt change of subject. "Yessir. It's a law the President of the Confederation makes by fiat, without going through Congress."

"That's right. I have here," he lifted a sheet of foolscap and turned it so Bass could see its ornate calligraphy and ornamentation, "an Executive Order empowering me to grant commissions as I find necessary."

The blood drained from Bass's face.

"You see, Charlie, President Chang-Sturdevant couldn't go to Congress for this legislation. Hardly anybody in Congress knows that 34th FIST is quarantined, much less the reason for it. She also understands that 34th FIST is better off if some replacement officers come from within than if they come from outside and get the shock of their lives when they find out what they're in for only when they get here."

He grinned. "Charlie, this document means I can make you an officer. You don't have to go to OTC for the small amount of training it offers that you're ever likely to need— there isn't that much in the way of 'polite society' on Thorsfinni's World." He shook his head. "Which is a very good thing. I've seen your scandalous behavior in 'polite company.'

"So, Charlie, all you can do at this point is smile and say, 'Thank you, sir!' "

Bass's face went from pale to flushed in a flash. He started to rise, but dropped back onto the chair when he saw Shiro and Parant start to reach for him. "Damnit, sir, I'm a gunnery sergeant, I outrank almost any damn ensign. You're busting me!"

"AS YOU WERE, GUNNERY SERGEANT!" Shiro bellowed.

Parant jumped to his feet and leaned over Bass, his fists clenched at his sides. "You've already been busted a couple of times, Bass. You're bucking for another!"

"But—"

They all turned to Sturgeon, who was almost doubled over with laughter.

"Oh-my-Charlie," he gasped as he struggled to get himself under control. He weakly waved at the two sergeants major to resume their seats. After a moment he gained enough control to assume a stern expression, but wasn't able to hold it and broke up laughing again. It took a few more moments before he calmed down to occasional laughing barks.

"Charlie, Charlie, Charlie," he said, and took a deep breath. "Yes, yes, your final enlisted rank does outrank the final enlisted ranks of most ensigns, but really, an ensign outranks a sergeant major." He held up a placating hand to Shiro and Parant. "*Technically* outranks." Shiro and Parant looked only partly mollified.

"As I was saying. Your pay remains the same, but you get additional allowances. Seniority for ensigns is a bit more complex than it is for other officers; as final enlisted rank enters into the calculation, it's not based simply on date of commission.

"Charlie, you've been doing the job, and in a most exemplary manner." He had enough control now to turn serious. "Any ensign doing as good a job as you've done would be strongly recommended for promotion to lieutenant—I think you know that. You don't lose anything by accepting a commission. Instead you gain. I've got enough officers now, so I have to fill your billet with an officer. I'd rather keep you in it, but there are things even the commander of a forward outpost FIST—even one under quarantine and with an Executive Order in hand—can't do."

"Sir, with all respect," Bass said, speaking more soberly as well. "You were an NCO yourself once. You remember how senior NCOs feel about ensigns. They're mostly kids, even if they were sergeants or staff sergeants before they got commissioned. They need to be nurse-maided and trained. I don't want to be nurse-maided."

Sturgeon shook his head. "That attitude was supposed to change when the Marine Corps decided only to commission officers from the ranks. Sadly, it hasn't, and that leads some senior NCOs who would make outstanding officers to decline commissions, thus depriving both themselves and the Marine Corps." He tapped the Executive Order. "There's something else this does. It authorizes me to promote officers under my command as needed."

"Sir?"

"There's nothing in Marine Corps regulations that says a lieutenant has to be a weapons platoon commander or a company executive officer."

"Sir?"

"There's nothing that says a lieutenant can't be a blaster platoon commander."

"Sir?"

"If I feel like it, I can make you, by rank, the senior blaster platoon commander in the infantry battalion." He nodded to van Winkle. "With Commander van Winkle's concurrence, of course."

"I have no problem with that, sir," van Winkle said.

"It's settled then." He looked at the assembled officers and senior NCOs. "After operations on Kingdom, 34th FIST has quite a few men who merit decorations and deserve promotions. There will be a combined award and promotion ceremony in a FIST formation four days from today." He looked back at Bass. "I'm glad the staff sergeant and the sergeant I'm going to commission then haven't given me the same grief over it that you have, Charlie.

"Now. The new officers will need new dress reds. Thirty-fourth FIST is going to revive a discarded tradition; their first set of officers' reds will be a gift from the FIST's other officers." He looked at van Winkle. "Two of the new ensigns are yours, Commander. Will you take care of that?"

"Yessir, gladly, sir," van Winkle said with a grin.

Sturgeon looked around the room again. "Gentlemen, this is Sixth Day. Why aren't you off base enjoying some liberty? Not you, Charlie. You're going to New Oslo with the other two who are about to be commissioned to get your new uniforms."

On the flight to New Oslo, Bass ignored the staff sergeant from Mike Company and the sergeant from the transportation company who were going with him to Thorsfinni's World's finest men's clothier for the final fitting of their dress reds. Instead he mused over the sequence of events that culminated in his getting a commission.

The scientific team on Society 437, more commonly called "Waygone" because of how far it was from inhabited worlds—an Earthlike planet that was being examined by the Bureau of Human Habitability Exploration and Investigation for possible colonization—had missed two consecutive routine reports. His platoon was detached from 34th FIST and dispatched to investigate. They discovered that Society 437 had been invaded by an alien sentience armed with acid-shooting weapons who wiped out the entire thousand-person team. In a harrowing operation, the platoon met and wiped out the small invading force. On their way back to Throrsfinni's World, their ship was intercepted by a major general from Headquarters, Marine Corps, who ordered them never to speak of what they'd encountered on Society 437. Any slip would result in automatic sentence without appeal to the penal world of Darkside—a prison from which no one was ever paroled.

Not long afterward, third platoon along with the rest of Company L was sent on a secret mission under the command of an army general. This time they went to Avionia, a world that was quarantined, the public was told, because of virulent pathogens that killed all who landed on it. The truth was far, far different. Avionia was home to yet another alien sentience, one that had only reached the cultural level of fifteenth-century Earth. Avionia was quarantined for the protection of its native population. But the world also held a unique commodity—a type of gemstone that became highly prized when some were leaked into the marketplaces of Human Space. Not only were outlaws secretly landing on Avionia and smuggling the gemstones out, they were providing some of its inhabitants with weapons four or five centuries beyond anything the local technology was capable of producing, thereby threatening to disrupt the natural development of the Avionians in ways that could conceivably lead to their extinction. Company L's mission was to put the smugglers out of business and retrieve the weapons from the locals who had them—to kill that technology.

Thirty-fourth FIST was normally a two-year duty station, but transfers had stopped without explanation or notice. Brigadier Sturgeon had made a trip to Earth to find out why. Assistant Commandant of the Confederation Marine Corps, Anders Aguinaldo, found out 34th FIST was quarantined to prevent knowledge of the alien sentiences from spreading. Not only were transfers to other units canceled, so were releases from active service due to end of enlistment or retirement—assignment to 34th FIST had, in effect, very quietly become a life sentence.

Thirty-fourth FIST had recently returned from Kingdom, a human world that had been invaded by a major force of Skinks—the name the Marines had given the aliens who invaded Society 437. They had been joined on that campaign by 26th FIST. Bass wondered if 26th FIST was also quarantined now. And what about Kingdom? Or the sailors of the CNSS *Grandar Bay*, the ship on which the Marines had gone to Kingdom and that supported them in the operation?

For that matter, was the civilian population of Thorsfinni's World also closed off from two-way contact with the rest of humanity?

Ah, thinking about it did no good. All that accomplished was to raise questions and make him think the situation wasn't fair. Great Buddha's balls! One lesson lengthy service in the Marine Corps had taught him was that nothing was ever fair. Anyway, through the window he could see they were on the final approach to New Oslo, the capital city of Thorsfinni's World. Capital city? With its million-plus population, New Oslo was the only *real* city on Thorsfinni's World, and it looked like a village compared to cities he'd visited on other worlds. New Oslo was on the southern part of Niflheim, a fjord-rent island roughly the same shape and size as the Scandinavian peninsula on Earth, and at about the same latitude. That, and the fact that it was the largest island on the continentless planet, was why Ulf Thorsfinni had selected it for his settlement when he'd led the first colonists there.

New Oslo. Bass wondered if Katie still lived there, and if she was still single and available—and still willing to talk to him after he'd been out of touch for so long. He flinched when he realized he hadn't seen her since before the Diamunde Campaign. She was probably a fat, contented hausfrau with three fat, happy babies by now. Still, they'd had a lot of fun together. It wouldn't hurt to look her up. Anyway, she was more pleasant to think about than aliens and quarantines. And certainly more pleasant than thinking about how he was going to walk out of that clothier with an officer's dress reds.

The bloodred tunic with its stock collar was fine; the only difference between it and the dress reds tunic he'd worn through his entire career was it was made of better material and was tailored. Not even that—he'd had his tunics tailored for the past fifteen years! But those gold trousers—the agony! He *liked* the blue trousers with blood-stripe outer seam that showed he was a noncommissioned officer. Like most enlisted Marines, he'd always thought officers' dress reds were entirely too gaudy.

And he had to turn in his hard-earned—and more-than-once-earned—chevrons, rockers, and crossed blasters for the lousy single silver orb of an ensign's rank insignia. They'd let him keep the wound stripes on his sleeve. As if he *wanted* entire worlds to see them and know how many times he'd done something dumb in the line of fire and gotten injured. If the tailor had put the wound stripes on his sleeve, he decided, he'd have him take them off. That was one benefit of being an officer—officers didn't have to show off that badge of error.

The aircraft landed. Bass and the other two soon-to-be officers piled into a waiting courtesy car and were whisked off to the clothier.

The other two were greatly impressed when they saw the mass of decorations and medals already mounted on Bass's waiting tunic; he had more than both of them combined.

In less than an hour they left, each carrying a bundle. On the way to the hotel where they would stay until returning to Camp Ellis in two days, Bass gave his companions directions to a not-too-disreputable establishment where they could find decent food, inebriating drink, and willing women.

As for him, once he stowed his new uniform, he got out his personal comm and punched up Katie's number.

She wasn't there anymore, which didn't much surprise him. Comm Central reported that while he was away on Kingdom she'd moved to—

Bronnysund?

Bronnysund—"Bronnys," as the Marines of 34th FIST called it—was a fishing town in the northern reaches of Niflheim. More to the point, it was the local liberty town for Camp Ellis. Why had Katie moved to Bronnys? Had she met and married a fisherman? That didn't seem at all like the Katie he'd known and very nearly loved. Did she go there in search of Charlie Bass? That didn't seem very likely either, but the thought certainly stoked his ego.

Maybe she'd like to come to his commissioning ceremony. *Yessir!* Katie pinning on one of his silver orbs. That would almost make having to go through the stupid ceremony worthwhile!

To hell with his orders to remain in New Oslo for two more days. He caught the next flight back to Bronnys and looked for Katie. He found her too.